BORROWED MEMORIES

By

J.R. Torbic

Published by Piscataqua Press
An imprint of RiverRun Bookstore Inc.
142 Fleet Street | Portsmouth, NH | 03801
www.riverrunbookstore.com
www.piscaaquapress.com

Printed in the United States of America
ISBN: 978-1-939739-43-4

DEDICATION

This book is dedicated to every individual out there—male or female, young or old—who has ever been abused in any way by another person. Abuse does not discriminate. The abuse may have been physical, sexual, verbal, or psychological; it doesn't matter because abuse—in whatever form—can change an individual's life forever.

If you, or anyone you know, finds themselves in need of help regarding an abusive situation, please consider contacting one of the numbers below (provided by the web site www.helpguide.org).

Help for women:

In the US: Call the National Domestic Violence Hotline
at 1-800-799-7233 (SAFE).
In Canada: Visit ShelterSafe to find the helpline
of a women's shelter near you.
UK: Call Women's Aid UK at 0808 2000 247.
Ireland: Call Women's Aid at 1800 341 900.
Australia: Call 1800RESPECT at 1800 737 732.
Worldwide: visit International Directory of Domestic Violence Agencies
for a global list of helplines and crisis centers.

Help for men:

In the US and Canada: Call the National Domestic Violence Hotline at
1-800-799-7233.
UK: Call the ManKind Initiative at 01823 334244.
Ireland: Call AMEN at 046 902 3710.
Australia: One in Three Campaign

AUTHOR'S NOTE

Do you believe that we all have a dark side to us? Well, I believe it's true. I don't believe it's anything we should be ashamed of either, because whether we want to admit it or not, we ALL possess those qualities that are characteristic of a darker nature. Those qualities may include emotions or actions reflected via anger, selfishness, jealousy, being overly judgmental, having a violent nature, or, having certain unnatural or unacceptable sexual desires or needs. If you can honestly say that you don't exhibit any of these darker qualities, then you may not enjoy reading this book.

My dark side first completed this novel on November 2, 1999— almost 10 years before I became a born-again Christian. I wrote it during a dark time in my own life, and I have re-written it now in hopes that it will bring hope and faith to someone who may need it. I apologize if the subject matter offends anyone, but, I do not apologize for writing this type of story. It focuses around a subject that, even today, is not talked about as much as it should be—sexual abuse of women and children. The statistics of these occurrences are staggering, and they are growing in number, rather than decreasing. So, as unpleasant a discussion as it might be, it is a topic that does not need to be swept under the carpet any longer. Children's lives are forever changed because of sexual abuse; some children overcome it, while others never do. This book is a work of fiction, but, if you look deeply enough into it, I am sure you will recognize someone you know—even if it is only a friend of a friend, of a friend. Our faith in God pulls us through so many of life's troubling circumstances. We can use that same faith to help someone else who has experienced this type of abuse. Please, don't turn away from it, and don't think that it could never happen to you, or to someone close to you. Get involved!

My inspirational fiction novels are written under my married name—J. T. Livingston. My darker, psychological thrillers are written under my maiden name—J. R. Torbic. The genres may be different, but, they share one common factor. They are page-turning mysteries that will open your mind, heart, and imagination to either a world you wished existed, or, to one that you hope and pray never does...

Happy reading! Please remember that word of mouth is an author's best friend, so, your reviews—good, bad, or ugly—are always appreciated. Be sure to visit my website at www.jtlivingston.com, or Amazon.com and leave your review of my books.

CHAPTER 1

October 1969

"Come on, Kacey..." the handsome teenager pleaded, while his inexperienced hands groped clumsily beneath the girl's sweater.

The equally inexperienced girl pushed him as far away from her as the compact interior of the 1969 Volkswagen would allow. Apparently, it wasn't far enough, and she flinched noticeably when his hands quickly resumed their frenzied search. She grabbed his hands, shoving them away with a force that belied her delicate, feminine strength.

"No! Stop it, Scott!" she practically hissed.

A surge of teenage hormones flowed like a raging river throughout the frustrated boy's well-developed body—not quite a man's body, but close enough. He growled and leaned forward once again. "Oh, come on, baby...please...don't be like that." His hands spawned a stubbornness all their own, refusing to accept the girl's vehement denial of his intentions.

She pushed him away again, hard enough this time for the back of his head to impact sharply against the closed, steamed window.

"Ouch!" he moaned in pain.

Scott Pennell rubbed the back of his head, checking tentatively for any sign of bleeding. His dark brown eyes, which had brimmed with unbridled desire just a few short moments before, now glared back at the young girl with transparent anger and disgust. He was suddenly tired of her endless games and adolescent teasing. He had lied to his friends for months now, bragging about his sexual exploits with the girl. He had not had the nerve to tell them what he believed to be the truth—that the girl had merely strung him along, teasing him with unfulfilled promises. His extraordinary tales of sexual gratification were simply a combination of vicarious experiences compiled through perusal of select magazines and a creative imagination.

He knew he would be the laughing stock of the locker room if his friends ever found out the truth. They would never let him live it down.

It was, most likely, the fear of ridicule from his friends that had convinced Scott that his relationship with the girl would change tonight. Even though it wasn't in his nature to force himself upon anyone, he now felt a kindred spirit with those males who felt the need to exert their control and power over women. He was trying to convince himself of something that he truly did not believe—that, although she was saying no, she really meant yes. He did not want to admit to himself that she didn't want it as badly as he did.

His sexual tension continued to grow as Scott glared at the young girl while she struggled to reassemble her disheveled appearance. He watched as she felt her chest, patting it nervously. He had managed to remove her bra during their passionate, albeit too brief, romantic episode. He gritted his teeth together when she spotted the bra peeking from beneath the driver's seat.

If he could have seen himself in the mirror, he would have realized why the weak smile faded from her beautiful, porcelain face when she looked up at him. He would have flinched, too, if he had seen the fury etched across his normally calm face. He shuddered inwardly when a terrifying thought came to him. *It would be so easy...so easy to just grab her by the throat and choke off her air supply...so easy..."*

"Scott?"

The hideous thoughts vanished as suddenly as they had appeared. He blushed with evident shame and silently chastised himself for his cruel, sinful thoughts. He had no idea from where those thoughts and images had come—they were so totally out of character for him. He shook his head and closed his eyes.

The girl's soft, warm hand reached out and timidly touched his cheek. "Scott? Are you okay? Did I hurt you? I'm so sorry...I didn't mean to push you that hard. It's just that..."

Scott opened his eyes, rubbed the back of his head again, and offered a retiring smile. He felt more in control of his emotions now. "No, Kacey... you didn't hurt me. I'm okay, but..." he offered up a sheepish grin. "You could kiss it and make it all better."

Kacey Wymer was vice-president of her junior class at Baker High School, and co-captain of the varsity cheerleaders. She sighed with visible relief and playfully bumped Scott's broad shoulder with the heel of her hand. "You scared me! You looked, I don't know...kind of spaced out. I thought I'd really hurt you."

Scott put on his best hound-dog expression, grabbed her hand, and placed it over his rapidly beating heart. "Naw, I'm okay...just my pride and ego wounded...again."

Kacey dropped her gaze, in a vain effort to hide her blushing cheeks from his view.

Scott couldn't help it. He slowly, but deliberately, pulled her hand lower until it rested against his groin area.

Kacey felt his arousal and immediately tried to jerk her hand away.

Scott managed to hold her hand firmly in place. His eyes glassed over with renewed desire. He took a deep breath and smiled. "You know, you could make it up to me, Kacey..."

Kacey jerked her trembling hand free. She stared at it for just a moment, silently condemning it for temporarily betraying her.

Scott saw her panicked expression and raised both hands defensively in mid-air. "Hey, I'm sorry! I'm just kidding...really...just kidding." He ran his fingers through his thick hair and exhaled deeply. "Seriously though, Kacey, are we ever going to do it? I mean, we've been seeing each other for months now. Everybody already thinks we're doing it anyway...and, hey...everyone else does it. I know you're a virgin, but you have to know how much I care about you; it's not just about the sex."

Kacey locked her hands in her lap and shook her head. She suddenly looked much older and wiser than her sixteen years. "You still don't understand, do you, Scott? I thought maybe you did. I thought we had it all worked out...thought we had an understanding. I really thought you were different from all the others."

Scott came dangerously close to losing control of the temper he had so valiantly managed to subdue only minutes earlier. Neither patience nor empathy had ever attributed to his limited list of great virtues. He was the only child of upper middle-class parents and he was used to getting what he wanted, when he wanted it.

His relationship with Kacey Wymer over the past several months had stirred a myriad of emotions within himself. For the first time in his life, he found himself wanting to place someone else's needs and desires above his own. He didn't want to do anything to hurt Kacey or to scare her away. He believed that she would give herself to him eventually—it was inevitable—and when she did, he wanted it to be because she wanted him as much as he wanted her.

Scott exhaled a final sigh of deep regret and reminded himself that Kacey was worth the wait. He reached behind him, fumbled for the door handle, and jiggled it until it popped open. His tall, lanky frame almost fell out but he managed to right himself at the last minute. He laughed softly and said, "Okay, okay! You win! I won't touch you again—ever! Not even if you get down on your knees and beg me!"

Kacey shook her head and smiled at his overly dramatic antics. She looked down at her hands, still clasped tightly in her lap. "I'm sorry, Scott. I really am, but there's more to it than what you think. I promise you, though, that the day will come when I will beg you—at least, I hope it will."

Scott stood beside the open car door but leaned down to look inside. He regretted his role that had brought about the frightened, helpless look on her face. He wanted to allay her fear—at least any fear she might have about him. Humor—a crutch he used often to bail himself out of embarrassing situations—had always worked for him, so he instinctively used it now to ease the tension that had almost ruined their evening together.

He posed his most offended expression and sighed, "Nope, it'll be too late then. You've missed your chance..." He reached inside the car and retrieved the white, lacy bra he had so inexpertly maneuvered off her less than an hour before. He brought it up to his nose and inhaled the sweet, mild aroma of her favorite perfume—Chantilly. "Yep...for sure... you've missed your chance."

Kacey's face reddened as she stretched across his seat and grabbed frantically for the bra. She couldn't even remember how he had managed to remove it. "Give me that!"

Scott laughed and pulled playfully on his end of the overstretched bra. He chose a strategically planned moment to release his end and laughed loudly when the unexpected action threw Kacey slightly backwards.

There was a momentary silence before he straightened himself and stretched his arms high above his head. "I'll be back in a minute, Kacey."

Kacey's own playful attitude quickly transposed into one of sudden alarm. "Where are you going? You're not going to leave me here alone, are you, Scott?"

It was almost midnight and the forest animals had projected their dominance throughout the immediate area. The dirt road was extremely isolated and ended in a dead end about fifty feet beyond where Scott had parked the car. There were no houses within a five-mile radius, but a full moon provided sufficient lighting for their surrounding area. A slight breeze stirred just enough to rustle the fallen October leaves and needles of the great oaks and pines that encompassed the secluded area.

Scott looked around him and shrugged nonchalantly. "Relax, Kacey. We're the only ones out here tonight; there's nothing out here to bother you. I've just gotta...well, you know." He glanced down and shrugged. The throbbing inside his jeans demanded a form of release that required some privacy.

4

Kacey looked adequately embarrassed, suddenly realizing what he meant. "Oh..."

Scott bent down again and extended his long body through the open door until he was half-way inside the car. He reached for her and gently pulled her toward him. He felt her tense at his touch. He admired her tenacity to hang onto her virginity, but at moments like this, he couldn't help but wonder why he was wasting his time on her when he could have his choice of any girl at school. He still didn't have an answer to that. He knew it wasn't love. Even though he felt she was worth waiting for, he also knew they were both too young for love—at least he was. He didn't intend to fall in love until he was at least thirty-five. He kissed the top of her head before she managed to pull away from him. "I'll be right back, I promise." He smiled again and teased her, still trying to lighten the moment. "You can *come* with me if you want." It was obvious to him that Kacey had not picked up on his innuendo, or else, she had chosen to ignore it.

She glanced nervously around the dark woods. "Scott, please don't leave me alone. I don't know...but, something just doesn't feel right out here."

The whine in Kacey's voice was almost all the gratification Scott needed. He ruffled her hair and turned on the car radio before turning to leave. "Roll up the windows and lock the doors if it'll make you feel safer. Relax, listen to the music. I'll be back in a shake...or two!"

Kacey managed a weak laugh, blew out a heavy breath and nodded. "Okay...go on...get out of here, but, please—hurry back!"

Her timid, feminine voice sent goose bumps traveling down his arms. She had that effect on him. Scott turned and waved back to her.

He walked at a brisk pace down a half-beaten path, off to the side of the road, and soon disappeared from Kacey's sight. He was about twenty-five yards away from his car when he spotted some tall brush to stand behind. He unzipped his pants and closed his eyes. He could hear the music coming from his Volkswagen. He nodded his head from side to side, keeping beat with the song. He smiled appreciatively when the deejay announced the next song; it was one of his favorites. Doing his part to relieve his sexual tension, he hummed along to a new hit by The Tokens—*The Lion Sleeps Tonight*. He didn't know all the words, but that didn't stop him from singing intermittently along with the chorus.

"In the jungle, ba dop...lion sleeps tonight, do, do doop, the mighty jungle..." He paused momentarily when he heard a noise behind him—a sudden, slight rustling of the dry, autumn leaves.

The song played on.

The rustling noise came again.

5

Scott opened his eyes briefly, glanced around and mumbled, "Probably just a raccoon or 'possum out for a midnight tryst..." He closed his eyes again and sang softly, "The lion sleeps tonight..."

The snapping of a twig interrupted his musical rendition and echoed loudly inside Scott's head. Once again, the noise seemed to come from directly behind him. He turned around sharply and realized—too late— that the movement was not caused by any animal.

It was human, but that realization came too late.

The music from his car continued to play, *The lion sleeps tonight...*

The moment that Scott turned to face the intruder, was the same moment he felt a whisper of air against his ear—the same moment that the club of wood slammed forcefully against his skull. A million bursts of white light exploded behind his closed eyes as he sank slowly to his knees. He collapsed to the ground, completely unconscious.

The man smiled and looked down at the boy's crumpled body. He had followed the young couple from the school dance, on to a popular burger joint, and finally to their present destination within the isolated forest. He had watched and waited patiently for the past hour, observing the hormonal contest between the girl and boy.

He gave the boy a final glance, zipped up his own pants, and moved silently through the forest toward the red Volkswagen.

The Tokens continued with their ominous serenade. *Hush, my darling, don't fear my darling...the lion sleeps tonight...*

Scott's slow return to consciousness was accompanied by clashing cymbals and the echoing beat of a bass drum. It was several seconds before he realized that the sound was only inside his head. The pain throbbed relentlessly as he blinked himself into awareness. In sharp contrast to the sounds inside his head, he gradually realized that an eerie absence of noise enveloped the woods. The breeze had died away and all the forest animals appeared to have adopted a mutual and respectful code of silence. Scott struggled to a standing position and looked down at his unzipped pants. He suddenly remembered why he was in the woods, and he remembered what had happened. Someone had hit him from behind!

"*Kacey!*" his throbbing mind screamed.

Scott began to run. "Oh, God..." he repeated continuously as he ran the short distance back to the car, "Please, God, please let her be okay... let her be okay!"

He stopped abruptly in front of the Volkswagen. The headlights attacked his vision but he could see Kacey through the windshield, and it only took one look for Scott to know that Kacey Wymer would never be okay again.

Kacey Wymer was dead—very, very dead.

The same face that Scott had envisioned earlier that night stared back at him now, but it wasn't a vision this time. It was real. Her swollen purple face and her terror-stricken eyes were real.

"NOOOOOOO!" Scott screamed into the emptiness of the night. He dropped to his knees and squeezed his head between his open palms. He forced himself to look at Kacey again. Her opened eyes stared back at him in what he perceived to be...accusation.

He remembered her last words, *"...something just doesn't feel right out here."*

Scott was cognizant enough to realize that he was in a state of shock. He moved cautiously around to the passenger door and looked inside. His entire body trembled, and threatened total non-support. He stuffed his fist inside his mouth to stifle a scream, and forced himself to look at her.

Kacey was fully clothed from the waist up, except for her bra. The white, lacy bra had been knotted tightly, around her throat. As bad as the strangulation was, it was another image that finally caused Scott to emit a scream—an animalistic, unholy scream that echoed throughout the forest—a scream that finally awakened the animals from their respectful silence.

Scott collapsed once again to the ground and continued to scream. He folded his arms tightly against his chest and rocked back and forth. Salty tears flowed freely down his cheeks. He forced himself to look at her again. "Oh, Kacey...I am so sorry...I shouldn't have left you alone. I am so sorry..." Scott closed his eyes. Maybe it was all just one horrible nightmare.

He opened his eyes slowly, hoping beyond all hope that the awful image of Kacey had disappeared.

It had not. Someone had not only choked the young girl to death, but they had also impaled her upon the stick shift of Scott Pennell's 1969 Volkswagen.

Kacey Wymer was a virgin no longer.

CHAPTER 2

Twenty Years Later

Martha Pennell paced back and forth across her son's expensive oriental rug, nervously wringing her hands together. "But I don't understand, Scott. Why do you have to move so far away?"

Scott smiled and walked over to his mother, who had moved to the bay window and appeared to be looking absently out at the late afternoon traffic. He came up behind her, placed both hands upon her shoulders, and rested his chin upon her head. "Mom, you know it's a great opportunity for me," he smiled and wrapped her in a protective bear hug. "Please...try to be happy for me. Have you told Dad yet?"

Mrs. Pennell glanced back at her son and shook her head. "Are you kidding? No, not yet. Besides, why should I be the one to tell him? I think you should do it...maybe over dinner tonight?"

Scott lifted his chin and planted a kiss upon his mother's head. "Nope, sorry, can't do it tonight, Mom. I've got a date with Cheryl. What if I stop by for brunch tomorrow and we can tell him together? He'll be happy for me...I'm sure of it."

Scott wondered if he was trying to convince himself more so than his mother. He knew that his father, Howard Pennell, would not be happy with his decision to accept a job so far away from home.

The senior Mr. Pennell had never made a secret of his hope for Scott to, one day, assume management of the family's lumber company—especially considering his own failing health. He accepted the fact that Scott's area of expertise was computer-science; however, Howard Pennell believed it was his son's duty to carry on the family business.

Martha turned to face her son and placed both hands upon her ample hips, a familiar gesture that meant she was not at all happy about a situation. "Care to make a wager on that, big boy? And, what about Cheryl…have you told her that you're pulling up roots and moving half-way across the country?"

Scott laughed good-naturedly and hugged his mother against him. "It's not half-way across the country, Mom, and…no, I haven't told Cheryl yet. I plan on telling her tonight."

"Well, it may as well be…" Martha muttered under her breath, not completing her thoughts.

Scott ruffled her hair and grinned down at his mother. "I still have two weeks before I have to report for work, Mom. That will allow me plenty of time to have everything packed and shipped. As for Cheryl, well…lately, it feels like that relationship is getting a little more serious than I'd like, so it's probably all for the best. The job, I mean…getting away, putting a little distance between me and Cheryl."

Scott's mother sighed and shook her head. "I just don't understand you, Scott. Cheryl is a wonderful young woman…almost as wonderful as Monika…and, Patty…and, that really cute, energetic one…what was her name…you know, the one who taught yoga or something?"

Scott's grin widened. He knew exactly who his mother was referring to—the acrobatic and flexible yoga instructor—Tammy. "Tammy…her name was Tammy, and…yes, she was wonderful. They were all wonderful women, Mom."

Martha threw her hands into the air in exasperation. "Then what's the problem? Why couldn't you have married any one of them, settled down, had a few kids, taken over your father's company, had a few kids, bought a house close to your aging parents, had a few kids…"

Scott laughed out loud at his mother's theatrics, some of which, he had inherited. The two of them would have made terrific actors. However, he grew serious for a moment while he contemplated an answer to her question.

He ran his fingers through his hair, which was still a rich, thick and lustrous mass of dark brown waves. He leaned backward and replied softly, "Honestly? I don't know, Mom. I really don't know…I wish I did. It just seems like something kicks in when things start getting too serious and…I pull away. To tell you the truth, the idea of having to make a lifetime commitment to a woman…hell, it scares me half to death. I mean, I know it's the right thing to do. I know it's what you, Dad, and everyone else expects me to do. But…I don't know. I…hell, I just don't know, okay?"

Martha moved toward her son and gently enfolded his hands into her own. "We've talked about this before, Scott. Maybe you should talk to someone about this."

Scott raised his eyebrows and grinned. "You mean a shrink, don't you?"

Martha sighed and nodded. "It's nothing to be ashamed about, son. Everyone, at some time in their lives, could benefit from talking to a counselor about things that bother them. I only want you to be happy, Scott. You're just going through the motions, pretending to be happy, but...until you're able to commit to someone, well..."

The conversation had turned much too serious for his liking, so Scott seized the opportunity to lighten the moment. "I am happy, Mom! Really, I am. Look at me! I'm thirty-seven years old, I drive a brand-new Porsche—well, almost brand new—make more money than I can find things to spend it on, and now I've been asked to head up the Technology Department of one of the finest data processing corporations in the United States. What's not to be happy about?"

Martha Pennell sighed in defeat. "I give up. Maybe your father can talk some sense into you before it's too late."

Scott watched the flurry of emotions cross his mother's face and wondered, again, about the real reason she resented the fact that he had accepted the job in Columbus, Georgia. He had left his family's protective nest more than fifteen years ago, and—up until now—his mother had never acted like a clinging vine. "Mom, what's the real reason you don't want me moving to Columbus?"

Martha paled at this unexpected question. "What...what do you mean?"

Scott shrugged. "I mean...are you upset because you're simply going to miss this handsome face, or...is there some other reason you don't want me to move back there? We lived there for a few years when I was a teenager, didn't we?"

Martha's normally tanned complexion remained pale. Somehow, she managed to stammer out another reply, "Yes, we did. We lived there for a short while, but...I didn't think you remembered that."

Scott shrugged again and replied, "I'd actually forgotten about it, to tell you the truth, until a few days ago, when I had some sort of—I don't know—a flashback I guess you'd call it."

Martha had not been aware that she was holding her breath until she tried to inhale and couldn't. "What kind of flashback? What exactly did you remember, Scott?"

Scott puzzled momentarily over his mother's concerned reaction. He shrugged his shoulders in indifference. "Actually, the flashback was of a car—one of those Beetle Bugs that teenagers used to be so crazy about.

10

They don't sell them in the States anymore, but I passed one on the street the other day, and I suddenly remembered that I had one. I did have one for a while, didn't I, a red one?"

Martha Pennell inhaled sharply and closed her eyes while she attempted to get her breathing under control. *"Please, God,"* she thought. *"Please, don't let him remember. I don't want him to remember."*

She opened her eyes and managed to claim control over the volatile emotions that still threatened to erupt within her at any moment. "Yes...I believe you did. It was a bright red one, with a convertible top, I think. But...you didn't have it very long. We sold it shortly before we moved here. It would not have been very practical for Pennsylvania's infamous winters. Is...that all you remember, Scott? The car?"

"Well," Scott mused, "The car and...some sort of forest, I think. Some place with lots of trees, anyway."

He rubbed the back of his neck before continuing. "I haven't thought about it much, but I must have been...what...about seventeen or eighteen years old about that time...certainly old enough to remember what kind of car I drove; but, the memory is like a blank...a void I have of that time frame in my life. Who knows? Maybe you're right, mom...maybe I should talk to someone. They could even hypnotize me or something...help me to remember."

Even though she had been the one to suggest it earlier, Martha suddenly panicked at the thought of what a psychiatrist might help her son remember. "No! Don't do that!"

Scott had only been teasing about being hypnotized. It really didn't bother him much that he had no memories of his senior year in high school. He just assumed it had been the stress over his father's initial, unexpected heart attack in 1969. However, his mother's reaction to his comment about being hypnotized intrigued him. His tone took on a more serious note. "Why, Mom? Is there something you don't want me to remember? Is that it?"

Martha suddenly began to busy herself by picking up a stack of old newspapers. "Don't be silly, Scott. Your senior year was just a difficult time for the family, that's all. I've told you before...your senior year was when your father suffered his first heart attack. You took it hard. The whole event upset you terribly, so you've probably just blocked out that time in your life. It happens sometimes."

Scott thought about continuing this line of conversation with his mother but decided that he had had enough of serious conversation for the time being. "Yeah, I suppose that's it. Okay then...enough chit chat. I've got a hot date to get ready for...be sure to tell Dad I'll see him tomorrow, okay?"

Martha Pennell accepted her son's subtle hint to leave and stretched on her tiptoes to reach his offered cheek. She gave him a quick kiss and collected her coat and purse. "I'll do that, son, and...please, be gentle with Cheryl. I really do like her. She would have made such a wonderful daughter-in law and mother to my grandchildren."

Scott nodded as he held open the door for his mother. "I promise to let her down easy, but I have a feeling she'll bounce back just fine. She's a great gal. She won't have any trouble finding someone else to help her have all the grandkids you're so anxiously awaiting. She might even let you be their godmother! Come on, old lady, I'll walk you to your car."

Martha punched him against his forearm. "Watch your mouth, smart ass!"

"Ouch! Man, that's a vicious right you've got there, lady!"

The two of them walked together down the stairs and into the parking lot. Scott gave her another hug and closed the driver's door. He waited until she had pulled out onto the main highway and merged with the oncoming traffic, before turning back to his apartment. He grinned and lumbered up the steps, taking them two at a time. He opened the door to his apartment and shook his head. "May as well make the most of our last night together!" he laughed, thinking of his date with Cheryl. "Who knows what tomorrow may bring..."

Martha Pennell travelled several miles down the road before she pulled off onto the interstate's emergency lane. She covered her face with both hands as great sobs of suppressed agony escaped her heaving chest. "Oh, God, it's going to happen. I just know it's going to happen. He's going to remember everything if he goes back there...and, if he does remember...it will destroy him!"

CHAPTER 3

THE GOODBYE DATE

Scott pulled Cheryl closer to him while they slow danced to one of his favorite tunes—*Unchained Melody*. Elvis was singing this version, rather than the Righteous Brothers. The song never failed to ignite deep emotions within Scott, and he sang along softly, holding Cheryl tighter and absently stroking her bare backside.

Cheryl Meckovich had taken extra care in selecting her dress for tonight's date with Scott, because he had told her there was something important he needed to discuss with her. She was expecting a marriage proposal tonight—something she had been anticipating for some time now; after all, she and Scott had been dating for almost a year. She knew they made a good couple; everyone said so, and she wanted him to be the father of her children. Cheryl knew that, at twenty-eight years old, her biological clock was indeed ticking, so she wanted to get started on a family as soon as they were married.

Scott's intentions, on the other hand, were to let Cheryl down as easily as possible, so he had attended to every possible detail for the evening. He had catered the best Italian cuisine the city had to offer, complete with candlelight and soft music. He had even instructed his maid to place clean, silk sheets upon the bed; it never occurred to him that he and Cheryl couldn't remain friends after he told her his news about leaving town.

Cheryl knew that Scott's preferred color of choice in women's clothing was black, so she had chosen her dress carefully. It was a mid-thigh, backless sheath, made of luxurious, black silk. The back of the dress followed a rounded curve that dipped to her slender waistline.

She closed her eyes while they danced and enjoyed the familiar closeness of Scott's body. Her hips swayed slowly from side to side in rhythm to the music and she reveled in the soft caresses he administered to her bare back.

Scott smiled as he looked down upon Cheryl's expressive face. Her eyes were closed and her lips slightly parted. He could see the tip of her pink tongue move beneath her snow-white teeth. He could sense her arousal as she pressed against his chest. He continued to watch as her mouth opened a little more when he applied more pressure to her back, forcing her body even tighter against him. His hand encircled the back of her neck and he pulled her to him for a long, seductive kiss.

Cheryl's left hand dropped from his waist and moved slowly to his backside. "Such a nice butt..." she sighed, never opening her eyes.

Scott offered a small chuckle and whispered in her ear, "Isn't that supposed to be my line?"

"Okay," Cheryl challenged him, "Say it." Her hands continued exploring and she felt his instant arousal. She willed herself to slow down. This night was going to be special and she didn't want to rush through it — not that Scott would allow that to happen, anyway. They were making memories that would carry over into their Golden Years, and she wanted to do her part to ensure this would be a night they would be remember for decades to come.

Scott inhaled softly and whispered huskily, "Such a nice butt..."

Cheryl smiled seductively. "How would you know, Mr. Pennell? You haven't touched it once tonight."

Scott's tongue probed the edge of her ear, knowing it was one of her most erogenous zones. "Oh, but I do know, Miss Meckovich." His hands moved from her neck and began a deliberate southern journey. He whispered into her ear, "You see, I have an extremely good memory...I was able to find my destination with no directions required from you..." He felt the slight trembling of her body when she pressed it firmly against his own.

"Oh, Scott..." Cheryl moaned, as she surrendered to a probing kiss that threatened to paralyze her mouth. "Let's go to the bedroom..." She lifted her arms upward to encircle Scott's thick neck. She could wait a few hours for his proposal if she had to, but some things couldn't wait.

Scott guided her toward the bedroom where gentle, flickering flames from the stone fireplace added just the right ambiance for seduction. His kisses deepened in intensity as he skillfully lowered Cheryl to the floor, atop a black, bearskin rug. The seduction wasn't happening in exactly the order of occurrence he had planned for the evening. His intention had been to tell Cheryl about the move, enjoy a good meal together, and then have one final romantic interlude to seal their friendship.

Their bodies were on fire and the lovemaking was inevitable, so Scott gave in to his physical needs and desires. He took the time to ensure that Cheryl enjoyed it as much as he did. It was a full hour later when they lay side by side watching the dying embers of the fire trying to sputter back to life. Sometime during that hour, the couple had moved from the floor to the silky coolness of Scott's king-sized bed.

After several moments, Cheryl rolled over and kissed him. "I can never get enough of you, Scott."

"Well," Scott moaned with blissful satisfaction. "I think you just got all that I've got to give—for the moment—anyway."

Cheryl laughed and rested upon her elbows. She kissed him again and sighed. "Scott...you said there was something important you needed to talk to me about tonight. We, ummm...we haven't done a whole lot of talking yet, you know?"

Scott offered a low growl when she began to caress his shoulder. His eyes remained closed as he replied, "That feels good...don't stop."

Cheryl placed soft kisses across his chest. "No, come on...what was so important? I'm guessing that there was something you wanted to ask me...am I right?"

Scott forced open his eyes. "*Ask* you? Well, no...not really...I mean...it wasn't a question; but, there is something we need to talk about.

The minute that Cheryl stopped kissing his shoulder blades was the same instant that it dawned on Scott what she had thought he had meant. He gently pushed her away and lifted her chin, forcing her to look at him. "Oh...wow...Cheryl...baby, I don't think we're talking about the same thing at all."

Cheryl's entire body tensed and her emotional guard automatically went up as she experienced a terrible premonition. What was he talking about? He was surely about to propose to her; she had been so certain that was what tonight was all about. She rolled off him and watched warily while he quickly assumed a sitting position. "I don't understand, Scott..."

Scott smoothed back his hair in a nervous gesture and dreaded having to tell her what she obviously wasn't expecting to hear. Her skin glistened with perspiration from their recent lovemaking. This probably wasn't the right time to tell her, but he knew that he had to somehow get the words out. He cleared his throat and his voice was hoarse. "Cheryl, there is something I need to tell you, but, I...have a feeling it's not quite what you're expecting to hear."

She folded her arms defensively across her chest. "I'm listening, Scott."

Scott was thirty-seven years old, but he suddenly felt as awkward as he had at sixteen when he broke up with a girl. "Okay...okay, well, you see, I've been offered this great job that I can't turn down. It's with CompuTech Industries in Columbus, Georgia. I accepted it, and...will be leaving in less than a month."

Cheryl smiled to herself and, once again, wrapped her arms around his neck. Was that it? Was he just worried that she wouldn't want to move from Pennsylvania, leaving all her family behind? She reached over and hugged him. "Scott! That's wonderful! I'm so happy for you... for *us*! Just think...no more getting snowed in during the winter. I hear it's beautiful down south...a little muggy, perhaps, but nonetheless, beautiful. I can't wait for us to move! Should we be married before we leave so that all our families can attend, or would you rather wait until we got settled in, what was the place? Oh, yes...Columbus."

Scott carefully removed her hands from around his neck. He suddenly experienced his own premonition that told him he was about to be in serious trouble. "Whoa, Cheryl...sweetheart. This...*relationship* we've had...well, you know, it's been great...hell, it's been more than great, but..."

Cheryl's demeanor changed and her entire body tensed noticeably. "But what, Scott?"

Scott rubbed the bridge of his nose between his thumb and index finger. "You...uh...you're talking marriage?"

Cheryl laughed at the absurdity of his question. "Well, of course, I'm talking marriage! Yes! The dreaded *M* word." She couldn't help but notice how uncomfortable Scott suddenly looked. Surely, she couldn't have misinterpreted his intentions; however, the look on his handsome, troubled face told her otherwise. "Oh, no...Scott..."

Scott tried to reach out to her but she backed away from his touch. "Cheryl, I'm sorry. If...if I've lead you on in any way, I sincerely apologize. Honestly...I never knew you were thinking along those lines."

Her anger finally conquered her embarrassment over the situation at hand. "God, what are you, Scott, some kind of idiot! What the hell did you think we've been doing together this past year?"

Scott raised his eyebrows and grinned sheepishly, "Having fun...great sex?"

Cheryl practically fell off the bed trying to get as far from him as she could. "Fun? Great sex! That's all it was for you? Fun! Why you...sorry son-of-a-bitch! I can't believe I've been so stupid, thinking all along..." She turned quickly, determined not to let him see her cry, and rushed into the adjoining bathroom. When she emerged a few minutes later, she was completely dressed. Her red eyes revealed her inability to control her tears.

Scott had put on his pants and was smoothing down the bedding, still trying to figure out how he had misread her true feelings. He really thought that she was in it for the sex and companionship—same as him. He heard her soft steps as she returned to the bedroom. He turned toward her and shook his head. "Cheryl...please. I really am so very sorry. I never meant to hurt you. I would really like it if we could remain... friends."

Cheryl stared back at him, somewhat pitifully, and shook her head. "Oh, this is great! This is just great! Friends? Scott Pennell, you're not only a son-of-a-bitch; you are a stupid son-of-a-bitch! The last thing I want to do is to be your damn friend!" She marched into the living room, grabbed her coat and purse, and turned to look at him one more time. "Have a nice life, you...you bastard!"

The door vibrated on its hinges when she slammed it behind her.

Scott grimaced when he heard tires squeal from the parking lot. "Wow," he sighed as he returned to the bathroom to shower, "That sure didn't go the way I expected." He stepped into the shower and allowed the hot water to stream over his tense body. He closed his eyes as a tune from the past suddenly crept into his mind. He began to hum along to the tune—one he had not heard in many, many years. He began lathering soap over his body and continued to hum along to the tune of *The Lion Sleeps Tonight.*

CHAPTER 4

RETURN TO COLUMBUS

Scott rolled down the Porsche's window and allowed the warm October breeze to pummel his face. He sped along Atlanta's Interstate 285 Bypass until he exited on Interstate 85, which would take him to his new home and job farther south in Columbus, Georgia. He kept his vehicle in the middle lane because he wasn't use to such intimidating traffic.

He smiled as cars passed him on both sides. *"Southerners might be slow about a lot of things,"* he thought, *"but driving certainly isn't one of them."* He estimated it would take him another couple of hours to reach Columbus, provided he went the posted 55 MPH speed limit, something none of his fellow drivers seemed to be practicing.

A black and chrome Chevy 2500 pulled alongside the Porsche and revved its mighty engine.

Scott nodded amiably at the young driver of the Chevy. The driver stayed even with the Porsche for a few minutes before finally speeding ahead and honking his horn in apparent dismissal. Scott noticed a Confederate flag proudly displayed in the truck's rear window.

The passenger in the pickup leaned out as they passed Scott and yelled, "Nice wheels, man!"

Scott threw up his hand in farewell and stretched his legs as much as the car's limited interior allowed. "The South shall rise again!" he yelled to no one in particular, and laughed out loud. He thought about stopping for a rest but decided against it. After seventeen hours of virtually non-stop driving, he was eager to see his new home.

CompuTech Industries had made all the necessary arrangements for an executive suite rental at an exclusive, adult community called Whispering Hills. Per the brochures they sent him, his new home was one of Columbus' ultimate apartment communities. His rental was a three- bedroom, two-bath suite complete with all the amenities. The complex also hosted six tennis courts, basketball and volleyball courts, four pools, and two large lakes.

As he drove along Interstate 85, Scott thought back to yesterday morning when he had driven to his parents' home to bid his final farewell. His father had looked pale and sickly, and his mother looked worried and withdrawn. Conversation was limited among them until the time came to say good-bye. His mother had hugged him tight and begged him one last time to change his mind. His father didn't say much at all, but he didn't have to—his body language more than revealed his true feelings. Scott knew his parents were proud of him, and of the opportunity that awaited him, but, he also knew that they felt betrayed by his leaving them when they needed him most. Scott almost lost his composure when he tried to hug his father good-bye, only to receive a handshake instead—that action on his father's part had hurt and upset Scott more than he let on. He just could not understand why his parents couldn't be happy for him. He hoped they would come around in time, but he had serious doubts of that ever happening.

Scott had felt, for years now, that his life was caught in a web of stagnation. He was almost forty years old, and beginning to think that life would pass him by before he had a chance to make an impact on something or someone. It had taken him a long time to decide that he wanted more out of life than a good job, great sex, and lots of money. That might be enough for some men, but Scott wanted more. He truly felt that the job opportunity in Columbus might be the solution to fill the void in his life. He couldn't explain it to himself, much less to his parents, but he felt that Columbus was reaching out to him, offering an anecdote to a fatal illness. He felt that something...or someone... was pulling him there.

Scott's incessant daydreaming almost caused him to miss the turnoff to Interstate 185, which would take him directly into the city of Columbus. He cringed at the sound of his screeching tires when he jerked hard to the right, just barely making the exit. The driver directly behind him blared his horn in protest and used a finger to execute the universal sign of anger and frustration.

"Shouldn't be riding my ass!" Scott yelled out the window, and exercised his own right to execute the universal sign.

He flipped the sun visor down and retrieved a city map of Columbus. He glanced at his watch. It was almost noon and the movers were expected to arrive at the apartment by two o'clock. Scott had only packed a few essential pieces of furniture, so he didn't think it would take the movers long to complete their task.

He arrived within the city limits of Columbus thirty minutes later. He pulled into the first fast-food restaurant he saw, went inside, and ordered a grilled chicken sandwich with melted cheese, large fries, and iced tea. He thanked the cashier, took his tray to a window seat, and began to devour his meal. He was ravenous; he hadn't stopped to eat a complete meal since he left Pennsylvania. Scott finished his meal in a matter of minutes and decided to go back through the line. He smiled at the cashier and placed a duplicate order to go.

The young, pimply-faced cashier returned his smile and batted her blonde lashes at him. "My goodness, you must really be hungry!" she grinned at him.

Scott wondered if she was attempting to flirt with him, and it took all his self-control to keep from laughing. He cleared his throat and handed her a ten-dollar bill, and couldn't help but notice her chipped front tooth. He nodded and returned the smile. "Yeah, I suppose I am. I've been driving for a long time. Guess I was hungrier than I realized."

The young girl looked him over as though she was considering the option of taking him for a test drive. "Well, with a bod like yours, you certainly don't have to worry none 'bout the calories, that's for sure."

Scott was a little surprised to find himself blushing at the compliment, if that's what it was. The last thing he expected, especially with his grubby and rumpled appearance, was a compliment about his body. "Uh...thanks." He watched as the girl placed his food upon a tray. "Could I get that to go, please?"

The girl ran her tongue along the bottom of her chipped tooth. "Oh, yeah...sorry 'bout that. You be sure to come back to see us now, you hear?"

Scott smiled as he took his order and turned to leave the restaurant. "Friendly town," he mumbled.

Twenty minutes later, Scott pulled into one of the most beautiful apartment complexes he had ever seen. The layout and beauty of the grounds was breathtaking, like something out of a horticulture magazine. He drove slowly through the gate, and followed the directional arrows that guided him to his building. He pulled the Porsche into an empty parking space facing his apartment.

He stepped out of his car and stretched his arms over his head. He was surprised at the sudden burst of energy he felt and realized that he didn't feel the least bit tired. "Beautiful," he sighed as he took a quick, cursory survey of the grounds. "Absolutely beautiful."

He noticed a woman dressed in navy slacks and a short sleeve white blouse closing the door to his apartment. Scott approached her and saw that she carried a clipboard tucked under her arm. "Excuse me..." he began.

The woman dropped the clipboard and cried out, "Oh my goodness! You scared me half to death!"

Scott was quick to retrieve the clipboard. He handed it back to her and offered a sheepish grin. "Sorry about that. It's just that I noticed you coming out of my apartment..."

The woman looked up at him with surprise evident upon her face. Surely this couldn't be her newest tenant? She had reviewed his application and knew that he was one of CompuTech's newly hired computer gurus; however, this man, most definitely, did not meet her expectations of a computer geek. He was much taller and thinner than she expected, and he didn't wear black, horn-rimmed glasses! "You're Mr. Pennell?" she sputtered.

Scott tipped an imaginary hat and grinned. "Scott Pennell, yes, that would be me...and you are...?"

The woman was totally flustered and embarrassed. She was aware that she had been staring at Scott with a dumbfound expression. She wouldn't blame him if he thought that she was a complete dimwit. It took a few moments, but she finally gathered her wits about her, offered a bright smile and held out a welcoming hand. "Oh, I am so sorry. Please excuse my manners. My husband, Jonathan, is the manager of Whispering Hills, and I help him out when he gets snowed under. My name is Peggy...Peggy Underwood. I...was just giving your apartment a final check to make sure the cleaning crew did everything that was on the final checklist."

"And did they?" Scott asked.

Peggy was still staring at Scott's ruggedly handsome face and the way he more than adequately filled out his worn jeans. "Did they what?" she asked.

Scott smiled and rubbed at his day-old stubble. "Never mind. I'm sure they did a wonderful job. I can't wait to see the apartment."

The two of them remained where they were for several moments, standing and smiling at each other.

Peggy was still mesmerized by the tenant's unexpected appearance. She really hadn't expected anyone so handsome. Oh, the single women of this complex were in for a real treat.

"Mrs. Underwood? Peggy..."

Peggy blinked when she realized the new tenant was speaking to her. "Goodness, you must think I'm short one screw, don't you? Well, of course, you want to see your apartment. Did CompuTech send you a key?"

Scott ran his fingers through his thick, dark hair. "No, they didn't. They said I would be able to pick it up from the manager's office, but...it looks like I won't have to do that now." He pointed to the key in Peggy's hand.

Peggy blushed and suddenly wished that she was still single. Jonathan probably wouldn't appreciate her train of thought concerning Scott Pennell. She handed him the key. "It's a beautiful apartment, Mr. Pennell. Would you like me to show you around?"

He reached for her hand and clasped it gently inside his own. "No, that won't be necessary, Peggy, but thank you for the offer...and, please, call me Scott."

Peggy swallowed the sudden lump in her throat that had quickly formed when he touched her hand. "Okay...Scott, it is. Well then, welcome to Whispering Hills, Scott...and, to Columbus. If there's anything I...we... can do for you, you'll find the manager's office located just around the corner. Feel free to drop by anytime."

"Thank you, Peggy," Scott smiled as he released her hand. He knew very well the effect he had on women and, at times like this, he allowed himself to have a little fun with it. There was no real harm done—just a little innocent flirting.

"Okay then, I'll see you later..." Peggy called out to him as she watched him practically run up the sidewalk. She watched until his front door closed slowly behind him. "Hmm...something about him is so familiar..." she muttered. "Something...oh well, he probably just looks like someone I used to know, or more likely, someone I wish I knew. Nice...very nice."

It only took Scott thirty minutes to unload the few boxes he had managed to pack into the Porsche. He was waiting outside for the moving company to arrive—they were late. He leaned against the Porsche, soaking up the warm October sunshine. He shielded his eyes with his hands as a white Rodeo whipped into a space directly across the street from him. He watched lazily from his position as a woman got out and walked to the rear of her car.

From his vantage point, Scott thought she was ravishing! Her hair was straight and almost the same color as his—a rich, dark brown, but with a blend of dark auburn highlights. She wore it in a loose ponytail, but wispy bangs framed her forehead. She wore sunglasses, so Scott couldn't distinguish much about her face except that her skin appeared to be ivory smooth.

Although the woman appeared to be stunning from the waist up, it was her legs that most captivated Scott's attention. She wore a pair of fringed Levi shorts and a white Nike tee shirt; he easily recognized the Nike emblem. She wore white sneakers—not Nikes—sans socks. He shook his head and blinked hard as he continued to stare. Her legs! They were long, sleek, tanned and toned in all the right places. He couldn't take his eyes off her.

The woman must have felt him staring because she turned to look in his direction after she grabbed two bags of groceries from her trunk. She quickly looked down at the pavement, avoiding any further direct eye contact.

Scott smiled and whispered, "She's bashful. I don't believe it! I didn't know there were any bashful women left on the face of this earth."

The woman turned away quickly and when she did, the bottom corner of her grocery bag ripped. Several cans began rolling across the parking lot in Scott's direction.

Being the gentleman that he was, Scott quickly leapt to the rescue. He gallantly chased after two cans of English peas and captured them just in the nick of time; they were headed straight for a storm drain opening. He sprinted back toward the Rodeo, cans in hand. "I believe these are yours," he smiled. "Do you need any help getting those bags inside? They look heavy."

Now that he was closer to her, Scott determined she wasn't as young as he first thought. In fact, she might even be closer to his own age. Nevertheless, he thought that she was even more beautiful up close than she appeared from a distance. He wished he could see her eyes, but the dark sunglasses prevented it.

The woman adjusted one bag onto her hip and took the offered cans from him. "Thank you...but I can manage." She left the trunk open and immediately began walking toward her own apartment.

He couldn't let her get away without at least learning her name. Scott grabbed a third grocery bag from the Rodeo and followed her to her front door. When she turned abruptly, they collided against each other, almost spilling the contents of all three bags.

"Sorry," Scott mumbled, embarrassed at his own awkwardness. He took the bag that had ripped at the bottom from her, cupping the torn corner in his palm. "Why don't you open your door and I'll set these inside for you. By the way, I'm Scott. I guess I'm your new neighbor. I've leased the apartment across the street."

She glanced in the direction of his apartment and smiled for the first time. "You mean the *suite* across the street, don't you?"

23

Just as Scott expected—her tiny, white teeth were perfect.

He shrugged as best he could while trying to maneuver the two bags of groceries. "Suite—apartment—whatever. It's my new home. I'm sorry, but I didn't get your name?"

She offered him a half-smile and shook her head while she unlocked her front door. "Just put those over there on the bar, please. And...thank you for your help. It really wasn't necessary, though."

She watched him place the bags upon the bar and a sudden shiver traveled over her. She removed her sun glasses to get a better look at him, but quickly put them back on. Something about him seemed vaguely and uncomfortably familiar. "What did you say your name was again?"

Scott thought her voice sounded like slow-moving honey. He sat his two bags of groceries on the bar counter and turned to face her. He saw that she still hadn't removed her sunglasses. He cleared his throat slightly and answered, "Scott...Scott Pennell at your service, ma'am." He bowed slightly and, therefore, did not see the sudden paling of her face. When Scott looked up again he was momentarily shaken at the look of *contempt* that registered upon her otherwise perfect face.

She held onto her own bag of groceries and backed toward the front door. She held it open for him. "Thank you, Mr. Pennell. Now...if you don't mind..."

It was apparent that she wanted him to leave and Scott wasn't sure how to handle her sudden, cool demeanor. It did not escape him that she had never offered him a name. "Sure, no problem, Miss...?"

"Garner...Macey Garner. Good day, Mr. Pennell. Would you please close my trunk when you go back out?"

Scott was still disconcerted at her sudden change in behavior. She hadn't been overly friendly to begin with, but for some reason, she had turned utterly frigid toward him once they were inside her apartment. He nodded and turned to leave. "Sure, no problem. Good-bye, Miss Garner. Maybe I'll see you again soon?"

Macey didn't respond. She couldn't. She stood in her doorway looking out at him as he walked back toward the parking lot. He closed the trunk of her car and looked back at her before turning toward his own apartment. Macey began to tremble. She had not realized that she had been holding her breath until she exhaled sharply. After all this time—after so many sleepless nights, wondering what kind of person could do what he did—she had finally come face-to-face with the man who had so brutally murdered her twin sister—almost twenty years ago.

CHAPTER 5

PAST MEETS PRESENT

Later that evening, Scott leisurely sipped at a few bottles of beer while unpacking boxes, hanging pictures, and humming along to his favorite collection of golden oldies from the sixties. The sixties were his favorite era for music.

A few hundred feet away, the atmosphere was very different in Macey Garner's apartment. The meeting with Scott Pennell had shaken her more than she cared to admit, and she couldn't fight off the ghosts from her past that infiltrated her thoughts so frequently...

It had been almost twenty years ago—Halloween night, 1969—when sixteen-year old Macey had given birth to her only child. She never knew if she had borne a daughter or a son because she had not been allowed to see the child after it was taken from her womb. She never got to hold it, to tell it how much she wanted it—how much she loved it. The only information she had been able to find out was that the adoptive parents had taken the baby and returned to their hometown.

Not one day had gone by during the past twenty years that Macey had not thought about her baby. She never allowed herself to indulge in self-pity because she knew that if she did, she would have given up hope, long ago, of ever being reunited with her child. The baby had come into the world, screaming at the top of its lungs, on the very night that Macey's twin sister had been brutally murdered.

Macey had never been much of a drinker, but she poured herself a half-glass of wine now and gulped it down in one quick swallow. The cool liquid did little to soothe her sore throat, which felt rough and dry from hours of incessant crying. So many tears—so many memories—most of them, very bad memories.

She reached for a tissue and blew her nose. The yellowed newspaper clippings lay beside the tissue box. Macey's hand trembled as she picked up one of the articles that she must have read a thousand times. She blinked her eyes continuously until they became focused enough to read the article.

The headline recounted the scene explicitly:

"LOCAL TEEN MURDERED!! BODY IMPALED ON STICKSHIFT!!"

Macey knew that such sensationalism sold newspapers, and gave little-to-no thought or consideration to the victim's family. She poured another glass of wine—a full glass this time—and continued reading, all the while, attempting to detach herself emotionally from the story.

She failed miserably. Her hands continued to tremble as she re-read the article.

"Kacey Wymer, a sixteen-year old junior at Baker High School, was found brutally murdered on Halloween night. It was not a holiday prank. The victim's semi-nude body was impaled upon the stick shift of a 1969 Volkswagen, registered to the parents of a classmate, Scott Pennell. Fellow classmates were interviewed and stated that Mr. Pennell and Miss Wymer had been dating for several months; although, parents of both these students denied knowledge of this fact. Scott Pennell allegedly ran several miles from the murder scene to report the incident. Police found him to be extremely upset, highly emotional, and incoherent. They stated he offered no explanation or insight into how the murder occurred."

Macey placed the wine glass on the coffee table and rose unsteadily to her feet. She clutched the article to her chest and closed her eyes tightly against the tears. She blew out a deep sigh and slumped back onto the sofa. She looked at the half-empty wine glass, reached for it, and swallowed the remaining liquid in one, huge gulp. She looked around the room and tried to remember if she had another bottle stored somewhere. She took another deep breath and continued reading the well-worn article.

"Police are withholding specific details about the case, known only to the killer and the police, until additional witnesses can be interviewed. Mr. Pennell's parents reportedly spent most of the evening at The Medical Center with their son, who is being treated for extreme post-traumatic shock. Mr. Pennell may have to undergo additional psychiatric therapy before he can be of any further assistance to the police.

Miss Wymer is survived by her parents, Ruth and Andrew Wymer of 314 Meridith Street, and a younger brother, Jacob. She was an honor student at Baker High School, and a member of the varsity cheerleading squad."

The article made no mention of a twin sister. Andrew Wymer had been adamant about that.

"They tried to pretend I didn't exist..." Macey whispered out loud.

She allowed the article to drift from her hands; it landed on the carpet between the couch and coffee table. Macey stepped over it and walked into the kitchen. She rummaged through the cabinets until she found another bottle of wine.

She sniffed, wiped her nose ungraciously on the back of her hand, and walked outside to her front porch. She inhaled several deep breaths of the cool October air and stared across the street to the lights shining within Scott Pennell's living room. She watched closely as his shadow made several trips, back and forth, in front of the curtained window.

Macey plopped down onto a chaise lounge chair and gulped a long swig of wine, straight from the bottle—who needed a glass? She sputtered hoarsely as several droplets seemed to get stuck in her windpipe. The raw membranes in her throat throbbed sharply. A small trickle of the burgundy liquid crept down her chin. She wiped it away, leaned her head as far back as it would go, and looked up into the spectacular display of October starlight. The light from thousands of brilliant stars illuminated her tear-stained face. "Oh, Kacey...why did things have to turn out like they did? Why? Why did you have to die? You were supposed to wait for me. We were going to get away from them, get a place of our own...just the two of us...and my baby."

The tears flowed freely and Macey felt embraced by the enveloping darkness. She closed her eyes tightly and, reluctantly, allowed her memories to once again travel back in time...way back to March of 1969.

The sisters, two identical fifteen-year old twins, sat on the back porch discussing plans for their future.

Kacey took hold of her sister's hands and cradled them inside her own. "Macey, please tell me. Who's the boy? Who got you pregnant?"

Macey lowered her head in shame while adolescent tears streamed down her cheeks. She shook her head and said, "I can't tell you."

Kacey squeezed her sister's hands. "That's not true...you can tell me anything. We've never had any secrets between us...we tell each other everything."

Macey shook her head and suddenly felt so much older than her fifteen years. "No, Kacey, not everything. There's a lot I haven't told you—or anyone. I can't—at least not now—maybe someday, though... someday soon, I promise."

Kacey hugged her sister close. "I heard Mama and Papa talking tonight. Papa wants to send you away, doesn't he?"

Macey returned the hug and sighed deeply. "Yep, he said he's sending me to stay with Aunt Chloe, up in Madison. He said that I'm a disgrace to the Wymer family, and he won't have me blowin' up like a beached whale for the world to see what a sinner I've been."

Kacey smiled. "That sounds like Papa, all right, but...what about the baby?"

Macey pulled away from her sister's embrace and stood up. She began pacing around the cement patio, being careful not to step on any cracks. She remembered the childhood superstition about breaking your mother's back if you stepped on a crack. She looked at the cracks for a long moment before issuing a snort of contempt, and deliberately placing her foot upon one. Why should she care about her mother, anyway? It was obvious to her that Ruth Wymer agreed with her husband that Macey's baby—her own grandchild—should be given up for adoption.

Macey stopped pacing and looked over at her twin. "Papa said that I have to give it up...he told me I have to give my baby away! He said that it's God's will...but I won't! I can't give this baby away, Kacey! It's...it's part of me. I'll run away before it comes, that's what I'll do. I won't let them take it from me...I won't!"

Kacey stood and leaned against her sister, shoulder to shoulder. "I'll help you. You know I will. You just tell me what to do and I'll do it...no matter what Papa says. He's wrong about this. He's wrong..."

Macey lived in an end unit, so she could sit on her front porch and see Scott's apartment across the parking lot; however, the sidewalk that led to her front door was to the right of her porch. Three large cypress trees separated her front porch from her front door, so she was unable to see who was at the door now. She heard the shuffling of feet as they wiped against her welcome mat. Waves of dizziness washed over her, and she had to steady herself before she could stand and walk quietly back inside her apartment.

She waited. The bell rang a second time...and, a third time.

Macey flipped on her outside light and forced her bleary eyes to squint through the peep hole. She couldn't believe it. A low moan escaped her lips when she saw that it was Scott Pennell who stood on the other side of her front door. Macey looked through the peep hole again and squinted her eyes. He was holding something in his hands. What was it? She looked again and saw what appeared to be a small bouquet of wilting flowers in his left hand. She backed away from the door and shook her head. "Oh, God," she moaned. "I can't handle this right now. Please make him go away. I just can't handle it...please, God..."

The doorbell rang a fourth time.

Macey closed her eyes and pressed her forehead against the door. "Please, go away," she whispered. "Go away...just go away."

She had to give him credit for his persistence. The doorbell rang once more but Macey forced herself to remain immobile. She had dreamed of this opportunity for so many years...the opportunity to confront her sister's murderer; however, now that the opportunity was literally knocking at her door, she found she wasn't quite ready for that confrontation. *"He probably thinks I'm crazy,"* she thought. *"But then... why the hell should I care what he thinks..."*

It took another few minutes before Macey gathered enough courage to look through the peep hole again.

Scott was gone.

She willed herself to stand still for another five minutes. She looked through the peep hole a final time before she slowly opened the door. The flowers were indeed wilted, and lay against her door, alongside a can of English peas. There was a note tucked under the rubber band that held the flower stems together. Macey retrieved the odd collection and carried them inside. She opened the note—a note that at another time, from another man, might have brought a smile to her face. She read its brief contents.

Miss Garner—this renegade can of peas somehow managed to escape you this afternoon, so I felt it my neighborly duty to return them to their rightful owner. I, also, discovered these flowers growing alongside one of the pools. I thought they might provide just the right ambiance for the peas. Wishing you a good evening...I hope to see you again soon.

Scott Pennell (your new neighbor)

The smile that had begun to form quickly faded. Macey crumpled the note in her hand and fresh tears spilled upon her cheeks. She closed the door behind her and placed the peas on the kitchen counter. She opened the sliding doors and carried the wilted bouquet onto her front porch. One by one, she ripped the velvety petals from their stems and threw them into the dirt around the shrubbery. She watched each petal—in slow motion—as they airborned to the ground below. She stood on her tip-toes and watched as the light in Scott Pennell's apartment dimmed. She retrieved the bottle of wine and quickly resumed her affair with it. The hurt, anger, and hatred she felt for Scott Pennell increased with every tip of the bottle. "How could you be so cruel? How could you!" she whispered hoarsely into the darkness.

It took another thirty more minutes of listening to the frogs and crickets harmonizing an unlikely symphony, before Macey came to the realization that Scott Pennell must not have recognized her. It was true that it had been almost twenty years, but was it possible for a person to forget a face that belonged to someone he had so brutally murdered?

Macey didn't think so.

She wanted to hate him—she *needed* to hate him. She had spent years convincing herself that she did hate the man; however, now that she was challenged with confronting the real Scott Pennell—not the one from her nightmares—Macey wasn't sure she had it in her to truly hate him, no matter how much he deserved it. It simply wasn't part of her personality to harbor permanent ill will against anyone. She, also, knew that Kacey would never have wanted her to hate anyone—not even the monster who had murdered her.

She had tried for years to hate Scott Pennell, to hate her father, to hate the man who had impregnated her...but, truth be known, she didn't hate any of them. Even though she didn't hate them, she, also, knew that she could never forgive any of them for the cruelty and damage they had inflicted upon her life...or, for the pain and loneliness they had forced her to endure. It would be so easy to hate them...to hate them all...but, she couldn't. It was not her place to judge their actions; that was God's duty. However, she knew that if she were to ever have any chance for peace in her life, she would have to find it in her heart and soul to forgive all of them.

Macey threw the remaining flower stems over the shrubbery and brushed her hands against her thighs. "I may not be able to hate you, Scott Pennell, but that doesn't mean I have to like you, either," she whispered against the cooling, southern wind. "I'll just stay as far away from you as I can, and once you realize who I am, I'm sure you'll want to do the same." She walked back inside, secured her doors, shut off the lights, and climbed into bed—fully clothed.

Her eventual sleep was inundated with nightmares and horrid visions from the past. She tossed and turned as she fought against the visions... visions of her father shouting biblical verses at her while he allowed and encouraged the man to have his way with Macey...visions of her baby's little hands reaching out for her as it cried incessantly after being ripped from its mother womb...and, visions of her sister, Kacey, screaming her last breath as her murderer choked the life from her.

"*Punishment for your sins*..." Macey remembered the words spoken by her own father to justify the part he played in her rape. She remembered him constantly calling her a Jezebel who needed to be punished and shown the ways of the Lord, so that the rest of her life could be lived in grace and peace serving Him.

While Macey tossed and turned in her sleep, suffering alone with her nightmares, Scott Pennell walked lazily in the woods behind his new home. A full moon bathed sufficient light upon the pebbled path. He found himself looking up into the same clear, dazzling sky that Macey had recently surveyed. He couldn't get his mind off Miss Macey Garner—at least he assumed she was a Miss. He smiled as he thought about her. Something about her seemed distantly familiar to him, but he couldn't imagine how that could be. Was it possible he had known her when he lived here twenty years ago? No, surely not...he would have remembered those legs!

He kicked some stones in the path and wondered why she hadn't opened the door for him. He knew she was inside her apartment. Her car was in the parking lot and she—or someone—had turned on the outside light when he rang the bell. He had written the note before he left his apartment in case she wasn't at home, and he suddenly felt silly and immature about leaving it with the flowers. "She probably thinks I'm some kind of Yankee geek..." he mumbled as he turned and headed back to his apartment. He kicked another stone that lay in his path and watched it skip across the grass. "But that's okay, Miss Garner, because I don't give up easily. Something tells me that you and I will become very close..." Scott shook his head at his last thought. "Man, where did that come from!" he marveled, laughing out loud. He hummed the theme music from an old television show, *The Twilight Zone*, and laughed again. He loved old music and old television shows. He grinned at himself and said, "Welcome to the sunny South, old boy! Let's hope Miss Garner shows us a little southern hospitality while we're here."

CHAPTER 6

THE WYMERS

Jacob Wymer sat at the breakfast table, drinking a glass of orange juice, and skimming the morning paper. He could hear his mother, Ruth, bustling about in the small laundry room off the kitchen; she was singing *Rock of Ages*. Jacob had no doubt that his mother was probably ironing a clean, white shirt for him to wear to work. He hated when she did that. His friends teased him unmercifully about how preppy he always looked in his starched, white shirts. It didn't help matters any that his mother always used too much starch on the collar, which irritated the back of his neck.

Ruth Wymer strode into the kitchen, holding Jacob's freshly-ironed shirt out in front for a closer inspection. Her long, thick hair was bound in a neat bun at the nape of her slender neck.

Jacob grinned as he watched her and thought she looked at least ten years younger than she was.

"Oh my," Ruth sighed. "I think I missed a wrinkle..." She hadn't noticed Jacob sitting at the breakfast table, and was startled when she heard his deep voice reverberate throughout the compact kitchen.

"That's all right, Mama, I'm sure no one will notice."

Ruth's slender hand slammed against her chest and she gasped in surprise. "Oh! Jacob, for Heaven's sake, I thought you were still in the shower. You scared me half to death!" She offered him the shirt and ruffled his hair in payback for being taken by surprise. "You're getting an early start this morning, aren't you, son?"

Jacob grabbed playfully at his mother's hand before smoothing his hair back in place. He pushed back from his chair, kissed the top of her head and took the offered shirt. At six-feet-two, he was almost an entire foot taller than his mother. "Thanks, Mama, I really appreciate it. Nobody irons a shirt better than you."

Ruth raised her brows and pursed her lips. "You didn't answer my question, son. Why are you leaving so early this morning? Your Papa's not expecting you for another hour or so."

Jacob knew that his father had reported to work at their family-owned service station at least two hours earlier; he, also, knew that the elder Wymer was more than likely waiting impatiently for Jacob to arrive.

He put the freshly-ironed shirt on over his tee-shirt, and tucked both into his equally impressive, starched and pressed blue jeans. That was just one more thing his friends enjoyed teasing him about—ironed jeans! Nobody still ironed blue jeans—nobody, that is, except his mother, who insisted on ironing *all* of his clothes. No doubt she would try to iron his Fruit of the Looms if he allowed her, but Jacob had to draw the line on starched briefs. He loved his mother unconditionally, and he knew that she loved doing things for him. There were times when he felt that her personality was a bit on the eccentric side, but that only made him love and want to protect her even more—especially from his father. His father was always quick to ridicule everything his mother attempted to do, no matter how large or small the project.

Jacob gulped down the last of his orange juice. "I've...got an errand to run before I check in with Pop."

A worried look crossed his mother's face. "Jacob, you know he's expecting you at nine o'clock sharp."

Jacob kissed her on the cheek and grabbed his windbreaker from a hook by the back door. "I know, Mama, and don't worry...I promise I will be there...on time."

Ruth attempted to shrug off her motherly concerns. "What sort of errand do you have to run at eight o'clock in the morning?"

Jacob failed to conceal a blush. He hated lying to his mother. "It's just...uh...something personal I have to take care of; I have to stop at the drug store before I get to the shop."

Ruth looked closely at her son. She knew he wasn't telling her the whole truth; she could always tell when Jacob was lying. "I don't think Big B opens up until nine o'clock, Jacob. You'll be late! You can't be late, son. You know how your father can get sometimes..."

"Don't worry, Mama. There's a drug store on Buena Vista Road that stays open twenty-four hours a day. It won't take me a second to run in and get what I need." He turned and waved to her on his way out the door. "You worry too much, Mama!" he laughed as he jumped in his truck and backed slowly down the driveway.

Ruth watched him leave, shielding her eyes from the early morning sunshine. She brought her hands together beneath her chin and spoke softly. "Protect him, dear Lord; please protect him...especially from his father..."

Across town, Scott Pennell was backing out of his parking space when he saw the black, 1982 Chevy pickup truck swing sharply into the empty space beside Macey Garner's Isuzu Rodeo. He watched, through his rear-view mirror, as a young man jumped from the truck and ran up the sidewalk to Macey's front door.

Scott allowed his vehicle to idle while he watched with curiosity. He watched Macey's front door open before the young man reached it; he saw Macey running out to meet the young man. He felt like a voyeur as he continued to watch, with unexpected disappointment, as Macey practically leapt into the young man's open arms and was swung around like a rag doll. They were both laughing when the man finally placed her on the ground and they walked arm-in-arm back inside Macey's apartment.

Scott was still watching as the door closed behind them. "Well," he sighed, "I suppose that explains the cold reception I got from her. But..." he added thoughtfully, "I didn't notice a ring on her finger...and, no ring means there's still hope! I don't give up easily, Miss Garner." He smiled and reached for the city map lying on the front passenger seat. "Okay, CompuTech, watch out! Scott Pennell is ready to rock your world!" He rolled down his window and let the cool breeze whip lightly against his face. "I love this place!" he shouted to an elderly woman walking a Pomeranian along the sidewalk.

Meanwhile, inside Macey's apartment, Jacob draped an arm over his sister's shoulder after accepting the cup of coffee she had poured for him.

Macey smiled at his youthful exuberance, and secretly envied him for it. "Jacob, I'm glad you stopped by, but this is a surprise. I'm afraid I can't talk long, though. I have a staff meeting at nine-thirty and, trust me, I *cannot* be late for this meeting."

"Why not?" Jacob asked, taking a quick sip of the coffee, which was much too strong for his own personal liking. He was more a cappuccino lover, while Macey preferred strong, black espresso. "What's so special about this particular meeting?"

"Come on," she motioned to him, "Let's finish our coffee outside on the patio, and then I really do have to get going." She led them onto the patio and smiled back at him. "This meeting? Well, Mr. Byce is going to introduce the new Director of the Computer Technology Department to everyone this morning."

Jacob smiled and managed to swallow another mouthful of the strong Java. "And we both know that's going to be you, right?"

Macey grinned at his abundant confidence in her ability. "I wish. Unfortunately, if the grapevine is as accurate as it usually is, well...he may have hired an outsider for the job."

Jacob smirked, "You mean he's hired a *man* for the job, don't you?"

Macey smiled at him again. "Well...yes, the grapevine does indicate it's a *male* outsider."

Jacob paced the length of the shrubbery-lined porch. He had no trouble seeing over the top of the manicured greenery. "That's just not fair, Macey! You're more than qualified for that position, and you've worked harder than anyone else for that promotion."

Macey placed her hand against his chest. "Whoa! Don't get upset, little brother. CompuTech is a great corporation and I count my blessings that I have a job there; and, if I were to be completely honest with you, and myself...well...I'd be lying if I said I didn't want that job. But...truth is, I really am considered pretty low on the totem pole as far as seniority goes. I've only been with the company for what...two years now? Trust me, I have a way to go before I make it to the top, executive level. Besides...I love my job. It's very interesting..."

Jacob shook his head and downed another swallow of the awful coffee. "Yeah, yeah, but we both know you'd rather have this new position."

"That's true," Macey sighed. "And who knows...maybe this new guy won't work out, or maybe he won't like the job, and it'll come open again sooner than we think. Enough about that, though. Aren't you supposed to be at work?"

Jacob nodded while he forced yet another swallow of the too-rich Java. "Yep, but I told Mama I had an errand to run before I went to work."

"And just what kind of errand at eight-thirty in the morning might that be?"

"Funny..." Jacob grinned, "Mama asked the same thing. She thinks I had to stop by the Big B."

"The drug store? This early in the morning...whatever for?"

Jacob displayed a serious expression before replying. "You know, Sis, there are times a guy has to purchase some...*personal* things..."

It took a moment before Macey caught his drift. When she did, however, her hand flew to cover her mouth as she failed to suppress a girlish giggle. "Oh, no! You mean, she thinks you had to stop and buy some..."

Jacob laughed out loud. "Go ahead, Macey, say it! I dare you! Say it!"

Macey blushed and shook her head.

"Come on, Macey," Jacob prodded. "If you don't say it, I'll tickle you!"

Macey backed away slowly. "Don't you dare! You know I can't stand to be tickled."

"Then you had better...say...it," Jacob teased as he inched slowly toward her with outstretched, wriggling fingers.

"Protection!" Macey shouted, as she dashed quickly back inside the apartment. "There! I said it!"

They both collapsed onto the sofa.

Jacob couldn't resist; he reached over and began tickling her anyway.

"They're called condoms, Macey! Come on, say it! I want to hear you say it...C-O-N-D-O-M-S!"

Macey's face turned red and she screamed with laughter while Jacob tickled her sides. "No! Stop it, please, stop it. I can't stand..." She began hiccupping and laughing at the same time. "Jacob, stop, please...I can't laugh anymore!"

"Then you'd better say the word..."

"Okay, okay! Condoms! Condoms! Condoms! There...I said it!"

Jacob ceased his relentless tickling and assisted his sister to a sitting position.

"Whew!" Macey exhaled, as she attempted to smooth her hair back into place. "Jacob, you are impossible!"

"I know, but you love me anyway, don't you?"

She looked adoringly at her younger brother. Her relationship with him, along with the hope of one day finding the child she had been forced to give up, had been her salvation over the past few years. If it hadn't been for Jacob, she may have given up all hope for some sense of a normal life, long ago. Her brother had helped her to hold on to her often-fragile sanity. She smiled and pushed a strand of thick hair off his forehead. "I love you more than life itself, Jacob. Please...don't ever doubt that."

He smiled, a little embarrassed at the raw emotion he heard in her voice, and glanced around the apartment. He noticed the empty wine bottle on the kitchen counter. "I know you do, Sis, and the feeling is mutual. Uh...not to change the subject, but..." he nodded in the direction of the wine bottle. "What gives with that? I didn't think you even liked wine. Or did you, like maybe, have company last night?"

Macey tweaked his nose in response to his questions. "You ask too many questions, little brother, but...no...to both your questions. I don't usually drink wine or anything else for that matter, and...I didn't have company last night."

"Too bad..." Jacob muttered beneath his breath.

"What did you say?"

Jacob shrugged his broad shoulders. "Nothing...hey, listen, Macey, I better get going before the old man blows a fuse; and, I don't want to be the reason you're late for your meeting either. I just wanted to stop by to check on you since I never made it over here Friday night. It's just that...something...came up. Maybe we can get together this weekend. I'll make up something to tell the folks."

Macey reached up and touched his ruggedly handsome face. He was such a good person. He wanted to make everyone happy, but in this situation, that would never be possible. Their parents would never forgive him if they found out that he had been in contact with his long, lost sister. They believed she had departed their lives, permanently, after she moved to Madison to have her illegitimate child. Macey shuddered to think what Andrew Wymer would do to his only son if he ever found out that Jacob had been secretly seeing his sister for the past five years. "I don't want to do anything that will get you in trouble with them, Jacob. You know that we have to be very careful. I've told you that time and time again."

Jacob grasped his sister's hand into his own and brought it to his lips. "I know, and we will. I only wish you would tell me the truth about some things..."

Macey shook her head vehemently from side to side. "I can't, Jacob; at least, not right now. Maybe...one day soon I can tell you everything."

Jacob shrugged again. "Okay. I won't pry. Just remember, if you ever need me for anything, you let Becca know, and tell her to get word to me right away. I mean it!"

Becca James was Macey's best friend; she was the only person Macey had allowed into her personal life. The only other person she had ever been that close to had been her twin sister, Kacey.

"I promise..." Macey smiled back. "Now, scat! We both have to get to work."

"Okay, I'm going," Jacob grinned back at her as he opened the front door. "But, promise me that you'll let me know if you need anything."

"I will...I promise. I'll see you this weekend; we'll work something out. Maybe we can go bowling or something."

Jacob was out the door and walking briskly toward his truck. He turned and waved. "Sounds like a plan! Bye, Sis. I love you!"

Macey waved and watched him drive away. "I love you too, Jacob," she whispered. "I love you, too."

Once back inside her apartment, Macey leaned against the door and closed her eyes in prayer. "Please, God...please protect Jacob. Watch over him today and protect him always...protect him from our father..."

CHAPTER 7

THE MEETING AT COMPUTECH

Macey only lived five miles from CompuTech so she made it to work with ten minutes to spare. She nodded hello to Janet Ward, the corporation's chief receptionist, an enterprising young woman who entertained aspirations of marrying her way into "the good life." Rumor had it that Janet had more than accommodated most of the members of upper management, and was the most recent mistress of CompuTech's Assistant Chief Executive Officer, George Byce.

Janet had been born and raised in Columbus, Georgia. She was twenty-four years old, and her beauty was incomparable to anyone within a ten-year radius of her age group. She was taller than most women, standing barefoot at five feet, nine inches, and her long, shapely legs seemed to account for more than half her overall height. Her thick and lustrous auburn hair cascaded across her shoulders, which were usually bare regardless of the current season. Her eyes were usually the most genuine emerald green that the latest technology in contact lenses could create. She wasn't well-liked by her female coworkers, nor, did that bother her. Her focus was strictly on the male population—most of which, found numerous reasons to stop by her desk several times during the day. She thrived on their continuous attention and compliments.

Macey had almost made it inside her office without having to speak to the notorious receptionist.

"Miss Garner! Wait!" Janet called out in her syrupy voice.

Macey turned and smiled politely, "Yes, Janet, what is it? I have a nine-thirty meeting to prepare for..." She didn't notice Jim Perry, CompuTech's Personnel Director, coming down the corridor toward Janet's desk.

Jim had been given the assignment of showing the new Director of

Computer Technology around the facilities and introducing him to a few of the employees.

Janet was quick to notice the two men approaching and immediately decided that the new Director of Computer Technology could be her new meal ticket off the employment rolls. She stood up slowly from behind her desk and straightened her black, silk skirt. She purposefully allowed her hands to linger a moment longer than necessary on her rounded hips. She walked slowly toward Macey in true southern style—one hip at a time—and waved the phone message she held in her hand. She handed the message to Macey. "There was a call for you a few minutes ago, Miss Garner. She said she was a friend of yours, but..."

Macey still had not noticed the two men, who had stopped their conversation long enough to admire Janet's deliberate progression across the room. She took the message from Janet's hand and inquired, "But...?"

Janet took her attention off the men long enough to look appropriately uncomfortable when she replied, "Well, it's just that I doubt this woman is *really* a friend, Miss Garner. She sounded...you know...well...*black*."

Macey bit her tongue, but the absurdity of the conversation finally got the best of her. "It's all right, Janet, really it is. You see, this is 1989 and...believe it or not...blacks and whites have learned to live together in relative peace. Some have even been known to develop actual *friendships*. Can you believe it?" She turned on her heel, not caring that she left Janet standing alone with a dumbfounded expression etched across her perfect face. She entered her office and slammed the door. Once inside the security of her own space, however, Macey sighed deeply. She was ashamed of herself for not handling the situation in a more professional manner. "Oh well..." she sighed again. She glanced down at the message she held between her fingers and wondered why Becca was calling so early. It was usually closer to the lunch hour before Macey heard from her best friend.

Janet stood staring at the closed door, trying to decide if she should be offended by Macey's remarks. A man's voice interrupted her thoughts.

"Miss Ward? Janet...excuse me, dear, but I'd like you to meet the new director for the Computer Technology Department. Janet, this is Mr. Scott Pennell. Mr. Pennell has just arrived from Pennsylvania. Scott, Miss Ward has been our receptionist for about three years now. Isn't that right, Janet, dear?"

Jim Perry didn't even try to contain his personal lust for CompuTech's chief receptionist. He had enjoyed the pleasure of her company many times in the past, until his wife found out about it. His wife had promptly threatened to cut off his manhood, gift wrap it, and personally deliver it to Janet if he even thought about seeing the receptionist again. She convinced him that it would, indeed, be in his best financial interest to end the relationship. Jim was no fool. He knew the price a divorce would cost him, so he heeded his wife's advice. He had not experienced satisfactory sex since.

Janet smiled at Jim and ran the tip of her tongue over her top lip. She offered her hand to Scott and sighed as she visualized their future together. "Yes, Mr. Perry, that's right…three years. Hello, Mr. Pennell. It is so very nice to meet you. Is there anything I can do to help you and *Mrs.* Pennell get settled in?"

Scott smiled at Janet's less-than-subtle attempt to determine his marital status. He held her soft, warm hand in his own and felt her thumb move sensuously across the palm of his hand. It was a common gesture—mostly among singles—to let the other party know that you were open to a relationship. He wondered if she was really expecting him to return the gesture. "Hello. It's nice to meet you, too, and…thank you for the offer, but that won't be necessary; and, by the way, there isn't a *Mrs.* Pennell." Scott smiled at the woman who was almost his height, given the three-inch heels she wore. "By the way, is it all right if I call you Janet, or do you prefer Miss Ward?"

Janet smiled with satisfaction as Scott discretely returned the thumb-caressing gesture. "Oh," she replied coyly, "You can call me Janet, please—everyone does."

Jim Perry motioned for Scott to follow him. "Come on, Scott. There are a few more people you should meet before the nine-thirty meeting."

Scott turned and glanced back at Janet who was walking back to her desk. He smiled when she turned back to look at him, too.

"Nice, isn't she?" leered Jim Perry.

Scott re-focused his attention back to the Personnel Director. "Excuse me?"

Jim nodded his head and grinned. "Janet…nice package, isn't she?"

"Well," Scott returned the grin. "She is easy on the eyes, for sure…" He turned to look back at Janet one more time and pressed his lips tightly together when she bent over to retrieve something that had fallen to the floor.

Jim sighed wistfully, remembering what great sex had felt like, and looked over at Scott. "Don't worry, Scott. She'll get around to you."

"Excuse me?"

Jim slapped Scott good-naturedly on the back as they continued down the hall. "I think you know what I mean. I'll give her…let's say…to

41

the end of the week, maybe not even that long."

Neither man had thought to mention the woman Janet had been talking to before they had stopped for introductions. Scott had been so engrossed in watching Janet's fluid hip movements that he had not paid attention to the other party.

Inside her office, Macey quickly pulled off her blazer and dialed Becca James' number. The phone was answered on the first ring.

"Macey? Is that you, girlfriend?"

Macey laughed at her friend's enthusiasm; it was contagious and always lifted her spirits. "Yes, Becca, it's me. You had me worried calling so early this morning. Is there anything wrong? Is your Dad feeling all right?"

"Oh, hell yeah, everyone's just fine. I didn't mean to worry you none, girl. I just wanted to catch you before you made any important lunch plans for today."

Macey laughed again. "Don't tell me...I know now why you're calling so early; your mama made her famous sweet potato pie, didn't she?"

Becca returned the laughter. "You guessed it, girl, and she said to tell you that you'd better high-tail it on over here before one o'clock or she'll be givin' your piece away to someone else."

"I wouldn't miss it and you know it. I've got a meeting this morning, but it should be over before noon. I'll see you then. Do you need me to bring you anything?"

Becca took a long drag on a cigarette before responding. "Not a thing, girlfriend. Just bring yourself on down here; I missed seeing you and that handsome brother of yours this weekend."

"Well, if I remember correctly, Miss James, you called and told me that you had gotten a better offer at the last minute!"

Becca exhaled an exaggerated sigh. "Oh, you have no idea how much better an offer it was, girlfriend...oh, yes it was! Anyway, his name is Carlton Brown, and, I'll tell you all about him at lunch."

Macey smiled into the phone. "I'll be there, Becca. Take care now and tell your Daddy hello for me."

"I'll do that...see you at lunch, girl! Bye now."

"Good-bye, Becca." Macey hung up the phone. Her mouth was already watering in anticipation of Mrs. James' sweet potato pie. She didn't even like sweet potatoes, but she loved the James' sweet potato pie. She exhaled softly and began digging through her files. Unfortunately, she had to get through her nine-thirty meeting before she could afford the luxury of thinking about today's dessert.

Macey was the last one to enter the filled-to-capacity conference room. She had received an urgent overseas call immediately after she had finished her call with Becca, so she was uncharacteristically late for the meeting.

"Well, well, we are so glad that you decided to join us, Miss Garner." The snide welcome came from George Byce, CompuTech's Assistant CEO, who—according to the office grapevine—ran the company with a firm hand and exigent phallus.

Macey avoided eye contact with the man. "I'm sorry, Mr. Byce. I had an unexpected overseas phone call…"

George Byce waved his hand in dismissal. "We don't have time for your excuses, Miss Garner. Please, take your seat. Everyone, before we hear status updates from the various departments, I'd like to take this opportunity to introduce the new director of the Computer Technology Department. Some of you may have already met him. Scott, will you stand up please?"

There was a small smattering of applause when Scott stood up and nodded his head in acknowledgment to his peers.

George Byce waved his hand again as a signal to end the applause. "Mr. Scott Pennell joins us from West Mifflin, Pennsylvania, where he was Assistant Director in charge of Computer World's Technology Department. He is a graduate of Penn State and has excellent credentials. I'm sure everyone will join me in welcoming him aboard. Scott, I'm confident that you will enjoy many productive years with CompuTech."

Another scattered applause was expended as Scott sat back down and replied, "Thank you, Mr. Byce. I look forward to working with everyone here."

George Byce nodded. "It is our practice, Scott, to assign a corporate sponsor to all new executive employees, especially those who join us from out-of-state. Unfortunately, your original sponsor was Ed McPherson, who was rushed to Doctor's Hospital late last night for an emergency appendectomy."

There was a culmination of expressed concern from the staff members.

"Now, now, everyone," George Byce said, holding up his hand to silence the gathering. "It's not that serious. Ed is fine but, unfortunately, he will be out of work for a couple of weeks; therefore, I have assigned you another sponsor, Scott."

"That's not necessary, sir," Scott offered. "I've got a city map and I'm sure I'll be able to find my way around with no problem."

"We wouldn't hear of it, Scott," Mr. Byce countered. "Besides, it really is company policy. So, since some of your work efforts will need to be coordinated through our training department, I thought the most appropriate sponsor for you would be...Miss Garner. Macey, would you stand please so that Mr. Pennell will know who you are."

Macey's emotions had surged from shock to total disbelief when Scott was introduced to the group. She couldn't believe it! What kind of cruel trick was fate trying to pull on her? She stood on trembling legs and smiled weakly at Scott.

Scott commiserated at her obvious discomfort, while at the same time, silently thanking fate for stepping in and lending him a much needed, helping hand. "Thank you, Mr. Byce," he rebounded, never taking his eyes off Macey. "And thank you, Miss Garner...you don't know how much I appreciate your help."

Macey didn't dare try to respond verbally, so she nodded in reluctant acknowledgement.

"Very well, then," directed Mr. Byce. "Now that we have settled that matter, let's get down to business. Miss Garner, we'll start with you. Give us your status report on the request for overseas training..."

CHAPTER 8

FIRST DAY AT WORK

Macey was in the middle of yet another overseas call when Scott knocked on her office door, which she had left standing slightly ajar.

He smiled at her and she motioned for him to come in.

"Thank you very much. I'll be in touch again soon, Mr. Hoechst. Yes... good-bye," Macey concluded her phone call. She glanced quickly at Scott Pennell and knew that it was important for her to find some sort of mental balance. She had to acquire a working relationship with the man, while at the same time, distancing herself from the monster who had brutally murdered her twin sister. It wasn't going to be easy to do. "*I've got to quit thinking this way,*" she thought. "*Come on, Macey, get control of yourself. You're going to have to work with this man...*"

Scott had moved inside the office, but was still standing. "I...hope I didn't interrupt some sort of global business deal?"

Macey did her best to ignore his smile and pleasant disposition. She stood and motioned to one of the chairs positioned in front of her desk. "No, of course not, Mr. Pennell. Please...come in...have a seat. What can I do for you?"

Scott watched her as she stood up and was awarded another view of her well-sculpted body. Even though her attire and demeanor were nothing but professional, the unintentional imprint of her nipples straining through her thin, white silk camisole was causing Scott to feel anything but professional toward this woman. He cleared his throat. "Thanks." He took the offered seat and stretched his long legs out before him. It had been a long morning. "First things first," he smiled again. "I would appreciate it if you called me Scott. I won't be Mr. Pennell until I reach at least the age of forty. Oh, and one other thing— I'm afraid I have a...slight problem. Since you are my corporate sponsor, I thought you might be able to help me with it."

Macey was winning her mental battle of ignoring the man's smile and pleasant disposition. "Of course, I'll be glad to help if I can...*Scott*?"

He smiled at her obvious discomfort in having to address him by his first name. "Well, actually, my problem concerns...food."

Macey was genuinely baffled at the serious tone to his voice. She shook her head and shrugged. "Food—you have a problem with food?"

Scott grinned and returned the shrug. "Well, not a problem *with* food; you see, I was so excited about work this morning, I completely forgot to eat breakfast, and now...I'm starving! I thought you might recommend a place where a man could get a good hot meal for lunch. Oh, and not fast food—I'm tired of fast food. Truth be told, I guess I miss Mom's cooking more than I thought I would."

"The murderer has a mother..." Macey rolled that thought around in her head. "Well," she sighed softly. "There are several places in the downtown area. If it's home cooking you're looking for, though, there's a great place on Eighth Street called Minnie's Uptown Restaurant. It's very clean and the food is excellent..."

Scott beamed and nodded. "That sounds great! Will you join me?"

The offer for lunch caught Macey off guard. *"Of all the nerve..."* she steamed inside while managing to keep her facial expression neutral. The last thing she wanted was to have to sit across from her sister's murderer and make polite conversation. It had become obvious to her that Scott did not recognize her, which meant that he had, also, erased Kacey from his mind. Macey wondered if it was a deliberate attempt on his part or whether he truly did not remember Kacey Wymer. She blinked hard. "I'm sorry...what did you say?"

Scott picked up on her immediate reluctance to accept his offer for lunch, but he had to try again. He flashed his captivating grin again. "Lunch—food—hunger! I was hoping to convince you to join me for lunch."

It was an internal struggle but Macey managed to return a half-hearted smile. She needed to keep her hands busy, so she started gathering and organizing papers on her desk that were already in perfect order. She looked back at him, made direct eye contact, and replied, "Thank you for the offer, Mr. Pennell...*Scott*...but, I have already made other plans for lunch."

Scott ran his fingers through his thick hair. "I should have guessed as much. I assume it's with the man I saw you hugging this morning?"

Macey's posture stiffened abruptly. Her face became flushed with a mixture of anger and anxiety, while she struggled to contain both. "Excuse me? What man are you talking about?"

Scott's eyebrows lifted in good humor. "This morning...back at the apartment...in the parking lot? I saw you come out and greet a young man, just as I was leaving. I couldn't help but notice that it seemed like more than just a casual greeting."

"Are you spying on me, Mr. Pennell?"

Scott shook his head and reiterated his preference for his first name. "It's Scott."

Macey stared at him as though he had suddenly grown two heads. "What?"

"Call me, Scott...please."

Macey suddenly felt awkward and simple-minded. "Oh..." was all she could say.

"Is it serious?" Scott asked.

"Is what serious, *Scott*?"

Scott grinned at her apparent dislike of having to use his given name. "Your relationship with this man...is it serious?"

Macey regained some control over her emotions. "Well...*Scott*...at the off-chance of sounding rude, I really don't think that is any of your business, do you?"

Scott bowed his head for a moment. He could tell he had upset her with his question, yet, she was still polite toward him. "Are you always this nice, Macey?"

Macey bit her lower lip. "Are you being sarcastic, Mr. Pennell?"

Scott held up his index finger and shook it. "It's Scott...and, no...it wasn't my intention to come across as sarcastic. It's just that I find you to be an extremely attractive woman, and I was hoping that we might have lunch together today. I mean, I am new to the area...all alone in a new city, and—in case you've forgotten—you *are* my sponsor."

George Byce was passing outside Macey's office and happened to overhear Scott's last comment. He tapped on the open door and peered inside. He smiled at Scott but turned a cold gaze upon Macey. "That sounds like an excellent idea to me, Miss Garner. Why don't you take Scott to Minnie's? The food is one to write home about, Scott."

Macey felt trapped. "I've made other plans for lunch, Mr. Byce. I hadn't planned on going to Minnie's today."

George Byce's cold glare demanded attention. "Then I suggest you take him wherever you *are* going, Miss Garner. Just make sure you're both back by two o'clock; there's a design meeting you'll need to attend."

Scott shook George's hand before he walked away, and watched while the man sauntered over to the receptionist's desk. He continued to watch while Janet refreshed her flawless makeup, gathered her purse, and left the building holding George Byce's offered arm. His eyebrows raised again when he saw George Byce's hand travel, indiscreetly, from Janet's waist to her shapely buttocks. He shook his head and thought, *"Bet he doesn't make it back in time for that two o'clock meeting..."*

Scott turned back to Macey and noticed that her face had visibly gone from flushed to pale. "I'm sorry, Macey...really, I am. I didn't mean to put you on the spot like that. Hey, don't you worry about lunch. I can find my own way to this Minnie's place. You said it was on Eighth Street, right?"

Macey squared her shoulders and shook her head. "Never mind. It's too late now. If I don't take you with me, I'll never hear the end of it from Mr. Byce. I'm meeting a friend for lunch. Her parents own a small cafe in East Columbus—not the best side of town—and, it's probably not like anything you're used to." She shrugged in defeat. "You're more than welcome to join us for lunch if you want to."

Scott knew that the polite thing to do would be to let her off the hook, but he had a feeling that she was right about George Byce. He didn't want to cause Macey any more trouble with the man—the tension between them had to be obvious to everyone. "That's great!" Scott replied excitedly. He was eager for any food that wasn't served between a bun. "What kind of food does this place serve? Steak— shrimp—pasta—pizza, maybe?"

Macey shook her head and was surprised to feel her mouth corners turn up at the eagerness in his voice. The semi-smile faded quickly, however, when she reminded herself of the importance of maintaining her mental distance with this man. Scott Pennell was bad news. She couldn't allow herself to like him. She had to maintain that mental distance because she, also, could not afford to let him know her true identity—no badly, how much she wanted to throw that information in his face. She wanted to hate him; she had every right to hate him, but, it just wasn't in her nature to hate anyone—not even the man responsible for killing her sister. She knew there must have been something good about him if Kacey liked him well enough to sneak around meeting him for months before she was killed. There was even the possibility—albeit remote—that Scott might not be the person responsible for Kacey's death. There had not been enough evidence twenty years ago to arrest and convict him of the crime; but, in her heart, Macey always believed he was her sister's killer.

Macey shook her current thoughts aside. She retrieved her purse from the bottom desk drawer, smiled, and walked briskly past him. "If that's the kind of food you're hoping to get, then—no—the food won't be any of those. You will, more than likely, be dining on something along the line of fried pork chops, black-eyed peas, collards, and sweet potato pie."

"Oh..." Scott rubbed his chin in confused contemplation. He held open the door for her when she hurried past him. He rushed to catch up with her and grinned. "I've never eaten black-eyed peas or sweet potato pie. Why do they call them that—black-eyed peas—or, do I really want to know? And...what exactly are...*collards?*"

CHAPTER 9

BECCA MEETS SCOTT

Becca James was working behind the counter when Macey walked through the restaurant door. Her curiosity and excitement showed when she saw the chivalrous man standing behind her best friend, holding open the door. Becca had nagged Macey for the past several years that she needed a good man in her life, or at the very least, some good sex — hell, maybe even some not-so-good sex. "Hey there, girlfriend! Over here!" Becca waved. "I've got us a table and the food is on its way...and just who do you have there with you, girl?"

Becca quickly sized up the handsome man standing behind Macey. Something about him caused the hair to stand up on Becca's arms. She rubbed at her arms absently and continued staring at Scott.

Macey joined Becca at the small table and gave her a quick hug. She turned away from her to introduce Scott so she never saw the sudden drawing together of Becca's brows and the bewildered look that briefly crossed her friend's flawless, ebony features. She didn't see Becca's mouth fall open in surprise.

Scott was so focused on Macey that he, too, failed to notice the look of amazement and disbelief that crossed the beautiful black woman's face.

"Hello, Becca," Macey smiled nervously. She was not use to having male companionship at lunch, or at any other time for that matter. "I'd like you to meet a new co-worker, Scott Pennell. Scott, this is my best friend, Becca James. Her mom and dad own this place, and Mrs. James makes the best sweet potato pie this side of Dixie."

Scott held out his hand to Becca, who turned steadfastly away from him. He got the distinct impression that the woman was intentionally ignoring the introduction. A look of embarrassment crossed his face, but he simply smiled and shrugged at Macey.

Macey had never known Becca to be intentionally rude to anyone, so she was mystified at the cool reception she offered Scott. She glanced quickly in Scott's direction, but, if Becca's behavior bothered him, it appeared that he was graciously ignoring her abrupt dismissal of their introduction.

The three of them sat down at the small table and for the next thirty minutes, the conversation was tense and brusque. Any attempt at small talk became pointless, so the conversation focused primarily on the delicious home-cooked food that had been prepared by Bertha James.

Scott didn't allow the lack of conversation to affect his ravenous appetite. He paid ample homage to the meal by respectfully cleaning his plate. He even ate the collards, which turned out to be some sort of green, leafy vegetable that dangerously resembled the weeds he used to pull from his mother's garden. He was thankful for the pepper sauce that Macey offered him; it reduced much of the vegetable's bitter taste. He especially liked the meat that was used to season the collards—at least he did, until Becca informed him the seasoned meat was *ham hocks*! He wasn't entirely sure what part of the pig the hock came from, and, he didn't think he really wanted to know.

Scott thought he noticed a slight thawing of Becca's initial reception toward him, by the time dessert was served; and, by the time he had finished his second serving of the sweet potato pie, he was even more confident that Becca James' tone actually bordered on one of civility. He hoped he was making progress with Macey's best friend.

Scott leaned back slightly in his chair and loosened his belt a notch. He wiped his mouth with the paper napkin and nodded. "That was, undoubtedly, the best pie I've ever tasted! Did you make it, Becca?"

Becca offered a stiff smile and lifted her chin upward. "No, it wasn't me. My Mama is the cook—best damn cook in Columbus, Georgia—ask anyone."

"You won't get any arguments here," Scott agreed. "And those green... leafy things weren't too bad either. I'm sorry, I can't remember what you called them, Macey..."

Macey barely managed to suppress a small laugh. "Those green... leafy things were *collards*, Scott."

Scott nodded. "Collards, right. Well, they sure were...interesting."

Macey grinned. "Yeah, it must be the ham hocks that makes them so...*interesting*. Right, Scott?"

Scott nodded in agreement. "Yep, ham hocks...that must be what gives them their uniqueness, all right. I don't think we have either collards or ham hocks back home in Pennsylvania. I'm pretty sure I would remember having eaten either of them."

Becca stood abruptly and pushed her chair back under the table. "Well, I've got a lot of work to do, Macey; I need to help Mama in the kitchen." She gave her friend a limp, tepid hug and whispered in her ear, "Call me when you get home tonight, girlfriend."

Macey nodded and watched Becca turn away. She yelled out to her, "Bye, Becca. Hey! Do you think I could get a piece of that pie to take with me?"

Becca looked back over her shoulder and threw a hand up in acknowledgment. "You got it, girlfriend." She stopped and turned to look back at Scott, her hand plastered to one hip. "You want one, too?" she asked gruffly.

The last thing Scott wanted to do was to offend Becca James any more than he already had, so he nodded eagerly. "Yes, please! I'd love a piece...of *pie*." He had absolutely no idea why he felt compelled to clarify his statement of affirmation.

Macey squirmed in her seat and smiled at Scott. "I'm sorry, Scott. I apologize for Becca's rude behavior. I've never known her to be so impolite to anyone before. I just don't understand..."

Scott smiled back and shrugged. "Hey, don't worry about it, Macey. I've got thick skin. Maybe she just doesn't like Yankees."

Macey sighed. She appreciated his inclination to overlook Becca's bad manners.

"She's very beautiful," Scott commented, feeling the need to make idle conversation.

"Yes...she is," Macey agreed, "And, not only on the outside. She has a heart of gold. There's nothing she wouldn't do to help a friend in need."

The two co-workers spent the next few minutes talking about their two o'clock meeting. Macey told him that all the department heads would be at the meeting, and, that she would make sure to introduce him to any he had not met at their earlier meeting.

Becca returned to their table, holding two brown bags. She smiled at Macey but did her best to ignore Scott's presence. "Here you go, girlfriend...two pieces of sweet potato pie to go."

Macey took the bags and offered one to Scott. "Thanks, Becca. Be sure to tell your mama I said thanks, too. It was a great meal, as usual."

Becca nodded. "Will do...and, hey, don't you forget to call me tonight, okay?"

Macey nodded. "I will, Becca."

Macey handed Scott her keys and the to-go bag once they were outside the restaurant. "Scott, do you mind waiting for me in the car, please. I, uh...forgot to tell Becca something important. I won't be long."

Scott took her brown bag and keys, and smiled back at her. "Take your time, Macey. We still have about forty-five minutes before the meeting starts. I'll just take a short cat nap in the car. All that food has made me sleepy. I bet it was those green...leafy things...or, the ham hock..."

"Okay," Macey laughed softly. "You do that. I'll be right back...and, don't you dare eat my pie!"

"Scout's honor!" Scott grinned and waved.

Becca had been standing just inside the door, watching the couple leave. She knew from the set expression on Macey's face that her friend was upset with her. She placed both hands upon her shapely, generous hips and readied herself for the confrontation.

Macey opened the door and saw Becca waiting for her. She took her friend by the elbow and guided her toward an empty corner of the room.

Becca's father, Alvin James, was working behind the counter and watched the two women. He had recognized the man that accompanied Macey at lunch—his face had not changed all that much in twenty years. He knew that Becca must have, also, made the connection. He had no doubt that his daughter would get to the reason behind why Macey was having lunch with Scott Pennell, of all people.

Macey folded her arms across her stomach and stood staring at her best friend. "Okay, Becca. We both know this won't wait until tonight. I'm listening."

"What?" Becca queried stubbornly. She really didn't want to get into this conversation with Becca in the crowded restaurant.

"Don't you *what* me, Becca James! You know exactly what I'm talking about! You were practically throwing daggers at the poor man! What gives?"

Becca's stubborn expression turned to one of stunned amazement. Could it be possible that Macey didn't recognize Scott Pennell? After all, she wasn't living in Columbus when her sister was murdered. Maybe she had never seen the photographs of Scott that were published in the newspapers and flashed across the television screen.

Becca, who towered four inches above Macey, placed her hands defiantly on her hips. She pursed her thick lips together and glanced sideways in her father's direction. She uttered a small growl when Alvin turned away from her stare and began clearing a vacated table. She turned her attention back to Macey and growled again. "What gives? Are you kidding me? Damn, girl, how can you stand there and ask me that?"

It was Macey's turn to be stunned. She honestly had no idea what had triggered her best friend's irritable mood. "What *are* you talking about, Becca?"

Becca stole another quick glance at her father, who now placed a finger against his generous lips and shook his head. There was so much Becca wanted to say to Macey, but maybe now wasn't the best time or place to do so. "Forget it—just forget it. It's nothin'. I'm...just havin' a bad day, that's all. Sorry...I didn't mean to take it out on your friend. Why don't you go on back to work, and, we'll talk some more about it later, okay?"

Macey shook her head and bit her lower lip. She sighed and said, "I'm not buying it, Becca. I want you to tell me what it is about Scott Pennell that obviously upsets you so much."

Becca's chocolate-colored eyes glared back at Macey. "And, I said we'll talk about it later, girlfriend. Now, scat! Get out of here! We're not all rich girls like you. Some of us have to work for a living."

"You're not fooling me one bit, Becca James. You're evading the subject, and, we both know I'm a long way from being a rich girl; but, you're right...I have to get back to work, too." Macey turned to leave but took time to wave goodbye to Becca's father, who had come from behind the counter.

Alvin waved back and stood beside his daughter. He placed an arm around her shoulder.

Becca leaned into her father's embrace and returned Macey's wave. "We'll talk later, girlfriend. Let's get something going for this weekend."

Macey nodded. "I'll talk to you later, Becca. Goodbye, Mr. James."

Alvin James smiled broadly and waved. "Goodbye, Miss Macey. Tell your brother we said hello."

"I will," Macey smiled as she exited the door. She stopped and looked back at Becca. "I *will* talk to you later."

"Right..." Becca mumbled beneath her breath. She stood at the door and watched until Macey and Scott drove away. She slammed her hand against the wall and cursed, "Son-of-a-bitch! What's *he* doing back in town? And what the hell are you doing with him, Macey? Girl...*what* are you doing with him..."

The few remaining lunch patrons kept their heads lowered and pretended not to hear Becca's outburst of profanity.

Mr. James came up behind his daughter and patted her shoulder. "Let it go, baby girl. When she's ready to tell you all about it, she will. 'Till then, it might be best if you don't let on that you know anything about her past—nothin' at all..."

CHAPTER 10

THE AMBITIOUS RECEPTIONIST

The next two weeks were a whirlwind of activity for Scott.

He knew he had a lot to learn about his new company, but he had not expected the learning process to be such a time-consuming endeavor. There were countless scheduled, and unscheduled, work group meetings with his subordinates. He devoured mountains of manuals and regulations, and quickly learned the general layout of the corporation, as well as its subsidiary agencies. He attended endless staff meetings chaired by George Byce. It had only taken one staff meeting for Scott not to be impressed with the man; however, the man was his immediate supervisor, so there was little he could do about that situation.

There had not been a lot of spare time, but what little Scott managed to acquire on the weekends was spent purchasing everything he needed for his new home. The time went by so quickly that he wasn't surprised that two whole weeks had gone by since his lunch with Macey and Becca James—two weeks, in which he had not had the opportunity to speak privately with Macey. Even though Mr. Byce had appointed her to be Scott's sponsor, their individual schedules had not allowed for any further one-on-one time.

On the third Monday after his arrival at CompuTech, Scott was in the corporate break room refueling his caffeine addiction. He had his back to the door, so he had not seen Janet Ward, CompuTech's heralded receptionist, enter the room. He did, however, sense that he was no longer alone.

Janet took a sweet moment to admire Scott's rear view before clearing her throat. "Well, good morning, Scott...you're in mighty early for a Monday morning."

It was only seven o'clock and Scott had hoped he might be alone in the building. He turned around slowly at the sound of the sultry, provocative voice. "Good morning, Janet...I didn't know anyone else was in yet. I came in early to do some research before an early meeting this morning, but, I left home without eating breakfast...so, I thought I'd scour the break room for something to eat."

Janet walked over to him and brushed against him when she leaned across the counter for a coffee cup. "Well...I don't know what you're hungry for, Scott, but *I* might have something you'd be interested in..."

Scott's body didn't need more caffeine to pick up on her less-than-subtle innuendo. He stared down at her and wondered, *"Was that another purr...or was it more like a growl this time?"* He answered his own question when she brushed against him again, causing his cup to tilt in his hand and spill coffee on the floor. No, the woman wasn't much for subtlety—it was most, definitely, a growl. He decided to play the innocent and feigned shock at her bold suggestion. "Excuse me?" he croaked. He reached past her for a paper towel to wipe up the spilled coffee.

Janet bent down to assist him, while managing to allow Scott a substantial view of her womanly attributes.

Scott was a man, so he looked. Her low-cut blouse barely secured the mammary beasts within; her tight, leather skirt rode up her milky-white thighs, offering him a palpable view of what she wasn't wearing underneath. The skirt was black leather—black had always been his favorite color for women's clothing.

Janet was well aware of the effect she had on men, and Scott was no different from all the others. She was use to the attention men gave her—they had been paying her extra attention since her body had matured into that of a woman at the age of sixteen. She would have been surprised and disappointed if Scott had not stopped to inspect her merchandise—even though, she could tell that he was trying to be discreet in his observation.

She swiveled her hips on her way to a standing position and, secretly, visualized their eventual union—she felt it was inevitable. She had used all the willpower she possessed during the past two weeks to deliberately distance herself from Scott; however, it was becoming increasingly more difficult to maintain any semblance of control. She was growing so tired of attending to Mr. Byce's aged, pliant organ day after day. Her affair with the Assistant CEO hadn't even gotten her off receptionist duties yet...much less off the employment rolls. Scott might not be able to help her in that department either, but, he would be a welcome change and distraction while she waited for her next contestant.

"You're staring, Scott." The female voice was silky and fluid.

Scott assumed the voice belonged to Janet.

It didn't.

He realized the voice came from behind him. He was still in a kneeling position but turned his head toward the voice. He groaned inwardly when he saw Macey leaning against the open door.

Macey held her own empty coffee cup and smiled awkwardly. "I can come back—if I'm interrupting something."

"Macey!" Scott sputtered. He immediately lost what little balance he had left, slipped, and fell unceremoniously on his butt. "Good morning...I...uh...I spilled my coffee..."

Janet bent down to assist Scott to a standing position. "And I was just...helping him clean it up."

Scott blushed and quickly turned away from the blatant viewing she offered him again.

"More than likely, you were helping him GET it up..." Macey thought to herself. She returned Janet's condescending smile. "I'm sure Mr. Pennell more than appreciates your help, Janet."

Oh, it's no problem at all," Janet purred. She straightened the too-tight skirt and directed her attention back toward Scott. "By the way, Scott, I wanted to make sure you're coming to the company's Halloween party Friday night. You are, aren't you?"

"Halloween party?" Scott mused as he used his foot atop the paper towel to wipe up the last of the spilled coffee from the floor.

"Don't tell me you haven't heard?" Janet pouted. "I typed up a memo and put a copy in everyone's distribution box." She took the saturated paper towel from Scott and tossed it toward the waste basket. She missed and smiled. "Oh, it'll be great fun! It always is. Everyone dresses up in costumes, gets looped, and...well, you know, we all have a really, really good time...if you know what I mean...and I do love to dress up..."

Scott looked genuinely puzzled. "Looped?" he asked, looking back and forth from Janet to Macey for clarification.

Macey educated him on the meaning of the word. "It means *drunk*, Scott. They all get disgustingly drunk, which is usually their idea of a good time."

Janet squared her shoulders and looked down her nose at Macey.

Macey returned the stare. In spite of her generally accommodating personality, she was not easily intimidated by the likes of Janet Ward— by others maybe, but not Janet Ward.

"Well, Miss Garner," Janet snipped. "I really don't think you should comment on what goes on at the Halloween party, especially since you've never been to one." Janet turned back to Scott and smiled sweetly at him. "We really do have a good time, Scott. I do hope you'll...*come*."

Macey took a few steps forward and deliberately walked between them. "Oh, sorry. Please excuse me, but I need to get in here." She poured herself a cup of coffee and leaned against the counter. She sipped leisurely at the steaming coffee.

It was obvious to Janet that Macey Garner was in no hurry to leave. She moved to close the distance that Macey's path had created between her and Scott. She leaned closer to him and whispered in his ear. "We *really* do have a good time, Scott..."

Macey couldn't help herself. She deliberately separated them again when she moved to the opposite counter. "Excuse me again, please. I need some sugar...for my coffee." She smiled sweetly at Janet. "I'm sure you have fun at the parties, Janet—all I'm saying is that maybe it's not everybody's idea of a good time." Macey took another long sip of coffee. "By the way, Janet...coffee wasn't the only reason I came in here—I saw your car outside, and figured you might be in the break room. I, also, thought you might want to know that Mr. Byce came in early this morning, too; he's already stopped by your desk twice during the last fifteen minutes."

Janet knew that she needed to remain in George Byce's good favor—for the time being. She practically snarled her response at Macey. "Well, why didn't you say something sooner! I'd better get back out there!" No matter how bored she had become with Mr. Byce and his sick, sexual fantasies over the past several months, she knew better than to induce his ire. She made a quick exit toward the door and yelled back over her shoulder. "Think about what I said, Scott...about the party!"

Macey's temporary bravado vanished when she found herself alone with Scott Pennell. She was still uncomfortable around him and found it difficult to look at him without seeing the seventeen-year old boy accused of murdering her sister. However, after observing Scott at a safe distance during the past two weeks, Macey thought her feelings along those lines were gradually altering. Something just did not feel quite right about the whole situation. The more she watched and listened to Scott interact with their coworkers, the less she could visualize him as a cold-blooded murderer. One thing continued to bother her, however. It was his reaction to Macey—or rather, his lack of reaction to her. She and Kacey had been identical twins, except for their eye color.

Scott cleared his throat. "We could go to the party together, Macey. You know...just to make an appearance—get the old man off our backs for a while."

Scott's deep, rich voice brought Macey's thoughts back to the present. "What?" she mumbled.

"You and I...go to the party together, maybe?

Macey looked stupefied. "The two of us...together?"

"Well, it might help take some of the pressure off...maybe make Mr. Byce ease up on you some. I can't help but notice that he...well...that he doesn't treat you very nice. I've been wanting to ask you. Does he always talk down to you like you're his...servant?"

Macey winced. "You've noticed, huh?"

Scott nodded and moved closer to her. "It's hard not to notice. What has the man got against you, anyway?"

"I think I need more coffee." Macey spoke softly. She moved quickly away from him and hoped she might be able to avoid having to answer his question. She exhaled deeply. "I could use another shot of energy right about now."

Scott allowed her the physical space she needed. "You're not going to answer my question, are you?"

"Which question, Scott? You ask a lot of them."

"You know which question. Mr. Byce—what does the man have against you?"

Macey turned her back on him and attempted to pour more coffee into a cup that was already full. She sat her cup down and turned back to face him. "I'm surprised our illustrious and ambitious receptionist hasn't already filled you in on that score."

"I'd rather hear it from you than through the office grapevine, Macey."

"Why?"

Scott ran his hand through his hair. He stared at Macey, and for just a moment—a very quick moment—he experienced a sudden, vivid flashback of a much *younger* Macey. The younger Macey smiled at him, reached out to hold him, and...*kissed* him. A shiver ran down his spine and the flashback ended abruptly at the sound of heavy, approaching footsteps.

"There you two are! I saw your cars in the parking lot," bellowed George Byce. He forged into the break room and stared at them both. "Taking a break, are we?"

"Yes, sir," answered Scott, glancing down quickly at his watch—it wasn't even eight o'clock yet. "How are you this morning, Mr. Byce?"

"Very well, Scott—thank you for asking." Mr. Byce turned a malignant glare upon Macey.

Macey avoided eye contact with the man and focused her attention on a nonexistent stain on the floor.

George Byce's voice practically dripped with venom. "And what about you, Miss Garner? Are you very well this morning, also?"

Macey finally looked up and stammered a meek response. "Yes, sir... thank you. If you two will excuse me..." She turned to leave, more than ready to avoid any confrontation with George Byce. He had treated her badly since the day, last year, when she had bravely renounced his sexual overtures. It had not mattered that she had refused propositions from other men in the company, as well; she knew that George Byce took her rejection as a personal affront to his senescent manhood.

"Not so fast, Miss Garner!" he commanded. "I came looking for you for a specific reason."

Scott caught the slight trembling of Macey's hands. "Something I could help you with, sir?" he implored. He hoped to ease the tension in the room and to divert Mr. Byce's attention from Macey.

George Byce stared at Macey and curled his hands into fists. He turned toward Scott and smiled. "Maybe you can help, Scott," he replied. He rubbed his chin in pretense of thought.

"Anything...anything at all," Scott offered.

George Byce turned back to face Macey, but directed his response to them both. "Miss Ward told me she was talking with you both earlier about this year's Halloween party. What she probably didn't tell you is that there will be several of our overseas' associates at this year's party. They will be in town over the weekend for a technology convention, so I am directing *all* my staff to attend this party."

Macey appeared visibly uncomfortable with the idea of attending the party, but she knew better than to counter his directive.

George Byce noticed her obvious discomfort and smiled.

Scott's natural chivalry kicked in when he saw how uneasy Macey was with the idea of attending the party. He found himself wanting to do anything he could to make her feel better, to take the pressure off. "No problem, Mr. Byce. As a matter of fact, Macey and I were just talking about the party. She's...uh...agreed to be my date for the party. Isn't that right, Macey?"

Macey spun around to face Scott. The blood rushed to her face, reflecting her silent ire. *"How dare he!"* she fumed inside. Instead of saying what she wanted to say, she found herself simply nodding in agreement.

"Good! Very good," smirked George Byce as he patted Scott on the shoulder. He turned to leave the room, and ensured his arm brushed close against Macey's breast. He smiled when he felt her recoil at his touch. He glanced at his watch and spoke gruffly. "Break time's over, you two. It's time to get to work!"

"It's not even eight o'clock yet..." Scott mumbled beneath his breath.

Macey waited until she was sure Mr. Byce was far enough down the hall not to be able to hear them. She took a deep breath to suppress her seething anger. She turned to face Scott. "How dare you!" she hissed.

Scott held up both hands up in defense. "Whoa, Macey! I was only trying to help...really."

"Help! By letting him think we're going to the party *together*?"

"Well, would you really rather go alone, Macey...and chance running into a drunken George Byce?"

Macey was speechless. She opened her mouth, closed it again, and shook her head as tears threatened to capture her Confederate-gray eyes.

Scott reached for her, intending to pull her gently into his arms.

She pushed him abruptly away and whispered hoarsely, "Don't touch me! Don't you ever touch me again!" She turned and fled from the break room.

Scott was left standing all alone in the break room, feeling shocked and bewildered at her strange reaction to his failed embrace. "What did I do?" he asked the empty room. He threw his hands up in defeat. "What did I do?" He sighed and shook his head. He had the distinct feeling that Friday night was going to be a long night for a lot of people.

Macey rushed to her office and slammed the door shut. She began a nervous pace—back and forth—across the length of the room. She rubbed the sides of her arms vigorously and furiously, trying to wash away the touch of Scott Pennell. She finally sat down on the leather sofa and allowed the tears their inevitable escape. "Oh, Kacey, what am I going to do! What am I going to do?"

There was only one thing to do...only one thing that would help her at this moment. Macey closed her eyes and did what she always did to calm herself. She prayed—she prayed to God, to her guardian angels, and...she prayed to Kacey.

After several minutes of continual prayer, she found the inner peace and strength she so desperately sought. A soothing calmness enveloped her entire being and she knew that she was no longer alone. Kacey was with her, and she would be with her Friday night to help her endure whatever was needed to survive the evening with Scott and Mr. Byce.

She rubbed her arms and closed her eyes. "Oh, Kacey, did you tremble at his touch, too? What is it about him that threatens to weaken our resistance to him?" Macey arose from the sofa and, once again, paced the length of her spacious office. She continued her muttering conversation with her dead sister. "I won't give in to him, Kacey. I won't, and...I won't let him hurt me like he did you. He should have been punished for what he did to you. He was never punished...never. He should have been... punished."

Once again, a soothing calmness returned to embrace Macey and she sighed softly. "But not by me, I know...not by me. It's not my place to judge him. Only God can do that...and He will...He has to..."

CHAPTER 11

ANDREW WYMER

He knew he was alone in the house. Neither Ruth's nor Jacob's car had been parked in the driveway. It had been one of those days, complete with rude customers, pushy salesmen, and no time alone. He really needed to be alone for a while. Everyone needed some time alone.

Even though he knew no one was home, Andrew Wymer walked through his small abode, double-checking to ensure that he was indeed alone. He walked into the bedroom he shared with Ruth, glanced at the solitary, twin beds they had purchased shortly after Kacey's death, and went directly to the closet. He shoved a heavy box from the corner, tapped softly against the back wall and shimmied a squared section until it popped loose. It wasn't the perfect hiding place, but he felt secure in his belief that he was the only member of his family who knew of its existence. He reached in, swiped absently at some stray cobwebs, and pulled out a tattered, dusty shoe box. He took it to his bed and emptied the contents upon it.

At least fifty pictures, depicting Kacey Wymer at various stages of her short life, spilled onto the bed. Most of the pictures had been deliberately cut in half. Andrew had tried for so many years to wipe away the image of his other daughter—Kacey's twin sister. If only it had been as easy as cutting pictures in half.

He sorted through the pile until he found his favorite picture. It had been taken two weeks before Kacey died. Andrew was smiling broadly in the picture, his muscular arm draped possessively around Kacey's frail shoulder. Andrew's brows drew together, and for the first time in twenty years, he thought he recognized the look on Kacey's face—it was one of fear. Her posture appeared stiff and cautious. Andrew traced the outline of her tiny frame with his callused finger and smiled as tears of remorse—too little and too late—trickled down his bearded cheek. He brought the picture to his lips, closed his eyes, and kissed it.

A scripture suddenly popped into his mind and he wasn't even aware that he had whispered it out loud. He quoted Psalms 127:3, "Behold, children are a heritage from the Lord, the fruit of the womb is a reward." Andrew bowed his head, and closed his eyes in silent prayer for a few minutes longer. He gradually opened his eyes and smiled wistfully at the picture he still held in his trembling hand. "Only four more days, Kacey... four more days until the anniversary of your death—your premature deliverance unto the Lord. Twenty years...twenty, long years...and still, no one has been punished for taking you away from me. Oh, Kacey! Do you know how much I miss you, how I long to hold you in my arms once again? I never got to say goodbye..."

The sound of the kitchen door slamming shut quickly returned Andrew's thoughts back to the present. He drew his bushy brows together and listened intently as his son, Jacob, whistled and rummaged through the refrigerator for something to eat, no doubt. The boy was always eating.

Andrew gathered up the photos and returned them to the shoe box. He replaced the show box in its hiding place and sat down upon his bed. He closed his eyes and began a rocking motion as he muttered softly, "Why couldn't it have been you, Jacob? Why couldn't God have taken you instead of my precious Kacey? It wasn't fair. It just wasn't fair..."

The telephone rang and Andrew snatched it up before Jacob could answer it. "Hello," he choked a harsh, unwelcomed greeting into the receiver.

"Brother Andrew! I was hoping you would answer..." The voice on the other end of the phone belonged to the Reverend Lucas Dudley, pastor of Pleasant Valley Church of God. Reverend Dudley had only recently returned to Columbus after a long absence. He had been pastor of the now defunct Morning Glory Church of God twenty years ago, until he had been requested to resign his post. His congregation had graciously given him the opportunity to resign in lieu of a public denouncement of him as their pastor. Twenty years had softened a lot of memories. It, also, didn't hurt that a large portion of the Morning Glory congregation had since passed on to their heavenly rewards. The congregation at Pleasant Valley welcomed Lucas Dudley with open arms and trusting hearts.

Andrew cleared his throat before answering, "Good to hear from you, Reverend. What can I do for you?"

"Well, now," Lucas Dudley drawled in his deep, exaggerated Southern accent. "I was hoping the Missus might be cooking her famous meat loaf tonight."

Andrew took a deep breath and prayed for patience. It did not surprise him that the good reverend felt comfortable enough to invite himself to supper. He somehow managed a civil response. "It's Friday night, Reverend. Ruth always makes meat loaf on Friday night, but...then again...you probably remember that, don't you?" Andrew had never been one to beat around the bush, so he exhaled and asked, "Is that the real reason you're calling, Reverend Dudley?"

There was an extended pause before Lucas replied. "You're right, Andrew. Although your wife's meat loaf is mighty tempting, I just thought we could all gather for prayer this evening. I know it's getting close to the anniversary of sweet Kacey's death. I just thought you and the family might need some...spiritual comfort."

Andrew exhaled deeply. He wasn't aware that he had been holding his breath. "You remembered? I didn't think anyone other than Ruth and I would remember. Yeah, well...they say time heals a lot of wounds for a lot of people, but to tell you the truth, Reverend, twenty years isn't enough time to heal the hurt I feel in my heart...the hurt I will always feel in my heart." Andrew wiped his nose with the back of his hand. He didn't want the Reverend, or anyone else, to suspect his frail, emotional state. "Thanks anyway, Reverend, but I figure Sunday's soon enough for...spiritual comfort. I'll tell Ruth you called though. It'll mean a lot to her."

Reverend Dudley cleared his own throat and replied, "Oh...well... all right then. Of course, I understand, but if you need me, please don't hesitate to call on me. I'm here for you both. I hope you know that, Brother Andrew?"

Andrew's response was curt. "Right." He hung up the phone and stared off into space, trying unsuccessfully to curb his torrential train of thought. "Oh, yeah...I'm sure it would mean a lot to Ruthie, Reverend. The *bitch*! She never loved Kacey, never...not like I did. She doesn't miss her...doesn't think about her. All she ever cared about...all she cares about now...is...*Jacob*. That worthless piece of shit I have to call a son."

Andrew put his hands together and looked upward. "Why, Lord...why couldn't you have taken him instead of my Kacey?" Great sobs of grief racked Andrew's body as he privately mourned the loss of his favorite child. Kacey had represented all that was good in the world. She was pure, kind, and good in a world filled with evil people and their decadent thoughts. He never doubted that Kacey loved him as much as he loved her. She had dutifully proven it to him time and time again.

Andrew's mourning had not been as private as he thought it was.

Jacob had been standing outside his father's bedroom door and heard his cruel declaration to God. He shoved his knuckled fist into his mouth to hold back his own tears and slowly backed away. He moved along the hallway, with its faded wall paper of ascending angels, and returned to the kitchen. He placed the sandwich he had made for his father upon the old, wooden table and collapsed into a chair. He closed his eyes tightly and was no longer able to hold back the threatening sobs of anguish. "Oh, Pop...why don't you love me? Why? What have I ever done to you? All I've ever wanted was for you to love me...even just a little..."

Jacob did not hear the approaching car in the driveway.

Ruth Wymer entered the kitchen and saw her son sitting at the kitchen table, his head bowed and his shoulders heaving softly. What had happened? Why was he crying? She closed the screen door quietly behind her and walked over to where Jacob sat. She placed both hands upon his bent and trembling shoulders. "Jacob? What's wrong, son? What's he done now?"

Jacob stiffened at his mother's touch. He was embarrassed for her to witness his weak, emotional state so he kept his head down, shaking it from side to side without answering.

"Jacob! Talk to me, please. Tell me what happened. What did he say to you? I know he must have said or done something—please, tell me..."

He finally raised his head and wiped his runny nose with the back of his hand. He looked back at his mother through tear-swollen eyes. "Nothing, Mama...it's okay. Never mind, I'm all right."

Ruth pulled up a chair and sat beside him. "No, you're not all right, son. What did he say to upset you so?"

Jacob pushed back from the table and walked to the door. He looked back at his mother and sighed. "Same old thing, Mama...same old thing... except, this time...before he asked God why it couldn't have been me instead of Kacey...he threw in that I was a worthless piece of shit."

Ruth cringed at Jacob's use of vulgarity, but knew that he was simply repeating what her husband must have said. "Oh, no...he said this to your face?"

Jacob shook his head sadly. "No, Mama, not to my face...to the good Reverend Dudley."

Ruth was stunned at the contempt with which her son referenced Reverend Dudley's name. "Reverend Dudley was here?" she asked, unable to disguise the crack in her voice.

"No," Jacob shook his head. "He called. Pop answered the phone before I could. I'm not sure he even knew I was here. I was going to surprise him...I made him a sandwich to hold him over till supper because

I knew he worked through lunch today. His bedroom door was cracked open, and I overheard him talking to the Reverend."

"And they were talking about you, Jacob?"

"Not at first, at least I don't think so. I heard Pop say that he wished it had been me who died instead of Kacey!"

Ruth shook her head in disbelief. "I can't believe he would say that to Reverend Dudley."

Jacob grabbed his windbreaker off the coat rack. "No, Mama. He would never admit anything like that to the good reverend. He said it to himself, after he hung up the phone."

"Oh, dear, God!" moaned Ruth. "Jacob...son...I am so sorry...so very sorry you had to hear anything like that, but...you have to know your father didn't mean it."

"For God's sake, Mama, don't take up for him! I've known all my life that he resents me for being alive. All my life I've tried to make it up to him; I've tried to make Kacey's death easier on him by being the best son I could be..."

"I know you have, Jacob. Please, son, don't take all this to heart. He's...he's just upset because Halloween is...well, you know..."

"Oh, yeah, I know..." Jacob agreed, pausing for a moment. "But, Mama...you and Pop both seem to forget something very important. Kacey wasn't your only daughter, was she? What about the other one?"

Ruth felt her chest contract sharply as she gasped for air that was reluctant to cooperate. "What are talking about, Jacob? What...other... daughter?"

Jacob turned and looked back at his mother's paled, expressionless face. He had not meant to say what he did, but he decided to continue. "The one nobody ever talks about, Mama. I believe her name is Macey?"

Ruth rushed toward him then but he was already out the screen door and half way to his car. "Who told you about her, Jacob? How did you find out? Your father has done everything in his power to erase all traces of her from our family tree."

Jacob looked back at his mother and didn't like what he saw and heard. He was suddenly just as angry with her as he was with his father. "He hasn't accomplished that by all by himself, Mama. There's a shoe box in Pop's bedroom closet. It's hidden inside the wall, behind that old cardboard box...sort of a secret hiding place, I guess. Check it out sometime, Mama. I did...several years ago. I know that Macey and Kacey were my twin sisters. I bet you and Pop both thought I was too young to remember them, didn't you? But I do remember some things, Mama... not much...but there are pictures of them both in that shoe box. Macey has been cut out of most of them, but there's still a few of the two of them together."

Jacob watched his mother's shocked expression. He regretted blurting out what he knew to be the truth, but he had been hurt, and his natural instincts demanded that he retaliate in like. It was unfortunate that it had to be his mother because he loved her deeply.

He walked back to where Ruth stood in a frozen, rigid stance upon the porch steps. They looked at each other for several moments before he leaned down and kissed her cheek, which was now damp from a steady flow of tears. "Bye, Mama. Don't wait up for me. I need some time alone, and...Mama? I'm sorry. The last thing I wanted to do was to hurt you. We'll talk about this later...maybe. Okay?"

Ruth didn't answer. She couldn't.

Jacob planted another soft kiss upon his mother's tear-drenched cheek.

Ruth touched her cheek and watched him drive away. She was still in shock to learn that her son had discovered the truth about Macey. All their efforts—especially on Andrew's part—to eradicate any memory of Macey from their lives had been futile. Jacob had discovered the truth after all. She shivered as a slight breeze rustled through the impending dusk. "What else does he know?" she spoke out loud. "Oh, dear, Lord... what else does he know?"

CHAPTER 12

BECCA'S COOL RECEPTION CONTINUES

Janet sat at her desk and filed away at a chipped nail. "Damn!" she exclaimed. "Now I'll have to redo the polish before the party tonight." She was so engrossed in her menial task that she failed to notice Becca James walk through the large glass doors and approach the receptionist area.

Becca was clad in her favorite outfit—a pair of well-worn, tight jeans and a brightly colored tee shirt. She used an exaggerated cough to get Janet's attention.

"Oh!" Janet gasped when her focused concentration was interrupted. "Excuse me, I didn't see you come..." She stopped in mid-sentence when she arrogantly assessed Becca's limited, and unprofessional, attire. "May I help you?" Janet asked with reluctant reticence.

Becca wasn't amused and didn't have time for pleasantries. She had to get back to the restaurant to help her parents prepare for the lunch crowd. "Probably not, but let's give it a shot anyway," Becca responded in kind. Her own sultry voice hinted at reciprocated reluctance.

Janet arose and stood behind her desk.

Becca watched her with silent amusement and thought, *"Damn, that is one tall white woman!"* Becca was almost four inches taller than Macey, but the receptionist towered over Becca by another two inches.

Janet continued to look down her nose at Becca, not even attempting to conceal her evident disapproval. "If you're looking for the Personnel Office, I can *assure* you we're not hiring, at the moment. However, if you'd like to leave your name and number..."

Becca placed both hands upon her hips, a gesture known to family and friends as one of impending directness and stubbornness. "Whoa there, girlfriend, don't go gettin' your panties in a wad. I don't need a job, thank you very much."

"Thank goodness," Janet mumbled beneath her breath. "Then... exactly how may I help you? *Perhaps* you're lost?"

Becca exaggerated every syllable while trying to reign in her temper at the woman's blatant rudeness. "No! I am not *lost*...I happen to be looking for a friend of mine. She works here. Her name is Macey Garner. *Perhaps* you know where I can find her?"

Janet walked slowly from behind her desk and smoothed down the ivory knit dress that clung to every inch of her curvaceous body.

Becca couldn't help it; she had to blink when Janet's perky nipples— more than evident through the thin material of her dress—addressed her at eye level.

Janet was genuinely astonished that Macey would keep company with the likes of the woman standing before her. "*You're* a friend of Miss Garner's?"

Becca's fingers curled into fists, with her nails digging into her palms. She was ready to give the receptionist a dose of her own medicine when she looked sideways and saw Macey turning the corner.

Macey glanced up when she heard the raised voices in the reception area; she recognized Becca immediately. She waved and rushed over to greet her friend. "Becca! What brings you here this time of the morning? I didn't think you got up until after ten o'clock! Come on into my office."

Becca returned Macey's hug and glanced back in time to see the astonished look upon the receptionist's face. She smiled at Janet and couldn't resist wrinkling her nose and sticking out her tongue in a juvenile victory.

Janet stared back in apparent disbelief. Did that woman really stick her tongue out at her?

Becca turned back to Macey and walked arm-in-arm with her inside her office. "I had to make an early run to the Farmer's Market. Mama insisted on fresh turnips for lunch. You know...I've passed this building a hundred times, but I've never stopped because I didn't want to bother you at work. Besides..." she grinned, as she patted down her casual and comfortable clothes, "I don't exactly dress for these fancy buildings."

Macey smiled and shook her head. "You look fine, Becca. You always do." She was cognizant of Becca's reaction to the plush surroundings. "So...what changed your mind this morning?"

Becca was duly impressed with the surroundings. Huh?" she mumbled back.

Macey laughed out loud. "I said...what made you decide that today was a good day to *bother me at work?*"

Becca trailed her hand along the white leather sofa; it was the softest leather she had ever felt in her life. Her mouth gaped open as she walked around the room, stopping every few feet to touch and admire the splendid accessories. The marble-topped tables glistened, the cherry-wood, executive desk was obviously not made from particle board, and the matching burgundy chair was the most comfortable-looking chair Becca had ever seen. The room was filled with a varied array of tropical plants, all of which, were displayed in expensive crystal vases and containers. "Wow!"

Macey laughed good-naturedly at her friend's first impression of CompuTech's open display of the best interior decorating that money could buy. "I know...that was my first impression, too. It sure makes it hard to go home to my meager and humble habitat at the end of a long, hard day."

"Wow!" Becca repeated. "Girlfriend...you are definitely uptown! Man, I had no idea this place looked like this. I mean, I've seen places like this in magazines and movies, but...not in Columbus, Georgia! Wow!"

"Yep," Macey agreed. "It's plush all right. Mr. Byce demands only the best."

Becca flopped down upon the soft, leather sofa with an unceremonious thud and leaned her head back. "Byce? That's the jerk who tried to put the moves on you last year, right?"

Macey nodded. "That's the one, yeah." She paused and waited for Becca to respond. "So...?"

Becca momentarily forgot the real reason she had stopped by to see Macey. She had not been able to shake the memory of seeing Macey with Scott Pennell, and they still had not found the time to talk about it—at least, Macey had not been able to find time. "Oh...right...well, the reason I stopped by was to see what we've got planned for tonight. Believe it or not, I find myself without a man-date, so...I'm all yours."

Macey watched her friend closely and recognized the signs of deliberate avoidance. "You could have called and asked me that, Becca. Come on, out with it. I don't know how many times I've tried to get you to visit my office over the past couple of years. What's the real reason for this visit?"

Becca continued her attempt at nonchalance. "I know, but...hey, girlfriend, if I'd known you worked in the lap of luxury, I would've been knocking on this doorstep a long time ago. Man, this is *really* nice!"

"Becca?"

Becca held her hands in defeat. "Okay, okay...I guess I'm procrastinating, huh?"

Macey folded her arms and stared at her friend. "Yes, you are...and that is totally out of character for you. Oh—and, by the way—what was with the dumb, black-woman routine out front with Janet?"

"Janet? That's her name?"

Macey nodded. "Yes."

Becca shrugged with indifference. "Stupid broad...she probably thought I was with the janitorial crew or something."

Macey nodded in agreement. "More than likely, she did; but, admit it...that's exactly what you wanted her to think, isn't it?"

Becca shrugged again. "No...not really, at least not at first. It's just that...I picked up on an attitude from the girl. What's her problem, anyway?"

Macey sat down behind her desk and smiled. "She has way too many to get into, but one of her big ones is that she's convinced we are still living in the Civil War era. She can't fathom the possibility of friendship between blacks and whites."

"I knew it!" Becca shouted and jumped up from the couch. "The girl thinks I'm just another dumb nigger! Attitude! I knew it! I told you, didn't I?"

There was a moment of subdued silence before both women suddenly burst out laughing.

Macey was the first to get herself under control. She looked at her friend and shook her head. "If only she knew you had a Master's degree in Education..."

"Yeah...and it's really coming in handy working in a mom-and-pop diner; but...shush..." Becca motioned with her finger to her thick, luscious lips, "Let's not spoil her fun...not just yet anyway."

Macey stopped laughing and stared intently at the only friend she had made in the ten years since she'd returned to Columbus. "So? Are you going to tell me the truth?"

"About what?" Becca asked in poorly disguised innocence.

It wasn't like Macey to lose her patience, but she was quickly losing it now. "Becca, neither one of us has time for silly games. Now, tell me... why did you really come here today?"

A short series of knocks on Macey's door interrupted their conversation.

Scott Pennell opened the door and walked in. His head was bent as he shuffled through the stack of files he carried. "Macey...Mr. Byce has called an ad-hoc meeting to go over these..." He looked up then and saw Becca standing off to the side. He noted how she crossed her arms obstinately across her stomach. "Hello," he smiled at her. "It's Miss James, isn't it?" He walked over to Becca, his free hand extended in welcome.

Becca turned away from him to deliberately avoid his handshake.

Scott was embarrassed and tried to bow out as graciously as possible. "I can come back, Macey. I apologize for the interruption." He looked at

Becca's turned back and shrugged at Macey's pained expression; however, good manners wouldn't allow him to exit without saying goodbye. "It was good to see you again, Miss James. Once again, Macey, I apologize for the interruption. Oh, don't forget...that meeting is in ten minutes. We'll need your international training file. See you there, okay?"

Macey could only nod in concurrence as she watched Scott slowly close the door behind him. She turned to face Becca, but before she could scold her friend for her rude behavior, Becca turned on her.

She pointed her finger in the direction of the closed door. "*He's* the reason I came here today, Macey!"

Macey was dumbfounded. "Scott? What in the world has he got to do with anything? And why have you been so rude to him? We've never gotten the chance to talk about how rude you were to him at lunch that day. It's appalling the way you treat the man, Becca. I've never seen you treat anyone like that before. What is it?"

Becca bit her top lip and nodded her head in angry agreement. "Yeah, you're right...I have been *rude* to him. What I can't understand, girlfriend, is why you're even giving him the time of day—*especially* after what he did!"

Macey's rubbery legs forced her to sit down again. Her breathing became uneven, but she stared directly into Becca's eyes. "What are you talking about, Becca?"

Becca leaned down until her face was only inches from Macey's. "You know damn well what I'm talking about. I've known you for five years, girl. Five years...and, in all that time, I've been waiting for you to feel comfortable enough with me to confide in me...to unburden that load you've been carrying all these years, but, you never have. Not about *him*, anyway."

Realization dawned and hit Macey like a ton of bricks. "Oh, no," she sputtered. "You know, don't you? You know who he is and what happened twenty years ago! How? How did you find out? I never wanted anyone to know who I was..."

Becca walked behind the desk and put her arms protectively around Macey's shoulders. "Daddy recognized you the first time I brought you into the restaurant. Later that night, he told me everything he remembered about what he had read in the papers. After that, I went to the Bradley Library and looked through old microfiche until I found the newspaper articles that reported what happened twenty years ago."

Macey stared at her friend and lowered her head. "You've known all this time? Why didn't you say something before now?"

Becca shook her head and shrugged. "It had to come from you. I guess I wanted you to tell me who you were...I didn't want you to know that I knew. Daddy thought it would be better for you if you trusted me

73

enough to tell me yourself; but, when you brought *that man* to lunch the other day...God, I just couldn't believe it! It's all I've been able to think about; I haven't been able to sweep it from my mind."

Macey exhaled deeply and looked up at her friend. "There's more to it than you know, Becca—a lot more—but, I'm sorry...I just can't get into it right now, but maybe soon. We'll talk soon...I promise..."

"How about tonight?" Becca urged.

Macey sniffed and shook her head slowly. "Sorry, I can't tonight."

"Why not?"

Macey attempted a half-smile. "Well, I've been *ordered* to attend the company Halloween party tonight..."

"And...?" Becca queried.

Macey sat up straight and squared her shoulders. "Scott's taking me."

Becca spun around and assumed her signature stance, hands upon her hips. "I don't believe this! I really don't believe this!"

Macey began to gather the files and papers she would need for the ad-hoc meeting, all the while, attempting to regain some control over her harried emotions. "Please, Becca, just let it go. I really, really cannot get into this with you right now. I promise to explain everything later this weekend. Why don't you stop by tomorrow, okay?"

Becca shrugged in temporary defeat. Her father was right—she shouldn't push Macey about her sister's murderer. "Okay, okay, go on. Go to your damn meeting. I'll let myself out. Besides...I can't wait to confront Miss Personality again."

Macey attempted another weak smile as she opened her office door. She turned back and pointed a finger at her outspoken friend. "Be nice, Becca!"

Becca raised her hands in defense. "I'm always nice, girlfriend."

Macey stopped Scott after the meeting and asked him to follow her back to her office. Once they were inside, she turned to him and smiled. "Scott, I want to apologize for Becca's behavior. I've never seen her act like that around anyone before. She's my best friend, but...she had no right to be so rude to you, and I've told her so."

Scott looked pleasantly surprised. "You came to my defense? Why, Macey?"

Macey stared into Scott's warm, gentle eyes—the same eyes that had probably bore into Kacey's during intimate moments. She shrugged and put some distance between them. "Let's just say that...I think my first impression of you might have been wrong, and, let's leave it at that, okay?"

Scott rubbed his chin thoughtfully. He didn't know where this was coming from—or why—but, he quickly decided not to look a gift horse in the mouth. "Okay, I can be gracious, too. Although...don't you think it's your friend who should be apologizing, rather than you?"

Macey smiled at Scott's condescending tone. "Well...if you're expecting an apology from Becca, you could be a very, very old man before that ever happened. I've never heard Becca apologize for anything in all the years I've known her. Not once..."

"Is it a southern pride thing?" Scott asked.

Macey shook her head. "No, trust me, being a southerner has nothing to do with it. It's just plain and simple pride with Becca; although, if I know her, she will more than likely try to make it up to you in some little way—like, maybe, serving you a larger slice of pie the next time you visit the restaurant."

Scott nodded. "Yeah, or maybe even an extra helping of those green, leafy things...*collards*?"

Macey grinned. She was relieved that he held no obvious resentment toward Becca. "Yeah, maybe even that." She smiled and shook her head before pushing him gently toward the door. "Now, go! I have work to do."

Scott laughed, glad that the air had been cleared. "Okay, okay, don't be so subtle; I can take a hint. Besides, I need to pick up my costume for tonight."

Macey grimaced at the mention of the party. "Do I dare ask what you're going as, Scott?"

"If I tell you, then it won't be a surprise. What about you, Macey? What's your costume?"

"No way am I telling you; I wouldn't want to spoil the surprise. Not me, Mr. Pennell. I will say, however, that it will be something that even Mr. Byce won't be expecting."

"Really? Now you've stirred my curiosity...come on, Macey. Tell me?"

Macey contemplated making him wait until the evening to see her disguise, but she weakened at his boyish charm. "Okay, but you've got to promise not to tell anyone else."

"Scout's honor," Scott replied, holding up two fingers.

"A nun...I'll be dressed as a nun..."

Scott's mouth fell open. "A what?"

Macey grinned mischievously. "You heard right—a nun."

"You're kidding, right? You're not really coming dressed as a nun."

Macey shook her head. "Nope, not kidding."

Scott ran his fingers through his hair and laughed out loud.

Macey surprised herself when she realized that she enjoyed the sound of his laughter.

"I can't wait!" Scott lauded. "I really can't wait to see this. Okay... hey, I've got to finish up some work, too, but...I'll pick you up at seven tonight. Is that all right? Did you want to stop somewhere and get a bite to eat before we go?"

Macey was beginning to relax around Scott, but, she still didn't want her friendly overtures to be misinterpreted as encouragement. "Uh... no...but, thanks, Scott. I'll eat something at home before we go. Seven o'clock is fine, but...maybe, we should take separate cars. I really don't intend to stay any longer than absolutely necessary, and, I wouldn't want you to leave early on my account."

Scott waved his hand in dismissal. "Don't worry about that. It'll give me a good excuse to bug out early, too. Okay, I'm out of here. I'll see you at seven."

Macey stood at her door and watched Scott hurry through the lobby.

Scott spotted the receptionist and did his best to bypass her desk; however, he wasn't quick enough.

Janet rushed to his side and touched his arm. "Where are you off to in such a hurry, handsome?"

Macey listened discretely while Scott told Janet that he had to pick up his costume for the party. She exhaled a deep sigh when Janet grabbed her purse, put her arm through Scott's, and offered to ride with him.

Macey shook her head at Janet's boldness. For one quick moment, she wasn't sure if what she felt when she saw Scott open the door for Janet was simple amusement, or something totally uncharacteristic for her—jealousy.

CHAPTER 13

THE HALLOWEEN PARTY

Scott and Macey arrived at George Byce's executive home at seven-thirty. The sounds of laughter intermingled with loud music indicated a party already in full swing. A butler was at the door to greet the collage of strange and spectacular costumes that illuminated the main drawing room. Groups of people, all of whom had a drink in hand, were trying in vain to talk above the music. A popular, local band was playing top-forty hits at full volume.

Scott felt Macey tremble at his side. He could tell that she did not feel comfortable in large crowds. He looked down at her and grinned. "I think I was expecting something a little more mellow and low-key from Mr. Byce." He spotted Janet across the room and pointed her out to Macey. "No surprise there, at least."

Macey nodded and winced at the distinct contrast in her and Janet's costumes.

He didn't dare say it, but Scott thought that Janet was much more convincing as a well-endowed, voluptuous Lady Godiva, than Macey was dressed in her humble imitation of Sister Teresa.

Macey watched Janet work the crowd for several minutes, and she was even more grateful for Scott's considerate, last-minute change-of-costume selection.

Scott had decided to forgo his knight-in-shining-armor costume for the less conspicuous, monk costume. Once Macey had confided to him what her costume would be, he thought she might feel more comfortable with a monk as her date. He hoped that she appreciated his chivalrous gesture.

A couple dressed as Raggedy Ann and Andy pulled Janet aside and pointed out the newcomers. The threesome had been regular visitors to the open bar since their early arrivals, and snickered behind their drinks. Janet eventually excused herself from the couple and slithered toward Scott and Macey. She had to make sure it was really Scott hidden under that baggy, unimpressionable costume. She wondered, fleetingly, if he wore anything beneath it—she hoped not.

Janet maneuvered herself among the crowd until she stood directly behind Scott. She wrapped her arms around his waist and purposely pushed her breasts into his back. The body suit of the Godiva costume was so thin and flimsy that Janet was sure he would be able to feel her reaction to seeing him. "Scott!" she cooed. "You made it! I am so happy to see you. Come dance with me, please?"

Scott whirled around to face her and barely managed to suppress a gasp at the closer inspection of the nothingness of her costume. He tried not to stare but it was hard to ignore the outline of her nipples through the thin fabric. "Wow! That is...some costume, Janet."

Janet purred and pushed herself into an embrace against his chest. She held onto his hands before backing away and twirling around. Her goal was complete—she left nothing to the imagination when it came to wondering what—if anything—she wore beneath the sheer, nude body suit. "Do you like it, Scott? Gee, thanks. The wig's getting a little hot though. I may have to come out of it before the night is over," she slurred suggestively. "Come on, Scott...dance with me. I promise to bring him right back, Miss Garner. Scout's honor."

"Wonder where I've heard that before?" Macey mumbled under her breath.

Scott looked imploringly back at Macey as Janet dragged him onto the crowded dance floor. A slow song was beginning and he lifted his eyebrows in mock horror.

Macey smiled and mouthed, "Have fun."

Once Scott had been dragged away from her side, it didn't take long for Macey to start feeling uncomfortable in her surroundings. She looked around the room and turned quickly toward the patio doors. She was intent on getting as far away from the crowd and the music as she could; she was already feeling the beginning of a whopper of a headache.

The cool, crisp October air offered a welcomed respite from the party atmosphere inside the Byce mini-mansion. Macey spotted a cement bench at the end of a brick path and sighed gratefully. She made her way over to it and sat down. It felt good to be away from the crowd, and she leaned her head backwards and closed her eyes. She was deep within her own thoughts and did not hear the approaching footsteps.

"Miss Garner...there you are." George Byce stood unsteadily before Macey. He held out the offering of a mixed drink.

Macey knew that she risked his wrath if she declined the drink, so she took it and lowered her eyes. "Thank you, sir. It's...uh...a wonderful party. You have a lovely home. Thank you for inviting me."

Byce plopped himself down beside her, sitting closer than the ample space necessitated.

Macey's skin prickled at his nearness.

His Robin Hood costume revealed much more about his aging body than he probably wanted anyone to see, but his wife had insisted he wear it, to complement her own Maid Marion costume. He stared at Macey through bloodshot eyes. "I'm glad you could make it, Macey. Several members of our overseas, sister-organization are here tonight. They're looking forward to finally meeting you, after having talked with you so much on the phone. I know for a fact that they are all very eager to meet you in person."

Macey grew claustrophobic at their forced closeness. She stood up abruptly. He had offered her the perfect excuse to go back inside. "I'm looking forward to meeting them, too..." she mumbled as she turned to walk away.

Mr. Byce grabbed her wrist and jerked her roughly back down onto the bench. He took her drink from her and threw it into the bushes behind them. "Not so fast, Macey. We have the whole night ahead of us; there's plenty of time for introductions later..."

Macey knew that George Byce was already drunk. Her palms grew sweaty and her breathing quickened. "But I thought you said..."

Byce pulled her roughly against him. He was so drunk he didn't realize his own strength; he was unaware that his rough handling would surely sport bruises upon her shoulder and arm tomorrow. "I said there's plenty of time for introductions...later." He looked at her for a moment longer.

Macey's gaze lowered once more upon the brick path, but she gasped when George Byce turned her toward him with a quick and sharp motion. She pulled her teeth over her upper lip when he cupped her face between both hands, and forced her to stare back into his drunken and lustful eyes.

He used his fat thumbs to caress her cheeks. His nails were buffed and painted with clear polish. "You are so beautiful, Macey...do you have any idea what I could do for you—for your career?"

Macey tried to pull to the left, but her movement only resulted in a tightening of his grip upon her shoulders. She winced and whispered, "Please...Mr. Byce...you're hurting me..."

George Byce wasn't listening. He had his own set agenda. "I could make it good for you, Macey; I could ensure your future with CompuTech before I retire next year. One year...is that asking so much..." His hands moved from her face to her long, slender neck. His drunken gaze lingered upon her breasts as they heaved against the costume's thick, dark material. He wanted her so badly; he had wanted her since the first day she began work at CompuTech. George Byce had grown accustomed to getting what he wanted. His touch grew bolder when she did not protest the caressing of her neck. He dropped his hand to rest roughly beneath her breasts. He assumed that her heavy breathing was indicative of her desire for him.

It never once occurred to him that Macey was too paralyzed with fear to protest anything.

Macey protected herself by doing what she did best—by shutting down her emotions. She removed her emotions from her present predicament, by forcing her mind to journey back in time—almost twenty-one years ago—when another man had forced his hands upon her in the same rough manner. This was the same man, who with the help of her own father, had tied her to a wooden work bench, and raped her virgin body. Both men had instructed her that the rape was a spiritual cleansing of her body and soul.

George Byce took her subsequent compliance as positive reinforcement of his actions. He was convinced that she really did want him as badly as he wanted her. Why had he waited so long to approach her again? He squeezed her breasts roughly together and lowered his slobbering mouth to what he assumed must be her nipples—it was impossible to tell through the thick material of her damn costume. He pulled at her bra and broke its clasp during his awkward fumbling.

Macey had not moved. She sat upright and rigid—still looking toward the ground—with her arms bent and resting on the top of her thighs.

Her boss continued his clumsy groping until he had managed to push Macey backward upon the bench. He removed her panties and adjusted her legs until they were straddling the bench. He grunted heavily against her while he used his free hand to attempt to remove his tights.

Macey stared up into the black sky that was littered with thousands of stars; her arms now hung as limply as her legs, on each side of the cold, concrete bench. In her mind, she was still enduring her *spiritual cleansing.*

The unexpected sound of a woman's piercing laughter, coming in their direction, startled George Byce. He rolled off Macey in an unceremonious manner. He pulled his tights up over his massive belly and grabbed for the plumed hat that he had previously tossed aside. He used it now to hide the conspicuous proof that he had been aroused. He returned his attention to Macey. What was wrong with the woman? Hadn't she heard the approaching laughter and voices?

Macey had escaped to her own imaginary world during Mr. Byce's unwanted exploration of her body. She continued to lie limply on the bench, her legs draped on either side of it, and her black tights pulled beneath her bare hips. She stared off into space, oblivious to the oncoming voices. It was several moments before she finally responded to the rough, deliberate shaking of her shoulders.

"Miss Garner!" George Byce whispered as loudly as he dared. "Macey!" He contemplated slapping her to bring her out of her apparent reverie.

After discarding the unwanted memories of her *spiritual* cleansing, Macey's natural defense against the unwanted invasion of her body had been to will her mind to remember more pleasant times. She had been physically aware of what George Byce was doing to her body; however, she had been mentally unable to respond to his actions—to make him stop, so, she had willed her mind to travel back in time to days spent with her sister, Kacey...days when they would run together in the meadow and make plans for their futures. The pleasant thoughts were doing the job, until the rough shaking of her shoulders caused her eyeballs to rattle against the sheer force of the shaking. Macey gulped in a deep breath of the cool air, held it inside her lungs, and gradually regained awareness of her immediate surroundings. She took another deep breath and looked through Mr. Byce staring down at her. "What...?" she asked, dumbfounded.

George Byce was frantic. "Someone's coming, Macey! For God's sake, woman, get yourself in order!"

Macey slowly glanced down and saw her bare legs straddling the bench. She sat up dizzily, dragged her right leg over the bench, and pulled her tights up to cover the nakedness of her lower body. She attempted to straighten her costume, and felt her breasts fall loosely from her unclasped bra. She stared at her boss with another dumbfounded expression. "What happened!" she shrieked.

George Byce was more than a little surprised at her obvious confusion; however, he regained his composure quickly and took advantage of her rattled reaction. "Quiet down, Miss Garner. You were all over me, that's what happened! We'll discuss the matter later. Suffice it to say, you practically attacked me on the bench just moments ago. I will admit, however, that I found it a rather pleasant experience...one that I'm looking forward to repeating."

Macey gasped a rebuttal. "No...I didn't...I...I don't know what you're talking about. I would never..." Macey's entire body began to tremble. *"Oh, my God...what happened?"* she whispered inside her befuddled head—the words echoed inside her head, battling against the confusion and disbelief.

George Byce grabbed her roughly by the shoulders again and hissed, "I said we'll discuss this later, Macey. Someone is coming this way, so pull yourself together—NOW!"

A familiar voice called out from about fifty feet away, but Macey and George Byce were still protected from sight by a small covering of shrubbery.

The familiar voice was closer now. Scott waved to them and quickly bridged the distance between them. "Macey! Mr. Byce! We've been looking for you."

Janet followed closely behind Scott. Her huge breasts bounced from side to side against the ultra-thin material of her costume as she ran to keep up with him.

Macey jolted toward him and practically fell into Scott's arms. "Scott! I want to leave. Can you take me home...now... *please!*"

Scott held her at arms-length and saw her ashen look for the first time. He saw the disheveled appearance of her hair and costume. His anger ascended quickly, and he fought to keep it under control.

George Byce ambled slowly toward them. He still held the large, feathered hat strategically in front of him to hide his rapidly deflating manhood. "Scott, my boy...it's good to see you. I ran into Miss Garner, here in the garden, and was just informing her that our international partners are inside, and are anxious to meet you both. Follow me, you two." He held a hand out toward his receptionist. "Janet?"

Janet took her boss's offered hand, but alternated her suspicious glare between him and Macey. It didn't take her long to assess the situation. Even though she was more than tired of keeping the old man entertained, she resented Macey trying to move in on her territory. She had already invested too much time in George Byce and his sick, sexual fantasies. He would be gone in a year's time and he had promised Janet a substantial promotion before he left the company. "Mr. Byce," she practically chirped as she folded her hand inside his own, "Have I told you how dashing you look in your costume? I simply adore Peter Pan!" Maybe I should have come as Tinker Bell!"

George Byce gritted his teeth and led the way back inside. "I'm Robin Hood, Janet! Robin Hood—*not* Peter Pan!"

"Oh..." giggled Janet. "I knew that! Of course, you're Robin Hood.

Peter Pan never wore a big, feathered hat, did he?"

The couple walked ahead of Scott and Macey, both of whom remained standing still and looking at one another.

"What happened here?" Scott whispered hoarsely. His private thoughts were rallying against hope, that what he was thinking, had not really happened.

Tears pooled in Macey's eyes and she blushed uncontrollably. "I...I can't talk about it now, Scott. I just can't. I...I'm not sure I even know what happened. I blanked out for a few minutes and when I snapped out of it..." She shook her head and began a brisk pace back up the path, toward the main house.

"Macey!" Scott hurried to catch up with her; when he finally did, he put his arm around her, and felt her immediately tense at his touch. "Macey?"

Macey shook her head and closed her eyes. A little color was returning to her cheeks. "I'm okay, really. Please...just help me find a restroom and give me a few minutes. We'll meet the international staff, and then—if you don't mind—I'd really like to leave this place."

Scott nodded. "Okay...no problem. I'll wait for you in the main foyer."

Macey found the ladies' room and quickly vanished inside. She was totally unaware that her movements were being steadfastly tracked by three separate sets of eyes—all three for very different and personal reasons.

CHAPTER 14

AFTER THE PARTY

Scott had just finished waxing his Porsche the next afternoon, when he saw Macey come out of her apartment. She was dressed in black sweats and wearing sunglasses. His wave was returned as she backed out of her parking space. He was surprised that she hadn't stopped to chat, but he dismissed it and began gathering his cleaning supplies. He smiled and admired his handy work. He had stroked and coaxed the Porsche to a brilliant shine—a simile he associated with making love to a beautiful woman. He turned and watched as Macey made a right turn out of the parking lot and—-for reasons he couldn't explain—he hastily threw his empty bucket and rag onto the passenger seat, jumped inside the car, and rushed to follow her. "She's probably just going to the gym or the grocery store," he mumbled as he swiftly passed the car in front of him and searched for her white Rodeo. He quickly dismissed that thought, too, because something about the intense expression on her face convinced him otherwise.

He was forced to stop at a red light two blocks up, and was undecided which direction to take until he spotted the tail lights of what he thought was Macey's car farther up the road. Scott counted about six cars that separated them, and he still wasn't convinced that he was following the right car. There were a lot of white SUVs on the road. He kept what he hoped was Macey's car in his sight, but found his thoughts drifting back to their drive home from the Halloween party the night before.

Macey had been more quiet and reserved than usual. She refused to talk about what happened between her and Mr. Byce, but Scott knew that something offensive must have occurred. The plumed hat to Byce's Robin Hood costume had failed miserably to hide the pulsating evidence.

Scott was sure the bastard had been harassing Macey. He tried to get her to open up to him on their trip home, but she had simply smiled, thanked him for his concern, and said that she could handle things. She told him that she didn't want to involve him with any problems she might be having with their boss.

Scott continued to keep an eye on the white car, and once it turned left onto Interstate 185, he knew for sure that he had followed the right vehicle. He stayed at least four cars behind until she turned off at exit 5 onto Macon Road. Scott switched lanes and moved up closer to the Rodeo when Macey took another left off the exit ramp. He made sure to keep a discreet distance between them. He was beginning to feel foolish for having followed her in the first place; after all, it wasn't any of his business how she spent her free time. He told himself that he just wanted to make sure she was all right. He really felt foolish when she made her next turn several miles down Macon Road. Scott hit his forehead with the palm of his hand when he saw her signal a left turn into Park Hill Cemetery. "Oh, great!" he chided himself as he drove past the cemetery. "Now I feel like a complete ass!"

He drove several blocks past the cemetery until he found a convenient place to turn around. His intention was to return home; however, as he approached the cemetery again, something compelled him to enter it. He drove slowly through the entranceway and pulled off to the side; he looked in both directions for Macey's car. He spotted the Rodeo parked on a slight hill, about a half-mile away, directly behind a black pick-up truck. Scott was sure it was the same truck he had seen at Macey's apartment several weeks earlier.

He wanted to get a closer look, but the Porsche wasn't exactly an inconspicuous mode of transportation. He didn't want to risk being seen by the couple so he decided to get that closer look on foot. "I can't believe I'm doing this," he scolded himself, all the while trying to decide on a suitable hiding spot. "What business is it of mine who she meets at the cemetery?"

He squatted behind a cluster of bushes, about a hundred yards away from Macey and her friend. His eyes were peeled on the couple as they knelt together before a grave. The young man placed a small bouquet of flowers upon the grave, and Macey bent forward to kiss the head stone. He was too far away to hear their words, but he assumed they must be praying. "Probably her mother or father," Scott mused. "Or maybe the boyfriend's mother or father—no, that can't be right—why would Macey be kissing the stone of his parents...unless, of course, they're serious about each other—no...that can't be right, either. I would have picked up on it if she were that involved with someone...wouldn't I?" Scott watched for another ten minutes while the couple embraced and continued to pray together.

The young man finally helped Macey to her feet and she stood on her tiptoes to plant a brief kiss. Scott wasn't close enough to tell if the kiss landed upon his cheek or his lips. He watched as Macey appeared to brush a tear from the man's cheek and kissed him again. "Why should I care where she kisses him?" he continued to rebuke himself. Scott crept backward and returned to his car, when he realized they must be saying their good-byes.

Jacob walked Macey back toward their vehicles. "Thanks for meeting me here, Macey. I can't really explain it, but...I needed to see where Kacey was buried. You probably think I'm weird or something for not coming before now."

Macey rubbed Jacob's back and smiled up at him. "No, Jacob, I don't think you're weird. After all, you don't remember much about Kacey... you were so young when she died; but, you know...I am curious...why now?"

Jacob exhaled softly and put his arm around his sister. "Do you have a few minutes?"

Macey smiled and hugged him back. "For you? Absolutely...I have all the time in the world. Do you want to go somewhere else?"

Jacob looked around at the immaculately kept grounds and shook his head. "No, this is fine. It's peaceful here and there's no one around. Come on...hop in the bed of the truck. We can talk there if it's okay with you."

"The bed of the truck it is—lead the way, little brother."

Jacob spilled his heart to Macey for the next two hours. He told her about everything he had kept inside since he had first discovered the pictures hidden in his father's closet. He and Macey had discussed their family and their historical circumstances many times during the past five years; however, neither of them had really opened up to the other about the way fate had affected all their lives.

Jacob confessed his contradictory feelings for their father. He confided to Macey how all he had ever wanted was for their father to love him and accept him as his son; yet, his father seemed to go out of his way to ignore Jacob's existence. He told her how their mother treated him just the opposite. She was full of extreme emotions and smothered him with too much love. Jacob told Macey that the only time their father ever talked to him was when he was issuing orders at the service station.

Macey listened quietly while Jacob spent his anger and frustration. She held him when he wept and provided the encouragement he needed to continue venting feelings that he had obviously kept buried for much too long.

Jacob bared his soul about his feelings toward their parents and Kacey; however, throughout their conversation, he never told Macey about the countless times he crouched, hidden in Kacey's bedroom closet. He never told her about all the times he secretly witnessed their father visit Kacey's bedroom after Macey had been sent away to Madison. He knew that everyone assumed that he didn't remember Kacey—but, he did remember her. He remembered, vividly, how the tears glistened against her pale, beautiful face during his father's late-night visits to her room.

Jacob never knew why Macey had been forced to leave home. His parents never mentioned her name, and, she never wanted to talk about that time in her life. He never knew about the rape or the subsequent pregnancy. He convinced himself that Macey must have left home as a teenager to escape their father; and, he couldn't help but wonder if his father had done the same things to Macey that he had done to Kacey. These were all the things that he could not talk to her about; he did not want to cause her any more emotional pain than she had already endured.

Macey had confessed a lot about her life to Jacob; however, she never saw the benefit in telling him the real reason she had been forced to leave their family. She hoped to be able to do that one day soon, but—for now—that was better left her secret.

A slight breeze blew clumps of leaves and pine needles softly across the grounds while the living children of Ruth and Andrew Wymer hugged each other for support. Their deceased sibling, who was always in their thoughts, offered the spiritual strength they would need to endure all that lay ahead during the next few months.

Scott moaned when he pulled into his parking space and saw Janet Ward attaching a note to his apartment door. She appeared to be holding a large stack of files. He thought about sliding down and hoping she wouldn't see him, but reminded himself that it wouldn't be the right thing to do. "Janet!" he waved to her. "Did you need to see me?" He hurried to his front door. "Here, let me help you with those. What have you got there?"

"Hi, Scott! I'm so sorry to bother you on the weekend, but Mr. Byce insisted that I bring these documents over to you today. He wants you and Macey to review them, and to be ready to discuss them Monday morning with those international fellows that are visiting."

"I thought they were leaving today," Scott replied while he gathered the files closer to him and unlocked his front door.

"No, there's been a change of plans. They'll be leaving after lunch on Monday. That's why the sudden rush on this. Mr. Byce wants you to write a synopsis of your programming analysis of the deal, or something like that...does that make any sense to you? Because it certainly doesn't to me!"

Scott laughed and pushed open the door. "Yeah, I think I know what he's looking for; I'll go over them tonight with Macey, if she's available. We'll have everything ready by Monday morning...no problem."

Janet flashed her award-winning smile. "Great! I'll tell Mr. Byce that you have everything under control then. By the way, it really sucked that y'all had to leave so early last night. It was a great party."

Scott nodded. "Yeah...I bet it was, but...Macey wasn't feeling well, so I..."

Janet had decided on the drive over that she had left Scott Pennell alone long enough. She didn't wait for an invitation; instead, she followed him inside and kicked the door shut behind her. She took advantage of Scott's disadvantage and wriggled up behind him while he was shifting the voluminous files in his arms. She pressed her breasts firmly against his back and rested her hands on his hips.

The stack of files fell out of his hands and scattered across the foyer as he turned to face her. "Janet!" He tried to gently push her away, but she pressed herself harder against him, groin-to-groin.

They were almost the same height, so Janet didn't have far to stretch to nibble at his inviting ear. She had read somewhere that the ear and neck were two of the male's most erogenous zones.

Scott sucked in air when her tongue began a gentle probe inside his ear. "Janet...what are you doing?" He wasn't aware that he had been holding his breath.

"You mean, you don't know?" Janet purred while her hands moved to his broad chest and her warm mouth suckled at his neck. She smiled with satisfaction when she felt the sudden, rapid beating of his heart against her hand.

"Janet...don't do this...we really...shouldn't be doing this..." Scott's protestations grew weaker with every stroke of her expert tongue.

Her hands dropped lower and squeezed assertively.

"Then again," Scott thought, *"It has been awhile..."*

Janet smiled when she felt his labored breathing against her own neck. It was always so easy to get a man to do what you wanted; all you had to do was remove their pants and they were yours for the taking.

Forty-five minutes later, after an unselfish display of Janet's sexual precision and expertise, Scott Pennell had finally lost control, and his earlier trip to the cemetery was the last thing on his mind.

CHAPTER 15

BECCA AND MACEY DISCUSS SCOTT

Becca James pulled into Wymer's Service Station and looked around quickly. She hoped to see Jacob working the pumps instead of his father, and honked when she spotted him through the large glass window. Wymer's Service Station was one of the few remaining, independently-owned, service stations that still provided full service to its customers.

Becca was more than capable of pumping her own gas and checking her car's fluid levels, but, she enjoyed the few minutes it allowed her to spend with Jacob Wymer. She had grown quite attached to Macey's little brother over the past few years. She had no brothers or sisters of her own—which, some would think a rare thing in black families—so, she had adopted Jacob as her own brother, even if he was a white boy!

A huge grin flashed across Jacob's face when he recognized Becca. He waved and hurried outside to chat with his sister's best friend. Jacob admired Becca's personality, which was strong and extremely opinionated—that meant that Jacob seldom worried about his sister if Becca was close by. He never dared to ask Becca how much she knew about Macey's past, but he knew the two women were as close as any two biological sisters might be. They were so totally opposite in personality and style, but Jacob understood how their bond of friendship managed to overcome all the complications generated by those differences.

Jacob also admired Becca's free-living and free-loving lifestyle, and secretly hoped that some of it would rub off on Macey. He thought his sister was much too reserved to have the looks she possessed—she needed to let loose and have a little fun. He grinned as he walked over and leaned his head in. "Hi there, Miss Becca!"

Becca had all the windows rolled down to better appreciate the crisp, October air. "Hey, yourself, kid!" Becca grinned at his youthful exuberance. He was almost twenty-five years old, but he looked more like nineteen. Becca wasn't fooled by his youthful appearance, however; she knew that any man with a well-developed physique like Jacob's was far from being innocent. On the other hand, his dimples and short, military-style haircut did offer the illusion of innocence when it probably didn't exist. His forever-immaculate appearance never ceased to amaze her either. She constantly marveled over the fact that anyone, in this day and age, still wore starched and ironed jeans! Becca looked around conspiratorially and whispered, "Is the old fart around?"

Jacob laughed out loud and shook his head. "No, Pop's out of town for a couple of days."

"Really, again? Seems like he goes out of town a lot lately, doesn't it?" Becca probed. She got out of her car, stretched, and yawned. Carlton Brown had stopped by, unexpectedly, the night before—needless to say, she hadn't gotten much sleep. Hell, truth be known, she hadn't gotten *any* sleep!

Jacob nodded and replied, "Yeah, I guess he does. It seems like it's been every other month or so, lately, that he's been taking a couple of days off."

"So...where does he go? Something to do with business?"

"Beats me," Jacob shrugged, as he cleaned her windshield. He wondered why she seemed so curious about his father's whereabouts.

"What do you think?" Becca continued to probe. "I mean...about where he takes off to when he goes out of town?"

Jacob stopped wiping the window and smiled at her. "I've never really wondered much about it, Miss Becca. Why are *you* so curious? Does Macey want to know?"

Becca shook her head. "Gawd, no! No...I'm too curious for my own good, I guess. So, where did you say he went?"

Jacob shook his head and laughed again. "I didn't say...because I don't know where he went. He never tells me—he just tells me not to screw up things too bad until he gets back."

Becca stretched and feigned nonchalance. "You mean he goes out of town, leaves you in charge of everything here, and doesn't even tell you where he can be reached? How about your mom? She knows, I bet."

Jacob threw the paper towel in the trash bin and looked back at Becca. "Nope, I don't think she knows, either. I've asked her before, but she just says he's probably taking care of some family business."

Becca twisted her lips and raised her brows. "Hmm...I thought all of his family was here in Columbus. What kind of family business do you suppose your mama is talking about?"

Jacob shrugged his broad shoulders again. "I have no idea. Pop comes from a pretty big family, though. I've never met any of them, but he has relatives spread out all over Georgia and Tennessee."

"What about your mama...does she come from a big family, too?"

Jacob shook his head as he lifted the hood to inspect the car's fluid levels. "Nope, I don't think Mama has any living relatives. She was an only child, and I think both her parents were only children...and they're both dead. They died a long time ago, before I was born. Macey might remember them."

Becca didn't know if Jacob was aware that Macey was a twin, but she decided to risk asking a question about Kacey. "Umm...Jacob...you never really knew your other sister, did you?"

Jacob lifted his head so abruptly that he banged it on the car hood. He looked around the hood and stared hard at Becca while he rubbed the sore spot on his head. "Miss Becca—no offense—but, you're asking an awful lot of questions...personal questions. I wasn't sure that Macey ever told anyone about our sister—not even you."

Becca stretched again to relieve her stiff muscles and to allow her time to think of an easy way out of this conversation. It was obvious that Jacob knew about Kacey, and, she couldn't help but wonder exactly how much he knew. "Well...she hasn't said much—no, I really don't know that much, Jacob."

Jacob continued to stare at her. "What exactly *do* you know, Miss Becca?"

Becca decided it was time to bring the conversation to a close. She didn't know how much of the truth Jacob knew about his family's history, and it certainly wasn't her place to educate him about it. She shrugged. "Not much, really. All I know is that Macey was a twin and that she was close to her sister. But, hey...none of that's important now, is it? It was all a long time ago."

Becca cringed at the pinched, confused look she saw cross Jacob's handsome face; it was time to change the subject. She certainly didn't want to be the one to tell him, if he didn't already know, how his other sister had died. She grinned at him. "By the way, kid, have you seen the old girl lately? We were supposed to get together this weekend. Maybe go bowling or something. Do you want to come along tonight if we do?"

Jacob was glad the topic of Kacey had ended, and, he welcomed any opportunity to spend time with Macey. It was, also, easier to be away from home for a few hours when his Pop was out of town. He knew his mother would be curious about his whereabouts, but he could handle her. He grinned enthusiastically. "Sure! Thanks for the invite. I saw Macey this afternoon but she didn't mention anything. Are y'all meeting at Peach Bowl Lanes?"

Becca nodded. "Yeah, probably around seven o'clock...sound okay?"

"Sounds great, Miss Becca. Will you meet us at Macey's or the bowling alley?" Either way, I'll make sure we have plenty of cold beer," offered Jacob.

Becca smiled as she returned to her car and started the engine. She handed Jacob a twenty-dollar bill and told him to keep the change. She waved as she drove slowly out of the gas station and shouted out the window, "Beer works for me, but Macey will probably want a Shirley Temple! I'll just meet you at her place around seven. See you later, handsome!"

Jacob had offered to drive to the bowling alley when they all met at Macey's apartment later that evening. The three of them had bowled for hours, enjoying one another's company. It was after eleven o'clock when Jacob dropped them off at Macey's place. "Thanks, ladies! Sorry I had to whoop you both so bad."

Macey leaned inside the car and kissed her brother on the cheek. "Just wait until next time, kiddo. Bye now...you be careful driving home, Jacob."

"Don't worry, sis, I will. I've only had three beers. Bye, Becca."

Becca waved as she turned toward the sidewalk that led to Macey's front door.. "See ya later, handsome! Keep those britches zipped!"

Jacob grinned mischievously and waved back.

Macey turned to walk up the sidewalk toward her apartment but glanced back to see if Scott's car was in the parking lot. It was, but she was quick to recognize the car parked beside it. It belonged to Janet Ward, and it had been parked there since Macey had returned home from the cemetery earlier that day. She glanced at Scott's apartment and noticed that all the lights were out. She sighed softly and was surprised at the unexpected feeling of disappointment that washed over her. *Oh well...so much for Mr. Pennell,* she thought. She sighed and unlocked her door, and motioned Becca inside. She welcomed Becca's upbeat company. "Want some coffee, Becca?"

"Sure, sounds good, but only if it's decaf. Hey, you don't mind if I crash here tonight, do you?"

Macey smiled at her friend and answered back, "You don't even have to ask a question like that, Becca. You know my guest room is always open to you."

Becca was unable to suppress a giant yawn. "Thanks...it's just that I didn't get much sleep last night, and I've been giving life a hundred and ten percent all day today. Guess I'm just not as young as I used to be, huh? I *really* need some sleep, and I'd probably fall out behind the wheel if I tried to make it home. Besides...this will give us a chance to have a nice, long talk."

Macey kicked off her shoes and walked into the kitchen. She watched Becca collapse onto the sofa. "Yeah...you're right. Something tells me we're probably long overdue for that talk."

"Humph!" Becca snorted, "About five years overdue, I'd say!" She pushed herself off the too-comfortable sofa and stretched her long, lean body to its fullest length. "But first...I'm going to take a potty-break, girlfriend. You get our coffee ready and I'll meet you back here in ten minutes."

Macey grinned and saluted. "Yes, ma'am!" She busied herself in the tiny kitchen and listened to the water running in the upstairs bath. She gathered coffee mugs and grabbed a bag of Double-Stuff Oreo cookies; she knew they were Becca's favorite snack. She carried everything into the living room and glanced toward the stairs. She could still hear sounds of water running from the upstairs bathroom, so she moved to stand before the sliding glass door that provided an unimpressive view of the parking lot. The lot was well lit for security measures and offered an unobstructed view of Janet's car. She exhaled hard enough to blow her feathered bangs out of her eyes. "Oh, Scott...I had hoped you could resist her..."

Becca bounded down the stairs and into the living room. She felt refreshed after a quick shower, and had rummaged through Macey's dresser to find a pair of old sweats and a tee shirt. She twirled around the room to show off her casual couture. She knew she looked comical with the sweats gathering several inches above her ankles. "Hey, girlfriend, hope you don't mind, but I raided your drawers..." She stopped short when she saw Macey staring absently out the sliding glass door, that led to the front patio. She went to stand behind her, and peered over her shoulder to see what had captured her attention. "Nice Porsche! Who does it belong to?"

Macey jumped. She had been caught completely off-guard. "Becca! I didn't hear you come down. For heaven's sake, you shouldn't sneak up on people like that!"

Becca shrugged. "I wasn't exactly sneaking. So...the Porsche?"

Macey took a quick survey of Becca's outfit and smiled. "Everything's a little short on you, but I guess it'll do."

Becca knew Macey well enough to know that she was either stalling the conversation or intentionally changing the subject. She shrugged and decided to let it go for the moment. "Hope you don't mind, girlfriend, but I just had to get out of those tight jeans. They were suffocating the hell out of my wussy!"

Macey punched Becca on her shoulder. "You are impossible! Come on, the coffee should be ready."

The two friends sat side by side on the sofa, dunking Double-Stuff Oreos into their creamy, gourmet coffees.

"So...you never said who the fancy wheels belong to?" Becca queried as she dunked another cookie into her coffee, totally oblivious to the fat grams she was eagerly consuming.

"The Porsche?" Macey asked innocently.

"No, Miss Einstein, the cute little Taurus parked next to it! Of course, the Porsche! First time I've ever seen one in this parking lot."

"Well..." Macey mumbled. "I'm sure you'll find out eventually, anyway. It belongs to Scott Pennell."

Becca almost choked on her cookie. "What! He lives *here*?"

Macey sighed and raised her brows sternly. "Yes, Becca. We work together and he lives in the same complex as I do. How's that for tempting fate?"

"Fate—hell! Girl, you have got to find a new place to live! It's bad enough you've got to work with the son-of-a-bitch, but to live right across the street!"

Macey grew quiet and composed herself before replying. "Becca, I want you to shut up for a few minutes."

Becca's nostrils flared. "What did you just say?"

Macey held her hands up to silence Becca. "I mean it, Becca...you need to shut up for a few minutes because I'm going to tell you some things that will probably shock even you. After I've finished, I think you may agree that fate has definitely intervened in this situation."

CHAPTER 16

MACEY'S PAST

Becca made herself comfortable and somehow found the will to remain silent while Macey began the painful process of finally sharing her shattered past.

Macey smiled at Becca and took a deep breath before beginning. "I grew up in a small town in Tennessee. You would probably refer to it as a *hick* town. I lived there until I was about fifteen years old. My father never had a real job; he just performed odd jobs around town—he was sort of a handyman type—he could fix just about anything. My mother helped by taking in other families' laundry. That's about all there was to do in that town to make a living, unless you could drive all the way to Nashville to find work. We were always poor, but, we weren't what you would call dirt poor. I remember…Mama always made sure our home was spotless and there was always plenty of food to eat. It may not have always been what we wanted to eat, but, we never went to bed hungry either. My folks did the best that they could to take care of us."

Becca kept her promise and didn't say anything, but she motioned for Macey to continue.

Macey knew what an effort it was taking on Becca's part to just sit back and listen, without interjecting or asking questions. She sighed softly. "You have to understand something about Kacey and myself. We were identical in looks, but, we were so totally opposite in personality. When I was a teenager, I was always the outgoing, adventurous one; I was *always* looking for something to get into. Kacey was always the sensible, practical one; she was *always* trying to keep me safe and out of trouble with our parents. My personality has turned a hundred and eighty degrees since I was fifteen; in fact, I'm probably more like Kacey would have been, had she lived. A lot of things happened along the way to—shall we say—alter my personality."

Becca grinned. "It's so hard to imagine *you* ever getting into any kind of trouble, girlfriend."

Macey smiled back at her friend. "Well, like I said—my personality has changed drastically since those days. I became the town flirt as soon as I hit puberty, while Kacey was always timid and shy around the boys. That's the only way people could really tell us apart. By the time I was fifteen, I had every boy in that small town chasing my skirts. Don't get me wrong, though—I promise you that flirting was all I ever did. None of those boys ever got past third base with me. Kacey, on the other hand, well...she never experienced anything along those lines until later...after the family moved to Columbus."

Becca could tell that the discussion about Macey's past was uncomfortable for her. "Why did your family move from Tennessee, Macey? And why didn't you come with them? Or did you?"

Macey shifted positions on the couch and poured another cup of coffee from the ivory carafe. She shook her head. "No, I didn't come with them. My father heard the Columbus mills were hiring and he'd been out of any real work for a long, long time. Even the odd jobs were getting hard to come by." She paused and stared directly into Becca's eyes. "What I'm about to tell you, Becca, is probably the hardest thing I'll ever have to tell anyone, and it's extremely personal and private. In fact, you are the only living person—besides my father and one other man—who know the truth about what happened."

"I'm listening, girlfriend...tell me what happened to you in Tennessee, Macey, because I have a feeling it must have been something pretty bad—am I right?"

Macey exhaled slowly and deliberately. She closed her eyes for a moment to gather the courage she needed to continue her story.

Becca was barely able to suppress a gasp when Macey opened her eyes—eyes that evidently hid some dark secrets and, maybe, some long-suppressed memories.

Macey nodded and exhaled again. "Something way beyond bad, Becca...something so horrible and painful—so very *painful*. No one should ever have to endure what I did...especially an innocent, fifteen-year old girl..."

Becca moved closer to her friend. She put a comforting arm around her and urged her to continue. "Go on, Macey."

Macey took another deep breath and forced herself to relive those painful memories. "Okay, there's no easy way to say it, so...I'll just say it. I was *raped*, Becca! I was a fifteen-year-old virgin, and I was raped by a well-respected member of that small town."

Becca's mouth fell open but no words came forth. This was *not* what she had expected to hear.

Macey squeezed her eyes tightly shut. "That's not the worst of it, either, because it was my own father who took me to this man after church one Sunday evening. It was my own father who held me down while this man strapped me to an old, wooden work bench, ripped off my panties and stuffed them into my mouth to...stifle my screams. It was my own father who stood off to the side and read scripture after scripture while this man raped me repeatedly...for more than four hours."

Becca had not realized that she had been holding her breath until she moaned and swiped at the tears that flowed freely down her smooth, ebony cheeks. "Oh, my God, no..." She pulled Macey to her and hugged her fiercely. "Who was it, Macey? What kind of man could do this awful thing to a fifteen-year old? Who?"

Macey bit her bottom lip and shook her head vehemently from side to side. "No, Becca, I can't...I won't tell you that. It's enough that I'm finally able to tell someone about what happened. Nobody else knows, and...please...you've got to promise me that this stays between the two of us. I don't ever want anyone else to know about it...I couldn't bear the shame and humiliation if anyone else ever found out about it..."

Becca jumped off the couch and stood trembling with anger for what her friend had been forced to endure at such an early age. "Girl, don't you go there—don't you dare—you have absolutely *nothing* to be ashamed of! For God's sake, *you* certainly didn't do anything wrong!"

Macey smiled up at her friend and watched while Becca paced busily, back and forth, in front of the sofa. "It's taken me a long time to come to that realization, too, Becca. I know that now—I really do, but even twenty years hasn't erased the shame and disgust that I have felt for myself since it happened. There is only one thing that has kept me going all these years...well, I take that back...actually, there are two things..."

"What's that?"

Macey grabbed the back of her shoulders with her finger tips and rolled her head from side to side, trying to relieve some of the physical tension in her body. "Well, number one is Jacob. I came to Columbus ten years after Kacey was murdered. I never wanted to step foot in the city where she had died, but something—some force if you will—drew me here. I couldn't shake this feeling that Jacob needed me. You may think I'm crazy, but I think that force might have been Kacey's spirit. I didn't even know if the family would still be here...but they were."

Becca shook her head. "No, girlfriend...I don't think you're crazy, but...Jacob thinks you've only been here for five years. That's how long I've known you, too."

Macey smiled and nodded. "Yeah, that's what he thinks—that I've only been in Columbus for five years, but the truth is, I stayed in the background for the first five years. I worked odd jobs, went to college at night—you know the drill—trying to decide what I wanted to be when I grew up."

Becca smiled in understanding. "Oh, yeah...been there...done that. Go on, girlfriend—tell me more."

Macey felt the worst part of her history had finally been told, so she found it easier to continue. "Well, as it turned out, the family hadn't moved away. All I had to do to find them was to look them up in the phone book. It was easy to find Jacob, but—and this is no lie, I swear—it took me another five years to get up the courage to approach him. I waited until he graduated high school and started night classes at Columbus College."

Becca drew her brows together. "So...he didn't know who you were, did he?"

Macey shook her head. "No, he was almost five when Kacey was murdered...his memories of his twin sisters—if he even had any—were fuzzy, to say the least. From what Jacob has told me over the years, it seems that our parents did their best to remove any evidence that Kacey and I ever existed. No pictures—no mention of our names—nothing at all. It's really eerie."

"Wow...so, Jacob really had no idea you were his sister?"

"No," Macey sighed, "But I managed to salvage a couple of pictures—with the three of us in them—before I left home. When I finally got up the nerve to approach him with the truth, I just shoved the pictures in his face and said, *"There's something you should see."* He was remarkable, Becca...so much like Kacey in a way. He never once doubted I was telling him the truth; instead, he was so happy—so accepting of me. He wanted to rush home and tell our parents that he had found me."

"But..."

"No, Becca...there was no way I wanted my parents to know that I lived in the same town. There have been a few close calls over the years, but I've somehow managed to avoid them. I truly believe that Kacey led me back here to help Jacob...to ensure his safety, and to help him in any way I can. He's almost at a point in his life where he can manage on his own. He's a grown man...sure...but, he still feels an obligation of some sort to our parents. My mother has a strong emotional hold on him. Jacob wants to be sure she'll be okay if he leaves town. No, Becca...my parents can *never* know that I'm living here...at least...not until Jacob is safely removed from their home and out of the picture."

Becca stood still for a moment and tried to digest everything Macey had told her. "Wait a minute...something just occurred to me. Your last name is Garner...why is that?"

"It was my mother's maiden name. I knew I couldn't come to Columbus using the Wymer name."

Becca nodded again. "Okay, okay...on with the story. What happened after the rape? You must have been a total mess."

"Oh...that would be an understatement. Yes, I was a genuine mess. I became pregnant by the man who raped me, but it was so easy for that man to convince my father that it must have been one of the local boys. Did I fail to mention that this man is also the one who convinced my father that I was a little harlot in the first place? He convinced my *very* religious father that he was the only one who could redeem my soul in the eyes of the Lord...he was the only one who could offer me true salvation...he was the one who convinced Papa that the only way to drive all the evil from my body was to...*purify*...me by means of what he called a *spiritual cleansing*."

Becca shook her head in disbelief. "And your father believed this psycho?"

"Papa was a very religious man. I guess he still is. He never went to church on a regular basis; nevertheless, he was a fanatic about religion. He was more than ripe for someone like this man to warp his thinking. You know, I think—at first, anyway—that Papa really believed this man could save me from my own damnation, and that I would be returned to the family a more pure and wholesome person—someone more like Kacey, who was always Papa's favorite."

Becca held up her hand. "Wait just a damn minute...you were a virgin when this man raped you, right? You had to bleed like a poked pig if he raped you for four damn hours!"

Macey bit her upper lip and nodded. "Oh, I did, but he convinced Papa that it was my monthly curse...yet another sign from God that my body sought physical purification from the evil within it."

"Good Lord, Macey...this is too much...I can't believe this! So...this man got you pregnant? I take it you miscarried?"

Fresh tears pooled in Macey's eyes and she cried softly at the mention of her baby. "No..." she whispered. "I didn't miscarry, Becca. Papa sent me away to stay with an aunt in Madison, Georgia until I had the baby. Oh, you would have loved Aunt Chloe, Becca...she made Betty Davis in *Hush, Hush Sweet Charlotte,* seem like Mary Poppins. It was awful. I was sick during the entire pregnancy, but Aunt Chloe never offered the slightest empathy. I don't think she was capable of any true emotion. She was the oldest of my father's sisters, and she always harbored deep resentment for having had to raise her siblings. She felt she was cheated of a life of her own because she was always waiting on them, sacrificing everything for them. She forced me to do manual labor during the entire pregnancy; it's a wonder that I didn't miscarry. I would sleep on a small cot every night, and I would promise myself that I would find a way to sneak away before the baby was born. I made up my mind to run away, have my baby, and never look back on the family that had deserted me. Anyway, my father moved the family to Columbus while I was in Madison with Aunt Chloe."

"So...something obviously happened to change your plans?" Becca asked hoarsely. "Because, I certainly don't recall seeing a kid around your apartment during the past five years." Becca slapped her open palm against her forehead. "Listen to stupid me...of course, it wouldn't be a kid any more, would it?"

"No, you're right about that, Becca. You see, my baby decided not to wait until its due date to enter the world. It was three weeks early—probably due to all the stress I'd been under. My aunt never took me to see a doctor, so I never had any prenatal care. I didn't really know what to expect—what having a baby would feel like, you know? Anyway, my baby was born on Halloween night—twenty years ago—the same night that my sister was murdered."

Becca jumped up and her hand flew to her throat as fresh tears sprang from her eyes. "Oh, wow...wow...these people sound like characters from a Stephen King novel! God, Macey, I can't even begin to imagine what it must have been like for you. What happened to the baby—or, do you even know?"

Macey stood up and walked slowly toward the sliding glass door. She stared outside at the raven-night shadows until she felt like she had gathered her wits and her thoughts. She turned and looked back at Becca who had sat back down on the sofa. "Another aunt came and took the baby away. They wouldn't tell me where. All they told me was that a couple up north was adopting it. They said it was the best thing for everyone…"

"Did you ever try to locate these so-called aunts again?"

Macey shook her head slowly. "No, not right away. You must remember—I was only sixteen years old when my baby was born. They stole my baby and left me all alone in that room. I ran away the night I gave birth—shortly after they took my baby. My poor, little baby…they never even let me hold it…"

"You ran away? Where did you go, Macey?"

Macey shrugged. "I'm sure you can probably guess. I lived on the streets for two years. I'm not proud of some of the things I did to keep myself alive."

Becca's surprise was genuine. This was not the Macey she knew.

Macey smiled and shook her head. "Everything except *that*, Becca. No—actually—I became proficient at pick-pocketing. Like I said, I did what I had to do to stay alive. I know, now, that God was watching over me during those hard years. One day turned into another—one year turned into another, and then, I walked into a church when I was eighteen. I'm not proud of it, but I stole a Bible when I left that service. I still have that Bible today. The pastor quoted John 4:24 that day and something just clicked inside my head—*God is Spirit, and those who worship Him must worship in spirit and truth.* I walked out of that church—with my stolen Bible—and decided to clean up my act. I decided it was time to search for my baby, but by then, it was too late. I had waited too long. The aunt who took the baby was one I had never met before. My father comes from a pretty large family and I probably have aunts and uncles out there I don't even know about. I can't even say for sure that this woman was really a relative at all. That's one reason it took me ten years to return to Columbus. I went back to Tennessee and traveled all over the southeast looking for my baby. I was young and inexperienced and didn't know enough to go through the proper authorities. I doubt they would have believed my story, anyway."

"This is all so incredible, Macey—so surreal. I guess you've pretty much given up on ever finding your child, huh?"

"No!" Macey exclaimed. "Oh, no, Becca…I'll never give up! I've even been searching the Internet for agencies that can help me. Most of them have told me that I probably won't find my baby until it decides it wants to know about me…something about keeping confidential documents sealed for the child's protection. But, Becca, what if my baby has never been told it was adopted? It will never know how hard I've searched for it all these years. No...even though my baby's all grown up now, I will never give up. We will be reunited one day—I know we will..."

"And if that does happen, Macey...what will you tell it when you're reunited? Man, I feel weird calling the baby *it*...sounds like something... alien, or better yet...another Stephen King character! I take it you never learned the sex of the child?"

Macey shook her head. "No...you're right. I never found out if it was a boy or girl. My gut instinct tells me it was a girl and that's really the way I've always thought of the baby. Yes...I want *her* to know the truth about what happened. I want her to know that I didn't give her up willingly. I hope that, someday, I will be able to tell her everything."

Becca glanced at her watch. It was almost one o'clock in the morning. "Macey, it's late. You don't have to go into any more of this right now if you don't want to. I'm glad you've told me what you have though."

Macey sighed. She was tired too, but if she stopped now, she might change her mind about confiding the rest to Becca. "Well, there's not much else, really, but if you don't mind...I'd like to go ahead and get it all out in the open with you now."

Becca leaned back on the sofa and propped her bare feet on the coffee table. "Okay, girlfriend, it's fine by me. We can sleep in tomorrow. Maybe God won't mind if I skip one Sunday at church."

Macey looked skeptically at her best friend. "You don't even go to church, Becca."

Becca nodded thoughtfully. "That is true. That is very true, however, God and I have an understanding. He knows that I do believe in Him, and—He and I have regular conversations, especially on Sunday mornings."

"Is that so?" Macey grinned. "Okay, I believe you. I'll go on then. As I said before, I wasn't living in Columbus when Kacey died, and, it's been hard for me to investigate her death without revealing my identity. I was hoping that Scott might be able to spread some light on that area, but... well, he doesn't seem to recognize me. Don't you think that's strange, Becca?"

"Here we go...Scott Pennell—my favorite subject!"

"Take it easy, Becca. You don't know him any better than I do. Besides, after being around him these past few weeks, I'm no longer totally convinced that he's the one who really killed Kacey. You know... they never were able to prove a case against him."

Becca grunted in blatant disapproval. "That's because he pleaded crazy and his folks moved him away! I guarantee you, if he'd been a black

103

boy, they would've hung him up by his balls! Didn't I read in one of those articles where he spent some time in the loony bin? If you ask me, I think he was faking being crazy—trust me, it's easy enough to do. Then again..." Becca paused because she was reluctant to admit this next part, "I suppose it could be possible that he really doesn't remember anything about what happened. I took a course once where we discussed cases involving people who built mental blocks around certain tragic events in their lives."

"Your degree was in education, with a minor in marketing, Becca! What kind of class required you to psychoanalyze mental patients?"

Becca threw up her hands in exasperation. "It was an elective, okay! I've always been sort of interested in what makes crazy folks tick, that's all."

"Well...whatever...Scott appears to be a sweet, sensitive man. He's caring and kind, Becca, even if you don't want to admit it. I'm just having more and more trouble believing that he's the type of person who could do all the horrible things the police report revealed."

Becca raised her eyebrows. "You read the police report?"

"Yes...shortly after I returned to Columbus. I needed to know exactly what happened to Kacey. A detective—I think his name was Detective Lance Windham—said the case was unofficially closed, but that it could be reopened if I had anything new to add to the case."

"Whoa, you go, girlfriend! You're a regular Nancy Drew, aren't you?"

Macey laughed for the first time in hours. "Not really, and to tell you the truth...after I persuaded him to let me look at the crime scene photos—I told him I was a cousin—well, let's just say, I wish I hadn't been so persistent."

Becca wrinkled her nose and shook her head. "Some detective this guy must've been! You mean to tell me he didn't recognize the twin sister of the murder victim?"

"I told him we were first cousins and people were always telling us how much we looked alike. Funny thing, though...I always had a feeling he never bought that story, but he didn't force the issue. Maybe he didn't think it was important after all those years. Besides, I didn't look much like the Kacey he'd seen in the crime-scene photos."

Becca shivered involuntarily. "I don't want to hear about those...at least not right now. Tell me something, though. You and Kacey were so close. Did she know about the baby? Did you two get a chance to talk or get together after you were shipped off to Mary Poppins?"

Macey smiled as she remembered her last conversation with her sister. "Yeah, as a matter of fact, we had a long talk the night before I left. I promised myself I would never tell anyone about what really happened—not even Kacey—but I broke down and told her...everything."

"Everything?"

Macey nodded and reached for a Kleenex. "Yeah...everything. I didn't leave out any of the gory details. She's the only one, besides my father, who knew the identity of the man who raped me. She held me and comforted me, like only Kacey could do, and we promised each other that we would run away and raise the baby together. She would have been such a perfect aunt, Becca. I wish you'd known her."

"I feel like I do, Macey. It must have been a real shock for your sister to hear the details of what happened to you."

Macey sighed and looked sadly at her friend. "Not as shocking as I thought it would be. I found out something that night that I never knew. It turned out that my sweet sister had been enduring her own kind of hell...with our own father."

Becca's undivided attention had once again been captivated. "Oh, no...that is just so sick! Tell me it's not what I'm thinking..."

"Nobody likes to talk about incest, do they?" Macey began. "But...it happens more often than people would like to believe. It seems that our Papa had been visiting my sister's room for almost a year before I left home, and...I never even suspected. She never told me. That last night that we were together—she told me about how he would come to her during the wee hours of the morning. She would awaken and beg him to stop touching her, but he kept telling her that it was his way of showing her how very special she was to him. There was never any penetration on his part, but he did force her to do other things..."

Becca felt sick to her stomach. "Oh, *Geez*... I don't believe this guy! Are you sure he never...?"

"No...I don't think so; although...I have no way of knowing what might have happened to her after I left home. We never got a chance to speak to each other again after Papa shipped me to Aunt Chloe, and Aunt Chloe never allowed me to contact any of my family."

Becca remained quiet for several moments before inquiring, "Macey? Do you suppose the police ever investigated your father regarding your sister's murder? I mean, do you think they could have considered him a suspect, maybe..."

It was Macey's turn for her own mouth to fall open—that possibility had never even occurred to her. Could her father have been responsible for Kacey's death? Had Kacey finally threatened to tell their mother about his nightly visits?

Macey blinked several times and shook her head in bewilderment. Why hadn't she thought of this sooner!

CHAPTER 17

HALLOWEEN 1989

Scott didn't see Macey all weekend—and, only briefly at work on Monday—when their presence was mandated at a last-minute meeting with the international staff. Scott had the distinct feeling that Macey was going out of her way to avoid him, even though he couldn't think of anything he might have done to offend her.

Janet, on the other hand, seemed to be at his side every time he turned around. Scott had pleaded a heavy workload as an excuse for her not to spend the night at his apartment on Monday night. He knew he had made a mistake by having sex with her, just as he knew that it wasn't wise to continue a sexual relationship with her. His mind knew that, but his body was a different story—his body betrayed his mental determination every time he remembered the twenty-four hours they had spent together over the weekend. Even though it had been difficult on his part, he had somehow managed to control his impetuosity to invite her back to his place for a repeat performance.

Scott rushed into his office Tuesday morning—Halloween—and discovered Janet bent over his desk. She appeared to be sorting through and arranging telephone messages in her own disorderly fashion. He couldn't help it—he paused and watched her for several moments. He shook his head at the way she filled out her skin-tight outfit, closed his eyes and inhaled softly. *"Get a grip, boy! You can't go there again..."* he chided himself. He closed the door behind him, and couldn't help but smile when she snapped around and lost her balance.

Janet slipped and was splayed across Scott's desk—her body supported, primarily, by her elbows. A conspiratorial smile crossed her lips when Scott moved quickly to stand behind her. She batted her long lashes at him and winked. "Well, now—this is a familiar position, isn't it?" She took her time to find her footing, but finally turned around— slowly. She re-positioned herself to ensure that there wasn't a spare inch between them. She watched while his eyes traveled from her chest to her eyes—and, back to her chest. Her smile was wanton. "Why...you scared me, Mr. Pennell."

Scott groaned inwardly when she pressed against him. His hands slipped easily around her tiny waist and he smiled down at her. "Sorry, Miss Ward...I didn't mean to catch you off guard."

Janet's hands moved surreptitiously inside his suit jacket and caressed the tense muscles in his back. "Why, that's no problem at all, Mr. Pennell. You can catch me anytime...anytime at all..." She leaned her head back. Her mouth opened slightly, exposing her perfect, white teeth. She moved her body slowly against his until she was rewarded with the physical reaction she fully expected from him.

Scott's body was working against him. He almost kissed her—almost.

Janet purred and went limp in his arms. "Oh...what you do to me, Mr. Pennell." She glanced around him. "Did you...uh...lock the door?"

The question—along with her sultry voice—snapped Scott back to reality. *"My, God! What was I thinking!"* he silently chastised himself. He knew that he had been without a physical relationship for too long, but, that was no reason to jeopardize both their jobs. He pushed away from her as far as her crushing embrace allowed. "No, Janet, I didn't lock the door, and, I don't think *this* is such a good idea after all. You should get back to your desk before Mr. Byce comes looking for you."

Her smile remained provocative as she ran her fingertips lightly across the front of his trousers. "You don't *really* want me to go...do you, Scott?"

Scott groaned and laughed at the same time. "No, not *really*, but...I do need this job, and if the old man finds out about us..." He gently removed her hands from their intended destination, and zipped up his pants. *"When the hell did she unzip my damn pants..."*

Janet cooed, "Don't worry about that old buzzard. He doesn't mind me seeing other people, as long as he gets what he wants once a week. He knows exactly what I want—what I expect—from that relationship." Her nimble hands returned to their favorite spot and started to unzip his pants again.

Scott pushed her hands away— more convincingly this time—and held them between his own. "Just the same, Janet, I'd rather Byce not know about us...okay?"

Janet pouted and pretended to think about his question. "Is he the only one you don't want knowing about us, Scott?"

"Who else do you mean?" Scott asked as he turned and eased away from her web.

Janet smiled mischievously. "What about Miss Garner?"

Scott coughed into his closed fist. "What about her?"

Janet shrugged and said, "Well...I wasn't sure if the two of you had something going on or not..."

Scott quickly became uncomfortable with the course the conversation began to take. "Leave Macey out of this, Janet. I mean it. I don't want her, or anyone else in this company, to know about us. If she does find out, I want it to come from me. You got that?"

Janet presented a mock salute. "Sure, Scott—no problem. I love things that *come* from you..."

Scott moved around her, sat down at his desk, and began sorting through files. He looked up and watched her slow retreat from the room. "And, Janet..."

Janet stopped at the door and looked back at him. She planted a hand on her hip and smiled. "Yes, Scott?"

Scott knew that it had been a mistake to sleep with her. Office affairs were never a good idea. They usually got out of hand and someone always got hurt. He stumbled out the words he needed to say. "Listen, Janet...I don't want you to get the wrong idea about what happened between us this past weekend. I mean—I don't want to mislead you in any way. I want to be up front with you about where I stand. I am not looking for a wife—I'm not even looking for a steady girlfriend right now. This job is my top priority—at least for the first year—until I get established in the company. After that...who knows? I know for a fact that my mom would love to see me settle down, but..."

Janet brought her hands to her mouth and gasped. "Your mom! Oh, my goodness, Scott—that reminds me—I put a message on your desk. Your mom? She called right before you came in—it sounded urgent that you call her back."

Scott looked quickly down at the disorderly stack of phone messages. Why would his mother be calling him at work? "My mom called?" He slapped his hand against his forehead as he suddenly remembered something. "Oh...I was supposed to call her this past weekend..."

Janet straightened her tight skirt along her hips and blew him a kiss. "Just tell her that you got all wrapped up in a *hot* project this past weekend, Mr. Pennell. Oh...and, Scott, I understand what you're saying about *us*. I'm a patient woman, but I have to warn you—if something better comes along...well...it will be your loss."

Scott exhaled when the door finally closed behind Janet. He looked down at his lap and knew that he would have to stay behind his desk long enough for the physical evidence of his recent desire to diminish. He shook his head and grinned. "I'm not sure I could handle you on a long-term basis, anyway, Miss Ward..."

Janet reached her desk just as Macey walked out of her office with the most handsome member of the male species she had ever seen. Her first impression of Jacob Wymer took her breath away.

Jacob looked especially handsome this morning. His short—but thick—black hair was still slightly damp from his morning shower. His body moved like a piece of well-oiled machinery beneath his neatly pressed white shirt and blue jeans.

Janet sighed as she silently appreciated how well he filled out those tight blue jeans!

Jacob smiled and nodded good morning to Janet on his way out the main entrance.

Janet Ward was utterly and hopelessly speechless for the first time in her twenty-four years. She walked slowly to the glassed entrance doors. She pressed her palms and her perky nose against the glass, and watched Jacob climb casually into a black, Chevy pick-up truck. It was obvious to her that this man was blue-collar all the way. She had made it a point to never waste her time on blue-collar men, so she shocked herself when she realized she had spoken aloud. "Oh my, goodness...I think I'm in love..."

Macey cleared her throat to remind Janet that she wasn't alone in the large reception area. "Janet? Are you all right? I do believe you look a little peaked." Macey shook her head and was barely able to contain a smile. She had been witness many times to the effect her little brother had on women of all ages. However, it never ceased to amaze her that he was neither cognizant of his good looks, nor of the impact he had on the overall female populace.

Janet moved from the window and walked slowly back to her desk. She flopped ungraciously down into her chair. She continued to stare toward the entrance and was totally oblivious to the ringing telephones.

Macey watched her for a moment longer before she moved around the desk and punched one of the blinking lights. "Good morning— CompuTech—this is Miss Garner, how may I direct your call?"

A woman's brusque voice—thick with a Yankee accent—answered back. "I'd like to speak with my son, please. Scott Pennell. Has he arrived yet?"

Macey's eyebrows shot up in surprise. Scott's mother! How interesting.

"Just one moment please," Macey offered politely. "I'll transfer you."

"Thank you, dear," Martha Pennell replied.

Macey handed the phone to Janet, who had finally regained her senses enough to attempt the most menial of duties.

Janet returned Macey's questioning look. "I'm so sorry. Thank you for answering that call, Miss Garner. Who did they want—I'll transfer the call?"

"Mr. Pennell. I believe it's his mother," Macey replied curtly as she turned to walk back to her own office. Macey was indeed amused at Janet's reaction to Jacob; however, she didn't trust herself to be civil to the receptionist for much longer. Her feelings were still hurt over the fact that Janet had stayed with Scott over the weekend. She knew she had no right to be angry at either of them because she certainly had no ties on Scott Pennell, but, she was indeed angry.

Janet paused slightly at Macey's cool attitude, but shrugged it off. She had regained her composure so she promptly buzzed Scott's office. "Your mother is on line three, Scott."

"Thank you, Janet." Scott punched line three and answered enthusiastically. "Mom...hi there! Hey, don't be mad at me...I know I was supposed to call this weekend, but my boss had me working on a real short suspense, and I was wrapped up in it all weekend."

There was a deliberate silence at his mother's end.

"Mom? Are you still there?"

"I'm here, Scott. As a matter of fact, so was Cheryl a few minutes ago."

"Cheryl's with you? That's great...put her on for a second and let me say hello..."

"I said she *was* here a few minutes ago," Martha barked. "She had to leave for work."

Scott smiled into the phone. "But she wanted to talk to me, right? I guess that means she doesn't hate me after all. So, you see, Mom...I told you everything would work out all right."

"Oh no..." Martha spoke slowly. "Cheryl certainly doesn't hate you, Scott; quite the contrary, son. The woman is very much in love with you."

"Mom..."

"I don't want to hear it, Scott, so don't say anything. She told me everything."

"Everything?" Scott doubted that.

"Shut up, Scott. Don't worry, she'll get over you. In fact, she mentioned that she's dating someone new."

"She came to see you and just happens to mention that she loves *me* but that she's dating someone new? Well, that's really...great. See, I told you it wouldn't take her long to find someone else, didn't I?"

"Humph," Martha snorted. "If you ask me, it's just an act. She still loves you and always will. I think she was hoping I would tell you about it, and you would get jealous enough to change your mind about things."

Scott attempted an expression of humility—a trait that didn't come easily for him. "It's all for the best, Mom. Cheryl was really nice, and we had some good—some *great*—times together, but, I never felt like...you know...that she was the one I wanted to spend the rest of my life with..." Scott felt more than uncomfortable talking to his mother about his love life, but he knew she wouldn't drop the subject if he didn't say something to appease her.

Martha Pennell switched gears quicker than Scott would have thought possible. "So...have *you* found a replacement for *her* yet?"

Scott choked on his reply. "Excuse me?"

"You heard me, Scott Pennell. I did not stammer. Have you met anyone yet?"

"Mom, I've been here less than a month...give me a break!"

"We both know that you're a fast worker...always have been. You have, haven't you? Met someone?"

It was images of Macey Wymer's smiling face and gentle nature that suddenly came to Scott's mind, instead of the more physical attributes of Janet Ward. He smiled to himself but didn't immediately answer.

His mother took his momentary silence as confirmation of her question. "Who is she, Scott?"

Scott blew out a deep breath. He knew he would never get any work done if he didn't offer his mother some token of confirmation. "Well, I certainly don't intend to discuss my love life with my mother, but—you're right, Mom—there is one woman. She's my neighbor and, also, a co-worker, but...Mom, it's not what you think—or what you hope for that matter. In fact, I don't think she even likes me very much. I think she just tolerates me because our boss more or less forced me on her."

"Hmm...sounds interesting. You're sure it's not serious?"

"Mom, be sensible! How serious could it get in just three weeks? I haven't even held her hand much less proposed to her!"

"Now you're being a smart ass, Scott Pennell. Just like your father."

"I'm sorry, Mom. How is Dad, by the way?"

"Don't ask. He's still mad at you for leaving, but, he'll get over it... especially if you would finally settle down and make him a grandpa before he dies of old age."

Scott laughed out loud. "You're crazy, old lady! I love you, you know.

Listen, I've got a meeting to get to. Can I call you back?"

"No, you can't. That's another reason I was calling. I'm coming for a visit."

"You're kidding—*here*—when?"

"Yes, *there*...and, I'll be there tomorrow night. I can only stay until Saturday morning, though, so—while I'm there—why don't you set up a lunch date with this young woman you're so infatuated with and let me meet her? My plane arrives at six-thirty tomorrow night; can you pick me up, or should I take a taxi to your apartment?"

Scott just smiled and shook his head. His mother had always been a take-charge kind of person, a trait she had, undoubtedly, passed on to her son. "Mom, I can't wait to see you. I'll be at the airport to pick you up. There is no way I would subject an innocent cab driver to your interrogations."

"Watch your mouth, Scott Pennell. I'll let you go now. See you tomorrow evening."

"Good-bye, Mom. Tell Dad I said hello. He's not coming with you, is he?"

Mrs. Pennell sighed. "Not this time, son."

"Okay then...I can't wait to see you. Have a safe trip."

"Good-bye, Scott. I love you."

"Love you too, Mom." Scott hung up the phone and thought about his mother's impending visit. He knew his mother all too well. She would scare Macey away for sure with all her insinuations and dreams about becoming a grandmother. He would have to do everything he could to keep his mother from meeting Macey; otherwise, she would have them engaged before she returned to Pennsylvania. *"Although...that doesn't sound like such a bad thing,"* Scott surprised himself at the unexpected thought.

He grinned all the way to his meeting.

CHAPTER 18

ANDREW'S PAST DESIRES

Andrew Wymer sat behind the old metal desk and shuffled the previous day's cluttered receipts from one stack to another. He glanced at the clock—it was after nine o'clock and Jacob was late again. Andrew suspected the reason for his son's tardiness might involve a woman. "Maybe I shouldn't begrudge him that," he spoke aloud. "Maybe that's what I need in my life—a woman—a real woman. A woman like my Kacey would have grown up to become if...if she'd only been given the chance. Oh, Kacey..."

Andrew's physical reaction to Kacey's memory was instantaneous. He had been ashamed of his actions back then, and he was ashamed of them today. His hands began to take control of the situation as they rested against his trousers, and he allowed his memories to travel back in time...

The night of the twins' fourteenth birthday party proved to be a turning point in Andrew Wymer's life—it was, also, a turning point for his daughter, Kacey. Andrew had always thought Kacey was extraordinarily special, but on that night, his favorite daughter proved to him just how special she really was.

He had waited until his entire family had been asleep for several hours before he slowly opened and entered the door to Kacey's room. He had done his best to fight the demonic temptations that had eaten away most of his soul over the past few years, but, he lost that fight the night the twins turned fourteen.

Andrew entered the dark room and locked the door behind him. He made his way slowly across the room, and retrieved a desk chair that he used to lodge beneath the door handle to a connecting door that separated the twins' bedrooms. He forced his breathing to slow down when he heard Kacey mumble in her sleep. He stood frozen in his step until she turned her backside to him and faced the wall.

A separate voice inside his head—the logical and sane voice—tried to talk him out of what he was about to do. *Physical—sexual—desire for his own daughter!* It was incest—pure and simple—and, he had fought those demons longer than he cared to admit. However, he simply could not help himself—he could not stop the physical yearning that he had for Kacey. There was something so genuine—so pure—about her. He did not want to share her with anyone; he wanted to possess everything about her. He was sane enough to realize that the feelings he had were not normal, paternal feelings, and, he had done everything in his power to suppress them over the years. He had managed to keep those feelings to himself, and, he only allowed them to exist in his dreams—in his most private thoughts. It was wrong—he knew it was wrong—but the urges were beginning to consume every hour of his day.

Andrew was not a drinker, but, he had consumed several glasses of wine earlier in the evening in celebration of the twins' birthday. He even went against his own rules—no drinking until the age of eighteen—and allowed the twins to each have one glass of wine. He had not been surprised when Macey eagerly accepted the wine and gulped it down quickly before he could change his mind. Andrew was repulsed when the girl giggled when some of the wine trickled down her chin.

If he had known Macey better, he might have realized that she giggled to hide the nervousness she felt in accepting the wine in the first place. He had wanted to slap her when she had held out her glass for a refill, but, her mother had been quick to overrule a second serving.

Andrew disregarded Macey with barely-suppressed disgust, and focused his attention on Kacey. Kacey was the more timid and demure of the twins. He smiled at her and touched her cheek, encouraging her reluctance to taste the wine. It was obvious that she did not really enjoy the taste of the bittersweet nectar, and he suspected that she was only drinking it, so as not to disappoint her father. The love and favoritism on Andrew's face was apparent to everyone in the room. Andrew ignored them all—except for one. "Kacey, sweetheart, would *you* like some more wine?"

Kacey flashed a nervous glance at her mother, who appeared to be ready to interject for her. "No thank you, Papa. I really don't like the taste all that much; it's made me a little sleepy. It's been a long day and the party was so much fun—but, I really am tired." She stood beside her father and put her arms around his neck. She kissed him on the cheek and said, "Thank you for everything, Papa. It was a wonderful birthday. I'll never forget it. I love you."

Andrew closed his eyes, revering the gentle kiss placed upon his stubby cheek. "And I love you, child. Go on to bed now. I'll see you in the morning."

Everything was put away and the members of the Wymer family all departed for their separate bedrooms—except for Andrew. He had sat at the table, consuming several more glasses of the cheap wine. He wasn't much of a drinker, so the alcohol affected him more than it would have a regular drinker. Several hours later—with the rest of his family sleeping soundly—Andrew crept into Kacey's bedroom. He told himself that he only wanted to watch her sleep; but, somewhere deep inside his wretched soul, he knew that wasn't the truth. After locking the door and bracing the chair against the connecting door, Andrew made a half-effort attempt to leave the room—before it was too late. That effort failed. His overwhelming desire to hold his daughter in his arms surpassed his failing good judgment. He knew that he was about to cross a line that might change his and Kacey's lives forever.

His bare feet made no sound as they moved across the hardwood floor to Kacey's bed. He stopped in mid-stride when Kacey mumbled once again in her sleep—he assumed she must have been dreaming. He wasn't aware that he had been holding his breath until Kacey turned onto her back and stretched her slender arms above her head. The thin coverlet slipped downward and Jacob saw the firm flesh of his daughter's smooth, flat stomach when Kacey stretched her arms over her head. Her long, dark hair fanned out in a million directions across the pillow.

Andrew took another step and perched himself carefully on the edge of the bed. He reached out to smooth a trail of fugitive locks from Kacey's face. His hand lingered on her cheek for a moment before it trailed across her chin, to her throat, and finally rested upon the small cleavage of her chest. He rubbed his thumb across the thin pajama material.

He was lost from that moment on.

He tried to swallow, but there was no spit in his mouth to accommodate the motion. He willed his hand away, but, it chose to remain steadfast upon her chest. Moonlight streamed through the open window and provided just the right amount of light for him to see the things he had no right to see. He was so engrossed in his hypnotic desire that he was not aware that Kacey had awakened.

The cool night air upon her exposed skin had stirred her awake from an unsettling dream. She had been dreaming that someone was touching her in places that had never been touched. She could not identify the man in the dream, but when she opened her eyes and saw her beloved Papa leaning over her, she realized that her dream—her *nightmare*—was real. She convinced herself, at first, that it was a dream—of course, it was a dream! Maybe the dream would dissipate if she spoke out loud. "Papa?"

Andrew's hand jerked back as if it had touched upon the very edges of Hell. His gaze flew immediately to his daughter's bewildered, light-grey eyes. The eyes were the only distinguishing feature of the identical twins. Macey's eyes were a darker grey in color, whereas, Kacey's were a much lighter grey. He watched those eyes now—the same eyes that had trusted him, unfailingly, for fourteen years. He watched as that trust was replaced with bewilderment and confusion.

Kacey propped herself up on her elbows. "Papa? What are you doing?"

Andrew's voice was raspy and thick—filled with unquenched desire—when he finally answered. "Go back to sleep, child. I was just checking on you to make sure you were warm enough."

Kacey continued to stare at her father. It had not been a dream after all. She knew—without a doubt—that it had been her father's hands she had felt upon her skin. She was completely dumbfounded. She didn't know what to do or say. "I'm fine, Papa. You can go on back to bed now. I'm fine...really, I am." Kacey watched while her father attempted to stand—it looked as though his legs wouldn't support him—they were shaking so badly. She, also, saw the bulge that pressed against his pants. She knew what that bulge meant, because Macey had recently taken it upon herself to educate her twin on the facts of life.

Andrew flinched when he realized that Kacey had noticed his arousal. He watched as her face paled, and he hated himself even more than he thought was possible. "Good...that's good, my little angel. You go back to sleep now, and...I'll see you in the morning." Andrew backed out of the room and pretended to close the door; instead, he remained outside the door and listened to Kacey's ragged breathing. He eased open the door just enough to be able to see her face—to see the fear etched upon her beautiful face—fear he had put there. He saw the tears flow down her cheek, and jammed his fist into his mouth to suppress his own tears. He saw her pull the covers up to her neck and rock back and forth on the bed. He saw her glance across the room—at the chair wedged beneath the door handle that connected her room to her sister's.

The last thing he heard was her raspy whisper that choked on her own sobs. "He wanted to make sure Macey didn't come in...oh, God... what am I going to do?"

Andrew couldn't listen to anymore. He backed away from the half-closed door and found his way to his own bedroom. He winced inwardly when he looked at his wife lying upon her own twin bed. Ruth was snoring soundly, oblivious to the horror that he had almost committed.

In his defense, Andrew had fought his demons and had tried his best to stay away from his daughter's room after that night. Unfortunately, he failed. That night marked the beginning of two years of emotional torment and agony for both Andrew and Kacey Wymer. Andrew continued the late-night visits—each one longer than the previous one—to his daughter's room. The strokes and caresses from his rough and weathered hands continued to explore her forbidden territory. He was always careful never to permit himself the gratification of actual intercourse with her; but, over the next two years, he manipulated Kacey into performing every other sexual act known to his own limited experiences.

Andrew knew it was wrong. He was convinced that Kacey, also, knew it was wrong; but, he was powerless to stop it. He didn't feel good about the emotional fear he inflicted upon her, by telling her that she would lose her father's love if she denied him—or, if she ever told anyone about what went on between them. Whenever Kacey gathered enough courage to doubt and question his reasoning, he used their religion to convince her that God approved of her physical expression of love for her father.

It wasn't until after Kacey's death—when Andrew found her hidden journals—that he learned of his daughter's secret liaisons with Scott Pennell during her junior year at Baker High School. She had written countless pages about her fears and doubts surrounding her *unhealthy* relationship with her father. She wrote that once she started meeting Scott secretly after school and on weekends, it had not taken her long to realize the true meaning of her father's sexual demands. She told her diary that she felt powerless to stop him...that she was too ashamed of her participation to confide her feelings to anyone—except to Macey.

The journals told of Macey's threat to go to the authorities, and of Kacey's subsequent plea for her sister not to interfere. Andrew read how Kacey had convinced her sister that she could handle the situation—that she was only enduring their father's demands until such time that she and Scott Pennell could elope. It had sickened Andrew to learn that Kacey believed that Scott Pennell was her ticket out of a bad situation. It had sickened him to think that Scott Pennell was touching and kissing his sweet Kacey.

The slamming of the shop's front door brought Andrew's thoughts back to the present. His brows drew together in a frown as Jacob rushed in—his cheeks robust with the cool, morning air.

"Hi, Pop! Sorry I'm late." Jacob hung his jacket on the back of an old, wooden chair and poured himself some coffee. He chose to ignore his father's purposeful lack of greeting. "Has it been busy this morning, Pop?"

"It's about time you made it in, boy. This is getting to be a habit with you."

Jacob tried to lighten the moment. "Come on, Pop. I'm not late that often. Besides—it's Tuesday—our slowest day of the week. You want some coffee?"

Andrew stood up and grabbed an old Auburn College baseball cap. He turned and walked toward the door that connected the office to the garage. "No, and you'd better get started on Alvin James' car. He'll be by at lunch to pick it up."

Jacob lifted his cup to his father and smiled. It was becoming harder and harder to smile at someone you knew didn't care whether you lived or died. "Not a problem, Pop. It's almost finished. I only have a few more adjustments to make on the carburetor and it'll be good as new. I like Mr. James, don't you? He's a friendly, old man."

Andrew looked back over his shoulder at Jacob and grunted. "He's a nigger, and he's just like the rest of them."

Jacob was truly offended at his father's ethnic vulgarity and blatant prejudice. "Pop!"

"You heard me, boy! Just fix his damn car and get him out of here. If we didn't need the money so bad, I'd send him somewhere else." Andrew stormed through the door into the garage.

"Alvin James is a nice man," Jacob clenched his fists after Andrew had left the room. "And, it doesn't matter if he's black, white, or purple...he's been more of a father to me the last five years than you ever thought of being..."

Macey managed to avoid Scott most of the day, speaking to him only when good manners mandated such. She was sorting through unexpected feelings of hurt and disappointment after discovering Janet's car still parked beside Scott's on Sunday morning. She knew that her feelings were unwarranted; she certainly had no claim on Scott Pennell—no reason to be jealous of Janet or any other female with whom he chose to spend his nights. She doubted that a man like Scott couldn't—or wouldn't—suffer the lack of female companionship for too long a period.

It was almost six o'clock before Macey locked her office and escaped to the parking lot. She was unaware that Scott watched her departure from his office window.

He waited for her to pull out of the parking lot before he rushed outside to his own car. He was intent on following her home and asking her why she had been avoiding him since the Halloween party. Today was Halloween and he was hoping that he could persuade her to go out to dinner with him—a sure way to avoid all the trick-or-treaters that might come knocking on their doors.

It took several lights for Scott to catch up with Macey's car. He maintained a three-car distance between them and followed her onto the interstate. He shrugged when she didn't turn at the exit that lead to their apartment complex, and continued to follow her to see where she might be going. It didn't take him long to figure out that she was probably headed to the cemetery again. "Man, I wonder who died?" he queried. "This isn't exactly the place I had in mind for a dinner date—especially on Halloween night." He pulled off onto a side road once he was inside the cemetery and watched as Macey drove slowly past the grave site she had visited over the weekend. "Now, why isn't she stopping?"

An old, green pick-up truck was parked alongside the curb, and a man kneeled at the grave that Macey and her boyfriend had visited a few days ago. It was obvious the man was crying and experiencing deep, personal grief.

Scott felt like a voyeur while he watched the man who appeared to be in his fifties; he had a stocky build and was nice looking. The man pulled a handkerchief from his back pocket to wipe his eyes. Scott continued to watch until the man dragged himself slowly back to his truck and drove away. The man never looked back.

Macey's car reappeared a few moments later. She remained inside her car for a few minutes, and Scott wondered if he had been spotted. "No," he whispered. "She can't see me from here."

Macey didn't stay long. She placed a bouquet of white and yellow flowers beside two similar bouquets that someone else had left; and, like the last time, she kissed the headstone. She turned and walked back to her car with her head down. She exited the cemetery from a side entrance.

Scott waited to be sure she wasn't returning. He parked alongside the grave site and cut his engine. He didn't know why, but his heart began a rapid pounding within his chest. The closer he got to the headstone, the faster his heart beat. He stooped to get a closer look at the writing on the headstone, and immediately began to hyperventilate. Another sharp, vivid flashback zoomed behind his eyes, and he had to catch himself from falling onto the grave. The flashback was one of him and Macey—as *teenagers*—and, he was holding and kissing her. Even though the flashback was one of a much younger Macey, he knew—without a doubt—that it was indeed Macey! "What the hell is going on..."

His next movement seemed to occur in slow motion—at least, that's what it felt like to Scott. He turned his head to read the headstone.

KACEY IRENE WYMER
BELOVED CHILD OF GOD
SEPTEMBER 12, 1953 - OCTOBER 31, 1969

It took another fifteen minutes before Scott's breathing regulated enough for him to feel it was safe for him to drive. He pressed his palms against his eyes and shook his head in denial. "Something isn't right... what is it?" He was perspiring profusely, even though the late-October air was comfortable and cool. "Why do I keep seeing your face, Macey... your *teenage* face? Why do I keep seeing us together?"

The name on the headstone flashed in his mind.

"And...who the hell is Kacey Wymer? How does she connect to you, Macey? I've got to find out what all of this means...and, something tells me that you're the only one who can help me. You've got to help me, Macey..."

CHAPTER 19

MARTHA PENNELL RETURNS TO COLUMBUS

Scott stood inside the door to Gate 1 and waited for his mother to disembark from the small commuter plane that had just arrived from Atlanta. It didn't take him long to pick her out from the crowd of thirty or so passengers. If her Clairol-dyed, copper-red hair wasn't enough to easily identify her among the crowd, her loud and boisterous voice more than sealed the deal. Scott shook his head—mostly in sympathy—for the unfortunate businessman on the receiving end of his mother's attention. Scott's head towered above the other people waiting for passenger arrivals, and he waved his mother toward him. "Mom! Over here!"

The unfortunate businessman glanced appreciatively toward Scott, and used the interruption to make a quick getaway.

Martha Pennell beamed with maternal pride when she spotted her only child. She yelled back at the retreating businessman, "There is he! There's my handsome and successful son!" She ran toward her only child with anticipation. She had missed him more than she thought she would during the past month. "Scott! Oh...it is so good to see you, son. I have missed you *so* much!"

Mother and son embraced for several moments while the other passengers ignored them and tried to maneuver their way around them.

Scott had always been close to his mother, and had probably missed her almost as much as she had him. "I missed you too, Mom.

Martha reluctantly pulled away from her son to get a closer look at him. "Look at you! You've gained weight! I expected to find you skinny as a rail—not eating right—but, instead, you look absolutely wonderful, son."

Scott grinned down at her and gave her another hug. "So, do you, Mom. It's great to see you. Although—I must admit—this visit came a little sooner than I expected. I told you I'd be home for Thanksgiving. What's the matter? Did you miss this handsome face?"

His mother punched him playfully against his shoulder and marched ahead of him. "Come on—help me find my bag. I can't wait to see your apartment. I want to see where you work, too. You don't mind if I come by your office tomorrow, do you?"

Scott grinned and shook his head. "Well, actually, I asked for tomorrow off, Mom; but, we can swing by CompuTech if you want. I'd love to show you around. It really is a great place, and—so far—I like everything about it."

Martha turned to look at her son while he spoke and decided that the new job must suit him; he really did look happy. "I'm glad to hear that, son...and, what about that young lady we were discussing the other day? Were you able to arrange a luncheon date so that I can meet her?"

Scott smiled and hugged his mother before moving ahead of her to lead the way to the baggage claim section. His intention had been to spare Macey a meeting with his mother, but, he knew that when his mother made up her mind about something, it was usually best to just roll with the flow and let her have her way. If he didn't arrange for the two of them to meet, he had no doubt that his mother would make it happen by herself. Persistence was her middle name. "I've done something even better—I've invited her to dinner tonight."

Martha raised her eyebrows in genuine surprise. "Tonight? Why, that's wonderful, son! Where are you taking us?"

"We'll be eating at my place. You'll be surprised to know that your son is cooking tonight."

"You're kidding! I don't believe it—but, that's a wonderful idea. The atmosphere will be much more relaxed. You did say she lived in the same complex as you, right?"

Scott nodded. "Yep, she lives right across the street from me. I stopped by her office as I was leaving today and persuaded her to have dinner with me tonight. The only way I got her to come was by agreeing to let her bring the dessert. There is one thing, though—I didn't tell her she would be meeting my mother tonight, so...promise me that you'll be nice and go easy on her, okay?"

"Well, well..." Martha smiled. "What do you mean—be nice—I'm always nice! I can't wait to meet this young lady."

Scott's forehead wrinkled with skepticism. "Yeah, I just bet you can't. Anyway, I told her to come over around eight o'clock. You have to promise me that you'll behave."

"Me—behave? Why, whatever do you mean, Scott?"

Scott's brows drew together in mock sternness. 'You know damn well what I mean, *mother*. Don't embarrass me—or Macey, for that matter."

"You should know me better than to even say that, Scott. Whatever makes you think I would do or say anything to embarrass either of you?"

"I mean it, Mom. I told you that Macey and I are friends—just friends—nothing else. I don't want you scaring her off by any offhanded attempts at matchmaking. The relationship isn't anywhere near that stage, and, may never be."

Martha pulled her lower teeth over her top lip. "My goodness! Will you look at the time! Scott, it's almost seven o'clock now! Come on, son, let's get a move on! I need to freshen up a little before I meet her. What did you say her name was again?"

Scott sighed. He knew that he had lost the battle, but prayed that he had not lost the war. "Her name is Macey—Macey Garner."

"Macey," Martha murmured. "That's a nice name, but...Macey Pennell—now *that* has a nice ring to it, too, don't you think?"

Scott pushed his mother gently ahead of him. He laughed out loud as they exited the automatic sliding doors. "Give it up, Mom...give it up!"

Becca stood off to one side and watched Macey rush around the kitchen.

Macey sprinkled the final touch of powdered sugar over her signature dessert—lemon-apricot pound cake.

Becca ran her finger inside the bowl of lemon glaze and rolled her eyes upward. "You do know that this is my favorite cake, don't you? I can't believe you made it for *him*!"

Macey wiped her hands on her apron and looked sideways at her friend. "Becca, you've got to get over these hostile feelings you have for Scott. My goodness, if *I* don't hate him, you certainly shouldn't. You won't even give the man a fair chance."

Becca was genuinely surprised at Macey's defense of Scott Pennell. "I didn't think you wanted anything else to do with him after seeing that hussy's car parked beside his for twenty-four hours straight. Or have you already forgotten about *that*?"

Macey removed her apron and tossed it at Becca. "No, I haven't forgotten, but let's face it. Why should I be upset about that situation? Scott has every right to see whomever he pleases. Now...I've got to run upstairs for a quick shower, and, I would appreciate it if you would be the great friend that you are and finish up those dishes before you leave, okay? I'll see you tomorrow at lunch and give you the whole scoop."

"I'm holding you to that!" Becca yelled back. "And save me a piece of damn cake!"

Becca finished the dishes and threw on her windbreaker before leaving the apartment. The days were still relatively warm, but the cooling November breezes often prevailed by dusk. She put the hood up on her jacket and looked up in time to see Scott's Porsche pull into its designated parking space. "Damn," she snarled quietly. "He's seen me."

Scott had indeed seen Becca leaving Macey's apartment. He waved to her as she made her way to her own car. "Hello, Miss Becca!" he yelled from across the parking lot. "Is Macey about ready?"

Becca threw up her hand in a weak acknowledgment, nodded, and quickly got inside her car. She hoped he didn't walk over to talk to her. The less conversation she had with the man, the better. She watched him through the rear-view mirror while he moved to the passenger side of his car and opened the door. The older woman he assisted from the sports car had the brightest red hair Becca had ever seen; it reminded Becca of one of her favorite soap opera characters—Sally Spectra, on *The Bold and the Beautiful.* "Now who the hell could that be?" she puzzled. "I thought he was having dinner with Macey tonight...the jerk!"

Becca adjusted her mirror and continued watching while Scott removed a small suitcase from his trunk. He draped an arm across the woman's shoulder and led her into his apartment. Becca was still puzzled, but she was determined to mind her own business this time. She started her car and drove away. She had her own plans for the evening with Carlton Brown and she didn't want to be late.

Once inside her son's executive suite, Martha walked around and inspected the immediate area. She particularly liked the cream-colored walls that were highlighted by a narrow strip of burgundy and hunter-green border paper. "Scott, this is absolutely beautiful! And, this view out back is breathtaking!" She turned back toward the dining room. "Oh, my...just look at this table! Real linen, fine china, and...candles, too! I am really impressed, son. You definitely did not learn the art of fine wining and dining from your father!"

Scott grinned and sat his mother's suitcase in the foyer. "Thanks, Mom. I hope Macey is as impressed as you are. This will be the first time she's ever seen the place."

"Too bad your old mom is here to ruin the ambiance, huh?"

Scott swept his mom up in a bear hug and laughed. "Don't be silly, old woman! I've got the rest of my life to try and romance Macey—*if*—that's what I decide I want to do, and, I'm not sure yet that it is. So, please remember—don't be pushy. I don't want to scare her off. She's...well, she's really different from most women I've known."

"Hmm...she sounds absolutely intriguing. I can't wait to meet her. In the meantime, why don't you point your old mom in the direction of the nearest ladies' room so that I can freshen up some?"

Scott smiled and pointed toward the hallway. "Your room is the first door on the left, Mom. There's a connecting bath off your room. I think you'll find everything you need in there, but, let me know if there's anything you need. I need to make a quick run to the package store for some more wine. I thought I had two bottles, but there was only one in the cupboard. I forgot that I...uh...opened the other bottle this past weekend. It's just down the road, so it won't take me long."

"Okay, son...hurry back."

It had taken Macey more than an hour to decide on the right outfit to wear. She wanted to appear feminine—but, not sexy—and, casual—but, not sloppy. She finally decided on one of her favorite outfits—black silk palazzo pants with a matching black, V-cut tee. Her only accessories included a silver chain belt accentuating her tiny waist, silver loop earrings, and a silver cross that nestled enviably between the slight cleavage between her breasts. Her dark hair was pulled up into a twist and secured with silver-studded combs that matched the earrings. She was confident in her choice of outfits as she made her way across the parking lot. She was both nervous and excited about having dinner with Scott tonight, and she wanted to look her best. She hoped this dinner would give them a chance to get to know each other better—outside of the office environment. She arrived at his door, took a deep breath, and rang his bell at exactly eight o'clock, being very careful to balance the crystal cake dish in her free hand.

Scott was quick to answer the door and smiled down at her. He held out his hand to take the dish she was holding. "Hi, Macy—you're right on time. Here, let me take that for you...wow...you look..."

They stood looking at each for several moments.

Scott was thinking how ravishing she looked in black—his favorite color.

Macey was reminded once again of the unspent emotions he stirred within her. No man had ever had that effect upon her, and she still felt guilty that *he* would be the one to stir them now.

Martha Pennell stood—hidden from view—behind her son. "Excuse me...Scott, dear? Do you care to introduce us?"

The sound of Martha clearing her throat was enough to break the spell that had seemed to suspend time for Scott and Macey.

Macey peeked around Scott's shoulder—she was too short to peek over it—toward the sound of an unexpected third party. Scott had failed to tell her that anyone else had been invited to dinner. The older woman had the brightest red hair she had ever seen.

Macey may have been clueless to the identity of Scott's other dinner guest, but, it only took Martha Pennell a split second to recognize Macey's face. "Oh dear, God!" she exclaimed. She grabbed her chest and gasped frantically for air.

Scott shoved the cake dish back into Macey's hands and reached frantically for his mother. He barely caught her before she collapsed onto the plush, cream carpeting.

Martha Pennell had fainted. She came to ten minutes later and found herself lying on the black leather sofa. She pulled a cool rag off her forehead. "What the hell happened?" she asked.

Scott moved quickly to kneel by his mother's side and put his hand to her forehead. "You fainted, Mom. How do you feel? Are you okay?"

Martha pushed his hand away and pulled herself to a sitting position. "Oh, quit your fussing! I'm fine..." It only took a split-second for her to remember why she had fainted. She quickly surveyed the room. "Where is she?"

Scott tried to touch his mother's forehead again. "Macey? She's gone upstairs to see what she can find in the medicine cabinet. I've gotta say, Mom...you really know how to make a great first impression. Way to go... are you sure you're alright?"

Martha slapped his hand away. "Oh, for Heaven's sake, I'm fine...quit your worrying. It's probably just...jet lag. I've never fainted before in my life."

"It was less than a three-hour flight, Mom. I doubt very seriously that jet lag is the problem," Scott reminded her. He sighed with relief and quipped, "Hey, I know! Maybe you're pregnant! Don't pregnant women faint a lot?"

Martha pushed herself to a standing position and squared her shoulders. "Oh! Such a smart ass I've raised..."

Macey hurried down the stairs. She carried a bottle of aspirin in her hand. "Scott, I'm afraid this is all I could find..." She stopped in mid-sentence when she saw Scott's mother standing. "Mrs. Pennell! Oh, I'm so glad you're alright." Macey walked toward the older woman and offered an extended hand. "Hello, I'm Macey Garner. I didn't know you would be here tonight. Scott told me who you were after you fainted. Is there anything I can get for you? Some water, perhaps?"

Martha shook her head and tried not to stare at Macey. Was her resemblance to Kacey Wymer coincidental? It must be. There was no other explanation. In all the articles Martha had read about Kacey Wymer, there had never been any mention of a sister. Still...the resemblance was uncanny. "No, Miss Garner, I'm fine, and...I apologize for fainting. I was just telling Scott that I've never fainted before in my life." Martha couldn't shake the eerie feeling that she was having a conversation with a dead woman. She continued to stare at Macey as though she had seen a ghost. She began to sense Macey's obvious discomfort under the blatant scrutiny. "I'm sorry, Miss Garner—excuse me for staring—but, is there any chance that...we've met before? Your face seems so familiar to me?"

Macey's spine stiffened when she stuttered a reply. "No, I...I don't think so, Mrs. Pennell, and, please...call me Macey."

Scott breathed an audible sigh of relief. "Well...now that I've got the two prettiest women in town prisoners in my apartment, what do you say we have a glass of wine?"

Martha reluctantly drew her gaze away from Macey. "I know I could sure use one!" she exhaled.

Macey emitted her own soft sigh of relief. "I'm not much of a drinker, Scott, but, I think I could probably use one, too."

"Coming right up!" Scott beamed. "Why don't the two of you go out on the terrace and get better acquainted? I'll bring the wine out in a second, with some cheese and crackers. I just need to put the steaks under the broiler and we'll be all set."

Martha led the way outside and sat down at the patio table. "This is a beautiful apartment. Is yours just like it, Macey?"

Macey took a seat opposite Scott's mother and shook her head. "Oh, no. Scott's place is much nicer than mine. His is what they advertise as an executive suite. Mine is much more along the lines of your basic apartment, and, my view does not compare to this one. He has nothing but peaceful, serene woods behind him. My front patio overlooks the parking lot, and my small, back balcony overlooks a few pine trees with a busy highway just beyond them. I hear much more traffic noise than Scott does."

"Yes, it is a beautiful setting. Scott tells me that you two, also, work together?"

Macey nodded. "Yes, we do. I've also been assigned as Scott's sponsor."

"Really? What exactly does that entail?"

Macey had been nervous when she found out the unexpected dinner guest was Scott's mother. It had been twenty years, and Macey knew that her own looks had not changed significantly over that time. She had been afraid that Mrs. Pennell would somehow make the connection between her and the resemblance to the younger Kacey Wymer. She felt some of the tenseness ease from her body, and she offered a timid smile. "Well, mostly, it involves showing people new to the city around town—recommending the best banks, doctors, restaurants, stores to go to—that sort of thing. However, things have been so hectic at work lately that I'm afraid I haven't been a very good sponsor for Scott. The only thing I've managed to do so far is to introduce him to some good, old Southern cooking—at lunch—at one of my favorite restaurants."

"Hmm...that's nice of you. I'm glad he has you to show him around, but..." Martha wasn't sure how much to say to Macey, but the more she watched and listened to her, the harder it was to shake the feeling that the woman had to be related to Kacey Wymer. The resemblance was simply too overwhelming.

"But...what, Mrs. Pennell?"

"Well...you do know that Scott isn't exactly a stranger to Columbus... don't you?"

Macey's heart skipped a beat. "Excuse me?"

Martha was quick to observe the tense look that suddenly shadowed Macey's beautiful face; but, before she could continue, Scott came outside carrying a tray bearing wine, cheese and crackers.

"All right ladies," he grinned. "What do you say to a little snack before dinner? We have about twenty more minutes before the steaks are ready. Allow me to pour you both some wine."

"Yes," Martha agreed. "That's a marvelous idea. Let's have some wine and...get to know each other a little better."

Macey shivered involuntarily but raised her glass to Martha Pennell. "Yes, I agree...let's get to know each other better."

CHAPTER 20

RESEARCH AND INQUIRY

Scott's initial plan to take Thursday off work changed when George Byce called him in to attend an unscheduled meeting with some foreign clients. He assured his mother, however, that he would be free for lunch, and told her to meet him at CompuTech.

Martha Pennell spent all of Thursday morning—after Scott left for work—at the Bradley Library, reading articles written about the 1969 murder of Kacey Wymer. The pictures of Kacey's smiling face loomed before Martha and brought back chilling memories of that long-ago Halloween night. After comparing the pictures of Kacey to the woman she had dined with the previous evening, Martha was more than convinced that the two women must be related in some way. She dissected every line of every available article about the murder and the subsequent investigation; however, there was no mention of a sister in any of them. "She's got to be related...the resemblance is too uncanny to be coincidental," Martha mumbled to herself. She leaned back and stretched her hands to the ceiling.

An elderly librarian walked by and heard Martha mumbling to herself. The old woman was curious by nature, so she didn't hesitate to lean over Martha's shoulder to see what she had been reading. She squinted at the microfiche screen and clucked her tongue hard enough to cause her false teeth to rattle. "Oh, I remember that...such a terrible thing to have happened to that poor, young girl," she whispered and shook her head sadly.

Martha glanced back at the librarian and figured she had to be seventy-five if she was a day. Her name tag identified her as Mrs. Page. "Yes," Martha agreed. "It was a terrible thing. I don't suppose you knew her, by any chance?" It didn't hurt to ask.

The old woman grinned and her false teeth popped loose.

Martha jumped back involuntarily.

Mrs. Page wrinkled her nose and jaw and, nonchalantly, managed to maneuver her teeth back into place. "Kacey? Oh, yes, Dearie," she nodded. "I knew Kacey. She and my granddaughter, Melissa, were both cheerleaders at Baker High School. As I recall...she and my Melissa had several classes together." The old woman sighed and shook her head again. "Melissa was heartbroken when Kacey was killed. I still think it's a mighty shame and disgrace that they never found out who did those horrible things to her. Personally, I think it was that young boy she was dating. Rumor had it, that his parents had enough money to keep him out of prison—sent him to the looney bin instead, I think."

Martha gritted her teeth—which she was proud to say were still her own—and decided to ignore the insinuation about Scott. She wanted to see what else the old bat might remember about Kacey Wymer. "Did your granddaughter know Kacey's family, Mrs. Page?"

"Well, of course she did, Dearie. Yes...Melissa used to go to their home to keep Kacey company whenever she had to baby-sit her little brother. I can't remember his name..."

Martha tried to keep the old woman focused on their main subject of conversation. "The articles say her brother's name was Jacob, but, they don't mention any other siblings. I was wondering if Kacey might have had a sister."

The old woman thought for a long moment before responding. "No... now that you mention it...I don't believe the papers ever mentioned the sister."

Martha practically fell off her chair. "You mean there *was* a sister?"

The librarian wasn't surprised that Martha didn't know about the sister; after all, the twin sister never lived in Columbus with the family. "Oh, yes, Dearie! Not only a sister, mind you—but, a *twin* sister!"

Martha gasped. That was it! That explained it! "A twin! Yes, a twin—that would definitely explain things."

A puzzled, glazed expression settled over Mrs. Page's wrinkled and leathered face.

It was obvious to Martha that the old woman's mind had momentarily drifted. She doubted the old woman would even remember their conversation ten minutes from now.

"What? What did you say, Dearie?" the old woman finally mumbled.

Martha quickly gathered her purse and notes together. "Oh nothing—but, maybe you can tell me, Mrs. Page, why there was never any mention of a twin sister in any of the articles?"

Mrs. Page had not forgotten their conversation. She looked around the empty library and whispered in a conspiratorial tone. "Well, I'm not one to spread gossip, mind you, but, my Melissa told me that the sister—I wish I could remember her name—anyway, committed some sort of...well...discrepancy...if you know what I mean. Rumor was that her daddy shipped her off to relatives and disowned the poor child. She wasn't even living in Columbus when poor Kacey was killed."

It was Martha's turn to look puzzled and confused. "By *discrepancy,* do you mean..."

The old woman clucked and nodded. "Oh yes, Dearie...the poor child went and got herself pregnant."

"Really?" Martha marveled. "Does anyone know whatever became of the twin sister?"

Mrs. Page shook her head. "Not that I've ever heard. Of course, my Melissa told me that Kacey confided to her once that the sister—I lost touch with most of her friends when she left. Melissa doesn't call or come to see me much anymore..."

Martha reached out to shake Mrs. Page's hand and nodded at the microfiche lying on the table. "Mrs. Page, you've been much more helpful than any of those articles were. I've really enjoyed our little talk. Thank you so very much. Have a nice day."

The old woman smiled a toothy grin. She looked like a bobble-head toy as her head literally wobbled atop her frail neck. "Yes, well...you are more than welcomed, Dearie. You have a nice day, too, and come back to see us real soon."

Martha waved good-bye and called for a taxi to take her to CompuTech. It was almost time to meet Scott and Macey for lunch.

Thursday was Janet's routine day to service George Byce. The two of them would leave for lunch at eleven o'clock and would not return until three o'clock. The routine was always the same. Byce rented a room at the uptown Hilton Hotel, treating Janet to an exquisite, room-service lunch. The next hour would be spent leisurely enjoying lunch with champagne. Janet spent the next two hours expertly fulfilling every fantasy George Byce could concoct in his sick mind. Their rendezvous always ended with Byce tucking a five-hundred-dollar bill inside her bra. Every Thursday—the same routine.

Most of CompuTech's executives, also, knew their routine. Scott knew that Mr. Byce would be unavailable for four hours every Thursday—

without fail. He decided to take advantage of the situation to show his mother around the company. He and Macey had agreed to take Martha Pennell to Alvin's Diner for a real southern, home-cooked meal—even though it might mean suffering through Becca's belittling scrutiny. How would he ever explain that situation to his mother when he didn't understand it himself? He always went out of his way to be nice to Becca, but, he didn't feel like he was making any real progress with her. He was glad Macey had agreed to join them; it might ease some of the tension between him and Becca.

Martha had excused herself to freshen up before lunch. While he waited in his office for her to return from the ladies' room, Scott thought about the dinner at his apartment the night before. He smiled as he remembered how well the two women had gotten along. His mother seemed to have fully recovered from her fainting spell, and, she and Macey had talked until almost midnight, when Macey reluctantly took her leave. There had been times during their conversations when Scott felt left out—like they had forgotten he was even in the room—but, he was glad that the two women had connected so well. His mother could be a hard one to win over, but he thought Macey had accomplished that feat.

Macey's soft voice penetrated his thoughts. "Penny for your thoughts, Mr. Pennell."

Scott turned around. The smile was still etched on his face. "Hi, Macey! You might not have enough pennies on you for that. Are you ready for lunch?"

"Yes, I am. Have you finished giving your mother the grand tour? Where is she?"

"She's freshening up in the ladies' room. We did agree on Alvin's, right?"

Macey wrinkled her nose and looked at him questioningly. "We did, but are you sure you really want to go there?"

Scott laughed. "You mean because I'm not Miss Becca's favorite customer, right?"

"Something like that."

"Yeah, I know, but, regardless of the way Becca feels about me—which, by the way, I still have no idea what I've done to deserve her spite—I want Mom to try those green things."

Macey laughed. "Collards, Scott—they're called collards—and, I do believe you've acquired a taste for those *green things*."

Martha Pennell knocked on the door. "I hope I'm not interrupting? There was no receptionist out front, and this place is so huge I got lost coming back from the restroom, so I just...followed my nose, hoping I could remember which office was yours, son." She nodded to Macy. "Hello, Macey. It's good to see you again."

Scott and Macey looked at each other and grinned because they both knew why the receptionist post was currently un-manned.

Macey interpreted Scott's acquiescence as proof that Janet's absence was of no concern to him. She smiled back at Martha Pennell and moved over to allow her the position by Scott's side. "It's good to see you again, too, Mrs. Pennell—and, no, you are not interrupting anything." Macy waited until Martha had hooked an arm through Scott's. "Listen, I know you're only in town for a few days, and I don't want to intrude on your time with Scott. Are you sure you wouldn't rather have lunch, alone, with him?"

Martha raised her brows and smiled. "Oh, don't be silly—of course not, Macey. Alvin's Diner, is it? Hmm...sounds...interesting. What do you say let's get going, you two? I'm starving!"

As it turned out, Becca wasn't at the diner. When Macey asked her father about her, he whispered in her ear that she was *sleeping in* because she hadn't gotten much sleep the night before. Macey blushed and smiled at Alvin James. She was sure that Becca's father knew exactly why she had missed work today.

Macey made the appropriate introductions. "Mr. James, I'd like you to meet Scott's mother—Martha Pennell. Mrs. Pennell, this is Alvin James, the owner of this wonderful restaurant."

Alvin James took Martha's hand in both of his and smiled broadly. "Why, it's mighty nice to meet you, Mrs. Pennell. You have a fine son... one with a mighty healthy appetite!"

"That he does, Mr. James—that he does," Martha agreed.

The trio laughed in unison as Mr. James led them to a table and took their orders.

Their meal consisted of buttermilk-fried chicken, real mashed potatoes with a kick of horseradish added for extra flavor, peas and butter beans mixed together and seasoned with fat back, collards, and, fried cornbread fritters. Dessert was a choice of Mrs. James' famous sweet potato pie or banana pudding. The threesome cleaned their plates, talking about insignificant issues such as the weather, local news, and an upcoming arts and crafts fair.

There was a long line of customers waiting to pay their bills, so once they finished their meal, Martha suggested that she and Macey wait outside while Scott took care of the bill.

Martha knew that she wouldn't have much time alone with Macey, so once they were outside, she decided the direct approach would be the best approach. "Macey?"

"Yes, Mrs. Pennell?"

Martha turned to stare directly into Kacey's dark-grey eyes. "I'm curious about something. Why haven't you told Scott who you really are?"

Macey's complexion turned crimson, but then paled noticeably. She glanced behind Martha to make sure Scott was still waiting in line to pay their bill. "Well...I could ask you the same question, Mrs. Pennell. If you know who I am...why haven't *you* told him?"

Martha bit down on her lower lip and nodded. "Actually, I was only able to confirm it just this morning. So, it's true then...you are Kacey's twin?"

It was obvious the woman knew the truth about her. Macey saw no need to deny the matter with Scott less than thirty yards away. "I am."

"Scott doesn't know, does he?"

Macey shrugged. She decided to treat the situation with feigned indifference. "If he does, he's keeping it to himself."

Martha Pennell shook her head in awe. "I don't understand it, Macey—I don't understand *you*! The police charged him with killing your twin sister! Why in God's name would you want anything to do with him? Help me to understand—unless—maybe, you're out for some sort of revenge. Is that it, Macey?"

Macey shook her head gently. "No, it's nothing like that, Mrs. Pennell. When I first met Scott, and realized who he was, my immediate instinct was to get as far away from him as I possibly could. Revenge? No... although, I do admit I felt tremendous hatred for him when I first saw him; but, as I've gotten to know him over the past few weeks...well...I just don't think Scott is capable of doing the things that the police thought he did to my sister."

Martha raised her eyebrows in genuine surprise. "So, you don't think he's guilty!"

Macey was equally surprised at Mrs. Pennell's reaction. "No, I don't... why? Do you?"

"Well, of course I don't! I know my son better than anyone. He could never do the things they accused him of doing...never." It was Martha's turn to glance back to make sure Scott was still in line. There were still two people in front of him. "Macey, he really doesn't recognize you, does he?"

Macey bit her lower lip and shook her head. "I can't be a hundred percent sure, but, no—he doesn't appear to. When I first met him, I thought he was just being insensitive...that, maybe, he had somehow *conveniently* forgotten about the murder."

Martha nodded her head. "In a way, you're right. He has forgotten it, Macey."

"What do you mean?"

"Well," Martha sighed. "Scott sank into a deep, deep depression the night of the murder. The doctors speculated that it was most likely brought on by the shock of what he saw. He spent a year at the Bradley Mental Health Center, with psychologists trying to help him through it. When he finally returned to reality—it took a full year for that to happen—well, he had no memory of the murder—no memory of Kacey. As a matter of fact, he couldn't remember anything that happened up to a year before the murder. It was as though his entire seventeenth year was wiped from his memory."

Macey didn't think this was possible, but she didn't know for sure. "Isn't that unusual—that he can't remember—after all this time?"

"I thought so, at first—but, now...well...I don't think so. I don't think he *wants* to remember, Macey. I think it's all still there—somewhere deep in his memory—and, there's always a chance it could resurface at any moment; but, the doctors said there's the possibility that he will *never* remember anything at all."

Macey looked thoughtful, but concerned. "He looks at me strangely sometimes, you know?"

"What do you mean?"

"I can't explain it really. He just gets a faraway look in his eyes sometimes."

Martha faced Macey directly and placed her hands upon the younger woman's shoulders. "Macey, don't get me wrong. I like you a lot, and it's obvious that my son likes you a lot too, but—for everyone's sake—I really think it would be best if you didn't get too involved with Scott."

Macey flinched at Martha's hands upon her shoulders. She willed herself not to jerk away. "I've never planned to get *too involved* with Scott, Mrs. Pennell, but...why not?"

"Well, the more time he spends with you, Macey, the more likely it is that he *will* remember something, or...everything."

"Would that be so terrible, Mrs. Pennell? Maybe he needs to remember everything. He might even remember something that would help the police? Have you ever thought about that?"

Martha shook her head vehemently in denial. "I doubt it. Besides...it's been twenty years. Some things are better left alone, don't you agree?"

Macey glanced behind her and saw Scott paying the bill. "No, quite frankly, I don't agree. I can't promise you that Scott and I won't become more involved; but, I can promise you that I would never do anything to intentionally hurt him."

"What about the rest of your family?"

"What about them?"

"What would they do to Scott if they found out he was back in town?"

Macey shivered involuntarily as an image of Andrew Wymer flashed through her mind. What *would* her father do if he ever came face-to-face with Scott Pennell?

CHAPTER 21

JACOB KNOWS

Scott sat across from his mother, at the small table, in the airport cafeteria on Saturday morning. The two sat together in amiable silence while they waited for her flight to be announced, and Scott couldn't help but wonder what she was thinking. "You're pretty quiet this morning, Mom."

Martha stirred absently at her cup of coffee. "What?" she asked and glanced up.

Scott grinned at her startled frown and threw his hands up in this air. He leaned back in his chair and yelled, "I said I'm getting married next month! What do you think about that?"

Martha's normal ruddy complexion paled. Her first conclusion to his comment was that he was referring to marriage with Macey; however, another quick glance at her son's smiling face instantly reassured her. He was only teasing. "That's not funny, smart ass," she replied sullenly. She paused slightly before continuing. "You *are* kidding, aren't you?"

Scott laughed good-naturedly and clapped his hands together with bravado. "I thought that's what you wanted, old lady...for me to settle down and make you a grandmother?"

Martha sighed and sipped at her coffee. "I want that more than anything."

"But...?" Scott implored. He was surprised at the hesitation he heard in his mother's voice.

"Well, son...you're right...I do want you to marry. If you called Cheryl and asked her to come out here, I can almost guarantee that she would be here quicker than a rabbit's litter."

Never mind where his mother might have heard that expression; instead, Scott wondered why his mother was bringing Cheryl into the conversation. Surely, she had picked up on the feelings he was beginning to have for Macey. "I don't want to marry Cheryl, Mom." The smile on his face faded. "What is it that you're really trying to say?"

Martha reached across the table and placed her hand on top of her son's. "Scott..."

"This has something to do with Macey, doesn't it, Mom?"

Martha winced at the disappointment evident in her son's face. "Macey is a wonderful person, Scott..."

"Why do I get the feeling there's a *but* in there somewhere?"

Martha shifted in her seat. She suddenly felt uncomfortable discussing her son's love life with him. She wasn't totally sure of Scott's true feelings for Macey, but it was obvious that he did like her. He had liked a lot of women over the years, though, so maybe she shouldn't be adding any fuel to a fire that might never be lit.

"Mom? I'm waiting. Is there something about Macey you don't like?"

Martha shook her head. "Oh no, son! Macey is a very personable young woman. She seems to have a lot going for her. I imagine she's very efficient at her job."

Something was off with his mother this morning, but Scott couldn't quite figure out what the problem might be. "You're right about that, Mom. She's so damn efficient, that she probably should have been promoted into the job I have."

"Oh, really?" Martha seemed genuinely surprised. "Then why do you suppose she wasn't?"

"Well, I think I know why...and, I probably shouldn't be mentioning this to you—or anyone else for that matter. I think it's because Macey rejected sexual advances from our boss."

Martha was only mildly surprised at Scott's supposition. "Then I hope she filed sexual harassment charges against the son-of-a-bitch! Companies don't tolerate that sort of thing like they did years ago, you know."

"Some companies, don't, that's true, Mom. Unfortunately, it's still a pretty common practice, and a lot of it probably goes unreported."

Martha shrugged. "So, I'm guessing that Macey must not have reported it—I wonder why? Maybe she's not as good at her job as you thought, or, maybe she didn't want to rock the boat because she really needs the job."

Scott shook his head. "I'm sure she had her own reasons for not reporting it—that's really none of my business. Macey is an excellent worker, though. She's extremely bright, articulate, patient, kind..."

"It sounds like you're speaking on a more personal level now, Scott, and not just about her work ethics."

Scott grinned and cocked his eyebrows. "I guess it does, doesn't it? Believe it or not, I am trying hard to keep my relationship with Macey on a professional level; that's mostly because she hasn't given me any reason to hope for anything else. Anyway—it doesn't really matter—I'm pretty sure that there's another man in Macey's life."

Martha was surprised to hear this news. "Really? Well, that's certainly never been a deterrent to you before, has it? If I remember correctly, there was another man in Cheryl's life when you first met her."

"Back to Cheryl, are we? Well, Macey's different—very different—from Cheryl, or any other woman I've ever known." He grinned at his mother and winked. "But, hey...be sure to give Cheryl my best, Mom, and tell her that I hope things work out for her and her new friend."

Martha pushed her coffee cup away. "So, what you're telling me is that you don't think there's a chance that you and Macey might ever become more involved—on a more personal level, I mean?"

Scott shook his head. "No, I don't think so. In fact, I'm not sure she even likes me all that much. I think she mostly tolerates me—in a nice way, of course. There were a few times after I first arrived...well, let's just say you would have thought I'd grown horns and a tail by the way she looked at me—especially when she thought I wasn't looking."

"What do you mean?"

Scott shrugged. "I don't know...it's just a feeling I picked up on. I always got the feeling that she didn't want to be in the same room with me."

"I wonder what changed her mind about you, son...because something obviously did."

Scott rubbed at the nape of his neck and stretched his shoulders backward. "I'm not completely sure that she has changed her mind. Sometimes, I think she's just being Macey—you know—nice. I don't think it's in her genetic make-up to be rude or obnoxious. She's too much of a lady to tell me to jack off...know what I mean? Anyway, the change has been a slow, gradual one. I think she's beginning to feel *safe* around me. I can feel her letting her guard down."

Martha sighed. "It sounds as though she's beginning to trust you."

"I hope that's true, because, I have a feeling that trust doesn't come easily for Macey. I have no idea what's happened in her past to make her so wary of people, but, you can feel her uneasiness sometimes—especially around Mr. Byce. You know, Mom—and, I don't want to hear any smart comments—but, Macey brings something out in me...something that I'm not used to. It's something that I'm not entirely comfortable with

140

myself just yet. I find myself wanting to—I don't know—*protect* her."

"Protect her from what?"

Scott threw his arms up. "Beats the hell out of me! I don't know—life in general, I guess. Sometimes she seems like a lost child, and, I want to be the one to help her find her way back home. That sounds corny, doesn't it?"

Martha bit at her bottom lip and prayed she was wrong about the relationship that might be developing between her son and Macey Garner. "No, son, it doesn't sound corny at all. You're a very loving, patient, and giving person. I think it's only natural that you would want to help someone you thought was in need; but, Scott—and, please don't get me wrong—but, I hope you're not considering any kind of long-term relationship with Macey."

Scott held up his hand and stood up. "Okay, let's stop there, Mom. I think this conversation has run its course. You know that I love you more than life itself, but, you should know that I am a grown man, perfectly capable of making my own decisions. I would never allow you—or anyone else—to interfere or try to persuade me, one way or another, regarding my choices for a long-term relationship."

"I'm not trying to do that, Scott."

The announcement allowing passengers for Flight 1340 to begin boarding at Gate Two startled them both.

Scott took his mother's coat from the back of the chair and helped her put it on. "That's you, Mom..."

Mother and son stared at each other for a long moment.

"You don't have to walk me to the gate, son," Martha smiled. "I would like a kiss for your old mother, though."

Scott turned her around and wrapped her in a tight hug. "I love you, Mom." He squeezed her tight and kissed her on the cheek. "I don't want you worrying about this thing with Macey. Even if I was seriously interested in her—and, I'm not saying that I am—but, if I was...well...I honestly don't think the feeling would ever be reciprocated." He grinned and winked. "As much as it pains me to admit it, I don't even think I'm her type."

Martha patted her son on the back and looked up at him with a forced smile. "Well, all I ask is that you just don't rush into anything. Okay, then—I've got to go. I'll see you at Thanksgiving, right?"

"Yes, you will. Be sure and tell Dad hello for me; tell him that I really miss our Sunday fishing expeditions."

Martha knew that was Scott's way of letting her know how much he truly missed his father—not any fishing expeditions. "I'll tell him. Good-bye, son."

"Bye, Mom. Call and let me know that you made it back okay."

"I will."

Scott waved and walked through the automatic sliding door toward the parking lot.

Martha turned to look back at him. *"I have a feeling that all hell is about to break loose. God help us all..."*

The relationship between Jacob and his mother had been strained since their earlier discussion about Macey. Ruth Wymer had become quiet and withdrawn after Jacob stormed from the house that day. She needed to talk to someone, but didn't know to whom she could turn. She briefly entertained the idea of confiding the gist of the conversation to Andrew, but she was terrified of what her husband's reaction might be at hearing Macey's name mentioned again. She had no close female friends with whom she felt comfortable enough to share her family's skeletal secrets. So, after almost two weeks of worrying about what to do, she decided there was only one person to whom she could commit her implicit faith and trust.

"Oh, but what would Andrew do if he knew I was talking to *anyone* about Macey?" Ruth asked aloud as she paced back and forth across the black and white linoleum kitchen floor. "Oh, Lord, please help me. I need your guidance to get me through this...to help me make the right decision." She got down on her knees and continued praying for another fifteen minutes. When she stood up, she wiped the tears from her eyes, picked up the phone, and dialed his number.

His phone rang five times. Ruth was about to hang up when he finally answered. His normally low and seductive voice sounded breathless when he finally answered. Ruth assumed that she must have interrupted his yard work.

"Hello?" he answered pleasantly enough.

Ruth swallowed the lump in her throat and whispered hoarsely. "It's me...Ruth...I need to see you...right away. It's very important."

He was still breathing heavily, but trying to get his breathing under control. "Of course, Ruth. You know that I am always here for you—day or night—anytime you find yourself...in *need*."

Ruth closed her eyes and swallowed another lump that had formed in her constricting throat. "It's not *that* kind of need. We need to talk. It's about Jacob. He knows about...Macey."

There was an interminable pause from his end.

His breathing had finally evened out. "Calm down, Ruth, and tell me *exactly* what Jacob knows?"

She plopped down at the kitchen table and finally released the tears she had been holding in. "I don't know! I'm not sure how much he knows, but, he knows that Kacey had a twin sister. He wants to know why we've never talked about her. He found pictures..."

There was a deep sigh from his end. "I thought you destroyed all the pictures of Macey," he piqued.

Ruth heard the sudden tightness in his voice. She wiped her nose on the back of her sleeve and said, "I did, but, Andrew must have kept a few that showed both girls. Jacob said Macey had been cut out of most of them. You know how Andrew felt about Kacey...he probably couldn't bring himself to destroy any picture with her in it."

Another deep sigh emanated from his end. "Yes...Andrew was unusually obsessed with that child, wasn't he? Anyway, I don't think there's any reason for concern. I doubt if Jacob would confront his father about Macey, do you?"

"A few years ago, I would have agreed, but—I don't know—Jacob has changed. He used to always follow my advice and listen to my opinions about everything."

"He's not your little boy anymore, Ruth. Why not leave him alone for a while? Let's just sit back and see how he handles it. Let me know if he mentions it to you again. The last thing your family needs is the resurrection of Macey."

Ruth sniffed loudly and sighed. She felt more in control of herself now. He was good for her. He always made her feel better. "I agree," she exhaled deeply. "You were right—from the very beginning—when you said that child was a sour apple in God's orchard. All those years ago—you tried to warn us about her promiscuous ways, and, just look at what happened to her! She went and got herself knocked up by some teenage punk, and, then ran away from her relatives in Madison. God only knows where she took her baby—my grandchild. Who knows what kind of life she's subjected them both to all these years."

He sighed and relaxed. "Yes, Ruth, it is true...Macey was bad news. I will always believe that she was a child possessed by Satan, himself."

Ruth was in total control of herself again and felt embarrassed at having called him. He was a busy man—his time was precious. "I'm sorry to have burdened you with all this..."

"Nonsense, Ruth. I'm here for you—always—for whatever reason."

"I know, I know...uh...by the way, Andrew is going out of town again the weekend before Thanksgiving. Can I...see you then?"

The lustful insinuation was evident in his quick reply. "I don't know how I can possibly wait that long; but, yes...I will most definitely see you then."

The man hung up the phone and smiled. He turned back to look at the nude, teenage girl strapped to the old wooden work bench. Her mouth was bound with electrical tape to muffle her whimpers of protest. Her father had left her there after having been assured that the good Reverend Dudley could expel all the evil spirits that possessed her young, licentious body. He had left his child there so that the good reverend could perform a *spiritual cleansing* of her body.

Lucas Dudley stroked himself as he walked toward the girl. "Just remember, Jennifer...this cleansing is for your own good." His tone was authoritative while he quickly unzipped his pants and exposed himself to the terrified thirteen-year old. "God will only forgive you for your many sins *after* I have submerged myself into your hot furnace of Hell. Only then will your family be able to accept you back into their embrace. It is the *only* way, child..."

The immobilized expression of fear etched on the child's face mirrored her involuntary capitulation of the situation. Her father had discovered her and Johnny Blaylock kissing behind the tool shed, and had chastised her for her un-lady like behavior. After a week of not speaking to her, her father informed her that the only way she would be forgiven was to receive a spiritual cleansing administered by Reverend Dudley.

Jennifer lay upon the table and ultimately decided that her father was right. Maybe this was what had to happen; maybe Reverend Dudley could cleanse her spiritually-lacking soul. She closed her eyes in paralyzed acceptance and tried not to choke on her silent prayer for forgiveness.

The spiritual cleansing began.

CHAPTER 22

GEORGE BYCE

George Byce picked up the phone and punched in Macey's extension. "Macey! I want to see you in my office right away."

Macey gulped a quick response. "Yes, Mr. Byce; I'll be right there."

Byce hung up the phone and walked over to the large, wall-to-wall bay window that provided an awesome view of the "Hooch", the local nickname for the infamous Chattahoochee River. The river became well known during the 1950's when several gangsters were suspected of sinking the bodies of their foes to the bottom of the deep, muddy river. Most of those bodies were never recovered.

He remained deep in thought while he watched the mighty current of the turbid river pull hungrily at anything that dared to venture along its destined course. Three weeks had passed since the Halloween party and he hadn't been able to get the encounter with Macey off his mind. He had deliberately avoided her since the party for fear that she would finally accuse him of the sexual harassment he had been so flagrantly guilty of since her arrival at CompuTech. It still puzzled and amazed him that she had not yet filed charges against him; he couldn't help but wonder why. He wondered what secrets surrounded her. He hoped to have some answers soon. The private investigator he had recently hired should be able to shed some light on her personal background—some leverage he might be able to hold over her, should he ever need it.

The knock on the door was so light and subtle that, had he not been expecting her, George Byce would not have heard it.

"Come in!" he snapped. He watched her fluid movements as she walked through the door, carrying several files in her arms. "Close the door, Macey. Come in and have a seat."

"Yes, sir. I didn't know which file you might want to discuss, so I brought them all."

Byce watched while she attempted to position the files on the small conference table, and smiled smugly at her apparent nervousness. He watched, with hungered anticipation, as she sat down and crossed her legs. He could almost feel the horripilation surging through her as she, most likely, wondered about the reason for this unscheduled meeting. He felt her stiffen immediately when he came up behind her and placed both hands upon her shoulders. He enjoyed the reflexive tension beneath his large hands. He began kneading the muscles in her shoulders and back while savoring the view of her modestly exposed cleavage from his standing vantage point.

"Please, don't do that, Mr. Byce..." she shivered involuntarily and cringed at his touch. She had been expecting this encounter since the Halloween party.

Byce sensed her want to withdraw from his touch. Maybe it was fear and not repulsion that paralyzed her body to his touch. He hoped it was fear. He closed his eyes and remembered how her body had felt beneath his invasive, massive hands. He pursed his lips together in suppressed anger when she tried to move from beneath his touch. "Oh, don't worry, Macey...I'm certainly not going to rape you. I won't have to. You will come to me on your own accord before long. I only have about six more months before I retire—a year at the most. This job, Macey—my job— could be *yours*. There is no reason why you could not be groomed for it during the coming months. That's why I called you here today. It's something I want you to think about...to think seriously about."

He looked down at her, saw her closed eyes, and increased the pressurized kneading of his hands upon her shoulders. He was no fool. He knew how unattractive she probably found him, but, he also knew the power he held over her. He never really doubted her repulsion for him. She probably wanted to do nothing more than turn around and spit in his face; but, he also knew she needed her job. They all needed their jobs, or needed him to make their jobs better. He was always more than willing to accommodate them—the young, modern women of today's high-tech work force. He would miss that part of his job more than anything.

Byce mistook Macey's sullen silence for consent. His touch became bolder as his huge hands travelled farther down her chest. He had just cupped her right breast when a sudden knock on the door jarred his hands from their intended prize. He spun around quickly when he heard the door open.

Scott hadn't waited for permission to enter. He had seen Macey walk by his office carrying a stack of files, and assumed Byce had summoned her. Something stirred in him and he once again felt the need to protect her from their boss. He poked his head inside and waved in greeting. "Good morning, sir! How are you this fine Friday morning?"

Macey's head slid forward in silent thanks for the interruption.

Byce positioned himself to intentionally block Scott's view of Macey. He hoped—but doubted—that the young executive would leave before he became aware of Macey's presence. "Pennell! What do you want?" he growled. "We didn't have an appointment."

"I know, and I apologize for the interruption, Mr. Byce; but, I finished those reports you said you needed for the meeting with the bankers later this morning. I stopped by Miss Garner's office to get her input, but..."

Byce stifled a groan as Macey pushed back her chair, which bumped against his generous backside. He briefly considered the possibility that the push had been intentional on her part.

Scott took in her paled expression and the glassy look in her eyes. "Macey? Are you all right? You...don't look so well." He took a step in her direction. "I didn't know you were in here," he continued. He looked back at Byce and, somehow, managed to hide his disgust and anger when he noticed the obvious bulge beneath the man's trousers.

Byce moved quickly to position himself behind Macey, hoping to remind her of his power and control over her situation. "Miss Garner is fine, Scott. She and I were just going over the quarter's final training figures for his meeting with the bankers. Isn't that right, Miss Garner? Leave the files. I'll look at them after I talk with Scott. I'll call you if I have any questions. Now, if you'll excuse us..." He waved his hand in dismissal.

Macey slowed her labored breathing and mumbled a quiet response. "Yes, sir."

Byce cleared his throat when she turned to leave. "Thank you again, Miss Garner. This data is exactly what I need. I will be speaking with you again—very soon—on that other matter we discussed. Make sure you are prepared."

"Yes, sir," Macey replied weakly. She looked over at Scott and nodded. "Scott? I'll see you later."

Some color had returned to her face, but Scott was still concerned about her. "You're sure you're okay, Macey?"

Byce motioned for Scott to take a seat and growled. "She's fine, Scott—probably just a touch of the flu trying to work its way in—don't you agree, Miss Garner?"

"Yes, sir," Macey mumbled. "I'll be going now."

The two men watched her leave. One was filled with lustful desire. The other one was filled with genuine worry and concern.

Once she was safely outside Byce's office, Macey leaned against the door and tried to catch her breath. She exhaled deeply, through her mouth, several times. She wondered if she had held her breath during the entire ordeal, because it now seemed as though she couldn't breathe in enough air to fill her lungs. She walked slowly to the elevator and was grateful that it was empty. She used the slow ride to the ground floor to regain her composure.

Janet was sitting on the edge of her desk, flirting with a man whose back was turned toward Macey. Macey was so wrapped up in her own thoughts and worries that she didn't immediately recognize her brother.

Janet's tight skirt had crawled upward, exposing her long, creamy thighs.

Jacob was no different from most men; he was not immune to the enticing display of flesh.

"There she is now!" Janet squealed and pointed in Macey's direction. "Oh, Miss Garner, you have a visitor."

Macey was half-way to her own office when she turned around.

Jacob took in her peaked condition and rushed over to her. "Macey! Are you okay? You look awful. Come on...you need to sit down." He put a protective arm around her and led her toward her office.

Macey appreciated Jacob's brotherly concern. It had been so long since anyone truly cared about her—no one had cared about her well-being since Kacey died; but, she had Jacob and Becca to care about her now—two people she could turn to whenever she needed them.

Macey had been so surprised to see Jacob that she forgot about their agreement to keep their relationship a secret. She knew instinctively that Janet became all ears when Macey blurted out, "Hey there, little brother. Me? No, I'm fine, but, it does feel like I'm trying to come down with the flu, maybe. What are you doing here, anyway? Aren't you supposed to be at the station?"

Jacob kept his arm around her. "Yep, but the old man's gone out of town again. My friend, Wally, is keeping an eye on things for an hour or so. It doesn't get real busy until lunch time. So...the flu, huh?" He reached out and touched her forehead. "Well, you're sweaty enough, but I don't feel any fever."

Macey gently pushed his hand away and walked toward her office.

"Come on in for a few minutes, *Doctor* Wymer."

"Okay, sis..."

Janet was practically foaming at the mouth.

Jacob turned to look back at her, smiled, and winked. He wondered if she was available; he would have to remember to ask Macey about the receptionist.

Macey motioned for him to side beside her on the leather sofa. "So... Papa's gone out of town again?"

Jacob plopped down beside her and stretched his arms overhead. "Yeah, but this time, the kid here is going to find out exactly where he goes on these mysterious trips."

The hair stood up on Macey's arms. "What do you mean? What are you up to, Jacob?"

Jacob smiled at his sister. He was glad to see that some of the color was creeping back into her cheeks. "Well, I paid a friend of mine twenty bucks to follow Pop."

"You did what? Why? I don't understand..."

Jacob shrugged. "I'm not exactly sure why I did it, Macey; but, don't you think it's a little weird? I mean...all these trips he takes...never telling anyone where he's going? Just call it a funny feeling that I need to follow up on. Besides, you know how tense things have been at home these past few weeks."

Macey nodded. "Yeah, I remember you said you told Mama you knew about me...which, by the way, was not a very smart thing to do, Jacob. Has she mentioned me at all since then?"

Jacob shook his head. "Not a word, and, I don't think she's mentioned it to the old man, either."

"Why do you say that?"

"Because I know Pop! If she'd said anything to him, he would've been breathing down my neck, asking all sorts of questions. He'd want to know why I was interested in knowing about you, and, he'd probably be able to get the info he wanted—if you know what I mean."

"But you only *asked* Mama about me. I know you didn't tell her that you and I have..."

Jacob pretended to have hurt feelings. "Don't be ridiculous, Macey," he jabbed playfully at her arm. "You know I would never tell anyone about us."

Macey sighed with obvious relief. "I just don't want them to know about us, Jacob—at least, not until you're safely out of that house."

"Well, that may be sooner than later, Macey. I've made up my mind to leave after Christmas. Mama's the only reason I've hung around this long, and...*you*...of course; but, after Christmas...watch out...because I'm heading to the sunshine state!"

Macey nodded and grinned. "Florida, huh? It will be hard on Mama when you leave, Jacob. You're her whole world...you always have been."

His love for his sister was obvious in his face. Jacob wished that he could permanently erase all the sadness he so often saw in her eyes. "Who knows...maybe you and Mama can become friends, Macey. God knows she'll need one when I leave."

Macey shook her head vehemently from side to side and shivered. "Now that's a chilling thought. No, Jacob...Mama and I could never be friends. She wasn't there for me when I needed her most, and, she wasn't there for Kacey either. Besides, you're her favorite; she always loved you best...her baby boy."

Jacob grew silent. His emotions were torn as he pondered whether to reveal the secret he kept to himself about their sister and father. He looked at Macey's still pallid complexion and decided that now was not the time. He tried to lighten the tone of the conversation—it had become way too serious. "Okay, okay, that's enough rehashing of ancient history. The reason I stopped by was to tell you about Pop being gone, which means—drum roll, please—that we can get together this weekend. How does tomorrow night sound to you?"

Macey nodded slightly. "Yeah, maybe. I've got some reports to work on over the weekend, but I should be able to take a few hours off. Should I call Becca?"

"Sure, but knowing her, she's probably got a hot date. That reminds me—speaking of hot—why don't you invite the babe out there at the front desk?"

Macey's eyebrows shot upwards. "Janet? Oh, no...I really don't think she's your type, Jacob."

Jacob beamed and said, "Maybe not, but, with thighs like that, she could become my type—really quick!"

Macey blushed and shoved him gently. "You are so bad. Go on...get out of here. We both have work to do." She smiled back at him as she pushed herself up off the sofa. "Jacob? You said you paid a friend to follow Papa?"

Jacob returned the grin. "Yeah...I was wondering when you'd get back around to that."

Macey was quiet for a moment before replying, "Do me a favor? Let me know what you find out about that trip?"

Jacob opened the door to leave and called back, "Will do, sis! I'll talk to you tomorrow. Bye now."

"Bye," Macey replied absently as she sat down behind her desk. Her curiosity about her father's trips had temporarily taken her mind off her recent meeting with George Byce.

Neither Macey, nor Jacob, had noticed Scott's presence as he was coming around the corner just as Jacob left Macey's office.

"*Sis*?" he mumbled. "Well, I'll be damned!" The grin that spread across his face was expansive!

CHAPTER 23

Ruth and the Good Reverend

Macey and Becca met at Macey's apartment later that night and shared a pizza. Becca drank a beer while Macey sipped on iced tea.

Becca listened—without interrupting—between bites of the greasy, meat-lovers pie, while Macey outlined the day's events. She knew that her friend desperately needed to talk about the situation with her boss.

Macey knew that she could confide in Becca because she was confident that Becca would keep the information to herself.

Becca wiped her generous lips with a paper napkin. "Girlfriend, I don't know why you haven't already turned that son-of-a-bitch in for sexual harassment! Now if it was me, I'd pretend to give him what he wanted, then bite that snake off and shove it as far down his rotten throat as it would go!"

Macey almost choked on her pizza. "Remind me never to get on your bad side!"

"I'm serious, Macey. I'll never understand why the hell you put up with that white man's crap."

Macey shrugged. "It won't be for much longer, Becca. He'll be retiring in a few months. I only have to wait it out for a few more months."

"Wait it out! Girl, don't be stupid! How much longer do you think this man is going to let you keep putting him off? You'd better wake up and smell the roses, Macey, or you're going to end up sitting in a bed or thorns." Becca searched inside her pocket and pulled out the folded money she always kept stashed there. She pulled a bill rom the stash and held it out to Macey. "'ll bet you twenty that sorry lard ass will find a reason to fire you before he leaves, especially if you don't start putting out soon."

Macey smiled when she snatched the bill and tucked it inside her own pocket. "He might not...especially if I pray hard enough about it."

Becca flicked her wrist at Macey and snickered. "You and your prayers, girl! Where were your damn angels this morning while the old fart was becoming your *bosom* buddy? And give me back my twenty!"

Macey laughed out loud, retrieved the twenty, and flung it playfully at her friend. "You're impossible, Becca James! Just you wait...one of these days you're going to have reason to believe in those same angels."

Becca began clearing up the remnants of their meal. "Well," she grinned and sighed, "If they'll just give me the stamina I need to keep up with Mr. Carlton Brown tonight, then maybe—just maybe—I'll believe in them."

The doorbell rang and since Becca was already up, she moved to answer it. She placed one hand on her hip and stared ominously at their uninvited visitor.

Scott stood outside holding a large pizza box in his hands. He smiled at Becca when he noticed the empty pizza box she held in one hand. "Uh-oh...looks like we both had the same idea. Hello, Becca. Is...uh... Macey home?"

Becca stood glaring at him, one hand remaining firmly planted on her hip. "No...I always let myself in whenever I feel like eating pizza *alone!*" Becca asserted. "Of course, she's here, Einstein." She turned away and walked into the kitchen.

Scott remained standing outside the door.

Macey shook her head and shot Becca a scolding look. She made her way to the door and motioned Scott inside. "Scott, come on in. Becca was just leaving...weren't you, Becca?"

"I am now," Becca muttered under her breath. She was careful to avoid any physical contact with Scott when she met Macey at the door. She hugged her and said, "Tell Jacob I can't wait until tomorrow night."

"I'll tell him," Macey nodded as she motioned, again, for Scott to come inside. She closed the door behind Becca and turned to face him. Her embarrassment was evident in her flushed face. "I really am so sorry, Scott. I hate to keep apologizing for Becca's rude behavior. You might not believe it, but, she really is a wonderful person..."

"I'll have to take your word for that, Macey. Besides...if you like her, then I suppose she can't be all bad." Scott offered an indifferent shrug of the shoulders and looked down at the pizza box he still held. He grinned and offered it to her. "You're probably not hungry, huh?"

"No, I'm not—I'm stuffed—but, thank you for the thought." It suddenly occurred to her that Scott might be hungry, even if she wasn't.

153

"You probably are though." She took the box from him. "I'll get you a plate for the pizza. What can I get you to drink?"

Scott followed her into the kitchen and stood behind her. He tried, in vain, not to notice the contour of her body as she stretched to reach for a plate. He cleared his throat when she bent over and looked inside the refrigerator. "I don't suppose you have any beer in there, do you?"

Macey turned and tossed a cold bottle to him. She smiled at his awkward attempt to catch it. "Compliments of our mutual friend, Becca James. Enjoy!"

Scott barely managed to catch the beer in mid-air. "Nice!" he laughed nervously while he made his way into the living room. It didn't take him long to make himself at home. He positioned himself on the couch, opened the beer, took a long swig, and lifted a slice of pizza from the box.

Macey raised her brows when she saw that he had taken her previous position on the couch, but she didn't say anything. She quickly positioned herself in the recliner opposite the sofa and watched him eat.

Scott saw her watching him, so he licked the pizza sauce from his lips with deliberate intention. His peripheral vision offered him the view of her inadvertently licking her own lips. He wondered if it was the pizza—or him—that made her mouth water. "Are you sure you're not still hungry, Macey? There's plenty here."

Macey blushed. "No thanks, I couldn't eat another bite. Don't tell me you didn't have anything better to do on a Friday night than to bring me pizza?"

Scott grabbed a second slice and shook his head. "Nope, sure didn't. Well...I did bring a lot of work home with me this weekend, but, I thought I'd wait until later to dig into it. I wanted to make sure you were okay."

"What? Why wouldn't I be..." Macey stuttered. "Oh...you mean because I wasn't feeling well this morning? The flu..."

"You don't have the flu, Macey. It was more than that and you know it," Scott interrupted. "Byce hit on you again, didn't he?"

Her glass of tea almost slipped out of her hands. She was so embarrassed! It was one thing for her best friend to know about Mr. Byce's unwanted advances, but not Scott! "I don't know what you mean, Scott..."

"Don't try to deny it, Macey. I've been here long enough now to hear all the office gossip and rumors."

Macey stiffened with indignation. "Janet told you, didn't she?"

"What makes you think it was Janet?" Scott asked while he tried to decipher the meaning behind the defensive tone that he suddenly detected in her voice.

"Well..." Macey stumbled. "You said it yourself—office gossip and all—rumor is that you two are an item, so, I figured it had to be Janet."

Scott shook his head. "Don't believe everything you hear, Macey. I'll be honest with you, though. I spent one night with Janet. I'm not proud of it, but it did happen. It shouldn't have—I wish it hadn't—but, it did. It was just that one time. There's nothing going on between us." He wished he could tell if was relief or disbelief that flashed in Macey's eyes.

Macey threw back her shoulders and lifted her chin. "Well, it's really none of my business with whom you spend time, Scott...is it?"

Scott smiled because he recognized the telling implication in her voice. It was jealousy! Macey was jealous! Life was good—really, really good! He stood up and moved to where she sat in the recliner, with her long legs curled beneath her. He bent down, took her hands, and gently pulled her upward. He felt her flinch at his touch, but, he continued to hold her hands firmly in his own until she stood before him in her bare feet.

Macey took a deep breath and looked up into his face.

"Quite the contrary, Macey..." Scott whispered. He tried to steady the heavy beating of his heart. "It *is* your business..."

Macey was unable to look away. She swallowed hard and asked, Why?" She tensed again when his face inched closer to her own.

Scott squeezed her hands and pulled her closer. "Because *you* are very important to me, Macey."

"I am?"

Scott felt her trembling against him, but he pressed on. "Yes," he whispered hoarsely. His lips were almost touching hers. "Let me show you how important you are to me..." He felt her wanting to pull away from him, so he immediately pressed his lips lightly against her own. He held her firmly in place when he felt her pulling her hands away from his grasp.

The kiss continued.

Scott felt her lips remain tightly closed against his, but after a few moments, he sensed their resistance begin to fade. He released her hands, pulled her closer to him, and rested his hands upon her waist.

Macey's own hands hung limply at her side.

It seemed like an eternity to Scott before he felt her hands move cautiously to his waistline; it was at that same moment that her lips parted—ever so slightly—for him.

The kiss deepened and became more passionate. It was several more moments before they came up for air.

Scott searched Macey's confused and pleading, eyes. They seemed to beg him for answers to the turmoil that threatened to catapult her very soul into oblivion.

Macey felt dazed when she finally murmured, "I...I've never been kissed like that before."

Scott was fighting his own unexpected flood of emotions; however, they were for very different reasons. When the kiss had deepened and Macey's hands rested at his waist, he experienced another flashback. Once again, it was a flashback of a much younger Macey. He was shaken at the inexplicable, overwhelming sense of Deja vu, because he knew—without a doubt—that he had never kissed her before tonight. He was certain of that, because he would have remembered a kiss like the one they had just shared. He took a deep breath and gently pulled away from her. "Macey? I...uh...I'd better go. I'll...call you later..."

Scott was out the door and half-way back to his own apartment before Macey fully realized that she was no longer in his arms. She touched her lust-swollen lips. A pool of tears filled her fevered eyes. "Oh, God... what I am doing..." she cried out loud. She fell to her knees in shame and humiliation. She had just kissed the man accused of killing her twin sister! *What was she thinking!*

Scott was inside his own apartment before it dawned on him that the kiss had been a successful diversion— even though Macey had not been the one to initiate the kiss. It had ended any further conversation about Macy and George Byce.

Several miles away—on the opposite side of town—Ruth Wymer was, also, on her knees. She was praying silently to her God and begging His forgiveness for what she was doing.

She was fifty-three years old, had been married for most of her adult life, and up until a few months ago, she had never experienced an orgasm...not once. That all changed six months ago, when the good Reverend Dudley re-entered their lives.

Ruth had not seen the Reverend since they left Tennessee, for Georgia, more than twenty years ago. He had disappeared from their lives shortly after the family made the decision to send Macey away to relatives in Madison, Georgia—to have her illegitimate baby. Ruth remembered his strength during the days preceding the decision to send Macey away. He had been a rock of support to the whole family during that ordeal, but afterwards, he had simply disappeared from their lives. The church said he had accepted a position up north to be closer to his aging parents.

Six months ago—that's when Ruth literally ran into him while grocery shopping. She had not been watching where she was going and had accidently bumped her buggy into his backside. "Oh my, goodness... *Reverend*...it's you!" she had exclaimed in disbelief. She had recognized him immediately. He had not changed all that much, other than being a little grayer at the temples, but that only enhanced his already handsome looks. Why was it that men always seemed to age much more gracefully than women?

"Pardon me, madam, do I know..." the reverend stopped in mid-sentence. His own recognition of the mother of the Wymer twins suddenly unfolded. "Sister Ruth! I don't believe it!" He reached out to take her hands into his own. He smiled when he felt her tremble at his warm touch—he knew he had that effect on women—especially the ones who had been married all their lives. He had met and counseled so many married women who suffered from a lack of marital intimacy—it was much more common than people thought. Ruth was probably no different from all the others. She had, most likely, not shuddered at her husband's touch in a long time.

"Reverend Dudley! Why...what on earth are you doing in Columbus, Georgia? I just can't believe it...seeing you here!"

"I can't either, my good lady. I've only been here a couple of months. I've been appointed to serve as pastor of a small church in the valley. My, my...but you do look wonderful! The years have certainly been kind to you."

Ruth felt herself blush at the wicked thoughts that unexpectedly permeated her mind. She silently reminded herself that she was a married woman, and gently pulled her hands from his firm grasp. She tucked a loose strand of hair behind her ear and stammered, "Thank you, Reverend. Well...now that we've run into each other, you'll have to come for dinner one night soon. What about tonight—does that work for you? It won't be anything fancy, mind you, only meat loaf, but, you would be more than welcomed. I just know Andrew will be as excited as I am to see you again after all these years."

Reverend Dudley pondered the invitation briefly before accepting. It was good to see a familiar, friendly face. "Why...thank you very much for the invitation, Sister Ruth. There is nothing I would like better than to sample your meat loaf. I'm sure it's delicious, and being the bachelor that I still am, well...I would be a fool to turn down a home-cooked meal, wouldn't I?"

The sudden pressure on the back of her head brought Ruth's thoughts back to the present moment. She was on her knees before the good,

Reverend Dudley.

His posture remained erect as he supported his weight by pressing his free hand firmly against the drywall. His legs were spread slightly and his pants were pooled around his ankles. "Ruth! Concentrate, woman! You must continue..." he moaned as he neared his moment of release.

Ruth blinked hard. Her eyes felt like they would surely bulge right out of her head, but, she refocused her attention to the task at hand—and mouth. She tried to will the act to an early end. She had never embraced the concept of oral sex, but Reverend Dudley had convinced her that it was the most acceptable act for a married woman to practice on someone who was not her husband.

Ruth could tell that it wouldn't be much longer. The Reverend's glorious moment was finally at hand.

Lucas pressed himself deeper inside her mouth. "Now, Ruth! Don't stop! Now!" he shouted in glorified anticipation.

Ruth's eyes bulged wider and wider before the ghastly, repulsive act finally ended.

The Reverend's hips jerked forward. He took her head between his two hands and smiled down at her. "Your body and soul will now be cleansed of any evil that may be lurking inside it, Ruth..."

Tears pooled in Ruth's tightly-closed eyes. Now—more than ever—she needed to feel cleansed of her sins.

CHAPTER 24

REVEREND DUDLEY RECOGNIZES MACEY

Scott and Macey spent all day Saturday, alone, in their respective apartments. They reviewed files they had brought home to work on over the weekend; however, they were both having more than a hard time concentrating on those efforts.

"Oh, hell!" Scott shouted out loud. He pushed himself up from the executive-size, cherry-wood desk. "This is ridiculous...it was only a damn kiss!"

Feelings were a little less dramatic in the apartment across the parking lot. Macey was curled up on her sofa with files scattered all around her. She twirled a loose strand of hair around her finger and stared off into space. "Why did I let him kiss me?" she asked the empty apartment. "And, why did he rush off the way he did? Was kissing me so distasteful that he had to rush home and...rinse out his mouth or something?" The ringing of the phone startled her. She leaned over hurriedly to reach the cordless extension lying on the end table. "Hello?"

There was no response.

"Hello? Is anyone there?"

Scott cleared his throat before replying. "It's...uh...me, Macey."

"Scott? You...don't sound like yourself. Is there something wrong?"

It took another long moment before Scott answered. *Was* there anything wrong? He couldn't even explain to himself—much less to Macey—the reason why he was calling. He cleared his throat again and said, "We need to talk."

Macey gripped the phone tight. She was sure she knew what was coming next. He would apologize for the kiss. He would insist that it should never have happened, and that it would never happen again. Her feelings were mixed. She was both relieved and saddened by this expectation. "I'm listening, Scott."

"No...not over the phone! Are you busy right now?"

Macey glanced around her at the disarray of files that demanded her attention. "Well, I'm sorting through some files..."

Scott sighed and exhaled softly. "Yeah...me, too. Can you take a break?"

Macey was curious about the hesitant tone in his voice, and convinced herself that she needed to make sure he was all right. No, that wasn't completely true; she simply needed to hear what he had to say. "Sure— why not. Do you want to come over here, or, should I meet you at your place?"

Scott's reply was quick and abrupt. "Neither!"

"Oh...okay..." Macey muttered. "Where then?" She waited for his reply. "Scott? Are you still there?"

"Yeah...yeah, I'm still here. Listen, what do you say let's walk down to that yogurt shop."

"It's at least a mile down the road, Scott. Are you sure you want to walk?"

"I know..." Scott sighed. "But I could use the fresh air...not to mention the exercise."

"Well, sure, okay. Meet you outside in about ten minutes?"

"I'll be waiting, Macey."

Macey took the stairs two at a time and quickly changed into black leggings and a loose white, sweatshirt that was emblazoned with an orange and blue image of the Auburn University Tiger. She decided she may as well be comfortable if she was going to walk a mile or two.

The day was slightly overcast, causing it to feel much cooler than normal this time of the year. She grabbed a light windbreaker on her way out the door. She saw Scott waiting for her—leaning against her car.

Scott smiled and waved as he watched her hesitant approach toward him.

Macey acknowledged his smile by blushing. She couldn't forget the kiss they had shared the night before. She felt her cheeks warming and quickly averted her gaze. A small gasp escaped her when she approached him and he took her hands into his own. Her stomach entertained a quick flip-flop of gymnastics. She pulled back slightly at his touch, but relented when he pulled her to his side.

"Come on, Macey—I'll race you!"

She smiled at his gentle tugging of her hands. She was confused but ultimately decided that she couldn't resist the challenge he offered. She nodded, jumped out ahead of him, and sprinted quickly toward the entrance to their complex. "Last one there has to pay!" she yelled back, over her shoulder.

Scott's immediate reaction was so slow in coming that Macey was at least fifty yards ahead of him before he almost caught up with her. "You cheated!" he protested loudly, watching as her retreating figure gathered more speed.

The distance between them increased a little more.

They were both so engrossed in their competition that neither of them noticed the dark blue BMW drive past them, make an inconspicuous U-turn, and drive slowly past them once more. The car eventually pulled off into the parking lot adjacent to the yogurt shop. The driver stared in his rear-view mirror and watched overtly when the woman stopped to catch her breath and waited for the man to catch up with her. The driver shook his head in disbelief. "No...it's not possible...it can't be her..." he whispered hoarsely as he continued to watch until the couple disappeared inside the yogurt shop.

Reverend Lucas Dudley exhaled deeply, took out his Bible, and silently read scriptures for the next thirty minutes. He only closed his Bible when Scott and Macey exited the yogurt shop. He watched them as they walked slowly in the direction from which they had recently ran. He maintained a safe-enough distance, so that they would not be aware they were being followed. He stopped and parked on the side of the highway every few minutes and continued to follow them for the next thirty minutes. He watched as they walked through the entrance to the Whispering Hills complex. He pulled into the complex and found an empty parking space that allowed him to observe the couple while they stood talking for a few minutes. He waited until they walked past a white Rodeo and walked down the sidewalk, stopping at apartment number 27. The woman reached in her pocket for the key and the couple went inside.

He had to know. Was it really her? After all these years...was it really her?

Most apartment complexes utilized a centralized mail-box system; however, tenants of the exclusive Whispering Hills complex were provided a convenient, individualized, and private front door mail service.

Lucas waited another five minutes before strolling toward apartment number 27. He found himself praying that the name on the mailbox would not say WYMER. He exhaled an explicit sigh of relief as he casually walked by and glanced at the name on the box. "Thank, God!" he mumbled beneath his breath when he saw the name GARNER on a stenciled plate. He glanced casually back at the mailbox as he walked back toward his BMW and whispered hoarsely. "And so very lucky for you, my dear—that your name isn't Wymer..."

It never once occurred to him that GARNER might be a married name.

All the blinds and curtains in Macey's living room were open—to allow what little sunshine was available on this dreary day—to filter inside to her plants.

Scott sat at the dining room table, and saw the silhouette of a man, in his peripheral vision, walk by outside. His first thought was that it could be the mailman, but he thought the mail had already been delivered today. "Macey, some man just walked by, looking at your mailbox."

Macey came up behind Scott. She held a glass of iced tea in one hand and a cold beer in the other. "Here...you choose," she said holding out both hands out for his selection. "What did you say?"

Scott got up from the table and walked over to the bay window located between the front door and the sliding glass door that led to the patio. He pulled back the curtain for a better look outside. He glanced out the window and nodded his head toward the man who had stopped beside a dark BMW. He opted for the beer and motioned for her to look out the window. "Look down toward the entrance. See that man standing next to the dark BMW?"

Macey maneuvered herself in front of him; the top of her head just level with his shoulder.

Scott closed his eyes and inhaled the soft, mild fragrance of her shampoo. She smelled so good.

Macey focused her attention on the man Scott had pointed toward. Her body tensed while she watched the tall figure of the man open the car door and position himself in the driver's seat. She shook her head softly, and closed her eyes until the tenseness evaporated. "What? Do you know him?" she asked. She was suddenly aware of the minute distance that separated their two bodies. She was afraid to turn around and face Scott, so she stood frozen in her stead. She continued to watch while the driver of the BMW made a slow U-turn toward the exit and turned left onto the main highway.

Scott leaned forward and whispered in her ear. "He walked by your apartment a few minutes ago."

Macey managed to suppress a grin and whispered back. "So? Last time I checked...that wasn't against the law, Scott." She shuddered involuntarily at how close their bodies were. She was standing next to the man who, supposedly, killed her twin sister; but, her heart was betraying her—sending a very different signal. Was she betraying the memory of her sister by allowing Scott into her life?

"I'm pretty sure he was checking out your mailbox." Scott pressed closer to her as he strained to see which direction the car had taken after leaving the entrance.

Macey's heart began to beat faster. She knew she would have to turn around sooner or later. "Like I said...it's not against the law, Scott. He's probably just a...salesman. The complex doesn't allow solicitation, but I'm sure salesmen slip in every now and then."

Scott's forehead wrinkled. He tried to shake off the abrupt feeling of foreboding. "I don't know, Macey...something about him...he didn't look like he was selling anything."

Macey laughed softly and finally turned around. She hoped to be able to move around Scott without having to touch him any more than she already had. It didn't work. She turned quickly to move away from him, but, Scott's hands shot out reflexively and pressed her against the wall. She was trapped. Macey managed a smile, although, it was becoming more difficult to breathe. She looked up into warm, inviting brown eyes. "I know," she mocked. "Maybe he's the infamous Stocking Strangler!" She used Scott's perplexed state to catch him off guard and slipped gracefully beneath his outstretched arms.

Scott turned to look back at her. "I remember reading about that—it made national news," he muttered and followed her to the sofa. "I thought they caught that creep—some black man—Carlton Gary?"

The Stocking Strangler—also known as The Chattahoochee Choker—was a serial killer who had terrorized elderly, white women in Columbus, Georgia from September 1977 through April 1978. He had raped and strangled eight women, only one of whom, had survived his attack. A black man, by the name of Carlton Gary, had finally been captured in May 1984 and found guilty in 1986 of three of those murders.

"Yes," Macey acknowledged. "But there are still some people who think they may have locked up the wrong man. Who knows...maybe they did get the wrong man...maybe the Stocking Strangler is still stalking the female residents of Columbus, peering into their mailboxes and looking for..."

Scott realized, too late, that she was teasing him. "Cute...very cute," he grunted.

Macey felt relieved to be free of his embrace, and laughed softly at his embarrassed response to her teasing. "Seriously, Scott...the man was probably just looking for a friend's apartment."

"Yeah...maybe...you're probably right. It's just that...I don't know...an eerie feeling came over me when he passed by...made my skin crawl..."

Macey was both touched and disconcerted by the wariness she detected in his voice. She was touched that he might genuinely care about her welfare, but, she was disconcerted that he might have ulterior motives for trying to win her over. Maybe he was trying to assuage his own guilty feelings for what happened to Kacey. "Well...I'm sure it was nothing, but...I appreciate your concern, Scott; it's nice to know that someone worries about my safety."

It happened that quickly for Scott. The truth hit him so hard and quick that he was momentarily speechless, and he had to remind himself to breathe—just breathe! There was no doubt in his mind. He stared down at the petite woman standing next to him—the woman smiling up at him. Yes, he knew in that very instant. The reality of it came barreling toward him like a bolting revelation from the heavens above.

Scott Pennell was in love!

He was in love with a woman he hardly knew and had only kissed once! There had been no real intimacy between them—just one kiss! This couldn't be happening to him. What would his mother say? Never mind, he knew exactly what his mother would say. His heart filled with what he could only describe as—relief!

He continued to stare at the beautiful creature standing beside him and warmed with the secret knowledge of this most recent discovery. "I do worry about you, Macey. I hope you believe that." He reached out to take her hands and wasn't surprised at her involuntary withdrawal. However, this time, he held onto her hands firmly and led her to sit beside him on the sofa. He waited until she opened her eyes and looked at him.

"That's...nice, Scott. I'm not use to having anyone worry about me."

"That's hard to believe...not anyone—not even your parents?"

Macey shook her head.

Scott hesitated briefly before he continued. If he had truly fallen in love with this woman, then he was determined to learn more about her. He didn't tell her that he already knew about the young man who drove the black pick-up truck. "What about siblings? Do you have any brothers or sisters, Macey? I don't know anything about your personal life? Hey, at least you've met my mother!"

The mention of his mother brought an awkward smile to Macey's face. "You have a wonderful mother, Scott. I really liked her a lot. Your personalities are very...similar. I can see how she must have influenced the person you've become."

Scott grinned and shook his head. "No...we're not all that much alike—not really. Mom's much more outspoken than I am. She's...how should I put it? She's very direct in her opinions on just about everything."

Macey smiled in agreement. "Yes...I certainly got that impression of her all right."

"What about your mother, Macey? What's she like? Do you look like her? Is she still alive?"

Macey squirmed and scratched the back of her neck. "Scott, please don't be offended, but, I really don't like to talk about my family. Suffice it to say, that I did *not* have a happy childhood. I have not been in contact with my parents for more years than I care to remember."

"That's too bad. I won't pry, but maybe one day, you'll tell me about them."

Macey watched him closely. She only wished that she could talk to him about her family. Instead, she smiled and replied, "Maybe..."

Scott smiled and rubbed his thumb across the top of her hand. "I...uh...I have a confession to make, Macey."

Macey was sensitive to his touch. She was torn between wanting him to never let go, and, to getting as far away from him as possible. "What kind of confession, Scott?"

Scott hesitated briefly. "I...know that you have a...brother."

A startled frown formed on Macey's face and her hands trembled. "What are you talking about?"

Scott held tightly onto her hands, and did not allow her to pull away from him. "I was outside your office yesterday when he was leaving. I heard him call you, *sis*."

"Oh, God..."

Scott looked genuinely puzzled. "I don't get it, Macey. Is there a problem? Is there some reason you didn't want me to know you have a brother? And stop trying to pull away from me, dammit! I'm not going to let you go." He pulled her closer into his embrace. He felt her body stiffen against him but, at least, she stopped trying to pull away from him.

"I...didn't want anyone to know about Jacob," Macey mumbled into his chest. "Becca's the only one who knows about the relationship."

Scott breathed deeply. It felt so good to have her body pressed against his. "I don't understand. Why the secrecy?"

Macey took a deep breath and willed her muscles to relax beneath Scott's embrace. Part of her wanted to tell him everything; another part resented him because he never acknowledged knowing who she was. "It's a long, complicated story, Scott...one I don't think you're ready to hear—and, one I'm not quite ready to share. Can you just let it go at that for now?"

Scott lifted her face upward, leaned forward, and gently air-kissed her trembling lips. "For now? Sure, Macey...I can do that, but, just know that I'm here—whenever you need me. I have never said that to anyone before."

Macey pushed back slightly from his embrace and touched her lips; they still quivered from his gentle kiss. "We really shouldn't let this go any further, Scott. I don't think either of us fully realize what we may be getting ourselves into, do you?"

"I can't speak for you, Macey, but, I know exactly what I'm getting into—at least I think I do. I'm not ready to put it into words just yet. Does that make any sense to you?"

Desire and confusion ran rampant through Macey's brain, as she tried to sort through her feelings for the man next to her. Desire won out. She shook her head. "Not really...but, maybe it would if...you kissed me again?"

The overcast day finally succumbed to an orchestra of thunder and lightning; however, the sounds of the storm dimmed miserably in comparison to the fireworks that exploded within Scott Pennell's heart. He pulled Macey to him and willingly fulfilled her request.

CHAPTER 25

THE BOWLING DATE

Macey had made plans to go bowling with Jacob, Becca, and Carlton Brown on Saturday night. She knew that Becca might not be overjoyed, but she decided, at the last minute, to invite Scott to join them. Aside from the physical attraction she had toward him, she had felt guilty—being his sponsor—for not showing him around Columbus more than she had. A night at Peach Bowl Lanes might not be his idea of a fun time, but she had asked him anyway. Macey had mixed feelings when he had jumped at the opportunity to join them; she was both pleased and apprehensive.

Scott paced back and forth inside apartment 11. He stood in front of the floor-length mirror with nothing but a towel wrapped loosely at his waist. He stopped pacing and ran his hands through his still-wet hair. He smiled back at his reflection. He had not wanted to appear over-eager when he accepted Macey's invitation to go bowling, but he had a feeling he had failed miserably at hiding his enthusiasm. He tried to convince himself that the invitation was Macey's way of finding ways for them to spend more time together, without having to be alone with him—especially after that last kiss they had shared. He wished he had not committed himself to going back to Pennsylvania for Thanksgiving, but he wouldn't be leaving until Wednesday, so that gave him a few more days to find reasons for him and Macey to spend time together.

Scott ran his hands through his hair again and grinned at his reflection. "You are a handsome devil, aren't you?" The ringing of his doorbell startled him back to reality. He glanced quickly at his Rolex and hoped it wasn't Macey—if it was, then she was twenty minutes early.

Macey stood outside Scott's apartment and shifted nervously from one foot to the other. She glanced at her own watch—which was *not* a Rolex—and realized that she was too early. She had told Scott that she would come to his place at seven o'clock, so that they could ride together. It was only six forty! She turned around—hoping to make a hasty retreat—but stopped short when the door open behind her.

"Hi, there," Scott grinned. "You're early." He smiled down at her, held open the door, and motioned her inside. "Come on in, Macey..."

Macey turned around slowly and stared in awe at the perfect male specimen standing before her. She had been so anxious to see him again—evidently, a little too anxious. It had only been two hours since he left her apartment, but it seemed longer to her. She knew that their relationship had taken an extreme turn earlier today, and she was more than a little anxious about her evolving feelings toward him. She was still very confused about her feelings, but, she did know that she no longer hated him—if she ever truly did. She knew, too, that she would have to tell him the truth, eventually, about who she was—and, that terrified her. It was obvious to her now that he did not recognize her.

These thoughts were circling inside her head like buzzards over road kill, and her hands flew to her mouth when she stood within touching distance to the half-naked man who was the center of those thoughts. "Oh my...Scott...I...am so sorry—I'm too early. I can leave and come back..."

Scott grinned and shook his head. It was obvious that she was embarrassed and uncomfortable seeing him standing in the doorway, wrapped only in the short towel. He reached out and grabbed her wrist. "Oh no, you don't!" He stepped aside and motioned for her to enter.

Macey pulled her hand away and tried not to notice the wet droplets that fell from his hair onto his broad shoulders. "Scott, I really am so sorry! My watch must not be working. I could have sworn it was seven o'clock already. Really, I can come back—it's not a problem—and give you time to...uh...finish getting ready."

"Don't be ridiculous, Macey. You're here now, and it won't take me ten minutes to finish up with what I need to do. Make yourself at home, okay?"

Macey's dry throat and mouth failed her as she tried to swallow. She couldn't take her eyes off Scott's nearly naked body—the most gorgeous male body she had ever laid eyes upon. The small mass of dark hair that glistened upon his chest didn't do anything to alleviate her dry throat—she couldn't swallow. Her eyes seemed to have a mind of their own as they lowered to take in his firm, muscular thighs. She finally managed to swallow when he turned his back to her, and she observed the outline of another part of his body that also appeared to be extremely firm and taut. *"Oh, my goodness..."* Macey closed her eyes in silent appreciation.

Scott stopped and turned to look back at her. He smiled again at what he perceived to be embarrassment on her part. He walked back towards her, reached behind her, and closed the front door. He took her hands in his own and guided her into the living room. "Macey? Earth to Macey..."

Macey shook her head and pursed her lips together. "What?"

"It's me...Scott...remember?"

Macey opened her mouth to speak but quickly closed it again. She looked around her and wondered when she had moved from the doorway into the living room. She didn't remember closing the door behind her. "Don't be silly...of course, I remember," she scoffed. She exhaled deeply and raised her eyebrows in obvious bewilderment.

Scott crossed his arms and grinned back at her. "Then what did I just say?"

The look of bewilderment remained plastered upon her face. "When?"

Scott smiled and shook his head. "You don't remember. Are you sure you're okay?"

"I'm fine!" she replied more hastily than she had intended. "So...why aren't you ready? You do still want to go bowling, don't you?"

Scott scratched his head. "Ten minutes, okay? Give me ten minutes and I'll be ready to go. There's tea in the fridge if you want some." He turned and bounded up the stairs, careful to keep a close grasp on the towel.

"Okay...ten minutes...sure thing..." Macey whispered. She collapsed onto the couch and watched him take the steps, two at a time. She sat on her hands and rocked back and forth. She looked toward the staircase and exhaled sharply. "I sure hope he wears more than that towel, or I have a feeling that I'm going to throw a lot of gutter balls tonight..."

Becca James and Carlton Brown arrived at the bowling alley about twenty minutes before the others. Carlton pulled into the parking lot on the west side. It was still relatively early, so his was the only vehicle currently parked on that side of the building. The fluorescent lighting from the huge sign reading PEACH BOWL LANES provided a soft, amber glow within the car.

Carlton took a quick perusal of the parking lot. "I don't see your friend's Rodeo, baby. It looks like we beat her here." He moved to open the car door, but the firm pressure of Becca's hand upon his forearm stopped him.

Becca raised her eyebrows and smiled seductively. She ran her tongue over her full lips and purred. "Well, then...that means we've probably got a few minutes..." She leaned over and kissed his neck.

Carlton released the door handle and leaned back against the headrest. "Oh, baby...don't you go starting anything you can't finish."

"Who says I can't finish..." Becca whispered in his ear while she caressed him.

"Oh...Becca...you know I can't go inside like this, baby..."

"You won't have to, Sugar..." Becca reassured him as she slid down in the seat. "I'm gonna take care of that problem...right now..."

Several miles away in an old but well-established, quiet neighborhood, the good Reverend Dudley backed slowly out of his driveway. He had been unable to get the woman off his mind. He had mulled it over all afternoon, and had finally convinced himself that the woman's resemblance to the Wymer family had to be more than just coincidental. He had, also, chastised himself for not immediately recognizing that *Garner* might be the woman's *married* name. If that was the case, then the woman he saw jogging down the road could very well have been Macey Wymer. If she turned out to be Macey, then he most definitely had an interest in pursuing the matter further, because Macey Wymer was the mother of his only child—a child she had kidnapped and deprived him of knowing for twenty years!

Lucas arrived at the Whispering Hills complex fifteen minutes later, just in time to see the woman and man leaving in a white Rodeo. The man was driving, but Reverend Dudley had a clear view of the woman who occupied the passenger seat. Lucas stared at the woman, and for one quick moment their eyes met and held before he quickly dropped his gaze. He was confident that the woman—if she was Macey—had not recognized him. That didn't really surprise him; after all, it had been more than twenty years, and, she had been a terrified, fifteen-year old at the time.

The Reverend kept a deliberate distance and followed the Rodeo. He was unsure of his intentions, but until he verified the woman's identity, it was imperative that he learn more about her. If the woman was indeed Macey, then she would be able to tell him what happened to their child. He didn't even know if he was the father of a son or a daughter. The only information he had been able to gather had come from Andrew Wymer, who simply told him that Macey had run away before the baby was born. Hell! Their child may even be living with Macey and her husband at Whispering Hills!

He continued to follow the Rodeo for several miles until it pulled into Peach Bowl Lanes. Lucas parked in front of the bowling alley and watched the Rodeo drive around to the west side of the building and park beside a 1977 red and white Cadillac. He pursed his lips tightly together when the man walked around to the passenger side, opened the door, and draped his arm casually across the woman's shoulder while they made their way to the building's side entrance.

Lucas was far enough away to go unnoticed, but near enough to get a closer look at the woman. Glory be to God! It was Macey! It had to be! Her body had developed into that of a woman, but the face and the way she moved had changed very little over the years. She was even more beautiful now than she had been at fifteen. Her tiny waist and narrow hips were shapelier now than they had been when she was younger, but, she could easily pass for a teenager from the back—dressed as she was, in jeans and a tight black shirt. Oh, how he remembered those hips!

Macey sighed when Scott draped his arm over her shoulder. It felt good. It felt right.

It didn't take her long to spot Becca and Carlton once they got inside. Becca was bent over searching for a bowling ball, and Carlton stood behind her with his hands planted indiscreetly, yet firmly, upon her voluptuous butt.

Becca wriggled her hips beneath his touch and said, "Just wait until I get you home tonight, Sugar!"

Macey blushed and Scott smiled as they stood—unnoticed—off to the side.

"We could always go back out to the parking lot, baby" Carlton groaned as he positioned himself directly behind her.

Macey cleared her throat loudly enough to get their attention. "Watch it you two! There are minors in the building, and, I'm pretty sure you can be arrested for what you're thinking right now!" she whispered. She walked around them and tossed her purse onto a nearby galley seat.

Becca and Carlton turned abruptly. They were both momentarily speechless.

Macey would have sworn that they both blushed in total embarrassment—as much as a person of color can blush.

Becca clutched her ample chest and gasped. "Girlfriend, you've done scared me half to death! What..." She stopped in mid-sentence when she noticed Scott standing off to the side.

Scott nodded and smiled in her direction. "Hello, Becca. I hope you don't mind that Macey invited me to tag along." He smiled again, hoping beyond hope that Becca's animosity toward him might warm up enough for them all to enjoy the evening. Scott held his hand out to Carlton. "Hello, I'm Scott Pennell, a friend of Macey's."

Carlton grinned congenially and shook hands with Scott. "Carlton Brown. Good to meet you. Hey there, Macey...it's good to see you again."

Macey smiled back. "Hello, Carlton. I'm glad you could come tonight."

"Oh, I came tonight, all right!" Carlton thought, unable to suppress a sly smile. He watched Becca's reaction to Scott's presence. He felt her shoulders tighten beneath his hand, and wondered about her obvious change in personality. It wasn't like her to be intentionally rude to anyone, but, she was, most definitely, giving Scott Pennell the cold shoulder.

"I thought Jacob was going to be your date," Becca quizzed. She offered a cool nod of her head to Scott.

Macey looked back and forth between Becca and Scott and decided that enough was enough! "Okay, Becca, this has got to stop—right here—right now. I shouldn't have to ask you, but I want you to be nice to Scott. He has become a...special friend, and I won't put up with you being rude to him any longer. If you can't at least be civil, then maybe we should just leave. Besides, he knows that Jacob is my *brother*."

Becca's head shot up and she stared hard at Macey. "What else does he know?"

Macey returned a warning glare and gritted her teeth.

Scott and Carlton grinned awkwardly at each other, neither of them brave enough to venture any interference.

Macey was spared having to answer Becca's question, by an enthusiastic shout coming from the front entrance.

"Hey, guys!" Jacob yelled out while he sprinted toward them. He wasn't alone. He, too, had brought along a date.

Janet Ward joined the group, smiling and offering an awkward wave. "Hi, everyone," she giggled timidly.

A timid Janet! Macey was in shock! How in the world had her brother hooked up with Janet Ward, of all people?

Quick and awkward introductions were made, and the group eventually settled down into a reluctant—yet oddly—comfortable order. It took several beers, but the tension among them gradually evaporated while the three couples bowled in friendly competition among themselves. The losing couple—more often than not—was Macey and Scott, who had to buy the next round of beer for everyone.

Jacob described to everyone how Janet had stopped by his father's station for gas that afternoon, and recognized him from the times he had visited Macey's office. He had been secretly flattered that she remembered him, and did not hesitate to invite her to be his date for the evening.

Janet had never thrown a bowling ball before in her life, but, she was determined to learn how, especially if it meant spending time with Jacob. She was more than willing to make a fool of herself to get to know him better.

By eleven o'clock, the three couples were having such a good time together that it no longer mattered to any of them who bought the next round. They were all genuinely enjoying the company of the others; even Becca found herself relenting to Scott's charming personality. She allowed herself to look beyond the teenage boy mentioned in the newspaper articles, and to get to know a little bit of the man he had become. She could always blame it on the beer if he turned out to be the jerk she initially purported him to be.

By midnight, Carlton was anxious to get Becca home, to reciprocate her earlier sexual generosity.

Janet and Jacob hadn't been able to keep their hands off each other all night, so no one was surprised when they were the first to call an end to the bowling.

Macey and Scott had not been quite as physical in their appreciation of each other during the evening, but, they had exchanged stolen glances all night. Each of them was wondering where it was all going to lead—or, if it would lead to anything at all.

Scott had further impressed Becca by offering to pay for everyone's bowling. She was almost inclined to relax her concerns about him—almost—but, not completely.

The three couples gathered in the parking lot to say goodnight. They all promised to get together again soon, and then went their separate ways.

Scott and Macey were the last to leave. When Scott moved to open the car door for Macey, his attention settled immediately upon the dark BMW parked in front of the almost-empty parking lot. "Probably not the same car," he pondered.

"Did you say something, Scott?" Macey asked as he slid behind the wheel.

Scott pointed to the BMW. "See that car over there, Macey? The BMW?"

Macey stretched her head in the direction he was pointing. "Yeah, what about it?"

"It looks like the same one that man was driving earlier today."

"What man, Scott?"

"That *salesman*...the *Stocking Strangler*... who was checking out your mailbox...remember?"

Macey took a longer look at the car before shaking her head. "No...I don't think it's the same one. Come on, Scott...it's late, and I'm sleepy... guess I'm not used to drinking beer."

Scott grinned mischievously. "Does that mean I can take advantage of the situation?" He started the car and made sure he exited the bowling alley through the main entrance so that he could get a closer look at the BMW. He slowed and glanced at the license tag when he drove by. He memorized the sequence of the six numbers and letters.

Macey punched him on the arm. "No! You certainly cannot—will not—take advantage of the situation."

"Ouch! Why are all the women in my life always trying to punch me out?"

They both laughed and relaxed in their newly-discovered camaraderie.

Lucas stumbled out the front door of the bowling alley, punched the remote to his BMW, and staggered toward the car. He had sat at the bar for the past five hours, downed beer after beer, and watched Macey and Jacob cavorting with their black friends. If there had been any doubt in his mind about the woman's identity, it had vanished completely when he saw Jacob join the group. No, there was no doubt in his mind now. "The lit'l bish..." he slurred as he tried, unsuccessfully, to unlock his car door with the remote.

"Hey, buddy!"

Lucas turned around too quickly, lost his balance, and gripped the BMW's door handle to steady himself.

The blue and white police cruiser rolled up beside him.

Lucas stared at the cop, through slit eyelids, and followed up with a proper salute. "Tassi!" he slurred.

The police officer opened the cruiser's back door and allowed Lucas to stumble inside.

Lucas saluted him again and croaked, "Take me...(*hiccup*)... home, tassi!"

"This isn't a taxi, buddy...but, I'm taking you home all right..." the officer said as he assisted the drunk who was having a very difficult time maneuvering himself into the cruiser.

"You...are a kind soul, my...(*hiccup*)...good man. God...(*hiccup*)... Blesshoo..."

CHAPTER 26

PLANS FOR THANKSGIVING

Everyone seemed to be lost in their own individual thoughts and worries as the holiday weekend approached.

Scott was unusually busy, tying up loose ends before leaving to spend Thanksgiving with his parents in Pennsylvania. He had tried his best to persuade Macey to make the trip with him, but she had been adamant in her resistance to accompany him. Scott had listened quietly while Macey explained how she didn't want to interfere with any plans his family might have for him, and, she certainly didn't want to run into Cheryl or any other long-lost girlfriends. Scott felt somewhat appeased knowing that Macey intended to spend Thanksgiving Day with Becca's family, as well as a few hours with Jacob.

Janet Ward had also been extremely busy the last few days. She had been uncharacteristically pleasant and humble, following her bowling date with Jacob. Much to everyone's amusement, she had even lowered the hems of her skirts an inch or two. She used her wily charms every chance she got to inject herself in Jacob's plans for Thanksgiving, but thus far, had failed to receive the desired invitation.

Jacob, on the other hand, was positively certain of what his parents' reaction to Janet would be—not to mention the implication she would make of an actual invitation to their home. However, his parents' opinion of Janet was not the only reason that he was reluctant of invite her. He could not take the chance that Janet would mention Macey's name. Macey already thought that the receptionist knew too much about the Wymer family, and could not be trusted with their secrets. Jacob knew how important it was for him to keep his relationship with his sister a secret—at least, until after the New Year—until he had moved away from Columbus, Georgia.

Macey sat idly at her desk, pondering over everything that had happened during the past few days—at how quickly her life was changing. The buzzing intercom startled her and she looked away from the figures and data on her computer screen. She punched the intercom button and mumbled, "Yes, Janet?" She tucked her pencil behind her ear and leaned back in her chair. She used her free hand to rub the tense muscles in her shoulder and neck.

"Miss Garner—Macey—Mr. Byce wants to see you in his office...right away."

"Now?" asked Macey. She didn't think her muscles could get any tighter than they already were, but they proved her wrong.

Janet paused for a moment. "Yeah...he said you should bring the overseas training data with you, and to be there in five minutes."

Macey's hand began to tremble and she almost dropped the phone. "Thank you, Janet."

"Sure, no problem...by the way..."

"Yes, Janet?" Macey asked while she quickly gathered the requested data.

"I...uh...well, I haven't had a chance to talk to you much this week, but, I...uh...well, I just wanted you to know that I had a really neat time Saturday night. Your brother is so cool."

Macey smiled despite her nervousness. "Yes...it was fun, Janet. I think everyone had a good time."

Janet hesitated before continuing. "I'm having lunch with Jacob today...do you want to come with us?"

"Lunch? Well...I appreciate the offer, but I'm afraid I'll have to pass. Where is Jacob taking you?"

"Some little place I've never heard of," Janet cooed. "I think he said Alvin's Diner. Have you ever been there?"

Macey smiled again and wished that she could be there to see Becca's reaction. If Janet had been uncomfortable at the bowling alley, then having Becca for a waitress would prove to be agonizing as hell. The little devil on her shoulder convinced her not to forewarn Janet. "Yes—yes, I have—I eat there quite often. The food is great. Be sure to tell Jacob hello for me."

"Oh, I will!" Janet replied eagerly. She hung up the phone and applied fresh lipstick.

Macey gathered up the necessary files, took a deep breath, and hurried to the elevator. Mr. Byce didn't like to be kept waiting, and she was anxious to be in and out of his office as quickly as possible. *"Only six more months",* she reminded herself while she waited for the elevator door to open.

Macey's eyes were cast downward when the elevator door opened, and she practically fell into Scott's arms as she rushed forward with the large stack of files she carried.

"Whoa there, Speedy!" he exclaimed. "Where's the fire?"

Macey blushed and straightened the file folders. "Oh, I'm sorry, Scott! You'll have to excuse me. I've...uh...been *summoned* by Mr. Byce, and I'm already two minutes late."

Scott looked concerned as he held her steady. "Do you need some reinforcement to go in there with you?"

Did she ever! Macey appreciated his offer, but knew she had to do this on her own. She shook her head and said, "Thanks, Scott, but...no...I can handle Mr. Byce."

Scott was still holding onto her arms and felt them tremble beneath his touch. As much as he would have liked to believe the trembling was a result of his touch, he knew better. "Are you sure about that, Macey? I hate leaving you alone with him...especially while I'm out of town."

Macey was touched at the genuine concern in his voice. "Scott, that's really sweet of you, but think about it. I've been fighting off his advances for two years before you came into the picture."

Scott feigned disappointment. "That is true. Is that your way of telling me that you don't need me around?"

She stared into his handsome face and remembered all the kisses they had shared over the weekend. Had it really been only three days since he'd held her in his arms and awakened feelings within her that she never knew existed? She closed her eyes and sighed. "Scott, this is neither the time nor the place for this conversation. Sorry, but I really have to go..."

He released her arms and offered a hesitant smile. "Okay...you have my permission to enter the lion's den alone...all alone. By the way, will you still have time to take me to the airport this evening?"

"Of course, I will," Macey replied. She moved around Scott and knocked on Mr. Byce's door. She looked back at him and whispered, "I'll pick you up at your apartment at six o'clock."

"Make it five-thirty," Scott said loud enough for George Byce to hear.

Byce bellowed out a command to enter.

Macey blushed and nodded her agreement. She took a deep breath before bravely entering the lion's den.

George Byce arose from behind his desk and motioned Macey inside.

"I have those files you wanted, Mr. Byce."

"You're late," Byce replied irritably. "Have a seat at the conference table, Miss Garner; we'll go over them there."

Macey moved to walk past him, and was ready to offer an apology for her tardiness when she felt his deliberate stroke against her breast. She gasped and collapsed into a chair. "Mr. Byce! Please...don't do that."

"Please, Mr. Byce, don't do that!" he mimicked. "And just exactly how do you intend to stop me from doing that, Miss Garner? If memory serves correctly, you most certainly did not attempt to stop me at the Halloween party!"

Macey looked toward the closed door. She wished, too late, that she had accepted Scott's offer of reinforcement.

Byce followed her gaze and stroked the front of his trousers. "Don't expect Mr. Pennell to save you this time, Macey. I've left strict orders that we are not to be interrupted." He walked over to his office door and locked it.

"But...I...thought you wanted to go over these files..." Macey silently berated herself at the pleading she heard in her own voice. She hated herself for being so weak and vulnerable to this man and his unwanted advances.

George Byce was standing directly behind her now. "You didn't answer my question, Macey. What exactly do you plan to do to stop me?"

"I...I'll submit a grievance...a sexual harassment grievance..." Macey mumbled.

Byce laughed out loud. "A grievance...really? Come now, Macey, you can do better than that. You and I both know that you would have already filed a grievance if that was your plan. After everything I've already said and done to you—come on, tell me—why *haven't* you already filed that grievance?"

Macey moved to stand up but George Byce held her shoulders down, forcing her to remain seated. She turned her head and looked up at him. "What do you want from me?"

Byce towered above her. He turned her chair around to face him and stood over her, his legs straddling her tightly-closed knees. He grasped the arms of her chair and growled. "You are a grown woman, Macey, so you know damn well what I want from you...what I fully intend to have from you..."

George Byce was almost fifty pounds overweight, so Macey had to take a deep breath when his extended belly pressed against her face when he leaned toward her. She glanced lower and shivered involuntarily at his obvious arousal. "Why me?" she begged. "Why?" She despised the weakness she heard in her own voice.

He lifted her chin up and forced her to look him in the eye. "Because I am the Deputy CEO of one of the most powerful technological companies in the southeast...because I have more than earned the pleasure of your company...because we both know that it will only enhance your promotional opportunities after I retire...because I love a challenge... because you are the only female in this corporation—under the age of forty—who is not willing to sleep her way to the top. I could go on. Do you need more reasons?"

Macey shook her head and sighed. "No...please...don't go on."

Byce became encouraged by the sudden resignation he detected in her voice. He stared down at her and moved his hands to her shoulders. He kneaded them briefly before moving them to her neck, and finally running them through her long, thick hair. He felt her tremble and accepted it as her acknowledgment for him to continue. His thick, fleshy hands inched downward until they rested on each side of her breasts. "Don't worry, Macey...it won't happen today...or, maybe not even tomorrow. In fact, you can relax over the holidays because my wife is insisting we spend them with her parents. I only called you in here today to give you fair warning."

"Fair warning...about what?" Macey whispered. She closed her eyes and tried to ignore the boldness of his caresses.

"My timeline for you, Macey...it's Christmas. I have decided that you are to be my present this year. So...be ready. It's obvious to me that you must need this job; that's got to be the only reason why you haven't reported anything. So, make it easy on yourself, Macey. I'm really not such a bad guy...you might even enjoy it."

The room was closing in on her now, and Macey was finding it difficult to breathe. "May I go now?" she cowered.

Byce paused slightly before taking her hand into his own. "Yes...*after* you touch me, Macey. Touch me...and, then you can leave."

Macey closed her eyes and shook her head. "Oh, no...God, please... no...I can't..."

"Do it now, Macey...or your pink slip will be on your desk before you leave today. No one will ever believe your side of the story. I will make sure of that, and I will make sure that no reputable employer in Columbus will consider you for employment. No one connected to the computer industry will *ever* hire you. Now...*touch me!*"

The sound of his pants being unzipped reverberated through Macey's brain. She suddenly remembered another time...long ago...another zipper...and, another man forcing himself upon her. She took a deep breath as tears pooled in her eyes, but she forced herself to do his will. She reached out and touched him, timidly, but quickly withdrew her hand.

"You can do better than that, Macey," Byce growled. "And you damn well better, or I won't wait until Christmas."

Tears flowed down her cheeks, but she knew they had no effect on Byce. "I can't...please don't make me, Mr. Byce."

She was crying openly now and George Byce almost felt sorry her. It didn't do much for his ego to feel he had to force himself upon a woman. He wanted her to want him as much as he wanted her; but—in the end— it really didn't matter. He knew that he wasn't as physically attractive to women as he had been twenty years ago, but he, also, knew that there was still much that he could offer them. He fully intended to have his way with Macey Garner—with, or without, her cooperation. He decided that it was time to use what he hoped was his Ace in the hole. He had never been one hundred percent positive, but he hoped the information he had collected could be used to his benefit one day. "If you don't, Macey...then, not only will you receive your pink slip...I will personally see to it that everyone knows about your little...*secret*."

Macey's head jerked up and she looked at him with uncharacteristic defiance. "What secret?" she hissed.

Byce grinned down at her. "Did you really think that changing your last name would help, Macey?"

It wasn't possible. He couldn't know. Macey shook her head in disbelief. "How...how did you find out?"

"I've known all along, Macey. Your sister's murder captivated me years ago. It was gruesome even by today's standards."

Macey's mind was racing. If he knew who she was, then he must also know about Scott's involvement. "Scott?"

"Oh, yes, my dear...I've known all along who Mr. Pennell was. It was I who made the final decision to hire him."

"But why..."

George Byce towered over her, unbuckled his belt, and let his pants and underwear pool at his ankles. "It was my Ace of Spades, Macey... it always has been...my trump card over you. I knew if I couldn't have you by threatening your job security...well...something told me that you would do *anything* to protect your real identity. I am right, aren't I? For whatever reason you might have...you would do *anything* to protect your past."

Macey took a deep breath and swiped the tears from her cheeks. "I'll touch you...if that's what I have to do...I'll touch you."

Finally! He had her right where he wanted her! After two long years of scheming and yearning, she would *willingly* do whatever he wanted. Why should he have to wait for Christmas? He had known who she was from the first day she entered his office for the interview. He mentally chastised himself for not having played his trump card sooner.

He grinned and closed his eyes before replying, "No, Macey...I've changed my mind. You will do *much* more than touch me...and, you will be gentle. One misguided bite or scratch, and you will live to regret it, my dear. Oh, come on, now...don't look so forlorn, Macey. It's only for six more months..."

She knew what he wanted. She knew what she had to do. Macey slid off the chair and knelt before George Byce.

Fifteen minutes later, she closed his office door softly behind her and groped her way to the ladies' room down the hall. It was blessedly empty, and Macey spent the next thirty minutes regurgitating George Byce's climactic victory. She splashed cold water upon her terror-stricken face and stared at her reflection in the mirror. "Merry Christmas, you son-of-a-bitch," she whispered in a raspy voice that was devoid of all feeling or emotion.

CHAPTER 27

THE DAY BEFORE THANKSGIVING

Ruth Wymer stood at her kitchen stove and stirred the fudge frosting for Jacob's favorite layer cake. She loved cooking special dishes for her son, especially during the holidays. She was already looking forward to her Christmas baking, which included all of Jacob's favorite desserts.

Ruth inhaled the rich aroma of melted chocolate and listened to the sounds coming from outside their small, but well-maintained home. Andrew was splitting logs for the cooler weather he anticipated. She thought it was probably a waste of his time because it appeared that this winter would be an even milder one than usual. However, even if they didn't need all the chopped wood for themselves, she knew that Andrew could always sell the extra supply and make a few extra dollars.

She set the frosting aside to cool and watched her husband from inside the screen door. She poured him a glass of lemonade and took a moment to admire his body. He had taken off his shirt, exposing the sleeveless tee-shirt he always wore beneath. Ruth couldn't help but appreciate the well-toned physique he had maintained over the years. Although his waistline was four inches larger than when she married him, his body had remained firm and compact. At fifty-six, two years older than she, she thought he had aged much more gracefully—but, then, men usually did. His thick hair, accentuated by a small amount of gray concentrated mostly at his temples, only served to enhance his rugged good looks.

Ruth was stunned when she realized that she had become slightly aroused as she remembered how things had been between them during their early years of marriage. "It's been so long, Andrew," she whispered under her breath. "Much too long...that's why I've had to turn to Reverend Dudley...to get the comfort that you can't—or won't—give me. What happened to us, Andrew? Why do you continue to punish *me* for what happened...and, why do I continue to put up with it...*why*?"

Andrew felt like he was being watched. He turned slowly to face the screen door and wiped the sweat from his brows. "What are you looking at?" he bellowed.

Ruth jumped and almost spilled the lemonade. "You looked hot. I made a pitcher of lemonade...would you like some?"

Andrew stared hard at the woman he had married so many years ago...a woman he had once shared a life with...a woman he had loved with all his heart...back when he knew how to love...and had a heart. He knew that Ruth would probably never know the full extent of the guilt he felt for the abusive way he had treated her since Kacey's death. He had never resorted to physical abuse—he would never do that. His had been emotional abuse.

He continued to stare at her through the screen door. If he were totally honest with himself, he would have to admit that he still loved his wife. They had not had a physical relationship in years—not so much, as a simple hug or a peck on the cheek. They continued to sleep in the same room, but had opted for twin beds years ago. He was careful never to encourage any physical intimacy; and, he knew that Ruth would never be one to initiate any sexual overtures. Whenever his sexual frustrations got the best of him, he made a quick visit downtown to Eighth Street—infamous for its abundant supply of prostitutes, who were more than willing to offer a temporary solution to his problem. Ruth had been a passionate bed partner during their early years of marriage; and, he wondered what—if anything—she did to alleviate her own sexual frustrations.

Everything changed between them when Kacey died. An integral part of him had died the day they buried Kacey. He did not dare to be alone, in the same room, with Ruth after that. He feared that she would read more into his grief than that of a father suffering the loss of a child. He could never admit it to anyone, but his sorrow was twofold; he had lost a lover as well as a child. The only way he had been able to maintain a grasp on his sanity was to turn his emotions inward. His entire personality changed the day Kacey was lowered into that dark, void hole. Any semblance of kindness or gentleness that had been part of Andrew's former character had been replaced with open displays of cynicism, rudeness, and selfishness.

Memories flooded his mind and he had no idea how long he had been staring at Ruth. Andrew finally shook himself back to the present moment and snarled. "Well! Are you gonna bring it out or do I have to come get it myself?"

Ruth blinked back tears at his gruffness and hurried out with his drink. She stood beside him while he gulped it down, and poured him another glass from the pitcher she carried. "Andrew?"

He wiped his mouth with the back of his hand and looked at her. "What is it, Ruth?"

She shifted nervously from one foot to the other and looked down at the ground. "I...uh...well, tomorrow is Thanksgiving..."

Andrew threw a victory wave into the air. "Well, give the woman a prize! So...it's Thanksgiving...so what?"

"Well...I was thinking that we might invite Reverend Dudley to eat with us...if it's all right with you, that is."

Andrew handed the empty glass to his wife and glared at her. A quick twinge of guilt flitted through him when she flinched and took a step backward. He didn't like Lucas Dudley, but he couldn't afford for anyone to ever learn the real reason why. He still fought his own nightmarish demons for having taken Macey to him for her *spiritual cleansing*, as the good reverend called it.

"Andrew?" Ruth asked. She hated the timid sound of her own voice.

Andrew rendered another icy stare. "Why would you want to invite him, Ruth...we don't even go to his church. He's not our reverend anymore."

"You don't go to any church," Ruth thought—she would *never* dare say that out loud. She knew that Andrew read his Bible faithfully every day, but, she also knew that he had not stepped inside a church since the day they buried Kacey. "He doesn't have any family, Andrew. I...just thought it would be a nice thing to do. No one should be alone over the holidays."

Andrew turned his back on her. "I'm sure he would find someone else to free load off."

Ruth turned to leave. "I understand, Andrew...all right, I won't ask him. I just thought..."

"Ruth!"

She stopped in her tracks but didn't turn around. She didn't want him to see the tears that pooled in her eyes.

Andrew saw her head drop and noticed the slight tremble of her shoulders. "It's okay...go ahead and invite the man."

Ruth was not aware that she had been holding her breath until a single sigh of relief escaped her. She smiled and began to think ahead to the Thanksgiving meal. She knew Andrew would only stay long enough to eat before finding some excuse to leave. She assumed that Jacob would probably have plans of his own, too, which would leave her all alone—free and available to entertain their guest. She was so desperate for some male attention. She told herself it was because a woman had needs, just as a man did. She was only fifty-four years old...too young to bury her physical desires simply because her husband no longer wanted an intimate relationship with her. She lifted her shoulders and turned to smile at her husband. "Thank you, Andrew. We'll eat around three o'clock if that's okay with you."

Andrew silently chastised himself for the apparent fear and anxiety he instilled upon his own wife. "Whatever..." he grunted as he returned to chopping firewood.

Macey knocked on the door to Scott's apartment.

"It's open! Come on in," he yelled from inside.

She took a deep breath and plastered a smile upon her face. "It's only me, Scott. Are you ready to go to the airport?"

Scott walked out of the kitchen and stopped abruptly when he saw how pale Macey looked. He hurried over to where she stood beside the open door. "Macey! You look awful...come on in...sit down. Are you all right?" he asked. He felt her forehead, positive that his hand would detect a fever; but, her skin was cool to his touch—extremely cool to the touch.

"I'm fine," she protested and glanced at her watch. "We'd better hurry. I wouldn't want you to miss your plane. Your mom would never forgive me."

"We've got plenty of time. Sit down. Let me get you something to drink."

"Really, Scott, I'm fine. Please...don't bother." She sat down on the leather sofa.

Scott turned back to her and said, "Well, at least sit down for a minute. Are you sure you're okay? Janet said you left early because you weren't feeling well." He waited for her to say something, but she remained silent. She had not looked directly at him since she entered his apartment. He saw her hands tremble in her lap. "Macey? What is it? I can tell something has happened. Tell me what it is."

Tears flowed down her cheeks as she shook her head from side to side. She used her hands to wipe away the tears. "Really, Scott...it's nothing. God, I'm so embarrassed for you to see me this way. I...I thought I had it under control before I came over."

"Had what under control?" He took her hands into his own and felt the tension in her weak grip. It had been a while since she had tensed at his touch; he thought they had gotten past that aversion.

Macey exhaled deeply and shrugged. "Oh, you know...it's just a... female thing..."

"You mean your period?"

His ease at talking about her period took her by surprise. "Yeah... hormones...PMS, I guess. I just get real emotional a couple of days out of the month. Just when I think I've got it under control, my body reminds me that it's the other way around. I usually try to stay to myself those few days and not inflict my moods upon anyone else."

"Are you sure that's all it is?" Scott wasn't convinced.

There was no way Macey could tell him about what happened earlier that day in Mr. Byce's office. She was much too ashamed. She doubted that she would even be able to tell Becca about it. Macey's immediate goal had been to drop Scott off at the airport, as she had promised, and hurry back home to crawl beneath the covers. "Yes," she lied. She stood up and offered a weak smile. "So...come on, fella; get a move on it, or your mother is going to have heart failure thinking you're not coming home for Thanksgiving."

Scott stood up and pulled her to him. He felt her stiffen at the embrace. "I still wish you would change your mind and come home with me."

Macey willed herself to relax and shook her head. "No...I don't think that would be appropriate, Scott. Besides...I'm sure your parents want you all to themselves for a few days. You'll be back on Sunday, right?"

Scott grabbed a small suitcase from behind the door. "Actually, I've changed my return flight for Saturday. I wanted to ask if you would be able to pick me up then, but, it's not a problem if you can't. I can take a taxi."

Macey smiled up at him. She was secretly glad that he would be returning earlier than scheduled. "Of course, I can. What time does your flight arrive?"

"Not until twelve-thirty. I was going to make it earlier, but I thought you might want to sleep in."

"How considerate of you, Mr. Pennell. I'll be there, don't worry. Now, come on...we really need to get going."

Scott held open the door for her and locked it behind them. "Macey, I never got to talk with you after your meeting with Mr. Byce. How did that go?"

She stumbled and Scott grabbed her elbow with his free hand to keep her from falling. She was even paler than when she first arrived at his apartment.

"Macey? You okay?"

"Clumsy me," she replied with a feeble attempt at humor.

"So, how did the meeting go?"

"I told you before, Scott...I can handle Mr. Byce."

"I know what you told me," Scott said, shaking his head. He opened her car door for her. "But...I'm not convinced that you can. The stories I've heard about that guy...well...I worry about you, Macey. I hate to think about what I would be forced to do to him if he ever did anything to hurt you."

Macey was touched at his genuine concern. It had been so long since anyone worried about her. She wished she could confide in him, but she was afraid that it would jeopardize both their careers if he knew the truth. No, it was only for six more months; and, she could endure anything for six months. She didn't want anyone to know about the pain and humiliation she had experienced earlier that day, or that she would continue to experience during the next six months. She slid behind the wheel and waited for Scott to enter the passenger side of her car. Once he had closed his door, she leaned over and kissed him on the cheek. "I really can handle him, Scott, but thank you so much for caring...you have no idea what that means to me."

Scott took her face in his hands and looked deeply into her eyes. He saw the veil in front of those eyes—a veil that, he was sure, hid many secrets. He wished that she trusted him enough to share those secrets with him. He gently brought her lips closer to his own and placed a light, non-threatening kiss upon them. He smiled when she closed her eyes and moaned softly. It felt so good to be with her, and he wanted desperately to be the one she needed—the one to look after her. "I do care, Macey... more than you know...more than I even knew I was capable of caring. I've never told any woman this, but..."

Macey touched her fingers to his lips and shook her head. She looked him squarely in the eyes and pleaded, "Don't say it, Scott...not yet. There are things you don't know about me...things you need to know before I can let you say what I think you were about to say."

Scott smiled mischievously. "What makes you think you know what I was about to say, Miss Garner?"

Some color was returning to her face. Macey smiled back and whispered, "Because I've thought about saying the same thing to you, but, the timing...it's just not right."

Scott's eyebrows raised quizzically. "Am I supposed to understand

187

what that means?"

Macey ran her thumb along his upturned brow and smiled. "No, but you will soon enough, Scott. Like I said…there are things you need to know about me. After you hear these things, then—if you still feel the same way—well…who knows what the future has in store for us."

Scott smiled and touched his forehead to hers. "Yeah, who knows." He kissed her again and thrilled in the way she wrapped her arms tightly around his neck.

Macey was eager to return his kiss with equal passion and deliberation. "Yeah…who knows…" she mumbled before becoming totally lost in the kiss and the moment. She refused to let George Byce's actions intimidate her to the point that she might sacrifice the best thing that had happened to her in more than twenty years.

They reached the airport with just enough time for Scott to rush inside and check his bags. They waved to each other as he boarded his flight. They were so engrossed in each other that they were oblivious to the people around them.

Neither of them had noticed that they had been followed by a dark-blue BMW.

CHAPTER 28

JACOB AND MACEY DISCUSS THE PAST

It took most of the holiday weekend before Macey felt like she truly had control over her emotions. The perverted experience with George Byce had shaken her badly, but all in all, she was thankful that oral sex was all that he had demanded from her. It could have been much worse. She had not had sexual intercourse with any man, since the rape occurred twenty-one years ago. Many men had tried over the years, but the act never came to fruition. Macey wasn't entirely sure if she would ever be able to be an active participant in sex again. She was smart enough to realize that she should seek psychological help concerning this aspect of her life, but, she had not gathered the emotional strength needed to do that yet.

"What are you thinking about, sis?" Jacob lay on Macey's sofa watching an Auburn University football game; as usual, his favorite college team was winning.

Macey sat in the recliner opposite him and pretended to watch the game. Instead, the horrible memories of what she had been forced to do with George Byce continued to drill through her mind. Scott's smiling face and welcoming kiss yesterday had not been enough to fully deplete her memories of what had happened to her last Wednesday.

"Yo! Mace!"

Macey glanced idly at her brother. That faraway look was still etched upon her face. "What? Did you say something, Jacob?"

Jacob pushed up on his elbows and stared back at her. "You were a thousand miles away just now. I bet you were thinking about your boyfriend across the street, huh?"

Macey blushed. She stood up and stretched her slender limbs. "No, and he's *not* my boyfriend. I was...just thinking about something at work."

"Hey, am I keeping you from getting something done? If I am, I can finish watching the game at home. Mama's visiting some of her church friends and Pop's helping old man Jernigan fix the roof on his workshop."

Macey smiled and shook her head. "No, don't be silly. You're not keeping me from anything. By the way, you never did tell me about your Thanksgiving. Did you have a nice one? I guess Mama fixed all your favorite dishes."

Jacob smiled and rubbed his belly. "Did she ever! She is one helluva cook. I'm gonna miss that when I move to Florida. She made a seven-layer chocolate cake and I ate the whole thing, except for one piece. Good manners demanded that I had to offer the *good Reverend* a piece."

"Y'all had company for Thanksgiving? I didn't think Papa liked company...especially during the holidays."

"He doesn't. He doesn't like much of anything to tell you the truth. You know, Macey, he seems like one of the unhappiest people I know. Was he always like that?"

Macey smiled as she allowed herself to remember times during her early childhood when their father would take turns spinning her and Kacey around and around, giving them piggy back rides, and spending time with them at the playground. Even though he always showered more attention on Kacey, he usually set aside a small reserve for Macey, too. Macey guessed his feelings for her began to change when she reached puberty and her body began developing. Regardless of her countless denials, Macey knew that her father believed her to be wanton and too lustful for her age.

"Macey?"

Macey shook her head. "No, Jacob...Papa was not always an unhappy man. I don't think that happened until just before y'all moved to Columbus. Then, of course, I suppose after Kacey died..."

Jacob hesitated before making up his mind to proceed. "You know...I do know how she died, Macey," he said in a low voice.

Macey's head shot up and she stared at him, dumbfounded. "What do you mean, Jacob?"

"I mean...you and everyone else don't have to pussyfoot the truth around me. I never told our parents, but kids used to tease me about it years ago. I never believed the things they said, so...I looked it up at the library."

"Oh, Jacob," Macey walked over to him, sat on the couch, and wrapped her arms around him. "I had hoped you would never have to know. It was bad enough that Kacey had to suffer like she did...I didn't want you to suffer, too."

Jacob swallowed hard. He felt more than a little uncomfortable at having brought up the subject; nevertheless, he hoped to learn more about his other sister. "She did suffer...didn't she, Macey?"

Tears trickled down Macey's cheeks and she nodded. "Terribly, I'm afraid. The coroner reported that she died from asphyxiation; the impalement was, evidently, an afterthought on the killer's part. Are Mama or Papa aware of how much you know?"

Jacob shook his head. "Naw, I always let them think that I believed their story about her being killed in a car wreck. I guess they both thought I was too stupid to find out on my own what really happened...at least, I'm sure that's what Pop thought."

"Yeah, I know what you mean. Papa had a way of making people feel...insignificant," Macey mumbled, more to herself than to her brother. "God, that reminds me, Jacob," she exclaimed. She slapped her forehead. "I can't believe I forgot to ask you about it!"

"Ask me about what?"

"Well, you know, about a month or so ago, you told me that you slipped up and asked Mama about me? Has she mentioned me to you since then?"

Jacob patted her shoulder and remembered how close he had come to blowing things for Macey and himself. "No...don't worry, sis. I know I screwed up royally by letting that slip out, but, trust me...Mama still has no idea that you live in town or that we've been seeing each other."

"Oh, thank God," Macey exhaled. "You do realize how important it is that we keep that information from them, Jacob...at least until you move to Florida? After that, it won't matter. I can deal with them on my own... if I must. I just don't want you to get caught in the middle of anything ugly."

"Don't worry, sis," Jacob said. He retrieved his jacket off the back of the dining room chair and put his arm around her. "Come on, walk me to the front door." He gave her a bear hug and said, "They won't find out, Macey...at least not from me, okay? Listen, I'm gonna get out of here and let you get some work done"

"You really don't have to go, Jacob. I can work later tonight. There's plenty of time."

Jacob opened the front door and looked upward at the company of clouds beginning to threaten the afternoon skies. "Well, I'd better get going anyway. It looks like it's going to be a nasty night. I'll talk to you later in the week though. Okay?" He was half-way to his truck when he turned around and ran back. "Man, I almost forgot to tell you what I came over to tell you today! Do you remember me telling you about that friend of mine—the one I had follow Pop on his last out- of- town trip?"

Macey thought for a moment before nodding her head. "Yeah...I remember...why? Did he find out anything?"

Jacob scratched his head and raised his eyebrows in question. "I'm not sure. I've got to do some more investigating. He told me that he followed Pop up to some hick town in Tennessee."

"Tennessee?"

"Yeah...weird, huh? I know he has some relatives up there somewhere, but we're talking like real distant relatives. Pete—that's my friend—said Pop stayed in this little run-down shack, and that the only other people there were some old lady—I'm talking like ancient, you know—and a young girl."

"A young girl?"

"Yeah...a girl, or a young woman. Pete couldn't tell how old she might be, but, he did say that she was quite a looker. He said she acted kind of weird, though."

"What do you mean...weird?"

"That's just it...I'm not sure. Pete's okay, but you can't really trust his opinion about anything. I think the best way for me to know for sure what's going on is for me to follow Pop myself the next time he leaves town."

"Why are you so interested in where he goes, Jacob?"

"Well, actually, I never was before...until Miss Becca asked me one day where he went on these trips. I guess I just got curious about it after talking to her."

Macey sighed. "Well, whatever he does or wherever he goes, I think you should just let it drop. If he ever found out that you were spying on him...well, I hate to think what he might do to you."

"Yeah, there's definitely no love loss there...at least not on his side. You know, I've always wanted him to love me, Macey, but, he never has. Hell, he's never even *pretended* to."

Macey looked at her handsome brother, who looked like a younger, taller version of their father. She wished that she could take away his pain; however, she was the last one who could do that because she had never known much of her father's love either—nor her mother's, for that matter. At least Jacob was secure in knowing how much their mother loved him. She pulled him to her and kissed his cheek. "He does love you, Jacob. I'm sure of that. Papa just doesn't know how to show it."

"Yeah, well...whatever," sniffed Jacob. He was suddenly ashamed for having let his sister catch him in a weak, emotional moment. "Hey, it doesn't really matter anymore, because...after Christmas...I'm outta here!"

Macey attempted to lighten the mood with her response. "Just save me a spot on the beach when I come to visit, kiddo."

Jacob grinned. "You know I will! Okay...I'm outta here," he laughed as he waved good-bye. "Talk to you later, sis."

"Bye, Jacob."

Jacob jumped into his truck and backed out of the parking space. His tires squealed in anticipation and he almost ran over Scott, who was returning from an afternoon jog. Jacob screeched to a half-stop, waved, and smiled apologetically. "Sorry, Scott!"

Scott returned the wave and poked his head inside the driver's window. "No problem! I got caught in a rainstorm—my pants were wet anyway!" Scott slapped the truck as it sped out of the parking lot. He glanced toward Macey's apartment just as her door was closing. He didn't know whether she had seen him, but something about her demeanor yesterday—when she picked him up from the airport—told him that she needed some time alone. He stood looking at her closed door for another minute, and fought the urge to invite himself over. He turned and walked slowly back to his own apartment.

Macey watched him from her living room window. A single tear escaped and gravitated downward. "One of these days, Scott, who knows...maybe I'll be worthy of your love; if not yours, then maybe someone else's. God, how I pray that really happens. I want to be able to really love someone...to trust someone completely. One of these days..."

Several miles away—across town—in a darkened bedroom, Ruth Wymer was indeed visiting one of her church friends. The good Reverend Dudley had become one of her best friends during the past year.

Ruth found herself in a position most requested by the good Reverend. Her hips were lifted off the bed and her feet wrapped tightly around his neck. She breathed heavily and tried to ignore the arthritic pain in her lower back while Lucas continued a relentless pump and grind motion. She found herself praying that his release would come soon because she didn't know how much longer she—or her aching back—could hang on. She was not nearly as young, or flexible, as she had been twenty years ago. Unfortunately, for her, Lucas Dudley's sexual demands normally mandated a great deal of flexibility on her part.

Lucas' incessant ramming ceased abruptly. "Damn! I can't finish this way—turn over, Ruth."

Ruth was still trying to catch her breath and was momentarily puzzled as to what he meant. "What?"

"Turn over! Quickly! Get on all fours."

"But..."

"*NOW* for God's sake! Do it now, Ruth!"

The look on his face terrified her, but she desperately needed her own release as much as he did, so she complied with his demand. She assumed he meant to enter her doggie-style. He often did that when he had trouble climaxing. However, she was totally unprepared for accepting him into the orifice in which he chose to enter. Ruth screamed out loud before her face was pushed down into the pillow.

The good Reverend's climax was immediate. Lucas left her lying in a fetal position and went into the bathroom to cleanse himself. When he came back into the bedroom, he noticed that she had not changed positions, and that she was crying. "What's the matter, Ruth?" he asked, nonchalantly, as he began to dress himself.

She exhaled deeply, rolled slowly onto her side, and stared at him through swollen, tear-filled eyes. "You hurt me..."

Lucas dismissed her admonishment with a flick of his hand. "Nonsense. Don't be ridiculous. If it hurt, then that only means you had a trace of evil trapped inside your body. What I did will help purify you... rid you of that evil from the inside out. You know all that. I've explained it to you at least a dozen times before. Sometimes...pain is the only way to renew the body and soul. Now, please...get dressed. There is something we need to discuss."

Ruth wrapped the top sheet around her and stumbled obediently to the bathroom. She ran a hot shower and remained there for several minutes. Her tears continued to flow, but when she finally exited the bathroom, some of the pain had dissipated and she felt calmer. She slipped into her bra and panties. When Lucas held out her dress for her, she stepped into it and nodded when he offered to zip it for her.

Lucas stood behind her like a proud peacock. He kissed her neck and placed both hands upon her shoulders. "Come into the living room, Ruthie," he whispered into her ear. He looked behind him at the disheveled bedding. "We must allow the evil to disperse from this room before we use it again."

Ruth shivered against him. "Again? You mean..." After what had just happened, Ruth wasn't sure she ever wanted to use the room again. She wasn't sure if she ever wanted to see *him* again.

Lucas kissed her neck again and laughed.

Ruth thought that his laugh sounded hollow—like it lacked any true emotion or sincerity.

He squeezed her shoulders. "Not *today*, silly woman."

Ruth tried to suppress her sigh of relief, but failed. "What do you want to talk about, Lucas?"

He pulled her into the living room and directed her to sit beside him on the couch. He decided to get right to the point, so he didn't hesitate in his reply. "It's about Macey. Did you know that she is here, Ruth—in Columbus?"

Ruth began to hyperventilate, and it took fifteen minutes before Lucas could calm her down enough to carry on with the conversation. "No... she...she can't be here," Ruth cried. She shook her head in disbelief. "You must be mistaken."

"No," Lucas replied with practiced confidence. "I've seen her myself... and, it gets worse, my dear woman. I've seen her...with Jacob."

Ruth covered her eyes with her hands. "Oh, God, no! No!" she wailed, "No, no...please, tell me it's not true."

Lucas rolled his eyes in exasperation. "You really must get control of yourself, Ruth, because...I'm afraid it is true. I saw the two of them together at a bowling alley...just a couple of weeks ago."

"I...I can't believe it, Lucas. Why? Why has she returned here? There's nothing—or no one—for her here."

"Jacob's here."

Ruth's head jerked up again. Her parental protection was evident in her grieved expression. "Do you think Jacob is the reason she's returned?"

Lucas shrugged. He could care less about Jacob. "I don't know, Ruth. There's a lot I need to consider before I come to any definite conclusions; however, I believe it's obvious that she doesn't want you or Andrew to know she's in town. Otherwise...I'm sure she would have been in contact with you before now."

Ruth shook her head vehemently from side to side. "No, I think you're wrong, Lucas. I don't think so. I think Andrew and I would be the last people she would let know." Ruth paused for a moment before asking. "How...how does she look, Lucas? What kind of woman has she grown into?"

Lucas wondered why Ruth would even want to know. She had never tried to hide her favoritism for Jacob over the twins. "Why...she's lovely... quite stunning, actually."

Ruth was still in disbelief. "Oh, my...if Andrew finds out she's in town...I don't want to think what he might do..."

Lucas was deep in thought about his own plans for Macey. He sighed in contemplation of the situation. "Well, let's not put the cart before the horse, shall we? I don't think you should discuss this just yet with

Andrew"

Ruth was dumbfounded. "What? Not tell him?"

"That's right, Ruth. After all, for all we know, Macey's stay may be short term...in which case, I see no need to upset Andrew unnecessarily. If she leaves, then he need never know she was ever here. No, I think it would be best for us to sit back and wait a while, until we see what Macey is up to."

A formidable look settled upon Ruth's troubled face. "I have a bad feeling about this, Lucas...a very, very bad feeling..."

CHAPTER 29

Two Weeks Before Christmas

Macey knelt before the toilet in Mr. Byce's private lavatory, quietly spewing out all evidence of their latest encounter. Once again, he had only demanded that she perform oral sex on him; Macey was eternally thankful that was all he seemed to want—for the moment, at least. She had remained celibate for the past twenty years, but, she had picked up some pointers about oral sex, from various discussions with Becca. She had been able to bring Byce to a quick climax, and end another one of his impromptu meetings with her.

Byce was fully dressed when she returned to his outer office, and looking quite pleased with himself. He straightened his tie and smiled at her as she picked up her files and moved quickly toward the locked office door. "Macey?"

She stopped but didn't turn around. She grasped the door handle tightly for support. "Yes, sir?"

"Thank you for stopping by again on such short notice. Unfortunately, these things can't always be scheduled."

Macey closed her eyes and pulled on her upper lip with her bottom teeth. "Is there anything else, Mr. Byce?"

George Byce stared hungrily at her rounded behind, accentuated beneath her black silk slacks. He was disappointed in himself that he had not been able to hold out longer than he had. It never dawned on him that Macey was deliberately keeping him from further sampling of her delicious commodities by speeding up the process. "No, Miss Garner, that's all...for now. I expect that we will need to meet again, very soon, to further discuss the international conference that you'll be heading. A lot of hard work will be involved in that effort. You may go back to work now. I will let you know when we need to meet again."

"Yes, sir," Macey mumbled as she eased open the door and slid outside. She was relieved to find herself alone in the corridor, and thankful that no one was nearby to witness her pallid, sweaty complexion. "Okay, Macey," she whispered. "You can do this...pull yourself together and just get on with it."

Work kept Macey busier than usual for the remainder of the week; and, fortunately, for her, it also kept Mr. Byce busy as well—too busy for her to be called up for any further *unscheduled* meetings. There were only two weeks to go before Christmas, and Macey was counting down the days for him to leave on an extended vacation with his wife. She would be free of his demands for two weeks while George and Sarah Byce accompanied their grown children to Colorado for their traditional family ski trip. If she was extremely lucky, Byce might not have the time and luxury of calling her back to his office before he left town; but, Macey doubted if fate would be that kind to her—it never had been before.

A light tap on her door dragged her attention away from the computer data she was analyzing. Macey glanced up to see Janet standing in the doorway. She did a double take when she saw the receptionist. She was not convinced that it was really Janet standing before her.

Janet looked like a different person, dressed in a demure, below-the-knee, empire dress. The change was remarkable! The gaudy, over-stressed makeup and hair were gone. A soft blush caressed her cheeks, while a pale-pink lipstick provided the merest hint of color to her lips. Her thick, red hair was tied loosely, with a white satiny ribbon, at the nape of her neck. A few wispy bangs framed her beautifully-transformed face. The bright nail polish—a characteristic trademark—had been replaced with a pale pink gloss that matched her lipstick.

"Janet?" Macey finally acknowledged.

Janet grinned and spun around to model her new look. "Quite a change, huh?" she bantered.

Macey came from behind her desk and walked forward slowly for a closer look. "That's the understatement of the year...yes...quite a change, indeed. I can't believe it's you. You look...stunning, Janet."

"Thanks." Janet took a deep breath and exhaled. "It's going to take some getting used to, though. I've never dressed like this before. It feels a little weird, you know?"

Macey was dumbfounded—pleasantly so. "Do I dare ask, what—or who—brought about this change?"

Janet raised her eyebrows at Macey. "I think you probably know."

Macey nodded and held her chin between her thumb and forefinger. "Jacob?"

Janet nodded and said, "Yeah, it's your little brother all right. He's really something special, Miss Garner."

Macey grinned back. "You won't get an argument from me about that, Janet."

"By the way, Miss Garner, I've...been meaning to ask...but, why is it that the two of you don't have the same last name?"

Macey's smile disappeared and her body tensed. "What?"

"You know...Garner...Wymer? I'm guessing that Garner must be your married name, right?"

Macey had no intentions of confiding any personal information to Janet Ward, no matter how much the young woman had managed to attach herself to Jacob during the past few weeks. "Right..." Macey mumbled softly, almost beneath her breath.

Janet looked puzzled before continuing. "Yeah...I sort of figured that must be what it was, but, you know...when I looked up your personnel records, they didn't indicate that you were divorced or widowed..."

Macey quickly lost patience with Janet's innocent interrogation about her marital status. "You checked my personnel records? You had no right, or business, to do that, Janet. Did it ever occur to you that my marital status was none of your business? Besides, a lot of divorcees categorize themselves as being single, don't you think?" Macey knew she had to get Janet's mind off the subject at hand. "Enough of that...I really do like the changes you've made to yourself. I hardly recognized you." It was so easy to manipulate the woman. Macey knew that turning the topic of conversation back on Janet would be the quickest way to sidestep the worrisome line of questioning into Macey's marital background.

It worked.

"Oh, yeah?" Janet grinned and ran her hands over the dress. "You know...Jacob has never said anything about the way I dress; but, sometimes I just get the feeling that...I don't know...that, maybe, he might be a little embarrassed to be seen with me."

"Oh, I doubt that, Janet. You're a very beautiful young woman. I'm sure any man would be proud to be seen with you."

Janet did not appear to be in any hurry to leave. She hesitated before she continued. "Miss Garner...there's, uh...something else I've been meaning to discuss with you. It's about Scott."

Macey's heart raced at the mention of Scott's name. "Mr. Pennell? What do you mean, Janet?"

"Well, you know how rumors fly around this place. I thought you might have, you know…maybe…heard some things."

"Such as?"

"Well, you know…about me and him."

Macey forced a smile. She had heard plenty of rumors, but she had believed Scott when he said he had only been intimate with Janet the one time. "I don't put much stock in rumors, Janet. Besides…what makes you think I would care about any rumors circulating about you and Mr. Pennell?"

Janet looked surprised. "Well, I guess I thought you had a thing for him. I mean…"

"A *thing* for him?"

"Well, yeah…I mean…I know he likes you…a lot."

"How do you know that, Janet?"

Janet's mouth gaped in mock astonishment. "God, you'd have to be like…blind…not to see that, Miss Garner! The man lights up every time you come near him. If you ask me, he looks like a man in love."

This conversation had definitely become much too personal for Macey's liking. She decided it was time to bring it to a close. "Well… Scott has been a good friend, but, that's all he is…a friend. Now…is there some specific reason you came in…other than to show off the new you? Something I can do for you?"

Janet slapped her hand lightly against her forehead. "Man, just listen to me going on and on. You must think I'm some sort of fruitcake! I came in to bring you these messages I took while you were in the staff meeting."

Macey took the messages from Janet's extended hand. "Thank you, Janet. Well…I suppose we both need to get back to work."

Janet made no move to leave and Macey looked at her questioningly. "Is there something else, Janet?"

Janet pointed to the stack of messages. "There's one in there that's probably more important than the others. It's from Mr. Byce. He wants to see you in his office at two o'clock. He said you should bring the international training conference files, and that you shouldn't keep him waiting."

Janet noticed the sudden paling of Macey's face; she, also, thought she knew what had caused it. "Remember how I told you about the rumors that fly around this place, Miss Garner?"

Macey's hands were trembling. She had prayed that she wouldn't have to accommodate George Byce before he left to go out of town, but, it didn't look like that prayer was going to be answered. Her voice trembled almost as much as her hands did. "I'm sorry…what did you say, Janet?"

"The rumor mill? Well, it says that you're...uh...Mr. Byce's latest play thing. The truth is...he hasn't bothered me in weeks, so I figured he must have found someone else. I just didn't know...I mean, I never thought it would be..."

Macey returned an icy glare and pointed a finger at Janet. "I've never put much stock in office gossip, Miss Ward, and, I suggest that you and everyone else in this company practice doing the same."

Janet was embarrassed. "Oh, Geez, I'm really sorry. I didn't mean to..."

Macey was embarrassed at her own harsh outburst, so she softened her reply. "It's okay, Janet, but, really...you cannot believe everything you hear. Please do me a favor, and try to refrain from participating and spreading rumors like that."

Janet was more than eager to make up for her unsolicited comments. "I won't, and I'm so sorry if I've upset you."

Macey only nodded as she returned to her desk.

"I'm really, really sorry..." Janet whispered as she backed out of Macey's office and closed the door softly behind her. She backed into Scott as the door closed, and she jumped when he grabbed her by the waist to keep her steady.

"Excuse me, Miss..." he stammered while trying to maintain his own balance.

Janet turned around and smiled.

Scott looked incredulous. "*Janet*? "Is that you?"

"It's me, all right! How do you like the new me?"

Scott stared in awe at the amazing transformation standing before him. "You look great—better than great—*wow*!"

"Thanks, Scott. I kind of like this look, too. I'm thinking I might keep it for a while, but, that means I've got a lot more shopping to do. I don't have many outfits like this in my closet."

"You really do look fantastic, Janet. I like the new you."

Janet lifted her head proudly. "The old me would have taken that comment as a proposition, Scott, but the new me will just say...*thanks*."

"You're welcome. By the way, is Macey in her office? I need to go over some training stats with her."

Janet put a hand on his chest to stop him before he opened the door. "Scott? Do you pay any attention to the gossip mill around this place?"

"Not if I can help it," Scott laughed. "Why?"

Janet sighed, unsure if she should continue, especially since she had promised Macey not to participate in spreading rumors. However, in the end, she decided that Scott needed to know what people were saying—

if he hadn't already heard. "Well...the latest rumors involve Mr. Byce and Miss Garner...if you know what I mean."

"What!" Scott blurted. "What the hell are you talking about, Janet?" He shook her by her shoulders hard enough to loosen the ribbon holding back her hair.

"Scott, you're hurting me," she whimpered.

He quickly released his hold on her. "I...I'm sorry, Janet, but...explain yourself, please..."

Janet rubbed her sore shoulders. "Well...the ladies are all saying that Macey has been locked inside Mr. Byce's office several times over the last few weeks."

"What do you mean...locked inside!"

"Trust me, Scott...I know better than anyone what goes on behind Mr. Byce's locked office door. Anyway...one of the ladies...I won't mention who...has listened in at the door more than once."

Scott couldn't believe what he was hearing, but the insinuations would explain Macey's sullen moods and returned frigidity these past few weeks. "And..."

Janet shrugged and looked uncomfortable. "Well...you know..."

Scott knew all right. "That son-of-a-bitch..." He turned and walked back to his office, hoping beyond hope that it wasn't true.

Scott was sitting at his desk a few minutes before two o'clock—head in hand—when he looked up and saw Macey walk past. He watched as she entered the elevator. She never lifted her head—she kept her eyes down, looking at the floor. She seemed to be totally absorbed in her own thoughts, and from the forlorn look on her face, he knew where she was probably headed.

He allowed her a five-minute lead before he grabbed a handful of files and took the stairs—in lieu of the elevator—to George Byce's office. He knocked quickly and entered the office before receiving permission to do so. He bumped squarely into his supervisor just as Byce was reaching across Macey to lock the door.

Scott literally pushed himself inside and grinned innocently. "Hello, Mr. Byce! Hi, Macey. I'm glad I finally found you. I've been looking for you all over the building."

George Byce was not a happy camper. He was seething with resentment at Scott's blatant interruption. "Something we can do for you, Scott?"

"Yes, sir, there is. I do apologize for interrupting your meeting, but

I've got the international folks holding on a conference call, and, I need Macey to corroborate some data she and I collected for them."

"I'm sure this can wait until Miss Garner and I finish our meeting, Scott."

"Ordinarily, it could, sir, but...these fellows are pretty insistent. They need to know some of the background research stats that went into the analysis, and Macey is the expert on all that." Scott looked at Macey and smiled.

Macey looked at Mr. Byce for silent permission to leave.

George Byce closed his eyes and sighed. "Very well, take her with you. We can continue our meeting after the phone call."

"Well, this may take a while, Mr. Byce," Scott spoke matter-of-factly. "And if I looked at my calendar correctly, you and I have that meeting with the Rotary Club at three o'clock, remember?"

Byce slammed his hand hard upon his desk in frustration. "Damn! I'd forgotten about that stupid-ass meeting."

"It's good for our public relations, sir, and I know they're looking forward to hearing your speech."

"Yes, yes, I know. Go ahead then, go on! I'll get back to you, Miss Garner."

"Yes sir," Macey replied while offering a silent prayer of thanks to God for sending Scott along when He did.

She and Scott rode the elevator down without speaking a word to each other. She rushed into Scott's office and saw the telephone, void of any blinking lights. She looked back at Scott with a puzzled expression. "There's no one on the phone, Scott...we must have lost the connection. I'll have Janet to get them back on the line..."

Scott closed the door behind him.

Macey heard the lock turn in place. She tried to decipher the strange expression on his face—it looked like *relief*—as he walked slowly toward her. "Scott?"

He placed a finger upon her lips and shook his head. He leaned down and kissed her.

Macey tensed when his arms folded her in a light embrace, but quickly relaxed as she accepted the comfort and security his arms offered her.

The kiss was gentle, but very long...and very sensuous. When it ended, Scott shook his head again and whispered, "No...don't say anything, Macey. We've got almost an hour to kill, so...what do you say...let's kill it."

CHAPTER 30

THE ATTACK ON BECCA

It was late Saturday afternoon, December 16, and Becca sat alone at her parents' kitchen table. She was drinking coffee and scanning through old newspaper clippings about the 1969 murder of Kacey Wymer.

Carlton Brown had left town this morning to spend the holidays with his extremely large family in Opp, Alabama. Becca was especially looking forward to his return before New Year's Eve, because she had some special plans involving the two of them to welcome in 1990.

She looked up from her reading and watched while her father shuffled slowly into the kitchen. Facet arthritis had invaded Alvin's back many years before, and it always pained Becca to watch him move— albeit—probably not as much as it pained him to do so. She marveled the fact that he never complained about any discomforts he might be experiencing. She knew that he had—quite simply—learned to live with it, and she admired him for that.

"Whatcha doin' sittin' in here all by yourself, girl?" he smiled back at her and poured himself a cup of the strong Java.

Becca returned his smile. "Well, Daddy, I just didn't feel up to watching another episode of Amos 'n Andy with you and Mama!" Amos 'n' Andy was an American-classic television comedy that ran during the 1950s. It was set in Harlem—the historic black community in Manhattan, and offered a look at how black families lived.

Alvin made a shooing motion with his large, callused hand. "Now you know that ain't true, girl! Your mama and me didn't watch that stupid show thirty-five years ago, and we sure ain't got no use for it now. Besides, I could be wrong, but I don't think the NAACP would allow any re-runs of that show to be seen! That would give them something to protest, for sure, don't you know!"

Becca laughed out loud and pushed back her chair. She walked over and hugged her father. "That's where you're wrong, Daddy." She kissed him on the cheek. "They did allow re-runs of the show from 1954 through 1966."

Alvin grinned back. "Well, ain't you just a bucket full of information?" He patted her hand and sat down at the kitchen table. "Are you hanging out with the old folks tonight, or are you seeing that young man again? We're not complaining, mind you, but we ain't use to seeing you on the weekends, girl."

"That young man has a name—Carlton Brown. No, I won't be seeing him tonight. He left this morning for Opp. His family is planning a big get-together over the holidays."

"Does he come from a big family?" Alvin asked. He positioned himself as comfortably as was possible in the straight back chair.

Becca nodded. "Yeah, he's the youngest of—let's see—thirteen, so, there are lots of grandkids, too."

Alvin sighed at the thought of grandkids. Becca was his only child, and she showed no signs of settling down any time soon and making him a grandfather—at least—not until Carlton Brown had entered the picture. Alvin had been wondering for several weeks if this young man might be the one to persuade his daughter to give up her care-free, single life style. He took another loud sip of coffee and nodded his head slowly. "Grandkids, huh?"

Becca leaned down and kissed him on the cheek again. "Let's not go there, Daddy. Besides, don't worry...I promise to make you a granddaddy one of these days."

Alvin raised his eyebrows in practiced doubt. "Just do me one favor, girl, and make sure you be married first!"

Becca laughed out loud and rubbed her father's bald head. "I can't make any promises along those lines, Daddy, but...I'll do my best. Hey, listen...I gotta go. I want to stop by Macey's before I head home. I know Mama's asleep in the living room. Give her a kiss for me and tell her I'll see her tomorrow after church."

"You know you don't have to keep helpin' out at the restaurant, Becca. Your mama's all better now. Her hip healed just fine. The two of us can run that place. You need to get yourself a real job. That's why we worked and saved to send you to college...so you wouldn't have to work as hard as we did for the rest of your life. We want somethin' better for you, Becca."

Becca exhaled softly. She had heard this same speech countless times during the past year. "I know, Daddy. I appreciate all that you and Mama have done for me...and, don't worry. I'm going to start teaching again. I've been giving it a lot of thought lately. There's a position opening in September—at one of the high schools. I've been thinking that I might apply for it. I think I'd like to work with teenagers."

Alvin James smiled and nodded. "That would make me and your mama happy, girl."

Becca folded the newspaper clippings and slipped them inside the back pocket of her jeans. She grabbed her car keys off the kitchen counter and opened the back-screen door, which squeaked in protest. She looked back at her father and offered a slight grin and wink. "Who knows, Daddy...the students may even be calling me Mrs. Brown by then, instead of Miss James."

"Lord a Mercy! That sure would tickle your mama to death, girl. Yessiree...tickle her to death."

"Bye, Daddy...see you tomorrow."

"Bye, Becca...I love you, girl."

Becca cast a quick, parting glance at her father and returned his generous smile. "I love you more, Daddy."

Alvin rose stiffly from his sitting position and ambled over to the screen door. It was only late afternoon, but the skies were dark and angry-looking as a light mist began to fall. He waved to Becca as she pulled out of the driveway.

A dark-colored BMW was parked across the street, and the driver started its engine and pulled in behind Becca as she drove away. Alvin didn't think anything unusual about this until the man and woman inside the car turned to stare at him as they drove past. He shivered involuntarily at the cold, calculating look they leveled upon him. "Mercy, me!" he shivered. "I sure would hate to pass them folks in a dark alley."

"I don't understand, Lucas. Tell me again why we're following this woman."

Lucas Dudley glanced idly in the direction of his companion and wished—once again—that he had never gotten mixed up with the Wymer family. Things had gone downhill for him ever since the night he had initiated his spiritual cleansing upon Macey. Ever since that night, his life had consisted of one episode of bad luck after another. He had offered his services to so many churches over the past twenty years, and they had all eagerly accepted his offer. However, after several months, they would rescind that offer and pay a small severance for his limited time and services. He had to squander aside a percentage of the congregations' weekly tithes to maintain his desired level of living. He figured it was only a matter of time before his present congregation decided on a similar course of action. It had been so much easier, twenty years ago, to convince church members of the importance for the body to be spiritually cleansed.

"Lucas? Did you hear me?"

He glanced sharply at Ruth Wymer and gritted his teeth. How could he *not* hear her—the woman never shut up! Although she was reasonably attractive for a woman her age, she was about forty years older than he preferred his women to be. The young ones! Oh, how he hungered for their firm, pure bodies. His need for them was like an addiction for which there was no cure. He wasn't entirely sure he would accept a cure if one was offered. "I heard you, Ruth. As I've already explained to you, this woman is a friend of Macey's. I've been watching her for several weeks now to see if she would reveal anything for me."

"But...she's *black*, Lucas! I really don't think Macey would take a black person into her confidence. I doubt this woman knows anything useful."

Lucas sighed and counted mentally to ten before continuing. "I disagree, Ruth. I think she may know quite a lot. Macey does not have a lot of friends, so, I think—if she has confided to anyone—that it will have been to this woman. Just trust me on this."

"But you can't just go up to her and make her tell you what you want to know. She'll go straight to Macey and tell her all about us."

Lucas forced a tolerant smile. "Maybe it would be best if I take you home, Ruthie. Maybe you don't really want to be involved in any of this? Maybe...you want Macey to corrupt Jacob's thoughts and feelings about you...to take him away from you? Is that it? Is that what you want, Ruth? Because you do know that is exactly what is going to happen...if it hasn't already."

Ruth shook her head vehemently. "My Jacob! Oh, God, no! You don't really think she would turn him against me, do you? Oh, Lucas, that can't happen. Jacob is my life. I...I'd rather see her dead than..."

Lucas raised his eyebrows in surprise. "You'd see your own daughter dead? Wasn't the loss of one child enough, woman?"

Ruth raised her chin in defiance to his questions. "Macey stopped being my daughter when she ran off with her baby and deserted her family. She made her decision then, and I will not allow her to influence my son with her selfish, thoughtless ways. Never!"

Lucas slowed the car and pointed up ahead. "Look...she's turning into Macey's apartment."

Ruth looked around at the elegant grounds surrounding Whispering Hills. "I can't believe Macey can afford to live here..." she mumbled beneath her breath.

"Oh, yes, Ruth...your daughter has done quite well for herself. I have uncovered a lot of information about Macey. She has a college degree in computer science, holds a very prestigious job with CompuTech Corporation, and—trust me—she can more than afford to live here." Lucas paused and sighed. "What I haven't been able to find out, however...is what happened to her child."

"What do you mean?" Ruth queried as they pulled into an empty parking space and watched while Becca let herself into Macey's apartment.

"I mean...there's no sign of a child anywhere."

"Well, for Heaven's sake," sniffed Ruth. "In case you've lost total track of time, Lucas, we're not talking about a *child* here. Macey's daughter would be twenty years old now...certainly no longer a child."

Lucas jerked around in his seat and glared at Ruth. "How do you know the baby was a girl?"

"What..." Ruth began as she squirmed within the small confine of the front seat. The angry look on his face terrified her.

He grabbed her by the shoulders and shook her so hard that Ruth feared her eyeballs would jar themselves lose from their sockets.

"Lucas, stop it...you're scaring me..."

Lucas was in a stupefied daze. His hands squeezed harder. "You said her child was a *daughter*! How do you know that?"

Ruth feared the black ire evident in Lucas's glazed expression. "Andrew told me...when he came back from Madison. He said...he said that Macey ran away one night about two weeks before the baby was due. She didn't want him to give the baby away, but he insisted it was the only thing to do. It was the best thing to do for the baby."

Lucas's grip on her arm tightened even more. He was trying hard to reign in his temporary loss of control. "You mean it was the best thing for Andrew to do, don't you...to save face!"

"No!" Ruth shrieked. "It wasn't like that! Yes...we were ashamed of what she had done, but...Andrew just said the baby would be better off with a family that could afford it...a family who could offer it all the things that Macey would never be able to on her own."

"You still haven't explained how Andrew knew it was a girl. If Macey left before the baby was born..."

"She wrote a short letter to her Aunt Chloe in Madison. There was no return address, but it was postmarked from some small town in

Tennessee. All it said was that she had taken her daughter away to raise her the way *she* saw fit, and that she didn't want any help from her family."

Lucas' mind was churning a mile a minute. A daughter! Somewhere, he had a daughter!

The thoughts continued to roil inside his head. Maybe this was the salvation his empty soul had searched for all these years...someone to love him unconditionally...to finally make him feel complete. He never had anyone to love him that way. There had always been stipulations attached to any relationship he encountered. Everyone expected him to change his ways and his thinking. No one wanted to accept that his way was the right way—the holy way—the only way. He sighed deeply and allowed himself to momentarily enjoy the sudden discovery that he had a daughter.

"Is she married, Lucas?"

He blinked a few times when Ruth's question dragged him back to the present. "What?"

"Macey...is she married?"

Lucas shook his head and turned to stare at the closed door to Macey's apartment. "No...not that I've been able to determine. She goes by the name of Macey Garner, so maybe she was married at one time...I don't know."

Ruth looked surprised. "Garner? Why that's my maiden name! She's using my maiden name? Why would she do that?"

It was Lucas' turn to be surprised. What reason *could* Macey have for using her mother's maiden name? An explanation—one that seemed reasonable—suddenly came to him. "Well, it's obvious that she can't use her real last name, woman. Use your head and think. Someone would surely remember what happened twenty years ago, and that would draw too much attention to her. I have a feeling that Macey has deliberately kept a low profile over the past twenty years. She may not be married, but she does have a boyfriend."

Ruth looked interested. "Really?"

Lucas nodded and pointed in the direction of Scott's apartment. "Yes, and he lives just over there."

"What's his name?"

Lucas shrugged and returned his attention to Macey's apartment. Several lights had been turned on after the black woman let herself in. "I don't know yet. I've been focusing all my attention on finding out about Macey, so I haven't really paid him much attention." He glanced quickly back toward Scott's apartment. "Well, what do you know...there's lover boy now...taking out his trash. Do you see him, Ruthie...over there? That's your daughter's current lover."

Ruth squinted her eyes for a better look, but had to wait until Scott walked under the street light before she got a better look at him. Her first thought was that he was a handsome man. She watched him as he bent down to pet a stray cat that had wandered over to him. There was something about him...something vaguely familiar about him...

She continued to watch him for several more minutes while he played with the cat. It came out of nowhere—the impact of her sudden recognition struck her like a bolt of lightning. "Oh my, God..." she gasped. "Oh, dear, God...it's *him*..."

Lucas turned back and became concerned at the shocked look upon her face. He grabbed her arms again in a tight grip. "Ruth, what's wrong? Are you all right? Ruth! Talk to me, woman!"

She turned her head slowly in his direction, and the tears flowed freely down her cheeks.

Lucas thought that she looked quite ridiculous—and very unkempt—as mucous leaked from her nose, and her bleeding mascara effected a raccoon-like appearance.

Ruth knew that Lucas detested weak women, and, especially, women who resorted to tears to get their way with men. However, she was helpless to stem the flow of tears that continued to ebb from her swollen eyes. She looked back toward Scott and whispered in awe and disbelief. "It's him...it's really him."

Lucas was quickly losing patience with her. "Who? Who is he?" he practically screeched. He shook her again—this time, hard enough to pop a button on her blouse. The exposure of her limp, saggy breast did not faze him.

Ruth continued to stare at him with a glazed look, but, somehow found the strength to respond. "Scott Pennell. That man is Scott Pennell, and...you say...he's Macey's *boyfriend*?"

Lucas immediately released his grip upon her shoulders and pondered this latest revelation. "Isn't he the one the police arrested for Kacey's murder?"

Ruth nodded. Her eyes were dry now, but her breathing was labored. "They arrested him, but, he didn't kill her. I know he didn't kill her..."

Scott turned to walk back to his apartment.

Lucas grew disgusted with Ruth's babbling and quickly focused his attention on Scott. He wasn't sure how he could use this newfound information, but, he felt it might prove to be invaluable in the days to come. He was so engrossed in his own thoughts that he almost missed

Becca as she was leaving Macey's apartment.

Ruth tugged on his sweater and motioned in Becca's direction. "Lucas! Look, that black woman is leaving. Please...can we go now? It's been a long day and I'm tired. I'd like to go home."

Lucas ignored Ruth's plea to leave and quickly opened his door. "Wait here, Ruth."

"Where are you going, Lucas?"

"I said...wait here, Ruth. I'll only be a minute."

"But, Lucas..." Ruth whimpered as he shut the door quietly behind him. She covered her face with her hands and resumed crying. She wanted to go home. She was so tired—so very tired. "I'll just lay down... close my eyes..." she whispered into the darkness of the early evening.

Lucas had acted on sheer instinct. He had not planned his next move. He weaved stealthily—in and out—between the parked cars. Becca had parked her car across the parking lot from Macey's apartment, and Lucas reached it at the exact same instant she did.

Becca gasped when she felt one strong hand press roughly against her mouth, and another grab her firmly around the waist. She was about to bite down on the hand when she felt something sharp poke against her side. She felt sure it was a knife.

"Do exactly as I say, bitch, or—trust me—you will not like what happens."

Becca's eyes grew large with fear when she quickly realized that she was completely overpowered by the man's size and strength. She struggled in vain, and tried not to panic when the man dragged her backwards. She continued to squirm as he moved quickly between two buildings, and around to the wooded area located behind Scott's building. Her muffled pleas grew louder when she saw Scott's shadow play against his dimly-lit dining room window. He was so close, but she was afraid no one could help her now—not even Scott. She had no idea who her attacker was, or what he wanted, but for the first time in her life, Becca James felt out of control and powerless to prevent what was about to happen to her.

CHAPTER 31

SCOTT FINDS BECCA

Scott woke up earlier than usual on Sunday morning.

A restless, fitful sleep the night before had generated countless mini-dreams. Most of them included Macey—a much younger version of the Macey he knew. The dreams were confusing in that he and Macey were teenagers, fumbling with each other inside a red Volkswagen, and swapping sloppy, passionate kisses and amateurish caresses. Songs from the late fifties and sixties flitted throughout the dreams. The focus in most of these mini-dreams centered around Scott's primary intention—to persuade the young Macey to have sex with him.

The last dream was the one that jolted him wide awake.

Instead of whispering gentle persuasions in her ear and enjoying her lustful expression, he found himself kissing her grotesquely swollen face—a face that laughed back at his panicked expression. Scott bolted to a sitting position in bed—wide awake—-with perspiration beading his forehead and chest. "Where the hell did that come from?" he croaked as he rolled out of bed.

He thought an early morning jog might be just the anecdote to clear his head and to dissipate the depression that threatened his normally good mood. He and Macey had made plans to go Christmas shopping later in the day, and, he didn't want this unwelcomed depression to spill over into their time together. He quickly threw on a pair of sweats and his running shoes, brushed his teeth, and ran out his back door.

He took a few minutes to perform his routine stretches. He breathed in the crisp December air, listened to the orchestra of birds perched in the trees, and decided to run the wooded trail behind his apartment building. He ran hard for a mile, made a U-turn, and began a slower pace back toward his apartment. The mood caused by the early morning dream was slowly evaporating, along with the lifting fog that surrounded the woods. He began whistling a tune—*The Lion Sleeps Tonight*—from the late sixties, and found that his mood had lifted with the fog. He began to anticipate his day ahead with Macey. He was within a hundred feet of his back door, and was not paying much attention to his surroundings.

That's when he almost stepped on it.

The fog was so thick when he first left his house, that he had not seen it then.

He came to an abrupt halt. Surely, his mind must be playing tricks on him. Scott inched forward and squatted down for a closer inspection.

There it was. He wasn't imagining it. A human hand—-a brown hand—clutched at the dirt beneath his feet.

"Oh, shit..." Scott's mumbled brain managed to convey his thoughts.

He remained in his squatted position and stared at the hand. His first thought was that it might reach out and grab him—like it would in any good horror movie. If that did happen, then it meant that whoever was attached to the hand had to be alive. When that didn't happen, Scott stood up and nudged it slightly with the toe of his Nike. If this was a crime scene, then he had seen enough television shows and movies to know that he shouldn't touch anything. His eyes followed the length of the hand to an attached arm. The trail of skin ended at the elbow. The remainder of the body had been sloppily hidden beneath a mound of wet pine straw and leaves.

His brain still refused to acknowledge the fact that there might be an actual body lying beneath the mound. He was terrified of what he might find beneath the leaves, but he reacted quickly after that. He dropped to his knees and brushed away the pine straw and leaves—so much for contaminating a crime scene.

The rest of the body was there—much to his relief. As much as he hated finding a body at all, he would have been horrified to have found only part of a body. The body lay belly-down in the softened earth. It was a black woman—a partially-nude black woman. Her face was turned away from him, but Scott could tell from her swollen profile that she had been badly beaten. Her back and buttocks were bare of any clothing— her jeans piled around her ankles.

Scott placed two fingers along the woman's neck, certain that she was dead and that he would not find a pulse. He uttered a small gasp when he felt a slight pulse. It was an extremely weak pulse, but it was there—she was alive! He racked his brain for the appropriate first-aid procedures to follow. It was cold outside and he knew it was important to keep her warm; but, he was reluctant to move her—fearful that his actions could result in more permanent damage.

It was a chilly, thirty-three degrees and frost still covered the morning ground. Scott was torn between carrying her inside, to his apartment, or, rushing home to call 911 for help. He quickly decided it would be better to leave her where he found her, so he removed his running jacket and used it to cover her bare shoulders. "Don't you die on me..." he whispered as he sprinted back to his apartment.

Once inside his apartment, he called 911 and explained to them what he had discovered. The operator tried to keep him on the phone after she obtained his address, but he said he needed to go get back to the woman. He grabbed a pillow and a wool blanket off the sofa and hurried back to the crime scene.

Part of him had hoped whoever it was had gotten up and walked away while he had been in his apartment—but he knew that wasn't going to happen. The body was still there—it had not moved.

Scott was still hesitant to move the body. The woman could have suffered spinal damage, so, he gently lifted her head to place the pillow beneath her. He left his jacket on her, but used the soft, wool blanket to cover her bruised and swollen body. "Dear, God..." he moaned when he imagined the pain she must have endured. He leaned in closer to look at the side of her face. Her eye was swollen shut, and her nose appeared to have been broken—it looked like it had bled profusely. Coagulated blood pooled in her right ear. Her lips were also swollen and caked with dried blood. Her face was grossly disfigured from the bruising and swelling, but, it was the dark marks upon her neck and shoulders that captivated Scott's attention.

Scott leaned closer to get a better look at the marks. They were human teeth marks! Something about those marks sparked a repressed memory for him, but it dissipated as quickly as it had manifested. He pulled the blanket up and tucked it in around the woman's body, hoping to ward off as much of the cold wind as possible. "Who would do something like this..." he groaned. He tucked the blanket beneath her bare hips. He lifted her limp hand and cradled it between the warmth of his own; there were teeth marks on the top of her hand, too.

Scott shook his head in disbelief as the gentle wind seemed to commiserate his thoughts throughout the woods. His peripheral vision caught a slight movement to the right of the body. He looked up in time to see several pieces of paper swirling in the wind. He gently released the woman's hand and reached out to grab the papers, just as they were about to blow away into the wood line. They appeared to be newspaper clippings, and judging by the yellowing of the paper, they were very old newspaper clippings. Scott turned one of the clippings over to read it, but stopped when he heard the wailing sirens. He shoved the clippings inside his pants pocket, without thinking, and ran to the front of his building to direct the police to the correct location.

He looked back once, at the broken body lying on the ground.

Scott never recognized Becca James.

Macey's bedroom window faced the parking lot, and she had left it slightly open the night before. Screaming sirens roused her from a deep sleep. She sat up in bed and listened intently to the hurried sounds outside. She could have sworn that she heard Scott's voice among the many that were rushing about. She jumped out of bed and pulled her curtain aside in time to see Scott leading a policeman to the back of his building. "Oh, God...what's wrong," she whispered as she quickly put on a pair of jeans.

She grabbed the first jacket she came to and threw it on over her flannel pajama top. The first shoes she came to were bedroom slippers, so she slipped them on quickly and rushed outside. She moved among the gathered crowd who were talking among themselves, trying to decipher what had happened. Several policemen surrounded the immediate area, but, they were all too engrossed in their respective duties to pay much attention to Macey's inquiries.

Macey moved toward Peggy Underwood, the apartment manager's wife, who stood among a small cluster of residents huddled beside a police car. "Peggy, do you know what's going on? I heard the sirens..." Macey began as she quickly maneuvered herself within the group.

"Macey...hi," Peggy shrugged. "Gosh, I don't know. I'm like you...I heard the sirens and rushed outside to see what was going on. I saw Mr. Pennell taking a policeman around back, but they won't let anyone back there."

An ambulance roared into the parking lot just then and two emergency medical technicians threw open the back doors, and pulled a portable gurney outside. They conferred with a policeman standing to the side of Scott's apartment building and disappeared around back. Several minutes later, the same technicians rushed back toward the ambulance. A body now occupied the previously empty space on the gurney.

Macey recognized the blanket that covered the body. She had seen it before in Scott's living room. The technicians pushed through the crowd and passed in front of Macey. She glanced down quickly at the victim's face. "Oh, God...NOOOO!" she screamed. Unlike Scott, she immediately recognized Becca James.

Scott heard Macey's piercing scream as he came around the building alongside a police officer. He made it to her side in time to collect her collapsing body. "Macey! Macey, what's wrong?"

Macey fell limp in his arms and looked up at him. Her hands covered her mouth in utter denial and she shook her head from side to side. Tears cascaded down her ashen cheeks and she stared back at him in bewilderment. She pointed toward the ambulance. "Bec...it's Becca..." she finally managed to gasp between her choking sobs.

Scott grabbed her hand and pulled her along behind him. He rushed to the ambulance just as the doors were about to slam shut. "Can we ride with her?" Scott implored. "She...she's a friend."

The EMT nodded hurriedly. "Sure, but hurry up, buddy. We have to get her to the hospital quick—hard to tell how long she's been exposed to the cold."

Scott jumped inside the ambulance and pulled Macey in behind him. "Thanks, appreciate it," he nodded to the technician.

Macey crawled over to Becca's side and took her cold hand between her own. Tears flowed fiercely down her cheeks. She closed her eyes in a silent prayer to God to please watch out for her best friend.

The crowd of bystanders watched the ambulance speed away, and the police began their questioning.

Nobody had seen or heard anything.

More than half-way across town, Lucas Dudley sat at his kitchen table. He was calm and relaxed while he drank coffee and perused the sermon he planned to deliver to his congregation later this morning. He was calm, but still found it hard to concentrate on the sermon; instead, his mind insisted on rehashing what had transpired the night before.

He really had not intended to hurt the woman. her. He only wanted information on Macey and the child.

He had slapped her around a few times, but, but the bitch refused to reveal any useful information. The slaps turned into punches, but the woman volunteered precious little information that he didn't already know about Macey. Lucas lost all patience with her when she denied knowing anything about a child. The punches turned to kicks when he knocked her to the ground. She stood up repeatedly, trying to fight back, until he finally stopped her. He picked up a large stone, and used it to hit her face and head—repeatedly—until she lost consciousness.

Lucas panicked when she lost consciousness. He lifted her by the shoulders and shook her hard. He needed her awake to answer his questions. The voices inside his head began to speak to him when the woman did not wake up. They taunted him and convinced him that the bitch had gotten the best of him. She had not provided any substantial information about his daughter.

Something snapped inside him at that moment. He looked down and saw the blood oozing from the woman's nose and ear. He thought he had killed her. He really thought that the battered body, lying before him on the ground, was void of any life.

The fact that she might be dead did not matter to him—it did not stop him from doing what he did next—from doing what the voices told him to do. He fell upon her and ripped her clothes from her battered body. He didn't want to take the time to remove her boots, so he left her jeans pooled around her ankles. He spread her legs as wide as the pooled jeans allowed. There was a moment—one quick moment—when he stopped and questioned himself; but, the voices inside his head continued to berate him. He looked around him for an object large enough to inflict the kind of punishment she deserved for her disobedience and obstinacy. He found what he was looking for when he spotted a half-rotted stump, approximately three inches in diameter. He lifted the stump heavenward and began chanting a prayer in a guttural, unknown tongue. He finished the prayer, opened his eyes, looked lovingly at the stump, and caressed it. Several splinters pierced his fingers.

There was no hesitation surrounding his next move. He kneeled between the legs of Becca James, lifted her hips off the ground with one hand, and used his free hand to bury the stump inside her womb. Pieces of the stump broke off—pieces of it remained inside Becca. Lucas flung what was left of the stump deep into woods. "Evil...so much evil is inside you, bitch...you must be purged of this evil..."

Lucas lifted Becca's limp body toward him and began the process of ridding her body of the evil hidden inside her. He began the process by biting and pulling at the skin around her neck, and eventually moved lower to her shoulders, chest, and midsection. He flipped her over on her stomach and bit her neck, shoulders, back, and buttocks. Pieces of her dark skin ripped away in the more tender sections of her body.

Lucas really thought she was dead.

He would have liked to continue with the spiritual cleansing process, but he remembered that Ruth was waiting for him in his car. It had been more than thirty minutes since he had followed Becca James to her car, and he was afraid that Ruth might come looking for him.

Lucas wiped the blood from his mouth and looked around him. He decided that these woods would be the perfect place to leave her—it would be days before she was discovered. He dragged the body further into the wooded area, and covered it with the plentiful pine straw and leaves that covered the ground. He zipped up his jacket to cover the blood stains on his white shirt and smoothed back his hair. He never noticed when the woman's hand crawled out from under the layer of needles and leaves. He moved quickly toward the parking lot and bumped directly into Ruth Wymer as he rounded Scott's building. She had indeed come looking for him.

"Lucas! Where have you been? I think I fell asleep. I want to go home, Lucas. Andrew will be wondering where I am."

Lucas avoided eye contact with her as he grabbed her arm and dragged her back to his car. "Let's go. I'm...finished here," he exacted.

They returned hurriedly to the parking lot, and Ruth allowed herself to be pushed unceremoniously onto the front seat of Lucas' car. She suddenly remembered what had happened before she fell asleep. She remembered Lucas had rushed to follow the black woman.

She quickly became suspicious of what may have happened. "What did you do to that woman, Lucas? You didn't hurt her, did you? Oh, God, please tell me you didn't hurt her..."

Lucas offered her an obligatory glance, and thought again about how much she disgusted him—how all women disgusted him. He forced a smile. "Don't be ridiculous, Ruth. No, of course I didn't hurt her. I only wanted to talk to her about Macey, but...she took off running. I chased after her for quite a while, but...never could catch up with her. You know how fast black people can run. Anyway...you're right, it is late. We need to get you home."

Lucas blinked hard and rubbed the bridge of his nose. He looked around him. He wasn't in the woods. It was Sunday morning, and he was getting ready to deliver another educational sermon to his flock. He closed his eyes briefly, exhaled slowly, gathered up his papers, and deposited his cup into the sink. He allowed himself one more memory from the night before. He smiled as he remembered last night's cleansing, and felt immense satisfaction for a job well done.

He threw back his head, closed his eyes, and recited Lamentations 3:1-6 and 3:26, the verses that would preamble his opening sermon this morning. "I am the man who has seen affliction by the rod of His wrath. He has led me and made me walk in darkness and not in light. Surely,

He has turned His hand against me time and time again throughout the day. He has aged my flesh and my skin, and broken my bones. He has besieged me and surrounded me with bitterness and woe. He has set me in dark places like the dead of long ago...It is good that one should hope and wait quietly for the salvation of the Lord."

Lucas was still thinking about Becca James an hour later when he closed his front door behind him. He felt pride in knowing that he had done his part to rid the world of the evil that lurked within the souls of so many. He looked heavenward and quoted another favorite verse. "Be ready, for the Son of Man is coming at an hour you do not expect."

CHAPTER 32

Becca Struggles to Survive

The carpet in the waiting room was already worn and tattered, and Macey added to it as she paced a slow, steady path across the small room. She looked nervously, back and forth, from Treatment Room Number Three to the emergency room's front door, where Scott stood giving his statement to a police officer. She watched as the two men shook hands and the officer left the building.

She and Scott walked quickly toward each other, and they came together in a fierce hug.

Scott pushed her hair back from her face. He smiled down at her and wiped away the tears that pooled in her eyes, and wished that he could wipe away the fear reflected on her beautiful face as easily. He led her back toward the waiting room. "Macey, did you call Becca's family?"

She wiped her nose on the sleeve of her jacket and nodded. "The police were going to do it, but they agreed to let me call them...they should be here any minute. Neither of them is any condition to drive—a neighbor is driving them."

Scott blew out a breath—one that he felt he had been holding in since he first discovered the body. "I still can't believe it." He shook his head in disbelief. "Who would do such a thing? Who would want to hurt her...like that?"

Macey lifted her head off his chest. "Scott, I still don't know everything...no one has told me exactly what happened. It looked like she had been beaten pretty badly."

Scott wasn't sure how much to tell Macey just yet. The police officer would not disclose any substantial information to him because he was not family, but, it didn't take a genius to figure out that Becca had been severely beaten, and—most likely—raped. Scott led Macey to a small sofa and, for the next several minutes, relayed how his early-morning run had ended with him discovering the body. He left out the gory details about the condition in which he found Becca's body.

Macey continued to cry.

Scott felt useless—he didn't know what else to do to ease her pain—so he continued to hold her against him while she cried. "So...the doctors haven't told you anything yet?" He pulled her closer to him.

Macey shook her head and swallowed a grievous lump that had collected in her throat. "Just that she's unconscious, has a severe concussion, and, some...internal bleeding. Oh, Scott! She's got to be all right! She's just go to be. She's my best friend..."

"I know..." Scott stroked her hair. "She's going to be fine...you'll see. We've got to believe that, Macey. Hey...can you just imagine what Becca would say if she knew we were this worried about her?"

Macey managed a small smile. "She would probably say something like, *get a grip, girlfriend.*"

"Yeah...among other things," Scott mulled.

The emergency room doors pushed open and Becca's aging parents stumbled inside. Alvin James was supporting his well-fed wife as best he could, but, it was obvious that every step was a test of endurance for his arthritic back.

Scott rushed toward them and assisted Alvin in lowering Mrs. James onto another cracked-vinyl sofa.

Mrs. James placed her hand over her heart and tried to catch her breath. "Where's my baby?" she cried, looking to Macey for reassurance.

Macey quickly joined her and put her arm around the woman who had been like a mother to her during the last five years. "They're working on her now, Mama James. The doctor should be coming out soon. He'll be able to tell us more when he finishes his examination."

Alvin's right hand moved to the crook of his back, while he tried to suppress the spasm of pain that ripped through it. He glanced quickly at Macey, but motioned Scott off to one side. "How is my Becca...really? What happened to her?"

Scott had enough respect for Alvin James not to attempt to sugar-coat what he knew to be the facts. He spent the next few minutes telling Alvin everything he knew. He saw the pain evident in the old man's glistening, aged eyes.

Alvin listened to everything without interrupting. When Scott finished his brief summation of what he knew, Alvin wiped away tears and looked him in the eye. "So, they think my girl was raped? They don't know for sure?"

Scott shook his head. "The police wouldn't give me any specifics on that, Mr. James, but, yes, it looks like she probably was raped."

Alvin moved slowly and stopped in front of the treatment room door. He squinted and looked through the narrow panels, trying in vain to get a look inside at his only child.

Scott came to stand beside him and placed a comforting arm across the old man's shoulder.

Mr. James sniffed loudly and smiled back when he saw the look of concern etched across Scott's face. "And you're the one who found her, son?"

"Yes, sir."

"Do they know how long she'd been there—laying outside in that cold?"

Scott ran his fingers through his hair and shook his head. "No, sir, not really; although, they think it was probably for several hours—maybe even overnight."

The old man's shoulders began to shake and he sobbed softly—careful not to let his wife see how upset he really was. "I just seen my girl last night. She left the house just after dark...said she needed to see Macey. I wonder if she ever got to see her?"

"I don't know," Scott pondered. "What do you say, let's ask Macey? That might be something the police would be interested in knowing, too."

Scott pulled Alvin away just as the emergency room door exploded outward, nurses and physician assistants running off in different directions. One of the assistants yelled out to the nurse at the reception desk. "Code Blue! STAT!"

Alvin and Scott leaned over to look inside the treatment room. Two doctors and several nurses were gathered around Becca. There were numerous machines and tubes hooked up to her body.

"We're losing her! Step back everyone!" the doctor closest to Becca yelled. His scrub suit was covered in blood...Becca's blood.

Scott felt Alvin stiffen and he pulled the old man away from the door. The Becca James fan club of four watched breathlessly, for the next several minutes, while the medical personnel fought to save Becca.

The medical team was on the verge of despair—about to give up—when the doctor who was most covered with Becca's blood shouted once again—this time in triumph. "She's back! We did it...she's back with us! Let's get her into the operating room, STAT. We've got to get the internal bleeding under control. Is anyone from her family here yet?"

An assisting nurse replied, "Yes, doctor, they're in the waiting room."

"Good. I'll talk to them now while you move this patient to the operating room. Let's go people!"

Alvin placed a hand on the doctor's forearm after Becca was wheeled past him. He hadn't even had time to touch her, to kiss her, or to wish her God's speed.

The doctor's initial expression conveyed impatience when he looked down at the old, black man who had grabbed his arm. However, it quickly dawned on him that this must be his patient's father. His expression softened and he led the old man to the sofa where an old, black woman sat quietly with a young, white woman. "You're Mr. James?" the doctor verified.

"Yessir," nodded Alvin, still clutching the doctor's sleeve. "I'm Becca's daddy...she's my baby girl. How's my girl, doctor? Is she gonna be all right? Where are they takin' her?"

"Mr. James...will you come with me, please?" The doctor guided Alvin to the sofa, and knelt in front of Mama James. He placed his hand upon the old woman's hand. "Mrs. James...?"

Mama James nodded and continued to hold tightly to Macey's hand.

The doctor stood up and motioned for Alvin to have a seat beside his wife. He rubbed the back of his neck. It had been a long night—one that did not promise to end soon enough. "Your daughter has serious internal bleeding. We need to find the source of that bleeding and stop it. That means we must operate. We do need your consent, however, before we can do that..."

Alvin nodded his head and touched the doctor's arm again. "Yessir... you do whatever has to be done to save our girl. Please...please, don't let Becca die."

Mama James began to cry again.

The doctor feared that the old woman might be in shock. "I'll send a nurse over to make sure you both are alright. They've taken Becca to the operating room," he replied, as he stood to leave. "Your daughter is in good hands. I promise to do everything within my power to save her. I'll be talking with you as soon as we finish—it could take a while. The nurse will bring you the consent form to sign."

Mr. and Mrs. James, together with Scott and Macey, waited in the emergency room for the next four hours, while the doctors operated on Becca.

The most difficult hurdle for the medical team had been to stem the flow of blood coursing from Becca's uterus. The doctor removed dozens of large splinters. They cauterized the tears and cuts inside her vagina

223

and womb that had been caused by her attacker's use of the stump's violent manipulation upon her body.

It was one-thirty, Sunday afternoon, when an exhausted Dr. Stephen Mullins walked into the waiting room to inform the James' family that they had been successful in stopping Becca's internal bleeding. He explained to them that she was still suffering from a severe concussion, and, that they were very concerned about swelling in her brain.

The next twenty-four hours would be critical in determining whether Becca James would live or die.

While Becca James was fighting for her life at the Medical Center, Ruth Wymer was busying herself with Sunday dinner. It was difficult for her to concentrate because of what had happened earlier that morning.

She had attended Reverend Dudley's church, and listened to him preach a powerful sermon. She had only recently admitted to herself that she feared the man. However, as much as she feared him, she still felt compelled by him—drawn to him through no control of her own. It was this compelling magnetism that drew her to his church this morning, with hope that he might invite her into his private office after the sermon. She lingered long enough, after the service, to feel conspicuous among the other church members.

Lucas had watched her and knew that she had something on her mind, so, he begrudgingly complied with her request to speak privately with him in his office. Once they were inside, he turned his back to her and absently shuffled some papers atop his desk. "Well...out with it, Ruth? What is it? I have a lot of visitation to do this afternoon."

Ruth wrung her hands nervously together, and used her tongue to wet lips that suddenly felt parched and dry. "I...umm...I can't get that woman off my mind, Lucas."

Lucas kept his back to her and pursed his lips together to suppress his rising anger. "What woman?"

Ruth recognized the impatience in his voice, but decided to continue. "That...that black woman we followed last night. Lucas...are you sure you didn't do anything to...hurt her?"

He turned so abruptly that papers scattered in all directions around them. He delivered a menacingly stare. "I told you she ran away from me! Why can't you believe that!"

Ruth cowered at his venomous tone and stammered, "I...I do...I do... believe you, Lucas. It's just that, well...you were gone such a long time, and..."

"And what!" he bellowed. He secretly enjoyed the notable fear that crossed her face. "You were asleep in the car, Ruth, and I was not gone all that long!"

Ruth gulped in some much-needed air. "Well, what about..." she whispered hoarsely. She lowered her head and began wringing her hands again. "I thought I saw...blood...on your hands."

Lucas fought with himself for some degree of self-control. He couldn't afford to alienate this woman. She knew too much about him. He wanted out of this relationship, but he could not afford the luxury of belittling or humiliating her the way he felt driven to do so. He knew he had to smooth things over—to, somehow, reassure her.

He moved slowly toward her and took her in his arms. He felt a temporary resistance and kissed the top of her head. She made it easy for him to manipulate her. Her desperate desire for love and attention made it too easy for him. "Ruthie—my sweet, Ruthie. That was not blood on my hands that you thought you saw. Why...I am truly hurt that you would think me capable of hurting anyone. I explained to you that I slipped and fell in the woods while I chased after that woman. That wasn't blood, Ruthie...that was *mud* you saw on my hands."

Ruth felt sure that he was lying to her, but, maybe it was a lie that she needed to hear right now. She sighed and nodded. "Oh, thank God...I didn't want to believe that you would hurt her." She looked up at him and asked, "So...you really didn't find out anything from her...about Macey?"

Lucas exhaled patiently. "No, I didn't. As I told you last night...the woman took off running. I fell chasing after her, but never could catch up with her. You know how fast blacks can run. No...I did not learn anything from her about Macey."

"Well, Lucas...maybe...we should just forget about Macey...let her be. Maybe she's not here to do any harm..."

"Nonsense!" exclaimed Lucas. "We have to find out about the baby... Macey's child."

Ruth looked perplexed. "But why, Lucas? Why are you so interested in the baby? You weren't even around during the time that Macey had the baby. We had left Tennessee by then and you had moved on to Virginia."

He knew he had to be careful. It wouldn't do for Ruth to suspect the truth. "That baby is God's child, Ruth. We must find out what Macey did with her daughter—if the child is even alive. It wouldn't surprise me to learn that Macey had given the child away after all."

Ruth shrugged and shook her head. "I don't think so, Lucas. I don't think Macey could have done that, and—besides—the child is grown now. She could be living in another state, going to college...maybe even married with a family of her own. She could be anywhere."

Lucas was lost in his own thoughts, but managed to reply, "It is God's will that I discover the truth about the child—if for no other reason, but to bring some kind of closure to the heartache your family has endured these past twenty years. Your family has suffered so much, Ruth. I feel I must do whatever I can to bring happiness and security back into your lives."

Ruth smiled back into Lucas Dudley's cold, dark eyes. She quickly convinced herself that his logic made perfect sense. "You are such a good man, Lucas. I...I don't know how I would have managed this past year without you in my life. By the way...Andrew told me this morning that he's going out of town next weekend."

Lucas seemed mildly surprised. "Whatever for? I'm surprised he would be going anywhere the weekend before Christmas..."

Ruth's hesitation was evident when she got up the nerve to press her body against the good Reverend.

It was a woman's body, so Lucas' own body naturally reacted when her arms encircled his neck and she moved herself against him.

Ruth purred. "I don't know...he says it's business...he has to go somewhere in Tennessee, but he'll be back on Christmas Eve. He's leaving Thursday after work and will be back Sunday night. That gives us three whole nights."

Lucas trembled slightly when she planted butterfly kisses against his neck and continued to rub against him. He lifted her roughly off the floor and growled when she wrapped her legs around his waist. "Why wait until next weekend. . ."

Ruth closed her eyes in ecstasy while Lucas ravaged her willing and yielding body.

Lucas closed his own eyes and smiled in victory. He found himself comparing this escapade to the one with Becca James the night before. The more he thought about Becca, the harder he pumped himself into Ruth's body, trying to inflict as much pain upon her as he had on Becca James. "*Aww! One less black whore to worry about,*" he thought.

His climatic release came quickly, without any regard to Ruth's attempt to do the same.

CHAPTER 33

SCOTT LEARNS ABOUT THE PAST

Becca was transferred immediately to the Intensive Care Unit after her four-hour surgery. Dr. Mullins told her parents that it might be several hours—or possibly days—before she regained consciousness. He encouraged them to go home to rest, but, he wasn't surprised when the elderly couple remained adamant in their decision to stay with Becca until she awoke.

Macey eventually convinced them that they would be of more help to Becca—whenever she did awaken—if they were more rested. She promised them that she would stay with Becca overnight, and they could return early the next morning.

Scott called a cab and offered to pay their fare home and back the next day. He and Macey stood outside the entrance to The Medical Center and waved goodbye to Becca's exhausted parents. It had been a long day for everyone. Scott pulled Macey against his shoulder as they turned to go back inside. "I don't suppose I could talk *you* into going home and getting some rest?"

She sighed wearily and shook her head. "Not a chance. I won't leave Becca alone tonight. You heard what the doctor said—the next twenty-four hours are the most critical. I know Mr. James would never have agreed to leave if he hadn't been so worried about his wife. She has a lot of health problems. No, Scott, I can't leave her...I won't leave her."

Scott rested his chin on top of her head and inhaled the cool breeze that blew gently past them. "I had a feeling you would say that, but, I thought I'd try anyway. Since I can't talk you out of it, I think I'll take a cab back to the apartment, grab a quick shower, and bring some files back here to work on. I'm having to shoulder part of Byce's workload, with him being out of town for the holidays. I could stop by your place if you want me to—maybe get you a change of clothes?" He smiled as he tugged gently at her pajama top.

Macey looked up at him gratefully and said, "You know, I rushed out so quickly this morning, I'm not even sure if I locked the door behind me. I may not have an apartment to go back to. Yes, please—if you don't mind—that would be great...thanks, Scott. You should be able to find everything in my bedroom. Oh, and if you don't mind, would you grab me a pair of shoes, too? There's an old pair of Nikes in the downstairs hall closet...and, check the bathroom for my tooth brush and tooth paste, please?"

Scott glanced down at her white, fuzzy bedroom slippers and grinned. "No problem. Truth be told, I have wanted to get into your drawers for quite some time now, Miss Garner. I finally have my chance!"

Macey groaned at his silly attempt at humor and punched him against his shoulder. "Go on! Get out of here."

They both turned at the sound of a loud horn from an approaching taxi that screeched to a sudden halt directly behind them. A nervous passenger nearly fell to the asphalt when he opened the front-passenger door. The driver was the first to make it to the back-passenger door. He gently pulled a very pregnant, young woman from the back seat. The male passenger looked momentarily confused and stunned before the driver rushed him inside to get an attendant and a wheelchair. The driver leaned against the taxi and wiped sweat from his weathered forehead as he watched the expectant couple disappear inside the Emergency Room doors. "Hey!" he called out, lifting his hand in their fleeting direction. "You forgot to pay!"

Scott walked over to the driver and handed him a twenty. "This should more than cover it, shouldn't it?"

The driver looked at the twenty, then back at Scott, before offering a wide, toothless grin. "Oh, hey, fella, that ain't necessary," he said as he tried to return the twenty to Scott. "I ain't really worried about the money none. I'm just mighty glad I got 'em here in time. I sure as hell didn't want to be deliverin' no baby tonight, that's for sure!"

Scott folded the old man's hand until it closed around the twenty. "Keep it, please. Maybe you could drop me at my apartment?"

The old man grinned and moved around to the driver's side. "Sure thing—hop on in, young fella! I'd be mighty glad to drop ya anywhere you be needin' to go."

Scott turned back toward Macey. "I'll be back in a couple of hours."

"Okay..." Macey smiled. She was impressed with Scott's generosity.

"Thanks again, Scott...for everything."

He tilted her chin upward and placed a light, butterfly kiss upon her lips. He licked his top lip and grimaced. "Hmm...I'll make sure I don't forget that tooth brush..."

Macey punched him hard and turned to walk back inside. She offered a backward, flippant wave before the door closed behind her.

Dusk had announced itself by the time the taxi let Scott out in front of his apartment. He withdrew another twenty and handed it to the driver. "Keep the change," he smiled at the old man as he closed the taxi door.

The old driver leaned over his seat and looked out the open, passenger window. He grinned his wide, toothless grin again and shook Scott's offered hand. "Why thanks, young fella. I sure do appreciate it. Anytime you need yourself a lift anywhere, you just call the company and you ask for old George, you hear?"

Scott nodded and waved. "I'll do that, George. Thanks again for the ride."

"Anytime, young fella," George waved back and savored the twenty between his fingers. "Any, old time, yessiree!"

Scott watched George drive slowly out of the parking lot.

"Scott! Hey, Scott!"

Scott turned to see someone running toward him—coming from the direction of Macey's apartment. He didn't immediately recognize Jacob Wymer until the young man was beneath the street lamp. "Jacob? Is that you?"

Jacob reached him in a few easy strides; he wasn't even out of breath after his short sprint across the parking lot. "Yeah, it's me. Hey, man, I'm looking for Macey. I've been here for hours! Her apartment door was unlocked, her car's still here, your car's still here...I've called the office, I've called Miss Becca to see if she's there, I..."

Scott placed both hands upon the young man's shoulders. "Whoa, Jacob! Slow down, okay? Macey's fine. She's...uh...at the hospital..."

Jacob looked panic-stricken as thoughts of Macey in a possible car wreck played havoc with his imagination. "Oh, my God...Macey's hurt! What hospital? What's happened, Scott?"

"No, no, Jacob," Scott spoke softly. "I said...Macey's fine; it's Becca... she's in the hospital."

Jacob bent over and grasped his knees while he gulped in air. Some color had returned to his cheeks by the time he stood up again. "Miss Becca? Man, she's never sick! What's happened?"

Suppressed exhaustion was finally attempting to lay claim to Scott Pennell. He sighed deeply and rubbed the bridge of his nose. "I promise to tell you all about it, Jacob, but I need you to do me a favor first. Will you go back to Macey's place and gather up a change of clothing for her? A comb...her old Nikes in the downstairs closet, and...oh yeah, don't forget her toothbrush and toothpaste. Grab her purse, too, and lock everything up...then come on over to my place. I need a hot shower, but, I promise to tell you everything that's happened. It's been a really long day."

Jacob was anxious. He wanted to know everything about what had happened to Becca, but, he could see the weariness evident in Scott's face and posture. "Yeah, okay...but, I won't be long. I'll be at your place in ten minutes."

Scott nodded and patted Jacob's shoulder. "I'll leave the door unlocked for you. Just come on in when you've finished at Macey's. There's beer in the fridge if you want one."

Once he was inside his own apartment, Scott grabbed a cold beer and dragged himself slowly upstairs. A hot shower was exactly what his tensed body so desperately needed. He sat the beer on the bathroom counter and reached inside the shower to turn the faucets on. He rolled his shoulders and moved his neck from side to side before bending slightly to remove his sweats. That's when he felt it—the crushed paper that he had shoved inside his pockets when he first found Becca in the woods. "What's this..." he sighed tiredly. He closed the commode lid, sat down, and opened the crumbled newspaper clippings. He took a long swig of the cold beer, rubbed the bridge of his nose again between his thumb and forefinger, and attempted to focus his tired, blurred vision on the newspaper articles.

There were three brief articles about the murder of a young, sixteen-year old girl. He scanned the first article—dated November 1, 1969—about the murder of a young girl by the name of Kacey Wymer.

"Wymer?" Scott murmured. "That's Jacob's last name."

Scott began to hyperventilate by the time he finished reading the second article. A picture of the murdered girl—the young girl from his flashbacks—accompanied that article. It was the same girl he had believed to be a younger Macey.

"What the hell..." he gasped when he found mention of his own name.

The article identified *HIM* as the murdered girl's boyfriend, and, as the immediate, primary suspect. Shock and turmoil reigned for control within Scott's tired, battered mind. Shock would have, undoubtedly, won out had Jacob not arrived downstairs at that moment and called out for him.

"Oh my, God," Scott cried in disbelief. "Oh, my God, what did I do..."

Jacob rushed up the stairs when he thought he heard a strange, gurgling sound. He stood outside the bathroom door and listened to the running water until he heard it again—the gurgling noise. He tapped twice on the door and put his ear to it. He could have sworn that he heard Scott talking to someone—or to himself. He knocked on the door a second time; and, when there was no response, Jacob opened the door slowly and peered inside. "Hey, man...I hate to bother you in here, but I thought I heard..." Jacob stopped in mid-sentence, as he took in the haunted, bewildered expression on Scott's face. The steaming hot water from the running shower fogged the mirrors, so Jacob stepped around Scott and turned off the faucets. "Scott? You okay, man?"

A dazed look imprisoned Scott's face. He finally looked up at Jacob while the newspaper articles floated from his numbed fingers. They landed on the ceramic-tiled floor at Jacob's feet.

Jacob bent to retrieve the papers and immediately recognized them for what they were—he had his own copies safely hidden at home. He had known, all along, who Scott was, but he had never talked about it to anyone. His emotions concerning Scott were confused, at best. He had been so young when Kacey had died, so, it was hard for him to feel the hatred for Scott that people might expect him to feel. His main concern—since first meeting Scott—had been the man's intentions toward Macey. The more that Jacob had gotten to know Scott over the past few weeks, the more he had wanted to find out why Scott felt compelled to impregnate himself into their lives. Then again, the more that Jacob had gotten to know Scott over the past several weeks, the harder it was for him to believe the man capable of murdering anyone.

Jacob's plan had been to follow Macey's lead. If she accepted the man into their lives, then so would he. The newspaper articles stated that Scott had required psychological help after the alleged murder, but, there had never been any definitive proof that he was responsible for Kacey's death. He kept hoping that Macey would eventually confide in him, about those things of which he was already aware. Jacob stared at Scott. Why did the man appear so shocked and disoriented? It was almost as if he were reading the articles for the first time.

Scott lifted his head and pointed at the articles that Jacob held loosely between two fingers. "Those...articles...say that I...killed...that girl..."

Jacob was more than a little worried about Scott. He wasn't sure if Scott was flipping out on him or not. If he was, he wasn't sure that he knew how to handle the situation. He wished Macey were here...she would know what to do. "That girl...was my...sister," Jacob blurted.

Scott looked back at him. The impact of what Jacob just said had not quite registered in his befuddled mind. "But...*Macey* is your sister..."

Jacob nodded. "Yeah...Macey and Kacey were...twins, but...you knew that...right?"

Scott lowered his head onto his knees and began to rock back and forth. He began to choke on the great sobs of agony that somehow managed to escape his constricted throat.

"Oh, man..." Jacob begged. "Don't go crazy on me. Scott? Hey, buddy..."

Loud, horrendous sobs racked through Scott's crumpled body as he continued his rocking motion.

Jacob didn't know what to do to help the man, so he ran a wash cloth under cold water and laid it against Scott's forehead. He put an arm around Scott's slumped shoulders and tried to comfort him. "Scott, it's okay, man. Come on...you've got to get control of yourself..."

It took several more minutes before Scott finally stopped the rocking motion. He took the wet rag Jacob had laid upon his forehead and wiped his face with it. He reached over, pulled a long length of toilet paper off the roll, and viciously blew his nose. His shaking legs threatened non-support when he stood up and looked at himself in the mirror. "God... Macey's never said anything to me...nothing at all," he whispered. "How can she stand to look at me? No wonder she acted like she hated me when we first met..."

Jacob's mind was quick to grasp the puzzling situation. "Oh, man... oh, man. I don't believe this. You mean...*you* didn't recognize *her*, man?"

Scott looked back at Jacob's reflection in the mirror and shook his head. "I swear to you, Jacob...I don't remember any...any of this. I don't remember Kacey...hell, I don't even remember having lived in Columbus, even though I know we did for a while." Scott paused and closed his eyes. "The flashbacks..."

Jacob raised his eyebrows in question. "Flashbacks?"

"Yeah. I've been having...flashbacks a lot lately...about...a young girl whom I thought was Macey, but now...it must have been..."

"Her name was Kacey," Jacob reminded him. "Man, you're serious, aren't you? You really don't remember what happened that night?"

"I swear to God," Scott answered as he straightened himself and bit his lower lip. "God, you must hate me, Jacob. How have you managed not to slit my throat before now? No...I don't remember ever being in Columbus, Georgia until I arrived here a few months ago, but, Macey had to have known who I was. God...how could she even stand to be in the same room with me?"

Jacob exhaled slowly. "Wow...this is all too weird, man." He shook his head and was thankful that Scott appeared to be regaining his wits about him. "Listen, Scott...my Mama taught me from an early age that it's not my place to judge anyone, no matter what they might have done to deserve that judgment. You're right, though...I probably should hate your guts, but slitting your throat? No, man...that would take some mighty strong hate, and to tell you the truth...I don't think I have it in me to hate you—or anyone—that much. Neither does Macey. I think you probably need to talk to her about all this." Jacob turned to leave and said, "I'll...uh...leave you alone and let you get ready. You're going back to the hospital, right?"

Scott was still trying to absorb the shock of his discovery, mingled with the realization that Jacob somehow forgave and accepted him. He looked at Jacob with renewed awe, wondering how he could be so forgiving of the man who had murdered his sister. "Yeah...I told Macey I'd be back in a couple of hours. I...uh...wanted to bring her something to eat."

Jacob recognized the defeated expression on Scott's face. "Why don't you let me do that? I'll grab a few Krystal burgers and head on over that way. Is she at Doctors Hospital or The Medical Center?"

"What?" Scott asked. He was still dazed. "Oh, yeah...The Medical Center."

"Scott?"

"Yeah?"

"I know your head has got to be pretty screwed up right now. You've got a lot to sort through and, well...you and Macey have a lot to talk about, but..."

Scott looked up when Jacob paused. "What is it, Jacob?"

Jacob suddenly felt ten years old. He was afraid to ask, but he also needed to know. "Becca? You said Macey was with Miss Becca?"

Scott pressed his open mouth tightly between the palms of both hands. "Oh, yeah...I forgot you didn't know. It doesn't look good, Jacob. I found Becca early this morning in the woods behind my apartment. She had been beaten...badly..."

"Beaten? Becca!" Jacob gasped. "Oh, man...Macey must be in knots about this!"

Scott nodded. "Yeah, she's pretty upset. She won't leave Becca until she knows for sure—one way or the other. The doctor said that the first twenty-four hours after surgery were the most critical."

"It's really that bad?" Jacob wondered aloud.

"Yeah...it's bad, alright. You...uh...you had better get on over there, okay? And, Jacob?"

"Yeah, Scott?"

Scott bit down hard on his upper lip. "Don't tell Macey...let me be the one to talk to her about...this," he said as he pointed to the newspaper clippings that Jacob had placed upon the counter.

"Sure, man...sure. I'll see you in a few."

"Right."

Scott forgot about the hot shower that he had been so looking forward to; instead, he splashed cold water over his face and stumbled into his bedroom. He looked longingly at the bed. He wanted, more than anything, to lie down and sleep for the rest of his life—to forget about everything he had just learned—anything to delay talking to Macey about everything. He turned away from the bed and put on a clean shirt and jeans. He returned to the bathroom to brush his teeth and to retrieve the newspaper clippings.

He took his time driving back to the hospital. The question of why the newspaper clippings were scattered among Becca's body finally permeated his troubled brain. "Oh, God," he spoke out loud. "If the police had found these, they would have connected me to what happened to Becca. They would think that I did this to her...oh my, God...what the hell is going on here?"

CHAPTER 34

TWO DAYS AFTER ATTACK

Janet sat dutifully behind her desk bright and early Monday morning. She was actually performing some light typing in lieu of her usual early-morning routine—painting her nails. Scott had been assigned responsibility for a large portion of Mr. Byce's workload during the assistant CEO's Christmas vacation; and, Scott demanded much more of her—professionally—than George Byce ever had.

She was dressed, once again, in fashionably-demure attire—a navy pin-stripe skirt and matching blazer. Her abundant cleavage remained concealed beneath the ivory turtleneck sweater she wore beneath the blazer. Her thick auburn curls had been tamed into a tight French twist and her flawless complexion was void of her usual heavy makeup.

Janet pulled on the neck of the sweater, trying to loosen its death grip upon her throat. She wasn't use to the total confinement this outfit exacted. Several phone lines were ringing in unison when she noticed Scott as he shuffled through the front door. She gasped at his appearance—the pallid, sunken expression that covered his usually calm, handsome face. The calamity of ringing telephones prevented her from speaking directly to him, therefore, she only nodded in greeting.

It was a full twenty minutes later before things slowed down enough to allow Janet to take a short break. She carried a cup of coffee into Scott's office and watched him for a moment. He was sitting behind his desk, with his head in his hands. His computer had not been turned on, nor had his blinds been opened. She wondered if he had been sitting in that exact same position since he first entered his office. She walked quietly up to his desk and placed the coffee cup on the corner of it. She wondered if he was even aware that he was no longer alone. She walked around to his side of the desk. When it was obvious he had not noticed her, she bent down, put an arm around his shoulder, and rested her head against his. "Anything I can do to help, big fella?"

Scott felt Janet's head pressed lightly against his own. He opened his tired eyes and looked over at her. It had been a long night for him. He had returned to the hospital with every intention of talking to Macey about the newspaper clippings. However, when he arrived and saw her sitting with Jacob, hungrily devouring the food he had brought her, he didn't think he could put her through any more emotional turmoil than she had already experienced that day. He decided it would be best to wait until tonight to discuss things with her. Maybe they would have good news about Becca by then. "Good morning, Janet. No, I'm fine... just a little tired."

Janet grinned mischievously and teased, "Let me guess...wild weekend?"

Scott favored an exhausted smile. "I wish..."

She began a gentle, yet firm, massage of the tense muscles in Scott's back and leaned down to whisper in his ear. "You know...I could make that wish come true...all you have to do is give me the word."

For one moment—one quick moment—Scott considered doing just that. Maybe some great sex would be the solution—albeit temporary— to take his mind off everything he had learned in the past twenty-four hours—twenty-four hours that had changed his life forever. He still needed the answers to so many questions that he still had. Was it fair of him to expect Macey to supply the answers to those questions? He realized that Janet had spoken something to him. "What..."

Janet smiled and ran her tongue over her perfectly white, even teeth. "I said I could help you relax...if you'd only let me."

Scott returned a weak smile and shook his head. "No...but, thanks anyway, Janet—although, I could probably use a hefty dose of wild, uninhibited sex right about now." He sighed wearily and continued. "You know, now that I think about it, I've only had sex once in the past three and a half months. That's not much of a record, especially when you're used to getting it two or three times a *week*."

Janet turned his executive-leather chair around to face her and knelt on the floor. She ran her hands up the inside of his thighs and rested them lightly against the front of his trousers. She was more surprised than disappointed when she did not receive the immediate evidence her touches normally generated.

Scott placed his hands firmly on top of hers. "I thought you and Jacob had a thing going."

Janet pulled her hands slowly down the top of Scott's thighs until they rested upon his knees. She looked up at him and smiled sweetly. "We do, Scott—at least *I* do—but, to tell you the truth, I'm not real sure where Jacob's head is."

Scott leaned his head back and closed his eyes. "Then why are you willing to sacrifice that relationship by doing...this?"

Janet shrugged. "I don't know, exactly. Old habits die hard, I guess. Besides, Jacob won't sleep with me, Mr. Byce is away, you're not interested, and—jeez—it's been more than a month! It's driving me up a wall! I've even had to resort to..."

Scott smiled as he watched Janet squirm and pull at the neck of her sweater. He welcomed the brief respite from thinking about his own problems. He maintained a stoic expression. "You've had to resort to what, Janet?"

Janet arose abruptly and turned to leave. "Oh, never mind! By the way, do you know if there's a problem with Macey? She's usually the first one here every morning, and I've got a half-dozen calls for her already. She hasn't called in..."

Scott closed his eyes as his thoughts returned to Macey and Becca. He ran his fingers along the bridge of his nose and down to his chin. "She won't be in today, Janet. There was an emergency over the weekend, and she's at The Medical Center..."

Janet's eyes grew wide with genuine concern. "Oh, no! Is she okay?"

"Not her...Macey's fine, but, a close friend of hers—you met her at the bowling alley—Becca James was seriously injured. Macey wants to stay close to her until she knows for sure that she's out of the woods." Scott grimaced at his inadvertent use of the expression, since it was *the woods* where Becca James' troubles had begun the night before.

"Yeah, I do remember her...the black woman. "What happened? Was it a car wreck or something?"

Scott shook his head. "No...nothing like that. Becca was attacked and beaten...in the woods behind my apartment."

Janet's hands flew to her mouth. "Oh, Scott, no! I heard something about that on the news this morning, but, I didn't pay much attention to the story—I didn't realize that it happened at your apartment complex. Oh...wow...they said it was a...black woman, but I never thought to make the connection to Macey." Janet's eyes grew misty. She had not really liked Becca James—she thought her to be rude and arrogant—but, she had sensed the close bond between the black woman, Jacob, and Macey. "I can't believe it...she was found in the woods behind *your* apartment?"

Scott nodded and took a sip of the now, lukewarm coffee. He hoped the caffeine would produce enough physical energy to get him through the next twenty-four hours. He had a feeling they were going to be even more traumatic than the last twenty-four had been—if that was even possible. Scott looked directly into Janet's eyes. "I was the one who found her. I found Becca..."

Janet stood up and pulled him up from the chair, into her arms. She hugged him close to her, and felt his ragged sobs of anguish as they released against her demure pin-striped suit.

Andrew Wymer sat behind the rusty, metal desk and read the morning paper. He glanced up and watched—through the large glass window— Jacob shaking hands with the old black man, Alvin James, who owned the diner two blocks away. Andrew remembered the many times that the old, black man had tried to be pleasant and neighborly in his encounters with him, only to receive Andrew's scorn and obvious prejudice in return. It amazed and surprised Andrew that Jacob had, apparently, not inherited his own discriminatory ways. Andrew couldn't help but wonder what the two were talking about, with their hands still clasped together.

The old, black man finally drove away, and Andrew continued to watch Jacob while he entered the office and deposited money in the old-fashioned cash register. Jacob had tried to convince him, on more than one occasion, to update and modernize the station; but, Andrew always countered that fancy computers were a waste of money. Andrew knew that Jacob would be shocked to learn that his father could care less whether the station turned a profit or not. He would be shocked to learn that the business was merely a means to an end—a temporary escape from Andrews's pitiful excuse of a life.

Jacob closed the cash register drawer and glanced at his father. "Anything good in the paper, Pop?"

"No."

Jacob flinched at the curt reply, even though it came as no real surprise to him. He had prayed countless times for a normal conversation between him and his father—a conversation where his father would treat him like a person—like a son. "That was Mr. James out there just now," Jacob offered. He was determined to force a conversation from his father. "He's had some pretty upsetting news."

"Humph!" Andrew growled in reply. "Whatsamatter? Didn't he get his welfare check on time this month? Damn blacks—everyone knows that's all they're good for—breeding babies and mooching off the government. It's a conspiracy, you know. They keep having all those babies, hoping to outnumber us. It'll happen someday, too."

Jacob stared forlornly at his father. It was no use. He had nothing in common with this man. He couldn't believe they were even related! Their views about people and life in general were so totally foreign to each other. "I wish you wouldn't talk like that, Pop," he muttered softly. "Mr. James is a good man, and he works hard for a living. He owns the diner down the street. His wife is a great cook."

Andrew glared suspiciously at his son. "How do you know so much about him?"

Jacob panicked. Had he revealed too much information? It wouldn't do for his father to find out that Becca and Macey were friends. "He stops in here every week, that's all. He's always real nice. He even brought me a piece of sweet potato pie one day that his wife had made—best pie I've ever tasted."

Andrew was only half listening. An article in the paper had suddenly captured his attention.

Jacob watched his father's expression and wondered what had caught his abrupt interest. "Pop, what is it? What are you reading?"

Andrew glanced up from the paper. "You said your friend out there received some disturbing news?"

"Yes, sir. His daughter...she's in the hospital."

"This here article must be about her, then. Says some black woman was beaten and dumped in the woods behind those fancy apartments on the north side of town."

"Yes, sir. That was his daughter—she was hurt pretty bad. Mr. James said she's still unconscious. Things are still kind of touch and go for her."

Andrew wasn't completely insensitive to Alvin James' predicament. After all, twenty years ago, the police had come to his home to inform him that his own daughter had been severely beaten, choked, and impaled upon the stick shift of a 1969 Volkswagen. He remembered it like it was only yesterday. Yes, he could most definitely empathize with Alvin James. He forgot his prejudice for a moment and—almost against his will—closed his eyes in a silent prayer. It was a prayer from one father to another—for Becca James—even though, he doubted that God listened to sinners such as himself.

Jacob watched his father's expression with concerned interest. "Pop? Are you okay?"

Andrew looked across the room at Jacob. When had his only son grown into such a handsome young man who exhibited such open compassion for other people? Had he been wrong all these many years in discouraging any type of relationship between the two of them?

Could such a relationship have made a difference in all their lives? No, Andrew knew he didn't deserve a real relationship with his son—he didn't deserve a relationship with anyone. He attempted to shake off his sudden, melancholy mood and regained his typical, sour expression. "Of course, I'm all right, boy—get back to work. You know how Mondays are around here, and I want to be sure to get everything to the bank before I leave on Thursday."

Jacob sighed and shrugged, disappointed in himself—again—for thinking that he and his father could sustain anything resembling a normal conversation. "Pop? Do you mind me asking where you go on these out-of-town trips?"

Andrew's head snapped around. He glared at Jacob with menace. "Pretty damn nosy, aren't you, boy!"

Jacob should have known better than to expect anything other than this reaction from his father. He swallowed hard. "Sorry, Pop...I was just curious. It's none of my business. Sorry..."

Andrew jabbed himself in the chest with his index finger and glared at his son. "You let me worry about my trips out of town, and *you* just make sure you keep this place afloat while I'm gone. Don't forget that I expect to see receipts for everything! Don't be giving your black friends any free service, or getting any sticky fingers, if you know what I mean."

Jacob was silently infuriated at his father's insinuation that he might steal money from the business. However, as always, he was quick to bow to Andrew's dominant and overbearing personality. He watched his father retreat into the bay area where, for several months now, he had been working on the motor to an old, red Volkswagen. "It won't be much longer, old man...not much longer at all...then you'll be rid of me forever," he whispered behind his father's back. He wiped away what he hoped would be the final tear caused by his father's uncaring and insensitive attitude toward him.

CHAPTER 35

THE INEVITABLE MEETING

Scott left work an hour early and drove directly to The Medical Center. He ran into Dr. Mullins outside of Becca's room and asked if there was any change in her condition.

"No, I'm sorry." Dr. Mullins shook his head and patted Scott's shoulder. "Her condition hasn't changed at all. She's neither any better, nor worse, than she was yesterday, I'm afraid. She has not regained consciousness, and, as I explained to you and Miss Garner previously, every day that goes by without her doing so makes her prognosis less than favorable."

"Thank you, Doctor Mullins. I appreciate your candidness. Is it all right for me to go in?" Scott asked, motioning toward Becca's room.

"Go right ahead, Mr. Pennell. Maybe you can talk Miss Garner into taking a break and getting some rest."

Scott nodded and watched as the doctor made his way down the long, quiet corridor—perhaps to someone else hoping and waiting for good news. He turned and peered through the small glass pane in the door that lead into Becca's room. He pushed open the door and saw Macey sitting beside Becca's bed, holding her hand.

Macey looked up and offered Scott a weary smile. She had been with Becca for thirty-six hours.

Scott returned the smile and pulled up a chair on the opposite side of the bed. "You look so tired, Macey."

Macey closed her eyes and did not even attempt to stifle a yawn. "I am, but—no offense—you don't look much better."

"Thanks," Scott grimaced.

"I'm sorry..." Macey began, fearing she had hurt his feelings.

He held up a hand to silence her. "It's okay. I know that I look like hell.

I didn't sleep much last night, and today was hectic with Mr. Byce being away and all. Are you okay, Macey? Where are Mr. and Mrs. James?"

"I'm tired, but I'm fine...really. Mr. James took his wife home for the evening. She's not handling all this very well and the stress has caused her blood pressure to skyrocket. Dr. Mullins is worried about her. Some of their church friends are going to stay with her at her home tonight. Mr. James is planning on coming back here to spend the night with Becca."

"I hope that means you'll go home and get some rest then. Dr. Mullins is almost insisting upon it, you know?"

Macey nodded as she cupped Becca's swollen, bitten hand between her own. "I know. Mr. James made me promise, too. He said he would call me the minute she wakes up. I...uh...feel bad not having asked sooner, Scott, but, is everything all right at work? I didn't even think to notify anyone this morning that I wouldn't be there."

"No problem. I filled everyone in who had a need to know. Don't worry about things at the office. I'll take care of your workload until you return."

Macey rose stiffly from her seated position and walked around to his side of the bed. She looked down at Becca, and at the seemingly endless tubes inserted into every possible orifice of her body. "I don't know how to thank you, Scott. That means more to me than you could possibly know."

"Work should be the last thing on your mind right now, Macey. I don't want you worrying about the office."

Macey nodded in silent agreement and turned to look back at Becca. "You know, she's been like a sister to me these past five years. She's my only real friend, other than Jacob."

Scott grimaced at the mention of a sister, knowing all too well the emotional pain he would be dredging up for Macey when he finally opened a discussion about her twin. "I had hoped to be included on that list of friends, Macey."

Macey faced him and lay her hands upon his shoulders. She smiled when he placed his hands protectively around her waist and pulled her toward him. "Make no mistake, Scott...you are most definitely on that list...most definitely."

Alvin James arrived in the open doorway and watched the young couple from a discreet distance. He knocked softly and cleared his throat.

Scott looked up from Macey's belt buckle and smiled. He threw up a hand in welcome to the old man. He stood up to shake Alvin's offered hand. "Hello, Mr. James."

"Hello, Scott. It's mighty good to see you again. I hope you're here to take Miss Macey out for a good meal and then home to rest. Lord knows the child needs some rest." Alvin smiled paternally at Macey.

Macey turned back to Becca, leaned forward to kiss her friend's swollen cheek and whispered, "I love you, Becca. You come back to us, you hear?" She turned back to face the two men and offered a tired smile. "I am hungry...I didn't realize how much until you mentioned food, Mr. James. Promise me that you'll call me—no matter what time it is—if there's any change at all?"

The old man smiled and nodded. "You know I will, Miss Macey. Now you go on, child, and get some rest. It won't be doing my Becca any good if you go and get yourself sick. You go and let this young man take good care of you."

Scott took Macey by the hand and pulled her gently toward him. "I plan to do just that, Mr. James. I'll make sure she gets a good meal and some rest."

Macey took one last look at Becca and quickly interjected, "But I'll be back first thing in the morning."

Alvin smiled in acknowledgment. "I'm sure you will, Miss Macey. You go on now. I'll take care of my Becca tonight."

Macey kissed the old man's leathery, weathered cheek and wiped a small tear from the outer corner of his eye. "Then I know she's in good hands," she whispered into his ear.

Scott made good on his promise. He took Macey to a local steak house and forced her to eat a large steak, baked potato, and salad. If she noticed him picking at his own food, he was grateful that she didn't say anything about it.

Dusk was imminent when they finally left the steak house and walked slowly, hand-in-hand, back to Scott's car. He wasn't sure how to approach Macey with his newly discovered information, but he knew that he couldn't put it off much longer. He was glad to see that she looked more relaxed after having had a good meal. He knew that she needed some rest, but he needed some answers—some that maybe only she could provide—to some pretty perplexing questions. He wished there was another source for him to go to get the information he needed, but his mind wasn't working at a hundred percent at the moment, and he couldn't think of one.

He looked over at her as he started the car. Her head leaned back against the head rest, and her eyes were closed. She looked so vulnerable, but Scott knew that she was stronger than her petite appearance led people to believe. She was obviously a survivor, and if anyone could help him sort through the turmoil his life had become, it was Macey Garner—or, rather—Macey Wymer.

Scott was about to suggest a stroll around Cooper Creek before heading back to the apartment, but a quick glance at the gas gauge alerted him to the fact that he was sitting on empty. He had meant to fill the tank up earlier but had forgotten to do so. The car's fuel light glowed a bright red, indicating that he probably had only a little more than a gallon of available fuel. He surveyed the neighborhood for a service station and spotted one down the block on the right. He flipped on his turn signal and quickly pulled alongside one of the station's two, self-serve pumps. Two other pumps indicated full service availability—an oddity and rarity in this day and age. "I'll be right back, Macey. I've got to fill up with gas. You keep resting."

Macey never opened her eyes. She was exhausted, so she sighed and mumbled, "Okay." She smiled as she listened through the open passenger window to Scott humming the tune to *The Lion Sleeps Tonight* while he pumped gas. "I always liked that song," she said dreamily.

"Me too," Scott agreed. He pushed the tank lever to the off position. "I'll be back in a few minutes. Don't go anywhere."

Macey parted her eyelids slightly and smiled back at him. If she had opened them all the way she might have been able to prevent the ensuing scene. If she had only opened them and observed her surroundings, she would have known they had stopped at the last place on earth that Scott Pennell or Macey Garner needed to be.

Scott had pulled into Wymer's Service Station—the last independent gas station in Columbus, known for its full-service pumps.

Jacob and Andrew were in the attached service bay completing the engine overhaul on the red, '69 Volkswagen.

"Think I heard the bell," Andrew bellowed from his position under the car. "Go wait on the customer. I'll finish up here."

"Yes, sir," Jacob acquiesced. He wiped grease from his hands onto his denim coveralls. His welcoming smile froze upon his surprised face when he recognized the customer walking through the door. He quickly glanced back into the service bay to make sure his father was still beneath the Volkswagen. "Scott!" he croaked. He cast another nervous glance behind him. "What are you doing here, man?"

"Jacob?" Scott asked with a mixture of shock and stupefaction. "I didn't realize this was where you worked."

Jacob nervously wrung his hands together, a trait obviously inherited from his mother. "Uh...yep...says so on that big red and white sign right outside the door there."

Scott shook his head and grinned. "I'm so tired, I wasn't even looking where I was going. I've got Macey outside. I took her to get something to eat..."

Jacob thrust his hands deep into the pockets of the coveralls. He knew he should get Scott away as quickly as possible, but he was curious about something. "Have you...uh...talked to her yet about...you know?" He stole another quick glance behind him for reassurance that Andrew was still busy with the Volkswagen.

Scott removed money from his billfold to pay for the gas. "No, not yet. But...that's what I'm about to do. I just wish I had a crystal ball so I'd know how she was going to react to all this."

"Well, I think she's probably already worked most of that out in her head. The only thing that will probably shock her, is that you don't remember any of what happened—in which case—that might actually work in your favor—might make her like you even more."

"Why do you say that?" Scott asked. He handed Jacob a twenty.

"Well, because all this time, she's probably been thinking you're a real jerk for not recognizing her. Maybe she thinks Kacey wasn't important to you, or that you forgot all about her over the years. I just think she'll feel better about things, knowing that—through no fault of your own—you just don't remember what happened. That's it, isn't it?"

Scott scratched his head and nodded. "That's it, all right. I'm hoping Macey can fill in a lot of the gaps in my memory."

Neither Jacob nor Scott heard the footsteps approaching from behind.

Andrew came through the door to the bay area and barked, "Jacob, I need you out here. Hurry it up, will ya!" He turned to go back into the bay area, but something about the stranger's profile stopped him in his tracks. He turned slowly back around for a closer look. That profile...the hair...the smirk on his face...

Scott had never met Andrew, so he was unaware that he was Jacob's father. He nodded at the man and assumed it was Jacob's boss. "Keep the change, Jacob," he whispered. "I'd better let you get back to work."

Jacob saw Scott nod and glance behind him—toward the bay door. His brain went into immediate overdrive and he sensed the approaching disaster that was about to unfold before his very eyes. He tried his best to hurry Scott out the front door.

It was unfortunate for them all when Macey picked that exact moment to rush through the door. She had finally opened her eyes, recognized where they were, and hoped—desperately—that her father had already left work for the day.

No such luck.

Scott and Macey collided into each other, while Jacob chanced a quick look over his shoulder at his father.

Jacob knew instantly that it was too late. Even if Andrew had failed to recognize Scott, he most certainly had not failed to identify the beautiful woman who had literally fallen into Scott's arms.

Macey looked around Scott and saw the nervous expression on Jacob's face—silently pleading with her to leave. The impact with Scott had left her breathless enough, but when she looked past Jacob to the man standing in the doorway beyond, she forgot to breathe. A violent gasp escaped her.

Andrew's eyes grew wide, and his complexion paled as he stared back at the woman.

For one fleeting moment, Macey thought everything might be all right. She tried to convince herself that her father didn't recognize her— or Scott. It only took her a split second to realize that her self-reassurance was short-lived, at best.

"*Kacey*..." Andrew honed.

Jacob took a step backward. "Pop..." He took two steps forward. "No, Pop...it's not Kacey."

Andrew looked befuddled as he glanced back and forth between Jacob and Macey. His attention quickly became riveted on Scott— affirmation of his initial recognition was confirmed. He lunged forward awkwardly. "You...son-of-a-bitch!" he screamed. His outstretched hands reached for Scott's exposed throat.

Jacob did not stop to think about his next move. He ever hesitated. He threw himself forward to become a human barrier between his father and Scott.

Macey had managed to regain some control over the initial shock of seeing her father for the first time in more than twenty years. She was not surprised at the intense hatred and condemnation she still harbored against him. Her every instinct told her to get far away from him—as quickly as possible. She grabbed Scott's arm and pulled as hard as she could, just as Jacob pushed himself between Scott and her father. "Scott, let's get out of here! Now!" she yelled.

Scott jerked his arm away and looked back at Andrew, who—by this time—had overpowered and thrown Jacob to the floor. Scott cringed at the hard thump Jacob's head made when it contacted against the uncarpeted concrete flooring. "No, Macey...wait. Mr. Wymer..." He never had a chance to fend off the blow. It came out of nowhere. He felt his eye immediately begin to throb and swell when Andrew's fist made contact against Scott's left temple. The unexpected impact of the blow forced him against Macey once again, who fell unceremoniously out the door, onto the sidewalk.

Andrew stepped forward and glared down at her. Waves of immense, reciprocated hatred permeated throughout his massive body. He spat out a thick wad of phlegm, which landed in Macey's hair. "You whore... you little bitch...*you* should have been the one to die...if it hadn't been for you, my Kacey would still be alive..."

Scott had pulled himself up and grabbed Andrew's arm when he saw the man lunging toward Macey. He thrust a knee deep into Andrew's groin.

Andrew groaned in obvious pain and held himself protectively, but, he recovered quickly from the unexpected assault. His defense reflex kicked in and he bent down and retrieved the hunting knife he always kept strapped to the inside of his boot. He forgot all about Macey while he glared at Scott. Saliva dribbled from the corner of his mouth. "You... *murderer*," he howled. "I'm going to do to you what the courts wouldn't do twenty years ago."

The blow to his head had shaken Jacob, but he pushed himself up, shakily, onto one knee. One more push had him standing almost upright, and he moved to push himself—once again—between his father and Scott. He never saw the knife until his father lunged forward, with a wide swiping motion. "Pop! Noooooo!" Jacob screamed at the same time he pushed himself up, in time to take the full, piercing point of the knife's whetted blade.

The move was inadvertently timed so that Jacob's midsection took the full impact of the stab that had been intended for Scott Pennell.

"Agghh," Jacob gurgled as the stinging blade sliced across the full width of his stomach.

"Nooooo!!" Macey shrieked. She pushed past Scott and caught Jacob under the arms before he collapsed to the floor. She pressed her hands again the large, open gash, hoping to ebb the flow of blood that was spreading much too quickly through her fingers.

Time and movement was suspended for an eerie moment. Silence prevailed—there was no sound—no car horns honking, no dogs barking, no people chattering, no machinery running—while the four people took their individual stock about what had just happened.

Nothing.

Nothing...until the tightly-gripped knife finally slipped from Andrew's hand and banged against the concrete flooring.

Andrew looked down at his blood-soaked hand. "Oh, dear God..." he cried as he knelt before his son. "Oh, God, what have I done…"

Jacob stared back at his father. There was an awed, dumbfounded expression upon his face. He opened his mouth to speak, but nothing came out. His head tilted slowly to rest against Macey's arm, and his eyes closed slowly. A single tear escaped and trickled down his ashen cheek.

The look on Andrew's face alternated from one of pleading—at Macey—to one of agony and forlorn—at Jacob. Tears flowed freely down his weather-worn cheeks as he reached out to touch Jacob's head.

Macey used her free hand to slap him away. "Don't touch him! Don't you dare touch him…"

Scott moved forward and knelt beside Macey. He checked for a pulse along Jacob's neck. He couldn't find one.

Macey searched Scott's defeated face before looking back at her father. The all-consuming feeling of hatred she felt for the man before her immediately turned to one of blatant terror when she realized that her brother could be dead. Tears blinded her vision when she locked eyes with her father's tear-filled eyes. "Oh, God, don't let him die! Papa, please…please, please, don't let him die…"

CHAPTER 36

BORROWED MEMORIES

Macey and Scott found themselves pacing the floor of the waiting room, for the second time in two days. It had not surprised Macey when her father had panicked and fled before the police and ambulance arrived at the station. She was surprised and concerned, however, that neither the hospital staff nor the police had been able to locate Ruth to notify her of the incident.

Dr. Mullins was on call, and was unable to hide his surprise at seeing the couple in the ER waiting room again. He smiled at them when the doors to Jacob's treatment room closed behind him. "We've got to quit meeting like this." He hoped his meager attempt at humor might allay some of their fear and anxiety.

Scott came forward to shake his hand and asked anxiously, "Is he going to be all right, Dr. Mullins?"

Macey stood rooted to her spot—needing to hear the doctor's response—but, fearing it at the same time.

Dr. Mullins glanced toward Macey but directed his reply to Scott. "Jacob has lost a tremendous amount of blood, but I don't think we're dealing with a life-threatening injury here. We were initially concerned about possible internal damage to some major organs, but, we managed to stop the bleeding for now. X-rays indicate there is a tear in the intestinal lining so he will require surgery to correct that. The trouble is...we are having trouble contacting his family. We need their consent—although—we can't wait much longer. I don't want to risk any more infection setting in. If we don't locate someone soon, we will go ahead with the surgery. Jacob's been in and out of consciousness, and hasn't been able to help us much in that department. Do either of you know how to contact his parents—or anyone in his immediate family?"

Macey moved closer to Dr. Mullins and spoke for the first time. Her throat and voice were dry and raspy from her earlier screams and tears. "I am Jacob's sister. Please, Dr. Mullins...do whatever you have to...I'll sign anything. You said there was a slight tear to the intestinal lining... isn't that serious? Are you sure he's going to be okay? You're not just saying that?"

Dr. Mullins placed a comforting hand upon Macey's shoulder. "He's going to be fine. His x-rays, show that it might be more of a scratch than a tear, but, we won't know for sure until we get in there for a closer look. If it was any deeper, I'd be concerned about possible peritonitis..."

"Peritonitis can be pretty serious, can't it?" Macey asked worriedly. "Isn't it a result of fecal matter being absorbed into the bloodstream, or something like that?"

Dr. Mullins nodded. "Yes, Macey, peritonitis can be a very serious condition—sometimes, with fatal results—but, as I said, I feel fairly confident that the tear is not a deep one. My main concern now is the amount of blood Jacob has lost. He's going to be extremely weak for a while, so he'll have to remain in the hospital for a few days so that we can monitor his condition closely, just in case infection does set in. He was lucky. Another centimeter in either direction, and...well, it might be a different story altogether. I've got to go scrub in now. Jacob will be in recovery most of the night, but if you want to wait around, you can see him for a few minutes when we finish. After that, young lady, the best thing you can do is to go home and get some rest before I have to admit *you* to the hospital."

Macey wished she felt as optimistic about Jacob's injury as the good doctor appeared to be; instead, she nodded and smiled her thanks.

A few minutes later, she walked along side Jacob's gurney when they wheeled him from the treatment room. She reached out, took his hand into her own, and squeezed it lightly. She bent down and kissed his forehead, hoping that he could hear her. "I'll be right here, Jacob. I love you so much..."

It was eleven o'clock by the time Macey was allowed into the recovery room to spend a few minutes with her brother. She held his hand while he moaned several times and rolled his head slowly from side to side, but he never woke up. She thought it looked as though he might be dreaming. She stood outside the door to the recovery room, when the nurse reluctantly told her she would have to leave, and watched as the nurse checked Jacob's vital signs.

She was so exhausted that she barely felt Scott's warm, reassuring arms encircle her from behind. She leaned back against him and closed her eyes. "He's okay, Scott...he's going to be okay. God...when I think about how close I came to losing him...I..."

"Shhh..." Scott whispered into her ear and pulled her tighter against him. "Don't go there. Come on, there's nothing more you can do here tonight. I'm taking you home and putting you to bed."

Macey sighed. She had not slept—other than a few winks here and there—in almost forty-eight hours. "Becca...I forgot about Becca! Scott, I've got to go upstairs and check on Becca."

Scott held her firmly by the shoulders. "No, you don't. I already did that while you were in with Jacob. Mr. James is sleeping on a cot beside her bed. There's been no change in her condition."

Macey's shoulders slumped in despair. "Oh, Scott...she's got to wake up soon. The longer she..." She choked on her unfinished thoughts.

"We've got to believe she's going to come through this, Macey. Becca is going to be fine. Hell, she's too feisty and mean to die! And, Jacob has already weathered the worst part. He's going to be damn sore for a few weeks, but he's young and strong. It's you I'm worried about right now. You've got to get some rest, so...come on...I'm taking you out of this dump."

Macey turned in his arms but her tentative smile quickly faded. She suddenly remembered that her father now knew about her existence—not to mention Scott's. "Scott! What about my father? Did the police find him? Please, please tell me they found him and locked him up?"

Scott ran one hand through his hair. Not only had he not been able to have his discussion with Macey as he had planned, but he had suddenly been thrown into a situation he wasn't sure how to handle. He could only presume the measure of hatred Andrew Wymer must feel toward him, but, why did the man apparently hate his own daughter just as much—if not more? He remembered that Andrew Wymer had seemed shocked when he saw Macey in the station, and what was it he called her? *Bitch*? *Whore*?

He led Macey to a small bench reserved for visitors, but they both remained standing. "No, they haven't found your father yet, but they do have an APB out on him. Your mother hasn't answered their phone at home either, but, the police have an officer standing by for whenever either of them show up. Macey...I know you're exhausted...and I know this is not the time to get into all this, but, there are some things I need to talk to you about. Things I hope you can clarify for me. Do you mind?"

Macey sat down on the bench and motioned for him to join her. "I am beyond tired, but that's okay. What kind of things, Scott?"

Scott looked down at the floor and made no immediate move to accept her offer to sit beside her on the bench. He paced for a moment or two before finally reaching into his pocket to retrieve the newspaper clippings he had found beside Becca's body. He took a deep breath before handing them over to Macey.

She recognized the articles at once. After all, she had her own copies at home. She looked up at Scott with a puzzled expression and shrugged her shoulders. "What?"

Scott stared back at her with a dumbfounded expression. "What do you mean...*what*! Macey...these articles say I killed your sister! All these months I've known you...why haven't you said anything to me about it?"

It was Macey's turn to be dumbfounded, but she was simply too tired. Her shoulders slumped and she shrugged with unfeigned exhaustion. "What was there to say, Scott? When I first met you in the parking lot... remember that first day you arrived? Well...naturally, I recognized you immediately, and to be perfectly honest with you, I hated you more at that moment than I've ever hated anyone before in my life. God how I hated you...so much. I couldn't believe you cared so little about what you did that you showed no reaction to seeing me...to seeing *Kacey's* face..."

Scott listened and nodded in agreement. "I would expect you to hate me, Macey. You have every right to hate me, especially after reading all... *that*," he spoke hoarsely. He pointed to the articles Macey held limply in her hand. "God, Macey, why? Why would you want anything to do with me at all? How could you even stand to be in the same room with me?"

Macey sighed. She really was tired, but she could tell this was something Scott desperately needed to talk about. "Well...it didn't happen overnight, Scott, but it did happen much quicker than I ever thought was possible—for my opinion of you to change, I mean. Sometimes I feel like I'm betraying Kacey by being so accepting of you. Trust me...I wanted desperately to hate you, I really did. I didn't want to like you. I wanted to continue hating you. It was easier to hate you than to...well—after all—I had hated you for twenty years, but...being around you every day at work, seeing how you treated people, how you handled yourself under pressure...how you even fed and cared for that old stray cat that hangs around the complex. Well...I guess I just started doubting the hold that hatred had on me. Even though I had judged you guilty for twenty years, I finally had to come to terms with the fact that maybe I had been wrong about you, that maybe there was more to it than I'd read in the papers. For my own emotional survival, I knew I had to find a way, within myself, to forgive you—no—to forgive myself for the thoughts I had about you...and, to move on. If you knew Kacey at all, you would know that she wouldn't have wanted me to continue harboring the hatred and anger I had for you."

Scott finally joined Macey on the bench. "Kacey? She really was your twin, right? Your identical twin?"

"Yes...we were twins, but I thought you knew that."

Scott leaned forward and put his head in his hands. "Macey...I have a favor to ask. It's a big one, and, I'll...I'll understand if you tell me you can't do it."

Macey had no idea what he was talking about. She placed an arm gently across his back and lowered her head to his level. "Scott, you know I would do anything within my power to help you in any way I could. What is it?"

He turned and looked at her with eyes gritty and red from lack of sleep. "You're going to think I'm crazy, and you have every right to say no, but...your memories, Macey...I need to borrow your memories."

Macey's brows drew together and she shook her head in confusion. "Scott, I'm sorry, but...I don't understand. What do you mean you need to borrow my memories?"

Scott exhaled deeply and looked at her with a hurt that went beyond any hurt he had ever felt. "Oh, Macey...you really don't understand, do you?"

She shook her head, suddenly oblivious to her exhausted state.

He took her hands into his own and stared directly into her eyes. "Your sister...Kacey? I don't remember her, Macey...I don't remember anything about her. I don't remember anything at all about having lived in Columbus, Georgia, and, I sure as hell don't remember anything about murdering anyone!"

Macey jerked her hands away and covered her mouth.

She couldn't believe it! Was it possible that all the times she had thought him to be insensitive and cruel for not having acknowledged her identity that...he didn't know her because he couldn't remember anything from that time in his life? His mother had hinted at that explanation, but Macey had not believed her at the time. She had not wanted to believe her, but, that would explain so much.

She continued to stare at him until a tear escaped his tortured eyes and slipped down across his stubbed cheek. She slowly spread open her arms and rocked with him until she felt his tears subsiding. "Oh, Scott... even though I was once convinced of it, I don't think—no, I know—that you could not have had anything to do with Kacey's murder. There was never any definite proof, you know."

Scott looked up and stared at her in disbelief. "The articles say I spent a year in a mental hospital."

"No, they don't," Macey countered. "They say you spent a year receiving psychological help."

"Which means I must have been in a nut ward, right?"

"No, at least, I don't think so. You mean to tell me, Scott, that you don't remember receiving all that care and counseling?"

Scott released a shallow breath and shook his head. "My mom—for God's sake—why didn't she tell me about all this? She *knew*...and she never told me..."

She wasn't sure why, but Macey felt obligated to offer a theory in Mrs. Pennell's defense. "I'm sure your mother had her reasons for not telling you, Scott. Maybe she didn't want to remind you of such a traumatic time in your life. She probably thought it would be too painful for you to remember it all. No mother wants to see her child suffer."

Scott pulled away from her embrace. "She talked to you about this, didn't she...when she came to visit? She recognized you! What did she do, Macey? Did she make you promise not to tell me?"

"Yes, she did recognize me, Scott; but—no—she didn't ask me not to tell you anything. She...did ask me not to get involved with you anymore than I already was."

"What!"

Macey held firmly to Scott's forearm. "Easy, Scott. She only had your best interest at heart. I think she probably thought I had some sort of evil plan devised to get even with you...and—if not me—then surely someone in my family. She loves you very much, Scott. I'm sure of that."

Scott closed his eyes and sighed. "Yeah, I know she does, but, that doesn't excuse her for keeping this from me all these years. It explains so many things. These flashbacks I've been having for the past year or so, my lack of commitment when it comes to members of the opposite sex..."

Macey sat up straight and looked hard at Scott. "Flashbacks? You've been having flashbacks? What kind?"

Scott looked at his watch and pulled Macey up from the bench. "I'll get into all that later...I promise, but, I need to get you home. You can sleep in my guest room tonight. We'll sit up all night if we have to and sort through all this."

Macey offered a weak laugh and quipped, "Sleep in your guest room? That's ridiculous, Scott. I live just across the parking lot from you. I can sleep in my own bed."

Scott was adamant that she concede to his demand. "Nope...you're staying at my place so that I can see to it—personally—that you get some rest. I'll call Janet in the morning and let her know that neither of us will be in. I can work from home tomorrow, and you can get back to the hospital in the morning to check on Jacob and Becca. Meantime, I need you to tell me all about Kacey...about anything you know about what happened that night in 1969...about your family...why your father seemed so shocked to see you. It was like he'd seen a ghost, Macey, when he saw you standing in the doorway of his station. As for me, well...I'll tell you all about these flashbacks and maybe we can figure out if there's a connection to any of this."

They walked, hand-in-hand, down the hall.

Macey leaned against him. "Okay, Scott, we'll talk as long as it takes... you can borrow all the memories I have to offer, but tell me something."

"What's that?"

"Where did you get copies of those articles?"

Scott touched his head to hers and sighed again. "We'll add that to the list of things we need to talk about..."

CHAPTER 37

MACEY AND RUTH MEET

Scott pushed against the guest room door with his shoulder while trying to balance the breakfast tray he carried. He sat the tray down on the dresser and walked over to the bed where Macey lay sleeping. They had sat up until four o'clock that morning talking about the past, the present, and even a little bit about the future.

He pushed away a stray lock of dark hair from her face, and thought how lucky he was they had found each other. It had to be fate. Why else would he—Scott Pennell—fall in love with the twin sister of a girl he was supposed to have murdered twenty years ago? He knew now that it was, indeed, love he felt for Macey. He wanted to spend the rest of his life with this woman, making her happy, making her forget about her sorrowful childhood, making a family with her...so many things.

Macey sensed Scott's presence. She opened her eyes and watched the kaleidoscope of emotions racing across his face. "Penny for your thoughts?" she whispered.

Scott smiled down at her. "You're awake..." He trailed a finger across her cheekbone. "God, you are so beautiful..."

Macey sat up and smoothed back her hair. She returned his smile and blushed. "Yeah, I just bet I am. What time is it anyway?"

Scott glanced at his watch. "Almost ten-thirty, why?"

Macey tried to scramble from beneath the covers, but her feet got tangled in the sheets. "I've got to get to the hospital, Scott! You promised to wake me at seven."

Scott blocked her progress by gently pinning her back against the pillows. He couldn't help it—he couldn't have stopped himself even if he had wanted to—and, he didn't want to. He bent lower and kissed her gently. He felt her initial reluctance to return his kiss, but relaxed when her body gradually began to respond to the kiss.

Macey willed her body to relax. So much had happened in the past few days. Her mind was reeling, trying to sort out everything. The one thing she knew for sure—or at least she thought she knew—was that, somewhere along the line, she had fallen in love with Scott Pennell. She wasn't convinced if that was a good thing or not. It might be best for them to go their separate ways and try to put their pasts behind them once and for all.

Scott pulled away from her and smiled again. "Just for the record...I came in here to wake you at seven, but...I just didn't have the heart to do it. Three hours of sleep over the past forty-eight hours? I don't think so, Macey. You needed your rest. You're not going to be of any use to Jacob or Becca if you drop dead from exhaustion."

Macey nodded and sighed. "You're right...I know you're right...but, I really do need to get over there right away."

"I agree," Scott said. "But, not before you eat something."

Macey pushed herself up on her elbows. "But I'm not hungry, Scott... you made me breakfast? What is it that smells so good, anyway?"

"I didn't think you were hungry."

"I'm not, but...if you went to all the trouble of making breakfast, then the least I could do is *attempt* to eat something."

Scott playfully pushed her back upon the pillow and retrieved the breakfast tray. "You bet your sweet ass you will, Miss Garner...or, should I refer to you as Miss Wymer?"

Macey smiled as he positioned the tray for her. "I think I prefer Garner, if you don't mind. Scott? Are you sure you're okay about everything you learned last night? That was an awful lot of information to absorb at one time."

Scott hesitated slightly before replying, "No, I'm not sure that I am. You gave me a lot to think about, Macey. I wish I could say I remember everything that happened twenty years ago, but I don't; however, I have made a decision. I'm going to see someone who *can* help me."

"What do you mean, Scott?"

"A psychologist...maybe he can hypnotize me or something— anything—to help me remember it all."

"Do you really think that will help, Scott? Don't you think they probably tried that when you were a teenager?"

"I have no idea. Maybe they did and it didn't work. Maybe they'll have more luck now. It's worth a try, anyway. I'm going to make an appointment today to speak with someone. In the meantime, you ravishing female, you need to eat and get to the hospital!"

"Yes sir!" Macey smiled as she offered a mock salute in return.

Macey was relieved when the ICU nurse told her that Jacob was doing so well that he had been moved to a private room earlier that morning. She wanted to immediately rush to Jacob's bedside, but she needed to check on Becca first.

Macey rounded the corner in time to see Mr. James walking out of Becca's room. She took in his defeated look and worried about what the tired lines etched in his old, weather-worn face might mean. "Mr. James?"

Alvin looked up and smiled at his daughter's best friend. "Good morning, Miss Macey. How are you today? You do look a might more rested than the last time I saw you."

"I'm fine, Mr. James. How's Becca? Is there any change?"

Alvin shook his head sadly. "'I'm afraid not, Miss Macey. The doctors— they ain't saying much—but, I'm getting the feeling that they're giving up on my Becca."

Macey put her arm around the old man and led him to a sofa in the family waiting room. "I doubt that, Mr. James. I'm sure they're doing all they can for her."

Alvin held his hand up and shook his head. "No, no, Miss Macey. I don't mean it to sound like they ain't doing anything for her. It's just something in the way they look at her when they think I'm not looking— you know—like they're just going through the motions, when what they're really doing is waiting for her to die. They keep saying that it's up to her now, because they've done all they can to patch her up."

Macey nodded. "Well, that's true, you know. It is up to Becca...and, that's exactly why I know she's going to pull through this. Becca is too strong—and too stubborn—to let her life end this way. If I know her, she's probably laying in there—inside herself—thinking of ways to get even with the man who did this to her."

Mr. James smiled and patted Macey's hand. "You could be right about that, Miss Macey. Yessirree...you're probably right about that, for sure. Why...now that you mention it, I can picture my Becca doing just that."

Macey stood up and smiled back at the old man who was more like a father to her than her own had ever been. "I think I'll just poke my head in for a minute to see—for myself—how she's doing."

Alvin tugged on her hand as she turned to leave. "You might want to wait a bit, Miss Macey. She's got another visitor with her right now."

"Oh? Who is it? Mrs. James?"

Old Alvin smiled a half-toothless grin and shook his head. "No, no. The missus will be here after lunch to sit with Becca for a few hours, while I go and check on some things at the diner. Someone is running it for us, but he's probably stealing us blind behind our backs—can't trust anyone these days. You know how people sometimes take advantage of us old folks. No, actually...her visitor is Mr. Carlton Brown...that who's in with my Becca right now."

"Carlton? I thought he was out of town for the holidays?"

"Oh, he was, but the missus called him last night and told him what happened. He was here bright and early this morning, and he hasn't left her side since. I do believe the young man is smitten with my Becca."

Macey smiled at the memory of the two lovers teasing and playing with each other at the bowling alley. "You could be right about that, Mr. James...you could be right. And maybe—just maybe—Mr. Carlton Brown is exactly the medicine Becca needs right now. Listen, I need to go visit someone else in the hospital, but I'll check back here after lunch, okay?"

Alvin took her hand into his own and patted it. "That's mighty nice of you, Miss Macey...mighty nice. You take care now. I'll be seeing you later."

Macey was still smiling to herself when she pushed open the door to Room 327. That smile froze upon her face when she entered the room and saw Ruth Wymer sitting on the foot of Jacob's bed.

Jacob and his mother turned toward the door at the exact same time.

Macey stood in the doorway—paralyzed—unable to move forward into the room, or retreat backward out of it.

"Macey," Jacob smiled weakly. "Come on in...please."

Macey finally found her voice, but kept her distance. "Maybe I should come back later, Jacob." She prayed that her voice did not reveal the stirring of emotions she felt at seeing her mother for the first time in twenty years.

Ruth's face had paled visibly once she fully recognized Macey. She took a deep breath to calm herself, stood, and walked slowly toward Macey. Her hands trembled as she drew closer to her daughter. "Please don't go, Macey," she pleaded. "There's...so much to talk about, so much I need to say to you...and, to Jacob."

Macey still hesitated, and her fingers still held firm to the door handle. "I'm not sure if that's a good idea, Mama. Maybe...I should leave and come back later."

"No!" Jacob rasped loudly from his bed. He tried to rise, but the jolt of pain that penetrated his side caused him to elicit a weak moan before dropping back down onto the pillow.

Both women were quick to rush to his bedside.

"Jacob!" Macey cried. "Are you okay? What's wrong?"

Jacob reached for a hand from each of them and looked at them pleadingly. He inhaled and exhaled slowly, trying to wait out the moment of pain and discomfort. "I'm okay, but...it feels like maybe...I've pulled a stitch or two loose."

"Oh, dear," Ruth moaned. "Let me go get the nurse."

"No, Mama, it's okay...that can wait," Jacob countered. "Right now, I just want the two of you here with me...in this room...together, okay?"

Macey raised her eyebrows questioningly when Ruth looked in her direction. She looked back at her brother and knew he was in more pain than he admitted to, so, she answered for both Ruth and herself. "Jacob, you've got to rest. I'm going to get a nurse to come check those stitches. Mama and I will wait in the family room. It'll give us a chance to talk and give you a chance to rest."

Ruth Wymer squared back her shoulders and looked at the beautiful, confident woman that stood before her. She envied her that—her youth and her beauty—but, most of all, she envied her the confidence that she exhumed. Despite the feelings of envy, Ruth surprised herself—she was very happy to see Macey. Lucas had convinced her for so long that Macey would try to turn Jacob against her, but standing face to face with her now, Ruth instinctively felt that wasn't the case. She had tried, for so many years, to block Macey from her memory. In the end, however, her maternal feelings for her daughter were fighting to resurface. Yes, her initial feeling of envy was slowly graduating to one of pride in the person her daughter had become. There really was so much they needed to talk about.

"I think that's a wonderful idea, Macey," Ruth concurred. She leaned over and kissed Jacob's cheek. "We'll be just outside your door, Jacob. Please, son, try to get some rest."

Jacob leaned back into his pillows. "Be nice, you two. I love you both too much to see any more bloodshed," he sighed, with a weak attempt at humor.

Macey looked back at him with a feeling of love and immense relief that he was going to be all right. "There will be no more bloodshed in this family, Jacob...not if I can help it." She held open the door for her mother and watched her go through it. How she wished her mother had taken her in her arms and told her how happy she was to see her...told her how much she had missed her over the years. It wouldn't have made up for all the years she'd been neglected and forgotten, but, it would have been a good place to start.

"Thank you," Ruth smiled as she walked through the door Macey held open for her. She found she had to physically refrain from reaching out and taking her daughter into her arms. She wanted desperately to hold her, to let her know she loved her, but she wondered if too much time, pain, and heartache had passed between them to prevent that from ever happening. She felt sure that Macey would have pushed her away if she tried to hug her. She had endured enough of Andrew's rejection over the years; she didn't think she was strong enough to endure the same from Macey—no matter how much she might deserve that rejection.

Both women were so self-absorbed in their own thoughts that they didn't hear Jacob's deep sigh of relief as he watched them leave together. Jacob closed his eyes when the door closed behind the two women, and he offered a silent prayer to God. He asked Him to bring them together once again—as mother and daughter—before it really was too late.

CHAPTER 38

BURYING THE HATCHET

Scott made several phone calls after Macey left his apartment to visit Jacob and Becca. The first call was to CompuTech, informing Janet that he would be working from home for the rest of the week. The second call was to a psychiatrist he had found by *letting his fingers do the walking* through the Yellow Pages. The psychiatrist had a recent cancellation, and made an appointment with Scott for the following afternoon. The last call was to the Columbus Police Department, where he requested to speak to Detective Lance Windham. Macey had identified the detective as being the one in charge of her sister's cold case several years ago. Scott had been relived when Detective Windham agreed to meet with him on his lunch break; they planned to meet at Minnie's Restaurant at twelve-thirty.

Scott arrived at Minnie's at twelve-twenty. There was no available parking in front of the building, so Scott had to park on a side street, two blocks away from the popular restaurant. When he walked inside the crowded restaurant, he noticed a well-dressed man in a three-piece suit waiting off to one side. Scott glanced around and noticed that there was only one other man who appeared to be waiting for someone. The second man was dressed casually in a white tee shirt, jeans, and a baseball cap; Scott quickly decided that the well-dressed man must be Detective Windham. He approached the man and held out his hand. "Detective Windham?"

The man in the three-piece suit looked down his long, arrogant nose at Scott, who was dressed comfortably in gray sweats and running shoes. "Excuse me?" the man snubbed.

Scott smiled, only slightly embarrassed at his obvious mistaken identity of Detective Windham. "Sorry, thought you were someone else," he apologized.

The businessman turned when the door opened and a meticulously dressed woman in her thirties entered the restaurant. He moved around Scott, careful not to touch him, and offered his hand to the woman.

Scott blew out his cheeks to hide his embarrassment, scratched his head, and looked around the immediate area. He turned to leave, and didn't notice the man wearing the jeans and baseball cap ambling slowly toward him.

"Come on, Mr. Pennell," the man smiled. "It's too crowded in here. Let's go around the corner, grab a hot dog, and find a quiet place to talk."

Scott's eyebrows raised in genuine astonishment. "Detective Windham?"

Lance Windham smiled again. He knew his casual appearance and demeanor was not the average person's perception of what a detective should look like. "In the flesh," he grinned broadly. He pushed the baseball cap up off his forehead. "I know...probably not what you expected, huh?"

It was Scott's turn to smile. "Not really, but...hey, you're probably undercover or something, right?"

They walked outside and Detective Windham motioned toward an older-model pick-up truck.

"Nope...I usually wear a three-piece when I go undercover. Come on, let's take my truck. I saw you drive around the corner. I can't afford to be seen riding in a Porsche in this neighborhood—might ruin my image if any of my informants saw me."

"Wouldn't want to do that," Scott smiled again, shaking his head. He liked this man and felt immediately at ease with him.

Macey and Ruth left the nurse to attend to Jacob's pulled stitches, and walked to the hospital cafeteria for a cup of coffee. Both women remained quiet, each of them waiting for the other to begin the conversation.

Ruth finally cleared her throat and began. "I...uh...heard several weeks ago, that you might be in town, Macey, but, I didn't really believe it."

Macey was so stunned to find herself sitting across from her mother that she didn't think to ask from whom Ruth had learned of Macey's presence. "You mean you didn't want to believe it—isn't that right, Mama?"

Ruth looked up from her cup and confronted the directness of Macey's stare. "This isn't easy for me either, Macey. I know you must... hate me, and, you have every right to hate me. I haven't been much of a mother to you, have I?"

Macey's first instinct—ingrained in her since early childhood—was to remain polite and not hurt her mother's feelings. However, she had put other people's feelings ahead of her own all her life, and she was suddenly tired of it. She continued to look directly into Ruth Wymer's tortured eyes. "No, Mama. You haven't."

Ruth turned her head and tried to discreetly wipe away a tear from the corner of her eye. She took a deep sigh and turned back to face Macey. She nodded and said, "You have every reason to hate me...and your father."

Macey finally looked away from her mother and shook her head. "I only wish I could hate you, Mama. You and Papa, both, but...maybe something's wrong with me. I...I don't know, but...I don't hate you, Mama. I've never really hated you. All I've ever wanted from you and Papa, was something you either couldn't—or wouldn't—give me. I wanted your love...your understanding...your acceptance." Tears pooled in Macey's eyes as she looked back at her mother. She sniffed and continued. "But that's all water under the bridge, as they say. I don't—I can't—dwell on the past any longer. If I'm going to have any kind of life, I know that I have to learn to put it all behind me somehow."

Ruth nodded her head in acknowledgment. "I agree...I know what you mean, Macey."

Macey knew that she had to get off the subject of her shattered relationship with her parents. "By the way, Mama...I assume you know what happened to Jacob. Have you heard from Papa? Do you know where he is?"

Ruth would have been mortified if Macey had known what she had been doing while Jacob was being so viciously attacked. She and the good Reverend had been enjoying a quick rendezvous, and she had not gotten home, the night before, until after eleven. She knew that Andrew had plans to visit a friend after work and wouldn't return home until around midnight. She knew she was taking a chance being out so late with Lucas, but, he had absorbed himself into her very being—as repulsed with herself, and as fearful of the man—Ruth's withered resistance always seemed to win out over her better judgment.

Ruth knew that she couldn't tell Macey—the daughter she had not seen in twenty years—about any of this. "No, Macey...I don't know where your father is. It was late when I returned home last night. A policeman was waiting at the curb and told me what happened to Jacob. He said the police were looking for Andrew and wanted to search the house. I wanted to get to the hospital immediately to be with Jacob, but, the policeman insisted that I remain at the house until they finished their search. I don't know what they were looking for—he had a search warrant—but, it didn't take him very long. He said it looked like Andrew might have been there earlier in the night. Some of his clothes were gone, and the money he kept in his sock drawer was missing. I...I still can't believe that Andrew would do something like this to his own son." Ruth lowered her face into her hands and sobbed softly.

Macey wished that she could comfort her mother, but she felt awkward with the thought. "Mama? Do you have any idea where Papa might have gone? It's important that the police find him. Did Jacob tell you that it wasn't him Papa was trying to kill?"

Ruth raised her head quickly and sniffed back a sob. "Why, no...Jacob didn't want to talk about it this morning. He just said you were there when it happened. He said he needed some time to think things out. I was just *so* thankful that he's going to be all right. I guess I just assumed it had to have been an accident because I know Andrew would never intentionally hurt Jacob. At least...not like that...with a knife. Oh, no... Macey! Was it you Andrew was trying to stab? Oh, please tell me that's not so..."

Macey did reach out to her mother this time. She placed her hand upon Ruth's and smiled. "No, Mama...it wasn't me, although...I think Papa would have preferred it to be me. There was someone else there. Someone Papa must hate even more than he does me."

Ruth welcomed the unexpected gesture of Macey's hand upon her own, and she reciprocated by placing her free hand on top of Macey's. "Oh, baby...your Papa doesn't hate you. He's never hated you. He's just been so...torn apart since Kacey's death. He's never been the same since the night the police called and told us about what happened to her, but...I'm getting off the subject. You said there was someone else at the station...who was it?"

Both their coffees had gotten cold, but neither of them seemed to notice.

Macey paused briefly before continuing. "It was Scott Pennell, Mama."

The name had been permanently ingrained into Ruth's memory. She would never forget that name. The name—and the man behind it—had been constantly on her mind, especially since the night she saw him at his apartment, taking out the trash.

"Oh, dear, God...no..." Ruth pushed up from the table and began pacing nervously back and forth. She was oblivious to the concerned stares from the other customers.

Macey looked embarrassed and pleaded quietly with her mother.

"Mama...please sit back down."

Ruth looked at Macey and quickly glanced around the room at the people staring at her. She slowly returned to her seat.

Macey took her mother's hands into her own, once again, to calm her.

Ruth's eyes glazed over with fear and disbelief as she stared back at Macey. "What was that...that *murderer* doing at our gas station? I can't believe he would have the gall to step foot in this town again...not after what he did."

"Mama," Macey responded hesitantly, but firmly. "Please, don't call him that. Scott is a friend of mine. We work at the same company, and live in the same apartment complex."

Ruth had momentarily forgotten about Lucas's previous revelation that Scott was Macey's boyfriend. "What..."

Macey shook her head firmly and answered in a low voice, "No, don't say anything else, Mama. Let me finish. Please?"

Ruth nodded her reluctant acquiescence.

Macey cleared her throat, unaware that she still held her mother's hands within her own. "He doesn't remember anything, Mama. Nothing. He remembers absolutely nothing about having lived in Columbus, about ever having met Kacey, much less...*murdering* her."

"How convenient for him," snipped Ruth. "That's the same excuse he used the night he killed her, too!"

Macey felt compelled to convince her mother of Scott's innocence. "Mama, please...listen to me. I believe him. I didn't want to at first, but I really do believe him. Scott has only recently learned about the murder. He found some old newspaper clippings, but he doesn't remember anything about that night...and, I really do believe him. I've told him I will do whatever I can to help him remember."

Ruth was shaking her head in denial, but Macey continued in a firm tone. "Now, Mama, I know how you must feel about him, but would you please...please try to put that aside for now and tell me all you know about that night. What do you know about Scott and Kacey's relationship?"

"*Relationship!*" Ruth rasped hoarsely. "What relationship? We never knew about any...*relationship*! We found out after Kacey died—from that boy's parents—that the two of them had been sneaking around for months seeing each other. Kacey would always tell us she was going out with girlfriends, when she was really sneaking off to be with *him*."

Macey patted her mother's hand and smiled her encouragement. "Go on, Mama. I know this is hard for you to talk about, but, I would really like to hear more of what you remember about Kacey's last few days and weeks. It's important..."

Ruth saw the pain reflected in Macey's eyes. "You two girls were always so close, weren't you? It was almost as though the two of you didn't need anyone else. You certainly didn't need...me."

Tears pooled in Macey's eyes again as she remembered all the times over the past twenty years that she had needed a mother's love and comfort. "Oh, Mama, you are so wrong...so very wrong. We both needed you desperately, each of us for very different reasons, but..."

"You didn't think I was there for you, did you?" Ruth interrupted.

Macey sniffed and shook her head. "No, Mama. You weren't there for us. You made it clear that Jacob was your life. He was all you ever seemed to care about. You thought I was a...whore, and, that Kacey was destined to be a...nobody; at least, that's how it seemed to us as frightened and confused teenagers."

Ruth shook her head adamantly from side to side. "That's so untrue, Macey—and, so unfair. I loved you both just as much as I loved Jacob. It's just that...well, I thought Jacob needed more love and protection from..."

"From whom, Mama?"

"Never mind, none of that's important now..."

"It's important to me, Mama. You mean from Papa...isn't that who you mean, Mama? You felt Jacob needed protection from Papa? Why? He was just a small child."

Ruth sighed and closed her eyes. "Yes, Macey...he was just a small child, but, he was a small child who had witnessed something horrendous. I had to protect him...I had to do everything in my power to keep him from telling anyone what he had seen—especially Andrew."

Macey was more confused than ever. "What are you talking about, Mama?"

Ruth gained strength from the touch of her daughter's hand. "It was after you went away, Macey, to have...your baby. There was this one morning when I went to awaken Jacob and he wasn't in his room. Kacey had already left for school, and I searched everywhere for him, calling his name over and over."

"Where was he, Mama?"

Ruth looked up again into Macey's dark-grey eyes. She thought they were kind eyes—eyes that might, also, be understanding and forgiving— one day. "I found him in your sister's room. He was curled up fast asleep... in her...closet."

"In her closet! I don't understand, Mama. What in the world was Jacob doing sleeping in Kacey's closet?"

Ruth hesitated briefly before continuing. "Well, after I woke him up and fed him breakfast, I got him to talking about why he was sleeping in Kacey's closet. He begged me not to tell anyone. When I asked him why, he said he had to stay hidden in her closet, so that he…so that he could… protect her."

Macey raised her eyebrows in surprise. "Protect her? From what? I'm sorry, Mama, I'm not following you. I don't understand…" Macey stopped in mid-sentence—maybe she did understand. Was it possible Jacob had witnessed his father's sexual abuse of Kacey?

Ruth watched the changing expressions travel across Macey's lovely face and closed her eyes again. "Oh, no…you knew, too, didn't you? Why? Why didn't someone tell me!"

Macey watched as fresh tears flowed down her mother's cheeks. "What would you have done, Mama? Would you have confronted Papa? Would you have stood up to him? Would you have gotten Kacey and Jacob far away from him? Tell me, Mama, I need to know…what would you have done?"

Tears continued to ebb slowly down Ruth's cheeks, causing the cheap mascara to blend and smudge into her skin whenever she attempted to wipe them away. "I…I don't know, Macey…I don't know…"

Macey wiped away her own tears. "I guess it really doesn't matter now, does it, Mama? So…Jacob saw *everything*? He's never confided that to me."

Ruth used a napkin to wipe away her tears and the smudged mascara. "I was so afraid of what Andrew would do to him, if he knew what Jacob had seen. Your father was a very angry man at that time, especially after you went to live with your aunt. He became an even angrier man after Kacey died."

"Yeah, I bet he did, Mama. Probably because his *lover* had been taken from him," Macey sneered.

Even though she didn't have it in her to hate—not even her father after all he done to her and Kacey—she did harbor tremendous anger and resentment toward him, for the pain and humiliation he had inflicted upon them all those years ago.

Macey stood to leave. "I think we've probably talked enough for one day, Mama. I'm going to spend a couple of hours with Jacob, and then I need to go up to ICU to be with a friend there."

"ICU?" Ruth asked in surprise. "I thought only family members could visit people in ICU?"

"That's true, Mama. The hospital is normally very strict about that rule, but…well, let's just say that this particular friend has a very persuasive father. The nurses pretend to look the other way whenever I visit Becca."

Ruth stood and placed a gentle hand on Macey's arm. She looked up into her daughter's beautiful face. "Macey, can we talk again? Soon? Please...there's still so much I need to say to you."

Macey bit her bottom lip and nodded. "Sure, Mama...we can do that. There's still a lot I need to say to you, too. Listen, if you hear from Papa—anything at all—you'll let me know?"

Ruth nodded. "Of course, Macey; but, how...how do I get in touch with you?"

Macey took a pen from her purse and scribbled her phone number on a napkin. "This is the number to my apartment. I check my messages several times a day, so if I'm not there, just leave a message for me."

Ruth nodded again. "Okay, Macey, but...I'm probably the last person Andrew would contact. By the way, your friend in ICU...Becca, you said? Is it serious? I guess it must be if she's in ICU, though..."

It was Macey's turn to nod. "Yes, Mama. I'm afraid it's very serious. Becca James is a good friend of mine...probably the best friend I've ever had. She's also black. I know how you and Papa feel about blacks, but, she was brutally beaten and molested Saturday night. She hasn't regained consciousness yet, and, we don't know if she's going to pull through or not. Maybe that's why the nurses in ICU are so lenient with my visitation."

"She's black?"

Macey sighed. "Yes, Mama." She was not the least bit surprised that her mother had focused on the race issue. "Becca's as black as the ace of spades, and, I love her like a sister. She's very important to me. Her entire family is very important to me."

"And she was beaten Saturday night?" Ruth rambled.

"Yes, Mama. Would you...would you like to come with me to see her, provided the nurses will allow it? I have to warn you though...she's not a very pretty sight at the moment."

Ruth very much wanted to see Macey's friend. Her mind was running rapidly over recent events. Could this Becca possibly be the same young woman she saw leaving her daughter's apartment Saturday night—the same woman that Lucas led into the woods? Oh, yes! Ruth Wymer very much wanted to see Miss Becca James. She squared back her shoulders and smiled encouragingly at her daughter. "Yes, Macey. I'd like very much to go with you to see your friend."

CHAPTER 39

Secrets Locked Away

The next several days went by too quickly for Scott, but, he knew that it had dragged eternally slow for members of the James and Wymer families. One week had passed since he had discovered Becca's body in the woods behind his apartment. One week had, also, passed since anyone had last seen any sign of Andrew Wymer.

Today was Sunday, Christmas Eve.

Scott was almost out of his apartment, leaving to pick up Macey from the hospital, when his phone rang. "Hello?" he answered hurriedly.

"Scott? Hello, it's Dr. Evans."

Dr. Marcus Evans was the psychiatrist Scott had enlisted to help him regain his memory of the events that transpired twenty years ago. He had only seen the doctor twice, but Scott felt extremely comfortable with him. He was confident the man would be able to help him.

"Dr. Evans, hello. Don't tell me you're working on Christmas Eve?"

Dr. Evans laughed heartily. He was an older, heavyset man with an easygoing, pleasant personality. He often volunteered to dress as Santa Claus, to entertain the children, at various functions during the holidays. "No, Scott...not really. The wife and I are getting ready to ride to Pine Mountain to spend Christmas with my son and his family. He has three children, and, well...Christmas just seems more like Christmas when there's a room full of children around to help celebrate it, don't you think?"

Scott returned the laugh. "I agree. Being an only child, however, I'm not used to being around a lot of people during the holidays."

"Were your parents very upset at your decision not to come home for Christmas?"

"Well," Scott sighed. "Under the circumstances, my mother really couldn't argue with me about it. She's upset that I've learned about what happened, and, I suppose she's feeling guilty for not having told me herself."

"I'm sure she had your best interests in mind at the time, Scott."

"Yeah," Scott concurred. "She probably did. Is that why you called? To talk to me about my mother? Want to know all about my childhood?"

Dr. Evans laughed good-naturedly. "No, maybe another time. I'm wrapping up some loose ends before I leave town, and, I was curious to know if you've taken Detective Windham up on his offer yet?"

Scott's expression turned more serious. "You mean his offer for me to look at the crime scene photos...to see if they trigger any memories?"

"Yes, exactly. It could very well be a turning point for you. I do have one suggestion, though; if you wouldn't mind, I would like to be with you when—if—you decide to do that."

"I appreciate that, Dr. Evans, I really do...but, if you don't mind, I think that's something I would like to do on my own. Well, not exactly on my own. As a matter of fact, I was just leaving to pick up Macey from the hospital. Detective Windham has offered to meet us at the police station today and let us look over the photos."

Dr. Evans expressed surprise. "Macey is willing to do that with you?"

"Well, actually, she's already seen them...a long time ago, but, yes, she wants to be there with me to look through them."

"And Detective Windham is giving up his Christmas Eve to assist you in this? Well now...I may have to change my overall opinion of our local police force."

Scott smiled into the phone. "I know what you mean, Dr. Evans. To tell you the truth, I've really come to admire this man a lot over the past few days. We've spent a lot of time together talking. I told him about finding—and taking—the newspaper articles I found by Becca's body last week. He agreed that I should have left them for the police, but, he understands why I panicked the way I did. I've been questioned again by the police, but all they had to do was match up the teeth marks on Becca's body, and they eliminated me as a suspect. They did say the articles were evidence, and that by taking them, I tampered with that evidence. Lance...Detective Windham...doesn't think they will charge me with that, though...given the circumstances. He has plans with his family later this evening, but, he agreed to meet us afterwards at the station to look at the photos."

"And you're absolutely sure you don't need me there? I'd be more than happy to tag along, you know?"

"I know, and I really do appreciate it, Dr. Evans, but, if all goes well, then maybe we won't have to try the hypnosis to help me remember what happened to Kacey Wymer."

"Yes, that is a possibility. Well...good luck, Scott, and please call me if there's anything I can do. Otherwise, I will see you next Friday?"

"You bet, Dr. Evans. Merry Christmas!"

"Merry Christmas to you, too, Scott."

While Scott rushed to pick up Macey from The Medical Center, Jacob sat behind the old metal desk, at his father's gas station. The hospital had released him the day before, with strict orders to stay home and rest, but, Jacob wanted to make sure the station receipts were in order. He and Ruth had had a long, heart-to-heart talk that included his plans to move to Florida. He knew that his mother was terribly upset at the thought of losing him, but Jacob had promised to visit often. He even suggested that his absence might give her and Macey a chance to become closer, since Macey had no immediate plans to leave Columbus. He and Ruth had also discussed what needed to be done about the station. They both agreed that it was probably best to sell it, although, that might prove to be difficult, since the deed was in Andrew's name only.

Macey and Scott had corroborated his testimony that Andrew had not intentionally meant to hurt him, and, Jacob had refused to press charges against his father. Regardless, Jacob doubted that would be enough for the police to drop their case against Andrew. He, also, doubted that they would ever find Andrew. He was just as sure that no family member would ever see or hear from him again. Jacob more than understood his father's ire toward Scott Pennell, however, he could not fathom why Andrew's anger toward Macey was so prevalent.

Jacob sighed as his thoughts continued to crowd his mind. He pressed the flat of his hand against his stitches as he bent to open the bottom desk drawer. The drawer was locked. "Hmm..." he spoke to the quiet that surrounded him. "Funny...I've never noticed this drawer being locked before."

He searched the desk thoroughly, but failed to locate a key for the drawer, so, Jacob decided to pry it open with a crowbar. The desk would be ruined, but, it was just an old metal desk—certainly not a collector's item.

The drawer offered little resistance against the crowbar. It popped open easily to reveal only one item—an old, dusty shoe box. Jacob lifted it out, took the top off, and began glancing through pictures of the most beautiful girl/woman he had ever seen. She was almost angelic in appearance, so pure and natural in her varied poses. Her smile was non-intimidating, and...trusting. Her porcelain skin radiated good health and was void of any makeup. She didn't require makeup. Her periwinkle eyes twinkled with what appeared to be innocent mischief, mixed with a measured timidity. Her dark, gleaming hair fell in thick strands to a minuscule waist, which only accentuated her overall petite frame.

She was undeniably *beautiful*.

Every picture was dated, and Jacob assumed they were all of the same woman, beginning from infancy in 1969 to the most recent one—dated October 1989. The name on the back of all the photos was the same—Gabrielle.

No last name, just. . . Gabrielle.

Jacob was more than intrigued. He continued to sift through the layers of pictures and letters, hoping to discover more information about the beautiful young woman. The letters were all addressed to *Paw Paw* and were signed, *Gabby*. Jacob shook his head in wonderment. "Paw Paw? Who the hell is Paw Paw?"

Even though Jacob knew the truth about his father's lewd relationship with Kacey—as well as the truth about how Kacey really died—he had never discovered the real reason Macey had been banned from the family. He never knew about her pregnancy. His parents had never told him, and Macey had never confided it to him.

Jacob shrugged and shook his head before bundling the letters and pictures together and returning them to the shoe box. "I'll let Macey look at these—see if she can make any sense of it all. I can't figure out why the old man had these locked away. Maybe she's the granddaughter of one of Pop's friends—maybe Pop had the hots for the kid, and was ashamed someone might find out. It wouldn't be the first time." Jacob looked down at the picture on top of the pile. "I can't say that I blame him, though...that is one beautiful girl..."

He moved around the office—slowly and deliberately—favoring the stitches in his side. He took his time, making sure all the windows were secured, before shutting out the lights, and locking the front door behind him. He never thought to check the maintenance bay. If he had, he would have noticed that something was missing.

The old, red Volkswagen was gone.

Detective Windham had three manila folders laid out on the conference table. He stood up when Macey and Scott entered the room.

"Hi, Lance," Scott smiled, waving a hand in welcome. "The officer downstairs said it was okay to come up. Lance, this is Macey Garner...

AKA, Macey Wymer. Macey..."

Macey extended her hand to Lance Windham. "We met a few years ago, Detective Windham. Thank you for seeing us on Christmas Eve."

"Good to see you again, Miss Garner. Have a seat you two. I've got all the files laid out for you. Miss Garner, you've seen everything before, so, I'm sure you can confirm for Scott that this will not be an easy task."

"I've explained all that to him, Detective, but, he's a little stubborn on this issue. He insists on doing this thing his way. Will you stay with us, please?"

Lance smiled and nodded. "Actually, I have to. Even though the case is twenty years old, these files—and your sister's clothing—are the only evidence we have. We can't take any chance on anything being misplaced or damaged. Okay, ready, Scott?"

Scott seated himself between Lance and Macey. He looked from one to the other several times before finally nodding his head affirmatively. "Let's do it."

Nothing could have prepared him for the violent, sadistic photographs that Lance laid out before him. Scott's eyes scanned down the rows of black and white photos, some of which had been enlarged to show specific, gruesome details of the murder. His hand flew to cover his mouth, and he thought he was going to be physically ill. "Oh, God...oh, God..." he moaned.

Macey moved to touch his shoulder, but Lance caught her eye and motioned for her not to interfere. He didn't want anything to interfere with whatever memories might come back to Scott.

Scott closed his eyes and leaned his head backward. He crossed his arms across his chest and began to rock back and forth. A small moan escaped his burning throat.

Macey and Lance noticed Scott's rapid eye movement behind his tightly clenched eyelids. They stared at each other but did not interfere.

Scott moaned again and clenched both hands into fists. He began to rock faster and faster as dozens of images materialized behind his closed eyes. A girl's soft laughter...a white lacy bra...soft skin...the taste of her lips...the feel of her small, firm breasts...and, then—suddenly— somewhere in the deep recesses of his memory, he saw a shiny, red Volkswagen parked along a narrow, dirt path. The forest was filled with beautiful trees and shrubs. The night was cool, but clear. Music was coming from somewhere close by. The song was one of his favorites— *The Lion Sleeps Tonight.*

Macey and Lance watched and listened while Scott, apparently unaware of what he was doing, mumbled portions of the song's lyrics.

"Umm...jungle...mighty jungle...la, la, umm...tonight, in the jungle, yeah...sleeps tonight. Awimaweh...umm, yeah...awimaweh..." Scott stopped singing—if you could call it that—and his body became rigid as more memories began to pour in.

The sudden noise that came from behind him.

Footsteps...he hadn't heard them in time because he was singing along with the song.

Ouch! The pain! His head throbbed with immense pain as flashing blisters of white light penetrated from beneath his lids.

"Wake up...must wake up...something's not right..."

The song continued to play inside his head, just as it had the night Kacey was murdered. *"Hush my darling, doop, doop...my darling...lion sleeps tonight..."*

Kacey! Kacey's in danger! Some madman must be on the loose! Must protect Kacey! Love Kacey! Must protect her! He pushed himself up off the ground where he had fallen, grabbed his throbbing head, absently zipped up his pants, rushed back to the Volkswagen, and STOPPED. The first thing he noticed was the busted windshield and broken headlights. "Oh, man...Dad is going to be so pissed!"

Kacey?

He touched his head, felt the sticky blood on his fingers, and walked slowly around to the passenger door, which stood wide open. He hadn't left it that way. He had told Kacey to lock it.

Music from the late fifties and early sixties filtered through the cool, October air.

Trick or treat!

He didn't want to look inside the car. He was scared to look, but in the end, had not been able to stop himself from looking. He bent down low and peered inside. Oh, God—this was no treat. It had to be someone's idea of a sick, sick joke—a trick. "Kacey...my sweet, beautiful Kacey..." Her chin rested upon the dash, her hands hung limp and useless at her sides. Her face...oh, God, her face...was swollen and purple; her eyes were open and stared straight ahead...accusing him? The white, lacy bra was knotted too tightly around her tiny, vulnerable throat. The vicious bite marks were everywhere...on her cheeks, her neck, her shoulders, her tiny breasts. Her dress pooled around her ankles...her panties pushed down below her knees. Her...

"Agghh! No...not Kacey!" Scott screamed out loud. He held his head firmly between both hands.

Macey jumped up and wrapped her arms tightly around him when she heard the raw, piercing agony rip from his dry, parched throat.

Lance managed to pry the last photo from Scott's fingers. He knew it was the worst one...the one that showed Kacey Wymer's virgin body firmly skewered upon the car's gear shift.

Scott's eyes were still closed. The rapid movement continued behind his lids. Scott finally allowed the suppressed, horrid memories to escape their prison. His screams filled the room and tormented the very depth of his soul.

There it was...a sudden movement...merely a shadow—reflected by the light from the full moon—that crossed from behind the car. The shadow's form evolved into that of a man dressed in black—a man who moved slowly and stealthily away from the rear of the Volkswagen. The man smiled at Scott and whispered hoarsely, "Silence the tongue, else evil find and befall you."

Scott felt reassuring warmth from the arms that held him, and he allowed his tears to flow freely. The warmth that emanated from those arms gradually brought him back to the present. He blinked rapidly and opened his eyes fully. He saw who held him. He opened his mouth to speak to her, but no words came out. He continued to cry.

Several minutes passed before his ragged breathing and tears finally began to subside. He glanced at the detective, who had somehow become a new friend, and smiled. It was a weak smile, but it gradually replaced the look of torrential agony that had filled his face for the past twenty minutes. He shook his head and closed his eyes. "I didn't do it, Lance. I didn't kill her...I really didn't kill her..."

"Scott," Lance spoke firmly. "You've got to tell me *everything* you remembered. Do you know who killed Kacey Wymer?"

Scott nodded for Lance's benefit, but his attention was focused on Macey. "Yes, yes...I do. It was the salesman, Macey. It was the salesman..."

Macey looked alarmed and confused. "Salesman? What salesman, Scott?"

Scott was aware that he probably wasn't making any sense, but, it felt so damn good to finally know for sure that he had not been responsible for Kacey's death. "You remember, Macey...the one I saw walking by your mailbox that day...the one in the dark BMW. *He* did it...*he* killed Kacey. *He* killed her...not me...I didn't kill her. I really did not kill her!"

Tears—formed from a mixture of immense relief and confusion—flowed from Macey's dark-grey eyes. "I don't think I ever really believed you did, Scott," she whispered into his ear. She drew him to her and held him close.

Lance had been about as patient as he knew how to be. He wanted some answers and he wanted them now. "Okay, guys," he lamented. "Someone tell me! Who the hell is the salesman in the dark BMW?"

CHAPTER 40

MACEY DISCOVERS THE TRUTH

Jacob was waiting in Macey's apartment when she and Scott dragged themselves inside at two-thirty that afternoon.

"Hey, guys!" he yelled from the kitchen. His smile faded quickly when he noticed their somber, exhausted expressions. "What's wrong now? It's not Becca, is it?"

Macey kissed his cheek and shook her head. "No, Becca's fine...or at least...there's been no change in her condition."

"Then why the long faces?" Jacob asked. "No offense, but you two look pretty bummed out."

Scott collapsed onto the sofa, gently tugging Macey down along side of him.

Macey lay her head upon his offered shoulder and closed her eyes.

"Come on, guys...what's up?" Jacob asked again, growing more worried with each moment of silence that passed.

Macey opened her eyes and smiled tiredly. She wished she could sleep for a week without any interruptions. She shifted her weight slowly on the sofa. "We've just come from the police station, Jacob."

Jacob's jaw dropped. "Police station? What for? Did they find Pop?"

Macey failed to suppress a yawn but managed to say, "No...it wasn't about Papa. Scott wanted to look at the...crime scene photos."

"You mean..."

"Yes, Jacob...those of Kacey's murder...every gory detail of them."

"But why would you want to see them, Scott?" Jacob mused. "I don't understand."

"Well, Jacob," Scott finally spoke. His voice came out sounding raspy and raw. "I thought it might help me remember what happened that night."

"And did it?" Jacob asked eagerly.

Scott sighed deeply. "I almost wish I could say no, but...yes...I remember almost everything. There are still a few gaps of things missing from the months leading up to that night, but, I think that—in time—I'll be able to remember everything about Kacey."

"Wow...man, that must've been really rough for you, Scott," Jacob sympathized. "So, does that mean you remembered anything that might help the police?"

"Actually," Macey interjected. "He did. In fact...he knows who killed Kacey."

Jacob's eyes widened in disbelief. "You're kidding! Oh, wow! Man, that's great! Who is the bastard?"

Scott shrugged helplessly and replied, "All I have is a face...and a voice. I never saw the man before that night, but...I have seen him since I returned to Columbus."

Jacob could hardly contain his excitement. "No kidding! When? Where?"

Scott stood up and walked to the bay window. "Last month—right outside this window—a couple of weeks before Thanksgiving. He was looking at Macey's mailbox."

"Why?" Jacob asked, puzzled.

Scott looked back at Macey. "Well, my guess is that maybe he saw Macey, noticed the resemblance between her and Kacey, and wanted to find out who she was."

"Wow, none of this makes much sense," Jacob scratched his head. "Why...after all this time, would the man be nosing around? It doesn't make any sense at all..."

"I don't know," Scott answered back. "But, we do have a fairly decent description of him. Detective Windham is going to have the police sketch artist create an age-progression drawing of what the man might look like today, based on the descriptions I gave him of the man I saw the night of Kacey's murder—and, the man I saw outside a few weeks ago. We, also, know that he drives a dark, BMW—either blue, or black."

"Man, this is all too weird," Jacob said as he returned to the kitchen to finish the sandwich he had been building. "You two want anything while I'm in here?"

Macey and Scott cried out in unison, "A beer!"

"Coming right up!" Jacob shouted back. "Hey, Macey, while you're just sitting there doing nothing...why don't you look in that box over there. It might take your mind off all this for a while...it's over there by the recliner. Take a peek at the pictures in that old shoe box I found

278

locked inside Pop's desk drawer down at the station. I'm beginning to think the old man was one of those pedophiles you read about..."

The last thing Macey wanted to do was look at more pictures, but, she reluctantly moved to the recliner and slowly lifted the lid to the old, dusty shoe box. The first picture she came upon was that of a newborn infant. A name and date printed on the back read, *Gabrielle, 2 hours old, 10/31/69.* Macey's face paled considerably as she continued leafing through the stack of pictures—more rapidly now than when she first began—until she came upon the most recent photo, inscribed, *Gabby, Oct '89.*

Jacob handed Scott his beer and walked over to Macey. He held out the remaining bottle to her and said, "She's some babe, isn't..." Jacob paused when he noticed his sister's pallid complexion. "Macey? What's the matter?"

Jacob watched as the tears suddenly began flowing from his sister's beautiful, dark-grey eyes. He knew, intuitively, that they were *not* tears of sadness.

Scott became alarmed at her sudden display of emotion and rushed over to her. Maybe the whole ordeal at the police station had been too much for her after all. He never should have allowed her to go with him. "Macey?" he stammered.

Macey held the latest picture of Gabrielle up to her lips and kissed it before pressing it tightly against her chest. She looked at Scott and then back at Jacob—at their worried, concerned expressions. She slowly held the picture out to them and spoke, through choked sobs. "My baby...this is my baby...it was...a girl..."

Scott and Jacob simultaneously dropped their beer bottles, paying no heed to the foamy suds being greedily absorbed through the rich, plush carpeting.

Across town, Lucas Dudley slammed the phone down, narrowly missing its proper return to the cradle. "Damn!"

He had been trying, for several days, to get in touch with Ruth Wymer. Any other time, she would have been pounding on his door, begging to be screwed—or, *spiritually cleansed*. She seemed to require a lot of spiritual cleansing these past few months—more than Lucas desired to provide her with, but, he needed his own physical release of the demon seed buried deep within himself. Ruth Wymer served that purpose well, though, he would have preferred one of the younger girls from his congregation. Ruth was so needy—he could do anything he wanted to the woman—take her in any form or fashion he so desired. He knew that she would never dare confess her sins to anyone. She was desperate for any means of affection—even his own, primal and demonic means. He knew there would always be women like her to fill his needs. The world was full of them.

His own aunt had been one of those women. The bitch!

He had loathed his mother—an alcoholic whore—who had abandoned him and left him to her spinster sister to raise as she saw fit. His aunt had seduced him when he was twelve years old, and used him to satisfy her own selfish needs, until he ran away from home at the age of sixteen. Oh, the things that woman had forced him to do—dirty things—unclean things. The images from his past forever haunted his present, as well as any future he had ever hoped to have.

The sexual abuse by his aunt was the primary reason he had never married. There had never been a woman pure enough to be worthy of his love and affection. He kept searching for that purity in the young girls to whom he routinely administered his spiritual cleansings. He had yet to find that purity—not even in those as young as twelve, and he dared not to go any younger than that. None of them had met his strict provisions and sanctions for purity and goodness.

That wasn't quite true. One had come close to meeting his requirements. She had been so sweet—the fifteen-year old Macey Wymer. It had been so easy to persuade her father otherwise—that her soul was in jeopardy of remaining forever in purgatory if he did not allow her physical body to be spiritually cleansed by a man of God. Lucas, however, had never intended to impregnate the girl. He prided himself in always being extremely careful not to mix his seed with that of his impure victims, but it had felt so different with Macey. He had shoved her own panties into her mouth to silence her, and Lucas had felt the heat of her innocence consume and tighten around him. Once he was inside her, he somehow sensed the genuine pureness within her, and quickly lost control of himself while she writhed beneath him. It took mere moments for all self-control to evade him completely. Even with her father looking on—nervously reading scripture after scripture, as Lucas had instructed him to do—he could not withdraw in time. He allowed himself to explode within Macey's young, virgin cavern. The spiritual cleansing had continued for hours, and each performance ended with Lucas releasing his seed inside the girl.

Weeks later—when Andrew told him that Macey was pregnant—Lucas had managed to shake his head sadly. He somehow convinced Andrew that they had not reached Macey in time—that she had not been a virgin the night she had been spiritually cleansed. They had been too late to cleanse her body and soul, because she was—undoubtedly—already pregnant when Andrew brought her to him.

The memories of a young Macey brought a temporary smile to Lucas's harshly set features. That smile did not last long. "But that baby was mine. Mine! Oh, and Macey, you just had to go and tell your sweet, little sister who the father was, didn't you? Too bad...so sad. Your sister might be alive today if you had only kept your stupid mouth shut. No...but you couldn't do that, could you? You told her, and after they sent you away and I came to Columbus, your sister saw me talking with your father one day. She caught up to me as I left and threatened to tell everyone the truth about...everything. Why...I couldn't let that happen, now could I? I would have been run out of town—or worse—locked away forever... never to know my own child. My child of God! Oh...where is my child, Macey? WHERE...IS...MY...BABY!"

Lucas pounded the table with his closed fists. He eyes were wild and unblinking. He ran his long, skinny fingers through his thick, dark hair and began pacing the room. He pursed his lips together and shook his head. "Someone...someone knows where the child is...and, I intend to find out," he whispered hoarsely.

He had hoped the black woman—Becca—would have told him what he needed to know, but, she had remained stubborn, refusing to the end, to tell him anything useful about Macey.

The ringing of the phone jarred him, and he shook his head to erase the web of memories that had imprisoned his entire being. He snatched the receiver from its cradle and growled. "Hello!"

"Lucas? Is that you?"

"Yes! Who is this?"

"You don't sound like yourself, Lucas. It's Ruthie. Is everything okay?"

Lucas took several deep breaths. He had to calm down. He couldn't let Ruth Wymer suspect his true feelings. She was already too suspicious, asking him questions about what had really happened between him and Macey's black friend. "I'm fine, Ruth. I was just going over some notes for Christmas services tomorrow. I've been trying to contact you for several days."

"You have? What for?"

Lucas emitted a low, guttural growl. "Do you really have to ask, Ruth?"

"Oh..."

"I was hoping we could get together...if you can get away from Andrew for a few hours. What do you think?"

"Oh, dear...I forgot...you don't know. Oh, Lucas, things have been such a mess these past few days."

"Whatever do you mean, Ruth? Has something happened? Has Andrew found out about us?"

"I wish it was that simple. No, Lucas...he doesn't know or suspect anything about us. I doubt if he even notices my absences. As I said, a lot has happened...too much to go into over the phone."

"Can you come over, Ruth? I know it's Christmas Eve, but..."

"That's not a problem. I can come, but...I can't stay long. I have to get started on Christmas dinner."

"Will I be invited?" Lucas purred.

There was a slight pause at Ruth's end. "I don't want to be rude, Lucas, but, well...I was hoping to invite Macey to dinner. I doubt if she will accept, but..."

"Macey! When in hell have you been in contact with your daughter?"

"Well..." Ruth stammered. "As I said, a lot has happened since I last saw you..."

"I think you had better get over here right away, Ruth."

"Yes, Lucas. I will. I'll be right there..."

Lucas hung up the phone and began pacing the floor once again. "What in the hell is going on here?" he wondered, gritting his teeth. "What are you up to, Macey? What have you told your mother about me? What..."

Ruth replaced her phone and sighed deeply. "This has got to be the last time...I just can't do this anymore...I *won't* do this anymore..."

CHAPTER 41

CHRISTMAS DAY

It was Christmas morning—a time for family, for sharing, for love...

Macey lay in her bed, drenched in dream sweat. She had tossed and turned all night, from the nightmares—different nightmares, that all ended the same—in Becca's death. Sweat beaded her forehead and her arms flailed relentlessly from side to side. In the last dream, she had entered Becca's hospital room to find a man—dressed in black—standing over Becca—yielding a thick, wooden tree limb. Macey knew the man sensed her presence, and she watched helplessly when he turned to look at her. His smile was malevolent when he returned his attention to Becca. His face was void of any features—other than the smile—but, Macey sensed she knew this man. She felt an ominous familiarity with him. The man raised the club, to administer the final, fatal blow to Becca's head.

Macey screamed in her sleep and forced herself awake. She sat upright in bed, oblivious to her own continuing screams of terror. Her sheets and nightgown were drenched with her sweat, but her body trembled from the coolness of the room.

Scott had stayed overnight in the guest room, but he awoke from his own restless sleep when he heard Macey's screams. He burst through her bedroom door, ready to defend her against any intruder. "Macey!"

Macey had been more than grateful, the night before, when Scott had insisted on staying with her. He had refused to allow her to stay alone, knowing that the man who had so brutally murdered her twin sister, might be roaming the streets searching for Macey—lying in wait, to find her alone.

Macey was vaguely cognizant of Scott's presence as he rushed toward her. She was even less aware that he was barefoot and wearing only boxer shorts.

"Macey!" he blurted out breathlessly. "What's wrong? Are you okay?"

She closed her eyes, cupped her hand over her mouth, and exhaled a gasped sigh of relief. It had only been a dream—it wasn't real—it was a terrible, terrible dream. Becca was still alive. She didn't say a word, but she opened her arms to Scott.

Scott never hesitated. He was beside her in bed in an instant, and wrapped her in a bear hug. Her arms trembled as they returned the hug. "What's the matter, baby?" he whispered into her hair, and placed a light kiss against her temple.

Macey shook her head against his shoulder. She felt safe and secure within his embrace. "Nothing...nothing. It was a dream...just a very bad dream." She tilted her head back and looked up into his handsome face—a face she couldn't help but notice was badly in need of a shave. "I'm sorry I woke you, Scott. I know how tired you must be. Please...go on back to bed. I'm fine." Macey closed her eyes when she felt his hands move slowly up and down the length of her bare arms.

Scott swallowed hard when his eyes zeroed in on the cleavage beneath her thin nightgown. She wasn't aware of how badly he wanted her, nor was she aware of his instincts telling him he would lose her forever if he didn't take things slow, very slow. If Macey could have seen inside his heart, she would have known that the time was right for Scott. It was always the right time for him when he was around her. He didn't think Macey was at that same point yet. He knew there were too many unsettled events going on in her life—Becca, Andrew, Ruth, the man in the dark BMW, and now...a child—a child she had never been given the opportunity to see, to watch grow up, or, to love. No, he knew that it was not the right time for the two of them...not yet.

Macey was wide awake when Scott lowered his head and kissed her gently upon the lips. Her eyes remained open and wary. She was physically attracted to him, and that attraction scared her—no, that attraction terrified her. She had endured many years of counseling to overcome her aversion to intimacy, but, she had never allowed herself the opportunity to test the results of all those years of counseling. She pulled away from him, embarrassed at the hint of intimacy permeating throughout the bedroom. She made an awkward attempt to push the remaining covers off her. This proved to be rather comical since Scott's weight made it impossible. It took some maneuvering and a few more tugs, but she finally released herself from the covers—with no help from Scott.

He grinned at her. "Don't tell me! Morning breath, right? I knew it!"

She stood beside the bed and smiled down at him. She was totally unaware of her body's sleek silhouette beneath the sheer white gown, but, she was quick to notice Scott's lingering gaze. She quickly folded her arms across her chest. "Scott...your breath is fine...well, sort of..." she smiled, wrinkling her nose.

He pushed himself off her bed, and Macey gaze shifted to his boxers. She swallowed hard and reached for her robe.

Scott recognized the quick aversion for what it was and tried to stifle the slight smile that captured his face. She *was* attracted to him! He knew it! All he had to do was be patient and bide his time. He wanted Macey as he had never wanted any woman before. He wanted all of her—not just her body, but her heart and soul, too. He wanted it all. "Umm...why don't I go downstairs and put on some coffee?" he offered, still trying to suppress a triumphant smile.

"Coffee sounds great," Macey responded eagerly. "I...uh...I'm going to take a shower and get dressed. I want to go see Becca. It's...Christmas. Today is...Christmas."

Macey held her breath when Scott walked toward her and took her protectively in his arms. She continued to hold it when he kissed the top of her head. She saw the raw passion in his eyes when he held her slightly away from him. She didn't trust her knees to support her weight for much longer.

"Do you want me to go with you?" he asked. His voice gruff with renewed desire.

Macey finally released her breath and shook her head adamantly. "No...no, Scott. You've done so much already. There's probably no change in Becca's condition, but I've got to see her...to talk to her. I don't want her to think that I would forget her on Christmas. It's always been her favorite holiday, you know. She's like a little kid. She loves getting presents and surprises, almost as much as she enjoys giving them."

"I know that she's been a good friend to you, Macey. You go ahead—be with Becca this morning. I'm going to wait a couple of hours before I call home."

Macey exhaled softly. "I guess your Mom blames me for your not coming home for the holidays, doesn't she?"

Scott ran his fingers absently through his thick hair. "Well, Mom's not exactly in a situation right now where she can blame anyone for anything."

"You're talking about the fact that she never told you the truth about what happened?"

Scott walked with Macey to the door of the master bath. "Yeah, I'm still having a hard time with that one."

Macey turned and placed a small hand against his chest. "She loves you, Scott. No mother wants to see her child hurt. That whole incident with Kacey must have been very traumatic—not only for you, but for your parents, as well. Try not to be too angry with her. Life's way too short to harbor ill feelings. Trust me...I know that better than anyone."

Scott took her hand into his own and brought it to his lips. "I know, and I'll get over the anger and disappointment I feel toward her in time, but...hey, let's make a deal not to talk about anything depressing for the rest of the day, okay? It's Christmas. How long do you think you'll be with Becca?"

"I don't know," Macey shrugged. "Probably most of the morning, why?"

"Well, I thought we could spend the day together...if you want to, that is?"

Macey squeezed his hand and nodded. "I'd like that. Jacob said Mama wanted me to come to dinner, but I don't think I'm ready for that just yet."

"Are you sure, Macey? It might do you good to spend some more time with her."

"Yeah, I know...and, I might go over later this evening, or maybe tomorrow. I think she's invited her Reverend to eat dinner with her and Jacob, and, I don't think I'm up to the stress of pretending to some stranger that we're one big, happy family."

"Can't say that I blame you there," Scott smiled down at her. "So...do you want to do anything special today? I'm sure we can find a restaurant open somewhere. If not, I can always grill steaks."

Macey returned his smile. "That sounds great, but, there is one thing I need to do after I visit Becca."

"What's that?"

"I need to visit the cemetery, and, before you ask, Scott...I need to do it alone. So much has happened over the past few days. I just need some time alone with Kacey. Can you understand?"

Scott brought her hands to his lips and kissed them again. "I understand perfectly, Macey. To tell you the truth, I could probably use some time alone with her myself."

"It will all come back to you in time, Scott. You will remember everything about Kacey. You must have cared about her, and she must have felt something special for you, too."

"What do you mean?"

"Well, she lied to our parents about seeing you."

Scott scratched his head and raised his eyebrows. "She did? I never knew that...or at least, I don't remember knowing that."

"Well, she did. She told our parents that she was going out with some girlfriends every time she met with you. She must have been terrified of Papa finding out."

"Your father? Why? Was he that over-protective? I thought you said he never showed much concern or affection for any of his kids?"

Macey sighed and squeezed his hand again. "I'll explain it all later. There's more to it than you know. Suffice it to say, however, that he did show affection for Kacey...much more affection than a father has any right to show. Listen, I've got to get ready. I want to be at the hospital before the shift change. There's a nurse working the night shift who has taken a special interest in seeing that Becca pulls through, and, I want to talk to her about how she did last night. I didn't get to visit as long as I would have liked yesterday."

"Okay, get going. We'll talk more about all this tomorrow. I don't want to hear anything else about it today. Agreed?"

"Agreed!" Macey grinned. "Now, how about that coffee you promised me?"

Scott offered a mock salute. "I'm on my way. Oh, by the way, Macey...I feel kind of bad," he said, looking uncomfortable. "I mean it's Christmas, but, with everything that's been going on lately, I...uh, well, I didn't have time to shop for a present for you. I feel bad about that."

Macey stood on her tiptoes and planted a soft kiss upon his lips. "You've already given me more than I ever expected, Scott."

Scott shrugged. "Thanks...I thought you would be more upset that I hadn't gotten you anything."

"Why would I be upset?"

"I don't know. Don't women usually expect fancy gifts for Christmas?"

"Not all women, Scott," Macey contradicted as she slipped into the bathroom and closed the door behind her. "Besides," she yelled through the closed door, "I didn't get you anything either!"

"You didn't?" Scott yelled back. "Now my feelings are really hurt!"

Forty miles from Columbus—in a small, well-maintained hunting cabin hidden deep within a forest abundantly filled with deer, coyote and fox—Gabrielle Wymer awoke to the smell of frying bacon and scrambled eggs. It was Christmas morning and she was ecstatic over being able to spend the holidays with her grandfather.

Andrew had left Columbus the night of the stabbing, rushed home and scavenged his belongings for whatever clothing and money he could quickly assemble, and left in the red Volkswagen. He had driven all through the night until he reached his intended destination—a small, isolated town in Tennessee—a town where nobody asked questions about other folks' business—a town in which he had entrusted the care and raising of his only grandchild to his oldest sister, Louise.

Louise had lost her husband and only child in a senseless fire when she was only eighteen. She received third degree burns over sixty percent of her body, and her face had been permanently disfigured in her repeated attempts to re-enter the run-down shack to save her husband and child. They had all been asleep when her husband rolled over in bed and inadvertently knocked the lit, oil lantern from their night stand. Louise had awakened to a smoke-filled room, gasping for any air she could find. Flames engorged the tiny bedroom in every direction she looked. The baby's crib—located only a few feet from their bed—was outlined by the wicked flames dancing off the curtains behind it. The baby's crying had awakened Louise, who immediately tried to rouse her husband, John. The sheets on John's side of the bed were smoldering, and when she turned him over she screamed at the horrible, blackened skin that had once been his handsome, loving face.

She had struggled out of bed and stumbled toward the crib—toward the sound of her baby's helpless cries. The flames surrounded her on all sides. She could just barely see her baby, who appeared to be standing up inside the crib, hands outstretched toward her mother. The baby's screams faded before Louise could reach the crib. She moved as quickly as she could toward the crib, feeling her way toward it—her arms moving frantically from side to side. She finally reached the crib and pulled the child's limp body to her. She fell to her knees and crawled into the living room and out the front door. She finally collapsed onto the front lawn—composed mostly of mud and stones, with a few weeds thrown in for the illusion of greenery.

Her baby had died in her arms. She took her last breath when her tiny lungs had been unable to arrest the damaging smoke that had so violently invaded them.

Louise Hicks was never the same after that night. She had no reason to go on—no reason to continue living—until Andrew presented her with baby Gabrielle. He had pleaded with her to help him raise the child. Louise never asked any questions about the baby's heritage. She didn't want to know Gabrielle's story. All she knew was that she was needed again. She loved Gabby Wymer more than life itself.

Louise had cried violently when Andrew arrived at their home and told her he was taking Gabby away—back to Georgia with him. She believed him, however, when he promised her it would not be for long—that they would send for her when they got settled in their new location.

Andrew really had no clue as to what his immediate plans entailed. He had not planned that far in advance. He certainly had never planned to stab his own son. Hell, he hadn't planned to stab anyone for that matter, but, it had happened. He knew the police were probably looking for him, but, he felt safe in the Georgia cabin that he had secretly purchased many years ago. It had served as a useful retreat for the many times he felt the need to get away from society—from life itself. He always felt closer to Kacey when he was in the cabin. Maybe because—in his eyes—it was like the beautiful forest in which life had left Kacey's body. He wasn't a psychologist—he didn't know why—but he always felt closer to Kacey when he walked through the woods and looked upward to the Heaven above.

"Something smells wonderful, Paw Paw! Merry Christmas!" Gabby threw her delicate arms around Andrew's neck and tightened them in a warm embrace. She loved her grandfather dearly, and was so excited about spending the holidays with him—even though it had meant leaving Aunt Louise behind.

Andrew hugged her back and kissed her forehead. He wanted to protect her always and he was thankful that the primal urges he had often felt with Kacey had never surfaced with Gabrielle. He had suffered a lifetime of overwhelming guilt over the relationship he had forced upon his daughter, and, he would never forgive himself for having subjected her to it. He had closed himself off from everyone after Kacey's death. He had convinced himself that he wasn't worthy of anyone's sympathy, love, or understanding. "Merry Christmas, angel. I've made your favorite breakfast."

"Bacon and scrambled eggs!" Gabby clapped excitedly. "I am so hungry, Paw Paw. Come on! Let's eat! Can I get you some coffee?"

"I already have a cup poured, angel. Go on...have a seat at the table. I'll bring you some juice."

The two sat companionably across from each other, each of them more than comfortable with the amiable silence. Andrew couldn't help but wonder what the rest of his family would be doing on this special day. It was a day that he should be sharing with them—even though he would pretend, as always, not to enjoy their companionship. It was a day that his family would never know how much he craved to be among them in celebration.

He watched Gabby cut her bacon into tiny, precise pieces and his heart broke with the love he felt for her. He wondered—not for the first time—if he had been wrong in taking this child from her mother. Had he been wrong not to tell Macey about her? To cheat her of all the wonderful childhood and teenage-year memories he had experienced? Would Macey even be interested? "Oh, hell...I've got to find out," Andrew whispered.

"What did you say, Paw Paw?"

Andrew smiled at Gabby and shook his head. "Nothing, angel...it's nothing for you to worry about..."

CHAPTER 42

PRAYERS ANSWERED

Macey stood outside Becca's ICU room and spoke to Nurse Brenda Jennings about her friend's condition. Becca still had not regained consciousness.

Carlton Brown was inside the room, sitting at Becca's bedside, holding her hand, and speaking softly to her about plans he had for the two of them when she was released from the hospital.

Nurse Jennings peered through the door's glass opening and smiled. "She's got some man there, that girl does." Brenda Jennings was an attractive black woman in her own right, and had ample opportunity to appreciate the near perfection of the male species so readily defined in one Carlton Brown. She envied Becca James because it was obvious how much the man loved her, and, she felt that love would go a long way in helping to snap Becca out of her current comatose state.

"Yes," Macey sighed. "I don't think even Becca realized the depth of his feelings for her. I only wish that she would wake up soon so she can find out first-hand."

"Well, the swelling in her brain has diminished considerably," Brenda offered in response, while she continued to admire Carlton's fine, chiseled physique. "The swelling and bruises on her face are fading, and I can tell now that she is a real beauty. I understand that she's pretty damn smart too...she has a master's degree?"

Macey smiled and nodded. "I bet her father told you that, didn't he? He's awfully proud of her."

"No, actually, Carlton told me," Brenda grinned. "Now, don't go getting me wrong, Macey. He's a fine-looking man, and any woman would be proud to call him her own, but it's obvious who the man is crazy about. He and I have talked a lot about Becca this past week. He stays during the night sometimes, so that Mr. James can go home to be with his wife."

Macey nodded. "Yeah, you don't have to explain yourself to me, Brenda. They are all good people, and they all love Becca...a lot. She is very lucky to have so many people who feel that way about her."

Nurse Jennings rubbed the bridge of her nose between her thumb and forefinger. "Yes, she is, Macey. Well, listen...my shift has been over for about thirty minutes, and my kids will be waiting for me to get home so they can open all their presents. Their Daddy is probably having a helluva time keeping them from it until I get there."

Macey touched the nurse's shoulder in gratitude. "Sure, I'm sorry. You go on now, Brenda, and thanks so much for waiting to talk to me about Becca. Merry Christmas to you and your family."

"Merry Christmas to you, too, girl. You try to get some rest over the holidays. Becca's beginning to look better than you do!"

Macey smiled and waved good-bye. She took a deep breath and tried to forget about how exhausted she still felt. The nightmare last night had not done much to induce sleep. It seemed forever since she had experienced a full, restful night's sleep. She smoothed back her hair and entered Becca's room. The sounds of the medical machines permeated throughout the room, but they could not drone out the smooth, calm resonance of Carlton's soft voice as he spoke lovingly to Becca.

Carlton must have sensed her presence in the room. Macey waved when he turned to look at her. She returned his smile when he gave her a thumbs-up.

Carlton whispered into Becca's ear, "Hey, baby...guess who's here to spend some time with you? It's Macey. I'm gonna go grab a quick shower and shave so that I can look good for you when you wake up, but I'll be back real soon. I love you, baby." He kissed Becca softly upon the lips and turned to look at Macey again. "Hi, Macey. Merry Christmas."

Macey placed a hand upon his shoulder as they both stared down at Becca, who really was looking considerably better every day. If only she would wake up! "Merry Christmas to you, too, Carlton. Why don't you go on now? Take your time. I'll sit with her until Mr. and Mrs. James get here. I'm sure they'll want to spend some time alone with Becca today, of all days."

"I'm gonna take you up on that offer, Macey. I think I'm probably long overdue for that shower and shave."

Macey shook her head. "You look fine, but you need your rest, too. It's hard to get any rest here in the hospital—at night—waking up every hour just to spend the fifteen minutes with Becca that they allow."

Carlton shrugged and grinned. "Actually, I've won Nurse Jennings over. She doesn't apply that fifteen-minute rule to me. She lets me stay in the room all night. In fact, she just took away the cot I slept on last night...made me promise not to tell the day shift nurses, though. She says they're sticklers for rules and regulations."

"She's a jewel all right. I'm glad the two of you take such good care of Becca at night. It makes me rest easier knowing that you're both here with her."

"I know what you mean. Okay, I'll see you later, Macey. Promise me that you'll call if there's any change? My number's in the table drawer over there."

"I promise. Now...go."

"Catch you later, Macey. Be sure and tell Scott Merry Christmas for me."

"I'll do that, Carlton."

Carlton had not been gone ten minutes when the strangest sensation suddenly came over Macey.

She was standing at the window that looked out over the empty parking lot—praying—and, wondering for the umpteenth time what her child—her daughter—was doing on this Christmas morning. A tingling feeling coursed through her when the strange sensation rocked through her. She shivered involuntarily. She knew that she was alone in the room with her comatose friend, but she suddenly felt a strong presence surrounding her. The hairs on her arms stood straight up and she shivered again. The room's temperature was maintained at a comfortable level, but Macey felt an extra layer of warmth wash over her. She could not shake the sensation that she was no longer alone in the room.

"Penny for your thoughts, girlfriend..." the weak, scratchy voice whispered.

Macey thought she had imagined the voice—that she was hearing things. She turned slowly away from the window, and another shiver ran up and down her arms. She knew that voice! She practically flew to Becca's bedside. "Becca! Becca!"

Macey was sure she had imagined hearing Becca's voice because Becca's eyes were still closed. She held onto Becca's hand and, within moments, felt a small squeeze in return. She watched her friend's face closely, willing her eyes to open. "Becca...please wake up...please." Macey leaned closer and saw the dark pupils of Becca's eyes through the small slits of her opening eyelids. Macey ran her fingers along Becca's cheeks while tears of pure, unadulterated joy ran down her own cheeks.

"You're awake...oh, thank you, God! You're really awake. Becca? Becca, do you know who I am?" The doctors had warned family and friends about the possibility of brain damage.

Becca's eyes opened a fraction of an inch wider, and, then...it was there. That smile—so often misconstrued as a smirk—for which she was so readily known. "Bet your sweet ass I do, girlfriend..." Becca turned her head slowly to the left and whispered hoarsely, "Where the hell am I? I... am so...thirsty..."

Macey wanted to pick her up and hug her tightly against her, but her best friend was still connected to all those tubes and wires. She bent down, instead, and stared hard at Becca, nose-to-nose.

"See something you like, girlfriend?" Becca smiled weakly.

Tears streamed freely down Macey's cheeks, and she took Becca's hands into her own. She nodded before finally choking out a tearful reply. "You bet your sweet ass I do..."

Reverend Dudley smiled graciously as members of his congregation filed from the church entrance. Each of them stopped to shake his hand and wished him a Merry Christmas. Even though he had held a larger service the day before—Sunday, Christmas Eve—he insisted on conducting a smaller service on Christmas morning. The turn-out had been lower than expected, but, he had felt obligated to offer the service to those who were willing to give up a couple hours of their Christmas morning to share with the Lord.

Ruth Wymer sat alone on the front pew. She waited until the last church member had departed from the parking lot before she approached Lucas. It was Christmas and she didn't want him to be alone on this most special of holidays—at least—that's what she wanted him to think. She wanted to be with him intimately, but, she also wanted to find out more about his possible connection to Macey's friend, Becca James. She had confronted Lucas earlier about the James' woman, but, he had convinced her that he had not had anything to do with the woman's assault. Ruth wasn't entirely sure she believed him. A part of her wanted to know the truth, while another part of her was terrified to know for sure. She wasn't sure if Lucas would agree to have dinner with her and Jacob, even though she had promised him the night before that Macey would not be there. Macey had turned down that invitation, much to Ruth's disappointment. It was obvious that Lucas did not want to be around Macey, but Ruth could not understand why. He had barely known Macey when she was a teenager. However, Ruth didn't want to think about any of that today. She was lonely, worried about Andrew, anxious about her potential relationship with her daughter, concerned that Lucas might have had something to do with the attack on Macey's friend, but, more than anything else—she was worried about losing Jacob.

So, on Christmas morning, Ruth Wymer found herself rising from an empty church pew, and moving slowly toward the man with whom she had a love/hate relationship. She wanted to know the truth about him and the James girl, but, the weak soul within her also needed him to offer a temporary distraction from all her worries. She thought she and Lucas could go back to his place after dinner, and that he could execute one of his spiritual cleansings upon her. As distasteful as they sometimes were, her spirits were often temporarily lifted after their sessions together. She tried to think of their encounters as a form of therapy, rather than the adulterous rendezvous she knew Andrew would believe them to be.

"Lucas," she began timidly. She placed a hand gently upon his shoulder as he waved to the last of his congregation. "Have you given any more thought to my offer of Christmas dinner?"

Lucas sighed. He suddenly felt very tired and unsure of himself—both of which, were completely out of character for him. "Are you absolutely sure your daughter won't be there, Ruth?"

"Yes, very sure. She's visiting that friend of hers in the hospital this morning, and she and Scott have plans for the rest of the day."

"Her friend—the black friend?"

"Yes," Ruth replied uneasily. "The woman that was found beaten behind Scott Pennell's apartment. Remember...I asked you if it was the same black woman you talked to that night we were there?"

Lucas tensed beneath her touch. "And I told you it wasn't," he hissed between clenched teeth. "I'm sure your precious Macey probably has more than one black friend."

Ruth was standing behind him. She moved closer and tentatively wrapped her arms around his waist. "You're right, of course. She probably does have lots of black friends. She didn't grow up to be as prejudiced as her parents. Maybe...maybe Andrew and I were wrong all those years, trying to keep our children segregated from the black kids."

Lucas turned around to face Ruth. He thought that she looked especially pretty this morning, with her hunter-green dress and red shawl. She looked very festive, indeed. He continued to stare down at her until she looked away from the heated intensity of his gaze. "Maybe we should just skip dinner and go straight for dessert," he growled. "What do you think about that idea, Ruthie?"

"Oh, my..." Ruth inhaled sharply. The mere thought of receiving one of his spiritual cleansings left her breathless and weak in the knees. "You don't mean...now? Here?"

Lucas's reached behind her to unzip her dress. His hands moved to the hem line and slowly lifted the dress until his hands cupped her buttocks. He grinned in triumph when her eyes lowered and acknowledged his immediate arousal. He whispered melodically in her ear. "You do feel a need for a spiritual cleansing, don't you, Ruthie? That is why you're here this morning, isn't it? I think maybe your soul needs one desperately. You have so many sins to atone for, and a cleansing would bring you immediate relief from those sins."

He slowly lifted the dress over her head. When she moved to lower her arms, he instructed her to keep them above her head. This forced her breasts to lift, which allowed him a momentary illusion of a younger, firmer bosom.

Ruth glanced nervously through the front entrance to make sure they were indeed alone. She was mortified to think that a parishioner might return to the parking lot and see her standing practically nude in the doorway. She hated the weak person inside her who mumbled, "Yes, Lucas...you're right...I do feel the need..."

"I thought so. Now...don't move, Ruth. Don't you dare move one muscle or this session will be over. Do you understand?"

"Yes...," Ruth inhaled when he lowered her panty hose to her ankles. She stood perfectly still while he removed her shoes and pantyhose.

"That's the last time you're allowed to move, Ruth," Lucas instructed. He moved behind her and unhooked her bra. He kicked her discarded clothing aside and moved to open the front door as widely as the hinges allowed. He smiled wickedly at Ruth's physical reaction to the unusually cold December air. "Remember, Ruth. Do not move...no matter what I may do...no matter how *uncomfortable* you may become. One slight move on your part, and it will be over. You will not receive what you so desperately need from me. In fact, I promise you...if you move—just once—this will be our last session. Do we understand each other?"

"You're going to hurt me..."

Lucas raised his voice slightly and repeated, "Do we understand each other?"

As much as she hated to admit it, Ruth Wymer was completely under the spell of the good Reverend Dudley. She prayed the day would come when she would be able to resist what he offered, but, she knew that today would not be that day. "Yes...yes, Lucas...I understand..."

"That's better," Lucas purred. "Much better. . ."

Ruth lost track of time, of how long she stood still and accepted the pain and humiliation that Lucas inflicted upon her body. When it was finally over, and she was permitted to lower her arms, she saw the savage bite marks left upon her body. She knew it would be several days before they disappeared, but she had done nothing to stop him during her cleansing. Instead, she had moaned in ecstatic pain—fearful of crying out and stopping the abuse—because she knew that he meant what he said...it would be their last session. She wasn't quite ready for it to be over.

Just when Ruth thought her cleansing had come to an end, Lucas walked over to a closet and retrieved a nine-inch candle from a storage closet. She wanted to ask him what he intended to do with the candle, but she knew better. Asking that question would ensure his absence from her life. Besides, by now, she had a pretty good idea of how he intended to use the candle. She had endured the use of similar objects over the past year with Lucas.

Lucas' eyes glowed with anticipation and excitement when he gave new meaning to the expression, *burning the candle at both ends*

When the cleansing finally ended, Ruth lay gasping on the floor. The reality of the whole situation suddenly hit her like a ton of bricks. How needy and gullible had she been? Why had she endured such treatment, such humiliation from this man for so long? What did that say about her? She couldn't blame it all on him—she blamed herself, too. She was a grown woman who had made some incredibly stupid, stupid decisions. But...no more...never again. She lay on the cold, hard floor inside the church foyer and watched Lucas Dudley smooth back his hair. She watched him assume his dominating stance—watched the sick smirk spread across his face—and, she decided something—a change was needed, one that was long overdue.

This was the last spiritual cleansing that she would ever need from this self-proclaimed man of God.

CHAPTER 43

CHRISTMAS DINNER

Ruth kept herself busy in the early afternoon, performing last-minute preparations for Christmas dinner. She wished that she could have retracted the invitation, but Lucas had finally agreed to have dinner with them. Jacob's new friend, Janet Ward, was also planning to join the family—or, at least, what was left of the family—for the holiday meal. Ruth was disappointed that she hadn't been able to persuade Macey and Scott to join them, but she felt good about the progress—albeit slow—that she and her daughter were making. They would probably never be confidantes, but hopefully, they might make peace with each other, and become friends.

Jacob walked slowly into the kitchen. He was still favoring the twenty-five stitches scheduled for removal next week, provided the healing process continued as well as expected. "Hey, Mama. Something sure smells good."

"Thank you, son. Well...," she paused and surveyed the immediate area. "I think I've done everything that can be done right now. Why don't we take a break? How about some iced tea?"

"That sounds good, Mama. I'll get it. You've been cooking for hours— why don't you sit down and rest for a while."

Ruth kicked off her house slippers and stretched her toes. It did feel good to rest, even though a sitting position wasn't especially comfortable for her at the moment. She experienced a quick flashback to the moment the candle had broken off inside her—the same moment that Lucas had climaxed. The two actions occurred simultaneously and Ruth had found no humor in the comment he had made regarding burning the candle at both ends. That was the moment that something had finally clicked inside her head. She knew when he made that crude comment, that her sick obsession with Lucas Dudley was finally over. Yes, she regretted extending the invitation for him to join them for Christmas dinner. She only hoped that her shame and disgust would not be evident to Jason. It would destroy her if her son ever discovered the truth about her relationship with the Reverend.

"Here you go, Mama," Jacob smiled and sat the iced teas on the table, and gently lowered himself onto the chair.

Ruth looked at him sympathetically. "Does it still hurt much?"

"A little—off and on—but not as bad as you might expect it to."

Ruth sighed tiredly and smiled at her son. "There's still been no word about your Papa's whereabouts. As angry as I am with Andrew for what he did to you, I...well, I'm also worried about him, Jacob. I just wish we knew where he went."

Jacob wasn't sure how much his mother knew about her only grandchild, but after the discovery Macey unveiled yesterday about her baby, he needed to broach the subject with his mother. "Mama, there's something I need to ask you...about Pop."

Ruth sipped her iced tea and shifted her weight to her other hip to accommodate the discomfort that the sitting position exacted. "What is it, son? I know you haven't wanted to talk much about what happened, but, it might do you good to get it all out."

Jacob shook his head. "No, Mama...it's not about that. I don't blame Pop for the stabbing, and I wish the police would just let the whole thing drop. Pop didn't mean to hurt anyone...I know that."

"But, Jacob..." Ruth began.

"No, Mama! I mean it. I don't want to talk about that right now."

"All right, then...what do you want to talk about?"

"I want to talk about Pop, but, not about what he did to me. I don't know how to ask this, Mama, so...I'll just spit it out. What do you know about...Macey's child?"

Ruth was stunned! The family never discussed Macey's pregnancy, and she was surprised that Jacob knew about it. She finally stammered a question. "Did...Macey tell you about that?"

Jacob sipped his tea and nodded his head. "I just found out...last night."

"What?" Ruth brows drew together. "I don't understand. Why did Macey feel the need to tell you—or anyone for that matter—about something so...tragic...and personal?"

"It's nothing for her to feel ashamed about, Mama. The only thing tragic about it, is that—thanks to this family—Macey has searched for, and worried, about her child for the past twenty years!"

Ruth pushed herself to a standing position, but held onto the table edge for support. She could not believe what she was hearing! Macey had been searching for her child? Andrew had always told her that Macey had taken her baby and ran away all those years ago—abandoning her own family—denying them the opportunity to know and love their grandchild.

"What do you mean...she has searched for the child for twenty years? My, God, it was Macey's fault I never got to see—and know—my first... my *only*...grandchild. She was supposed to give it up for adoption...to one of your father's sisters...at least, that way we would have been able to see the child occasionally...to keep it in the family. But, no, Macey saw fit to run off with the child in the middle of the night. No one ever knew what happened to either of them!"

Jacob thought he was confused yesterday when Macey revealed the fact that she had a child, but, he was way beyond confusion now. "Mama, what are you talking about? Macey never ran off with her baby. She was planning to, but the baby came early—it was taken away from her as soon as she delivered—she never even knew if it was a boy or girl—at least, not until last night."

Ruth shook her head in total disbelief. "I don't understand...all this time...your Papa told me Macey took her baby...our granddaughter...left town, and wrote a note saying she didn't need help from any of us...that she would raise the baby on her own."

"That's what Pop wanted you and everyone else to believe, Mama. Listen...I don't know what all of this means, but I found an old shoe box in a locked desk drawer at the station. It contained pictures and letters from a girl named Gabrielle. I took the shoe box to Macey yesterday for her to look at. Hell, Mama, after looking at those pictures, I was thinking that Pop was some sort of pedophile or something!"

Ruth was still reeling over the news about her only grandchild, but she still managed to interject. "Please don't curse, Jacob."

"Sorry, Mama."

"What about the pictures, Jacob? You're saying that Macey recognized the girl—after all this time?"

"She's never seen the girl before in her life, Mama, but she's not stupid. She put two and two together, from the dates on the back of the pictures. The girl was born on Halloween night, 1969."

Ruth plopped back down on the chair and felt the mildly throbbing pain in her backside. "That...was the night that Kacey was killed..."

"I know, Mama. I know everything about Kacey."

Ruth reached out and touched her son's hand. He was such a good son and she was going to miss him terribly when he left home. "Of course, you do, son. You...uh...told me about some pretty awful things that your Papa did to Kacey."

Jacob nodded in affirmation. "Macey confirmed everything I said, Mama. She knew about everything that went on. She and Kacey were pretty tight; they told each other...everything."

"But...how can Macey be so sure this girl—Gabrielle—is her daughter? There could be some other explanation."

Jacob stood up slowly and reached into his back pocket. Macey had allowed him to take the latest picture of Gabrielle, dated October 1989, provided he returned it to her as soon as possible. He looked at the picture for a long moment before handing it to his mother.

"What's this?" she asked as she reached hesitantly for the photo.

"You tell me, Mama? Who does she look like?"

Ruth took a deep breath and stared at the picture. It was as though time had turned back twenty years. The resemblance was undeniably remarkable! Gabrielle was the spitting image of her mother—except for the eyes. Ruth's focus was drawn to the eyes. They weren't Macey's eyes, but, they looked so familiar to her. Tears pooled in her own eyes as she smiled at Jacob. "This is my granddaughter, Jacob. This is her! Oh, my...she's so beautiful...just like Macey."

Jacob allowed his mother a few moments of her private reunion with the grandchild she had never been allowed to hold and love. "Mama?"

Ruth wiped her nose with the back of her sleeve and looked questioningly at her son. "Yes?"

"Mama, why do you think Pop would have a drawer full of photos and letters from Gabrielle? That must mean he knows where she is, don't you think?"

The ringing of the front doorbell ceased any continued discussion about the mysterious Gabrielle.

"I'll get it," Jacob offered. "It's probably Janet. She wanted to stop by early to see if she could help you with anything. Are you going to be okay, Mama?"

Ruth composed herself and smiled proudly at her son. She nodded and took a deep breath. "Oh, I'm going to be just fine, Jacob, just fine—and, so is everyone else in this family."

Lucas leaned back in his whirlpool tub, leisurely enjoying the pressure of the pulsating jet streams against various parts of his body. He closed his eyes and, once again, visualized Ruth's cleansing earlier that morning. It had been a wonderful cleansing, but, he wondered if he might have finally carried things too far with her. Her reaction to his use of the candle—not to mention his inappropriate remark after it broke off inside her—caused him some minor concern. He couldn't afford for Ruth to break away from him—not just yet. She could still be useful to him, as a tool to obtain more information about Andrew and Macey. He was sure that one of those two could tell him the truth about what had happened to his child, and, he was more determined than ever to uncover that truth.

He smiled as he thought came to him—about the Wymer women. "I've had all three. I've cleansed all three of them enough, to ensure that any evil that threatened to infiltrate their family, has been completely wiped out—sent back to Hell! That entire family should be down on their knees—thanking and praising me for all that I have done for them!" He sighed contentedly as the jet streams swirled deliciously around him. "Although... it really is a shame about what happened to poor Kacey...oh, well...some things are just meant to be, I suppose. Besides...it was the girl's own fault. She would have destroyed everything I had worked so hard to build. She would have made sure that I never saw my child. I simply could not allow that to happen, now could I?" Lucas sighed and closed his eyes. "But...my God has forgiven me for my temporary loss of control that night. I was only trying to make Kacey see the error of her ways. If only she hadn't fought me...if only she would have participated in her own cleansing...things might have turned out so differently for her..."

The ringing of the phone interrupted his memories. He took another sip of wine before settling the goblet on the corner of the tub. He stretched and reached for the cordless phone that he had placed atop the pile of plush, soft towels. "Hello," he answered in a lazy, mellow tone.

"Lucas? It's Ruth..."

He thought he detected a colder—more formal—tone to her voice. "Ruthie, my dear...how wonderful to hear your voice. I was just relaxing in the tub, thinking of our little...rendezvous. I don't suppose you would care to join me?"

Ruth bit down on her lower lip to keep from telling him that he could take a flying leap into the deep end of his oversized Jacuzzi, and drown! Her thoughts both shocked and delighted her. "No, Reverend Dudley. That won't be possible."

Lucas smiled because he thought he understood her obvious predicament. "Ahh...yes...I understand...you're not alone, are you?"

"That's right. I was calling to remind you that we plan to eat around four o'clock; however, if you've made other plans for today, I would understand."

302

Lucas lifted his hips slightly to allow the pulsating water better access to its intended target. "Nonsense, Ruthie. I can't wait to have dinner with you and your lovely family. You have always been a wonderful cook, and, I can only imagine the delicious dessert that will be served."

Ruth counted silently to ten and, once again, captured her lip painfully between her teeth. Janet and Jacob were sitting at the kitchen table just a few feet from her, and she didn't want them to suspect anything out of the ordinary from her conversation with Lucas. She would have given anything to be able to gracefully withdraw the invitation she had extended for him to join them. "Why, yes, Reverend. There will be several desserts for you to choose from...Janet even brought a cheesecake, and it looks delicious. Well, then...we'll see you soon?"

"Yes, my Dear...very soon. You've gotten me so excited thinking about dessert that I find it may take me a few moments longer than I thought. You do know what I mean, don't you, Ruthie?"

Ruth gritted her teeth, but somehow managed to smile for Janet and Jacob's benefit. "Yes...well...we'll see you soon then. Good-bye, Reverend."

Lucas laughed out loud as he listened to the phone's dial tone. "Oh, Ruthie, my sweet. You are hooked, aren't you? I knew it. I shouldn't have been worried that I had scared you away. You are part of me! You cannot get enough of me! Oh yes, I can't wait for dessert, Ruthie. I can't wait..."

CHAPTER 44

The Day After Christmas

Macey had moved back to her own apartment—against Scott's protest—on Christmas Day, and, they had sat up until the wee hours of the next morning discussing all the events that had unfolded during the last few days.

They had called ICU and were informed that Becca was sleeping peacefully, and would be moved to a private room the next day.

They had discussed Scott's memories, which were returning in bits and pieces. He was quick to share those memories with Macey—memories about his teenage crush on a very pure and wholesome young girl—a young girl who had somehow managed not to succumb to his adolescent charm.

They had both visited Kacey's grave—separately—on Christmas day, and had cried openly later that evening, when they talked about the young girl who had meant so much to them both. Macey had left the cemetery at dusk. She picked up Scott, afterward, and they ate Christmas dinner together at the Torch 280 Truck Stop Restaurant—one of the few local restaurants open on Christmas day—located across the river, in Phenix City, Alabama. There was nothing gourmet about the meal, but neither of them had been in the mood for a formal—or more traditional—meal. They were content to simply spend Christmas together.

Macey had called her mother, during the late afternoon on Christmas, to wish her a Merry Christmas. Her mother had company for dinner—Jacob, Janet, and the Reverend who presided over her church—but, she invited Macey and Scott for dessert and coffee. Macey politely declined the offer, citing exhaustion and the need for an early night. She spoke to Jacob, briefly, when their mother passed the phone to him. Macey thanked him when he offered to check the station for any additional information that might offer a lead to Gabrielle's whereabouts.

Scott had called his parents and wished them happy holidays, as well. Things were still rather tense between them, but he knew that he would eventually forgive them for their well-intended silence regarding Kacey's murder. He had to hope that they really had had his best interest at heart, by keeping silent about the past.

It was seven 7:45 AM, the day after Christmas.

Scott rang Macey's doorbell for the second time. He glanced at the Danish he had brought for her to enjoy with her morning coffee, and wondered why she wasn't answering her door. "Maybe she's still sleeping..." He sighed and rang the bell again. He was in a hurry to get to work. He knew the building would be practically deserted today, and he wanted to take advantage of the quiet, to catch up on some work before George Byce returned the following week.

He turned from her door, and noticed—for the first time—that her Rodeo wasn't parked in its usual space. He scratched his head and wondered where she could have gotten off to at such an early hour. They had not parted company until two o'clock that morning, and he assumed that she would want to sleep late—especially now that things in her life were beginning to take on a vague sense of normalcy. "Oh, well...guess I'll have to eat all these pastries by myself." He walked back to his car, tossed the bag of pastries onto the passenger's seat, and drove off in the direction of CompuTech.

The dark-blue BMW was parked outside the entrance to Whispering Hills. The driver waited several moments before pulling back onto the road, and maintained a discreet distance behind Scott's Porsche.

Lucas Dudley—unlike Scott and Macey—had gotten plenty of sleep the night before. Ruth had politely insinuated that he should leave, almost immediately following dessert and coffee. Much to his dismay, dessert for him turned out to be just that—dessert. It was just as well, however, because Ruth's spiritual cleansing—along with the hot bath—had relaxed him more than he thought. He found that he was quite content to reach home at a respectable hour and get a good night's rest.

Lucas had arrived early at Whispering Hills, but not nearly early enough, to see Macey drive off in her Rodeo; if he had, he would have followed her rather than Scott. He doubted that Scott knew anything about Macey's child, but, it couldn't hurt to find out more about the man. It was obvious that Scott was attracted to Macey, so, Lucas felt that it might be possible that Macey had confided personal information to him.

Reverend Dudley was only a couple of cars behind, when Scott pulled into the CompuTech parking lot. Lucas glanced at the front parking lot as he drove past it—it was deserted, except for Scott's Porsche. Lucas rounded the corner—prepared to leave when he saw the empty parking lot—and spotted Macey's white Rodeo, parked close to the door near the side entrance. "Well, now...what do we have here, children?" he cooed. "A rendezvous, perhaps? Hmm...maybe Mr. Pennell plans to administer his own special type of cleansing on Macey. Now, isn't that sweet..."

Lucas drove around the block and returned to the front of the building. He parked along the curb across the street from CompuTech. He stretched to retrieve a pair of binoculars from the back seat. The BMW's windows were tinted, which made it easy for him to discretely monitor the building from this distance.

Scott had parked in the front parking area and had not seen Macey's car parked along the side entrance. He was more than a little surprised when he unlocked the large glass doors that led into the lobby, and saw the light on in Macey's office. The rest of the first floor appeared to be completely empty at this hour of the morning—most of the employees had taken the day after Christmas off.

He walked quietly toward her office and peered in through the half-open door. He removed the warm, brown leather gloves she had given him for Christmas. Her back was to him and she was inputting information into her computer.

Macey was so engrossed in her work, that she never heard her office door close shut. She was dressed in black jeans and a soft, pink V-neck sweater. She was wearing the pearl earrings and matching necklace that Scott had given her as a Christmas present.

They had both lied to the other about not having had time to buy presents.

Scott tiptoed closer until he stood directly behind her. He looked down—a great vantage point for him—and appreciated a bird's-eye view of the soft swelling of cleavage. His voice was husky with desire when he whispered, "Very impressive, Miss Garner."

Macey nearly jumped out of her skin at the unexpected intrusion. She jerked her head to the left and saw Scott. "Scott Pennell, don't you ever sneak up on me like that again!" She pushed up from her chair and thumped him hard against his chest, with the flat of her palm.

Scott laughed heartily and smiled down at her. She was beautiful...so beautiful. Her face was flushed and her chest was still heaving with the fright he had inadvertently caused. "I'm sorry, Macey. Really! I am, but, I couldn't resist. What are you doing here anyway? I thought you were going to sleep in today and come back tomorrow. At least, that's what I thought we agreed on last night, or was it this morning…"

Macey returned a reluctant smile. "I know. You're right, but, with Mr. Byce coming back next week, well…I just didn't want to give him any reason to…"

Scott held his hand up and shook his head. "You don't have to explain, Macey. By the way…there's something I haven't told you, and…I probably should have, I guess…"

"What?"

"Well…it's about you and Mr. Byce."

Macey stiffened at the comment and prayed that Scott had not heard any rumors about her and their illustrious boss. She had tried so hard to keep the rumors at bay, but, in an organization the size of CompuTech, that wasn't always possible. "Go on, Scott."

"It's just that…well, you don't have to pretend with me, Macey. I'm here for you. I will always be here for you, so…that means you don't have to worry about George Byce any longer."

Macey looked stupefied. Did he know the truth? How long had he known? She cast her eyes downward, shamed and horrified that Scott might know the truth about her new relationship with George Byce.

Scott lifted her chin and looked intensely into dark-grey eyes that consumed him.

Macey closed her eyes when she felt tears began to pool in the corners of them.

Scott lowered his mouth to hers and placed a soft, delicate kiss upon her lips.

She accepted the kiss and opened her eyes. "How long have you known, Scott?"

He shrugged and feigned nonchalance. "Couple of weeks, I guess."

Macey bent her head and closed her eyes again. "You must think I'm awful."

Scott pulled her against him and gently massaged the tense muscles between her shoulder blades. "No, Macey. I could never think that you were awful. You're too good a person. I know you never would have allowed this to happen without a reason."

Macey willed herself to relax against his embrace. "Oh, Scott," she sobbed. "He is a horrible, horrible man. He threatened to tell everyone who I really was…everything about Kacey! I couldn't let that information get out. I couldn't let my parents know I was living in Columbus. I…I had to protect Jacob...at all costs. God...Scott, do you...hate me?"

Now was the time. He had wanted to tell her since Thanksgiving, but something always held him back—the timing never seemed quite right. "No, Macey," he argued. He ran his hands gently across her back. "No, I could never hate you...and, do you know why? Oh, Mace, you've got to know...surely you've figured it out by now."

Macey liked the way he shortened her name. She was speechless, and could do nothing but shake her head.

Scott smiled and held her face between his hands. "I could never hate you, Macey, because...I love you. I love you, Macey Garner. I love you more than I've ever loved anyone else in my life. I...love...*you*..."

"Oh, Scott..." Macey lifted her face and eagerly accepted the kiss he offered. It began as a gentle caress—a slight touching of the lips—but quickly grew into an eager, throbbing hunger for them both. Tears of happiness coursed down Macey's cheeks.

Scott smiled at her when they finally drew apart, and wiped away her tears with the tips of his fingers. "I meant what I said, Macey. You don't have to worry about George Byce ever again. It may cost us both our jobs—though I doubt it—but, I plan to have a quiet talk with him when he returns from his holiday. Trust me, unless he welcomes the embarrassment of a sexual harassment suit against him, he *will* back off. If he ever lays another hand on you..."

Macey shook her head and whispered, "I can't believe this is happening. I...I never thought I would find anyone to love me. I didn't think it was possible for anyone to love me."

Scott smiled and ran his index finger across her lips. "You and me, both! I've pushed women away for years, whenever it felt things were getting too serious, and now—well, at least now—I know why I've always been afraid of commitment. There is so much I have to resolve within myself...regarding Kacey and what happened, but, I promise you, Macey...I *will* resolve those things; and, it won't take long—and when I do, I'm giving you fair warning...I want you to marry me."

Macey jerked her face upward to stare into his handsome face. "Marry you!" she exclaimed hoarsely. "Scott...oh, I don't know. I mean...marriage? I don't know...I can't promise that I will ever be ready for marriage to you... or to anyone for that matter. I feel like I am damaged goods, and, there are still so many things that you don't know about my past..."

Scott silenced her protest with another kiss. "I don't care about the past, Macey, and you shouldn't either. That's all behind us now, and let's face it...there's not a damn thing either of us can do about it. We've both wasted so many years as it is; we shouldn't waste another minute of our future together. Hell, we can go to therapy as a couple if you want to!"

Macey smiled and shook her head. "You are impossible, Scott Pennell. Impossible..."

Scott returned her smile and pulled her chair out for her. He hoped that she wouldn't see the look of disappointment that he was sure had registered on his face. It did not escape him that she had not reciprocated his own declaration of love. "Before you go back to work, Miss Garner, there is one thing we need to clear up between us."

Macey sat down in front of her computer again and turned to look up at him. "What is that?"

"Well, I've stood here and spilled my guts to you about my undying love for you, and my undeniable need to make you my wife..."

"And?"

Scott assumed his most helpless, hound-dog expression. "Well, not only did you not give me an answer to my proposal of marriage, but, well...hell, I'm not even sure if you feel the same way about me!"

Macey stood up again, turned to face him, and pressed both hands firmly against his broad chest. "Scott Pennell...yes...yes. I do love you, and, you have no idea how much I would love—more than anything—to become your wife."

"Well, ALL RIGHT!" Scott shouted.

Macey pressed a finger to his lips. "Wait...I'm not finished, Scott. Like I said...I do love you, and I do want to marry you, but, I cannot do that until I've told you everything about my past. The past may not be that important to you, but I cannot— will not—start a new life with you, without first wiping the slate clean. It's just that...well...I'm not ready yet to tell you everything."

"When do you think you will be ready, Macey? We're not getting any younger, you know; and, I know we've never discussed it, but...well...I would love for us to try to have a child together...if...you think you might want that."

Fresh tears of joy flooded Macey's eyes as she threw her arms wildly around him. "Oh, Scott...there's nothing I'd like more than to have a child with you, but, you need to understand something."

"I'm listening, Macey."

"It's about my daughter—Gabrielle. Before you and I can move forward with our lives, I should tell you about her father. I, also, need to find out what happened to her. According to those pictures that Jacob found, she was alive and well just a couple of months ago. Papa knows where she is—I know he does. I've got to find Papa, and, I've got to find Gabrielle. I'm so sorry, but I just can't promise you a future until I know for sure..."

Scott kissed her again and held her tightly against him. *"We'll* find her, Macey. I'll help you, and whenever you're ready, you can tell me all about the father of your child. I can tell you, though, that no matter what you tell me, it won't make a difference. There is nothing you can say to me that will change the way I feel about you. I promise you that."

Macey sighed deeply and closed her eyes. *"I just hope and pray that's a promise you can keep, Scott,"* she thought as she pressed herself against him, feeling safe and secure within his embrace.

CHAPTER 45

ANDREW'S CHANGE OF HEART

Andrew sat on the porch of the old hunting cabin, and stared absently toward the rippling lake a hundred feet away. The fish were jumping now that he had put away his old cane fishing pole. His granddaughter—Gabrielle—was in his sight, walking in the woods off to the right of the lake. "This has gone on long enough," Andrew spoke aloud. "Too many years of deceit, too many scars, too much hurt, too much..."

Gabby moved lazily up the path that led back to the old, rickety porch, and smiled as she approached her grandfather. "I love it here, Paw Paw! Everything is so peaceful and beautiful. I just wish the animals weren't all hibernating, though." She sat down on the top step and leaned against one of the strong pine support beams, with which the entire cabin had been built.

Andrew looked at her thoughtfully. She may have been twenty years old, but his granddaughter's spirit and enthusiasm for life reflected that of a much younger person. She was so innocent and unassuming. "I know how much you love the animals, Gabby. Who knows...maybe some of them will decide to pop out of their hiding places long enough to make your day."

"Don't be silly, Paw Paw," Gabby blushed.

Andrew could sit and watch her for hours. He never tired of her beauty and her purity—her overall goodness. He had made it a top priority to protect her from life's sadness and disappointment. The saddest thing that had ever happened to her had probably been the death of a wild animal she had tried to domesticate. He watched as the early morning light bounced off her gleaming hair, and a dark cloud passed over his heart. He suddenly felt the need to be reassured of her purity and her innocence. He never doubted that she was still a virgin, but—nevertheless—he needed that affirmation today. "Gabby, tell me something. Did your Aunt Louise ever let you...well...did she ever let you date any of the young men back in Hayden?"

Gabrielle blushed again and looked at the ground. "Of course not, Paw Paw! Besides, Auntie Louise always said there weren't any young men left in Hayden. She said they all left during the Civil War!"

"She could be right about that," Andrew laughed in agreement.

Gabby waited a few moments to see if her grandfather would say anything else. "Why did you ask me that, Paw Paw?"

Andrew shrugged with practiced indifference. "No reason, really. Just an old man being curious...that's all."

"Well," Gabby grinned. "Even if there were any young men in Hayden—and, I don't believe there are—I don't think Auntie Louise would have allowed me to date any of them."

Andrew smiled. "You're probably right about that, but, she was just doing what I had asked her to."

"You told her not to let me date, Paw Paw? Why?"

Andrew picked at the wood on the porch railing. There was so much he needed and wanted to tell her, and he knew that time was running out. He couldn't stay hidden forever, and no matter what might happen to him, he needed to know that Gabby would be safe—that she would be happy. "Oh...that's not really important right now, Gabby. Tell me something, though. What about college? Have you ever given any thought to going?"

Gabby was astounded and laughed out loud. "Who...*me*—college? Heavens, no, Paw Paw. We could never afford anything like that. Aunt Louise always said that was the reason she home-schooled me—because we were so poor that we couldn't even afford to go to public school!"

Andrew nodded his head and waited several moments before he continued. "That's not what I asked you, Gabby. I know your Aunt Louise home-schooled you, and, it's obvious that she did a fine job of that, too. I just wondered if, well...maybe it's time that you got to know some people your own age. College might be a good place to start."

Gabby couldn't figure out where her grandfather was headed with this conversation, but, she wasn't eager to close the door on it either. She had harbored a secret wish for many years now—to someday go to college—but, she knew that their lack of money hindered any hopes of that ever happening. However, something about her grandfather's demeanor sparked a ray of hope within her. "Are you serious, Paw Paw? Really? Do you mean I could go to college here?" Gabby asked, looking around her at the magnificent forest surrounding the tiny cabin.

Andrew grinned. "Well, not here in this particular spot, exactly...and, maybe not even in this town. It's just that...well, I've put a little money aside over the years, and, I'd like for you to use it—for college—if you think that's something you'd like to do."

"That is so kind of you, Paw Paw. You have been so good to me, and, I am so lucky to have you in my life," she spoke softly and smiled up at him.

"I feel the same way about you, Gabby. You—sweet girl—are the only thing that has kept me going these past few years. You are the one thing that I've had to look forward to."

A dreamy expression crossed Gabby's face. She smiled and looked away, toward the lake. "Hmmm...college. You know...I think I'd really like that, Paw Paw, but, well—maybe not the same kind of college you're thinking about."

"What do you mean, Gabby?"

Gabby hesitated only briefly before continuing. "You'll probably think I'm silly."

"Never," denied Andrew. "Never. I only want you to be happy, and, it's important that I make sure you have a chance to make something out of your life because..."

"Because why, Paw Paw?"

Andrew sighed and shook his head. He did not want to cause his granddaughter any unnecessary worry. "Well," he sighed again and stood up. "I'm not exactly a young man anymore, Gabby, and—like it or not—I won't always be around to protect you. I want you to be able to take care of yourself when that time comes. I know I haven't allowed you much independence so far—always keeping you close to your Aunt Louise and myself—but...you are twenty years old. So, back to what we were talking about. What did you mean when you said not the kind of college I was thinking about—what other kind is there?"

"You've got to promise you won't laugh, okay?" Gabby asked demurely. She was unsure of what Andrew's reaction might be to what she was about to propose.

"I promise. What are we talking about here? Not one of those fancy, all women colleges that you have to sign away your life in blood to attend, I hope?"

Gabby shook her head and smiled. "No, no. Actually, Paw Paw, for several years now, I have...well...I have felt a strong calling to go to... seminary."

It was Andrew's turn to be astounded. "What!" he exclaimed. This was the absolute last thing he expected to hear.

Gabby grew quiet. "You're not happy about this, are you? Then, I won't go, Paw Paw. If you don't want me to go, I won't go. I'll go to whatever school you want me to. Really, any place you pick will be fine."

It took Andrew a few moments to recover from the shock of her request. "No, Gabby...tell me more about this...seminary. Help me to understand."

Gabby's eyes sparkled with joy and anticipation. "Are you sure, Paw Paw?"

Andrew sighed and nodded.

Gabby grinned eagerly and began to explain. "Well, I read an article last year in the newspaper about a woman who attended Luther Seminary."

"Where's that?"

She scratched the back of her neck, a nervous gesture she had carried over from childhood. "Well, it's not in the south, Paw Paw. It's in St. Paul, Minnesota. It's the largest seminary operated by the Evangelical Lutheran Church in America."

Andrew could only shake his head in disbelief. He never expected this. "Does this mean you want to be a...preacher?"

Gabby's laugh was so genuine, so pure. "Yes, Paw Paw. In all seriousness, I do. I want to study to become a pastor. I want to be able to really make a difference in people's lives."

"You've already made a difference in my life, Gabby," Andrew spoke low and soft. "More than you may ever know."

"I'm glad, Paw Paw, and, I hope you know that you and Aunt Louise are the two most important people in my life."

Andrew offered a half-smile. "Isn't there one of these...seminaries a little closer, maybe?"

Gabby grinned again, suddenly glad that she had done her homework on this subject. "As a matter of fact, there is one in Maitland, Florida. It's just as good as the one in Minnesota, and—yes—it would be closer."

"It sounds like you've given this a lot of thought, Gabby."

Gabby nodded. "I guess I have, Paw Paw—but, I wouldn't expect you to pay for all of it! It's going to be expensive. Probably close to...fifty thousand dollars, but, I can work part-time and take out student loans to help."

Andrew shook his head. His mind was already resolved to her suggestions about what college to attend. "No need, precious. Like I said, I've saved since the day you were born. If this is what you want to do, then I'll do all that I can to help make it happen."

Gabrielle threw her arms around her grandfather and hugged him fiercely. "This is the best Christmas I've ever had, Paw Paw. Thank you so much! Thank you for bringing me here to this beautiful cabin, for wanting to help send me to college..."

"We should have discussed this yesterday, I guess, and made it your official Christmas present, huh?"

Gabby hugged him again. "I am so happy, Paw Paw! When do you think we can start checking out the seminaries?"

Andrew smiled and shrugged. "How about after the first of the year, Gabby? They're probably all closed until after the holidays. Tell me some more about them."

"Well, that's all I really know about them, Paw Paw. I wasn't sure about how to go about finding out anything else."

Andrew suddenly thought about Macey and wondered if she had a college degree. Had she ever married? Did she have other children? What kind of job did she have? Was she happy?

"Paw Paw? Did you hear me?"

"I'm sorry, precious. I guess my mind was wandering."

"What were you thinking about just then, Paw Paw? You looked so... sad."

Andrew had vowed, for twenty years, never to reveal any information to Gabrielle about her mother. She had asked a few questions as a child, but, she had never pursued the matter. Maybe she had picked up on how unsettling the questions were for Andrew and Louise.

Andrew could not shake the memory of seeing Macey at his service station. His first reaction had been intense anger—the same reaction he had the day—at only fifteen years old—she told him she was pregnant. Her announcement had come almost three months after her spiritual cleansing had been administered by the good Reverend Dudley. Andrew had done a lot of thinking since Jacob's stabbing. He had taken time to review the actions and incidents that had occurred during the past twenty years, and, he deeply regretted his self-imposed separation from his family. His anger and hurt had caused him to become someone that even he couldn't stand to be around. He had treated his wife abhorrently; he could only pray that she might—one day—find it in her heart to forgive him. He knew that she was sexually involved with someone else; he had known it for several months now, but, he had not cared enough to pursue the matter—to discover the identity of her lover. He had thought an awful lot about his son, Jacob, too. He had failed him miserably—as a father, as a man, and, as a friend. How could Jacob ever forgive him for the love he denied him all his life, for the stabbing...for so

315

many things?

"You're doing it again, Paw Paw."

Andrew shook his head and stared blankly at Gabby for a moment. "What? Doing what, precious?"

"You're thinking about something else...something that makes you sad. I wish you could talk about it with me."

Andrew was hesitant, and took a deep breath before finally responding. "You know, precious...I think maybe I can. Yeah, I think I finally can...more importantly—I think I *have* to. I only hope that—after you hear what I have to tell you—that you will still love me. I couldn't stand it if you stopped loving me, Gabby."

Tears pooled in Gabby's eyes. "I'll always love you, Paw Paw. You must believe that. There is absolutely *nothing* you could say to me that would ever change the way I feel. Please believe that."

Andrew was not immune to her tears. His own eyes began to mist over, at the true sincerity of her remarks. "I do believe you, Gabby. I do. Come on," he sighed as he started down the steps. "Let's go for a walk. There's someone I want to tell you about...someone very special."

Gabby jumped up to follow her grandfather. She was suddenly very curious about what he had to say. "Who, Paw Paw?"

Andrew reached for her hand. "Your mother, precious."

They began a slow walk, hand-in-hand, toward the well-beaten path that lead into the forest.

Gabby stopped in her tracks and grinned. Her heart began to beat rapidly within her chest. "My mother! You mean it, Paw Paw? You really mean it?"

Andrew nodded. The time had finally come. "I mean it. Come on, precious...this is going to be a pretty long walk."

CHAPTER 46

BECCA REMEMBERS

Scott scheduled the appointment with Detective Windham for one o'clock on December 26th. He invited Macey to come along, but she had plans to visit Becca, so they agreed to share an after-Christmas dinner at Deorio's Italian Restaurant, later that evening.

Lance was waiting for Scott inside the front entrance to the police station. Storms and showers were predicted over the next several days, and the skies were already overcast and ominous.

The two men shook hands.

"Scott, it's good to see you again," Detective Windham smiled and shook hands. He directed Scott down the corridor, to the computer specialist who would attempt to construct a drawing of their suspect.

Scott returned the smile. "Hello, Detective—Lance—it's good to see you, too. How was your Christmas?"

Lance rubbed his flat, muscular stomach and grinned. "It was great. Mom did too much cooking and baking—as usual—but between me, my kid sister, and my Dad, we managed to put a pretty good dent in the leftovers. How about you?"

"It was a quiet Christmas, actually," Scott replied. "Except for one thing—you may not have heard yet—but, Becca James finally came out of her coma. You remember—Macey's friend—the one I told you about, that was so badly beaten."

"No kidding? That's great news. Have any of our guys been up to see her yet? Maybe she can help identify the son-of-a-bitch who did this to her."

Scott rubbed the back of his neck. "You know, I'm not sure. Macey hasn't mentioned anything. I think everyone is just so relieved that

Becca finally woke up, they haven't thought about what happens next."

Lance shrugged his broad shoulders. "Don't worry about it. I'll check on it when we finish up here today. If her doctor agrees, we'll send someone over."

"She's still pretty weak," Scott replied. "And I'm not sure how much—if anything—she remembers about what happened. She took a pretty good beating to the head."

"Yeah, that might take a few days. We'll see what happens. Here we are," Lance nodded and pointed to a closed door. "Come on. I'll introduce you to Sergeant Dey, and, the two of you can get started on that composite drawing. I've got another meeting downtown, so I don't know if I'll get back in time before you finish up here."

"No problem," Scott smiled and extended his hand once again. "I really appreciate all your help, Lance. Just knowing that weirdo is on the loose—maybe keeping tabs on Macey—well...it doesn't do much to guarantee a restful night's sleep."

"I know what you mean," Lance nodded. "I'll be in touch, okay?"

"Okay, thanks again...for everything."

Scott assisted Sergeant Dey—for the next three hours—in creating a computerized, graphics image of a killer. He left the station with two copies—one of what the killer looked like in 1969, and another—age-progression image—of what he might look like today. The latter image was an almost-identical one to the man Scott saw walking outside Macey's apartment—the man behind the wheel of the dark BMW.

He glanced at his watch and thought idly about killing a couple of hours at CompuTech before it was time to pick up Macey at the hospital. He was eager to show her the photocopies of Kacey's killer. He changed his mind about working at the office, and called Janet from his car phone. He told her that he had decided to work from home, and to fax anything important to his apartment. He made an illegal U-turn and turned the Porsche in the direction of The Medical Center. He gritted his teeth and looked down at the computer-generated images. "Time's running out for you, asshole."

Macey and Alvin James sat in the hospital cafeteria and sipped on another endless cup of coffee. They had been asked to leave Becca's room while the doctor conducted a more thorough examination, now that she was fully awake. A string of nurses and specialists had filtered in and out most of the morning, and, Becca joked that she would have been better off staying in the coma—where she could at least get some sleep!

Macey smiled at Becca's father. "So, Mr. James, it looks like Becca's done it. She's pulled through this."

Alvin returned a smile and nodded. "The power of prayer is a mighty powerful thing, Miss Macey...a powerful thing, indeed. Her doctors... well...I know they'd pretty much given up on my Becca, but, the Lord never gave up on her. It wasn't her time to go. He has plans for my girl. You've gotta have faith—yessiree, the Bible tells us that—*If you have faith as a mustard seed, you will say to this mountain, 'Move from here to there, and it will move; and nothing will be impossible for you.* No, I never gave up on my faith that God would pull my baby girl through this." Tears misted the old man's cloudy and blood-shot eyes.

Macey took his heavily-veined and wrinkled hand into her own, and nodded her agreement. "I believe that's in the book of Matthew. I truly believe that, too, Mr. James...and, Heaven knows that Becca had enough prayers going out for her."

Alvin patted the top of her hand. "She's mighty lucky to have a friend like you, Miss Macey. Mighty lucky indeed."

"Maybe...but I consider myself the lucky one, Mr. James." Macey smiled with embarrassment. She didn't think she deserved his compliments and sincerity, and, she had never been any good at accepting compliments. "By the way, has Carlton Brown been by today?"

Alvin threw back his head and grinned a mostly toothless grin. "My goodness—yes! That man has hardly left her side! If we didn't force him to go home and shower every now and then, well...let's just say, the smell alone would've woke my Becca up before too much longer!"

"Oh!" Macey laughed out loud. "You're awful, Mr. James!"

Alvin shook his head, a grin still spreading across his face, and wiped the sparkling tears from the corners of his eyes. "Just kiddin', Miss Macey. I reckon that young fella loves my Becca almost as much as I do."

Macey smiled and sighed. "I agree. Becca's lucky to have two such wonderful men in her life. By the way, have the doctors told you anything more about her condition—now that she's awake?"

Alvin released a tired sigh. "They just say that it might be a few days before everything comes back to her—*if* everything comes back to her. She took quite a beating against that hard head of hers, you know."

"What about..." Macey began, searching for a delicate way to ask her next question.

"I know what you're thinking about, Miss Macey. You're wondering about her female parts, aren't you?"

Macey blushed and nodded.

Alvin rubbed the back of his neck and shook his head. "Well…as you know, an awful lot of damage was done to my Becca in that area. They say it's too soon to tell, but, they more or less told me that I shouldn't be holdin' my breath to become a granddaddy no time soon."

"Oh, no…" Macey moaned. "Does…Becca know?"

Alvin shook his head again. "No. We haven't told her about any of that. I don't think she even remembers that part of the beating…"

Macey glanced at the clock behind Mr. James. "Well, that could be a blessing, I suppose. Listen, I think we've given those doctors their fair share of time with Becca. What do you say we go rescue her from all their poking and prodding?"

"Sounds like a mighty fine idea to me, Miss Macey—if she hasn't already given them the boot herself."

Macey smiled and tucked her arm through his. They walked, arm-in-arm, back to Becca's room.

When they arrived, they grinned at each other when they saw that Carlton Brown had beat them to it. The room was temporarily cleared of all medical staff, and, Carlton was leaning across the bed rail gently kissing Becca's slightly-swollen lips.

"All right, you two," Macey intoned. "There will be none of that."

Becca and Carlton were startled by the interruption, and pulled reluctantly away from each other. Carlton grinned at Alvin who was standing directly behind Macey. "Afternoon, Macey…Mr. James."

"Good to see you, Carlton," Alvin acknowledged. "Again…"

Carlton grinned and looked back at Becca. He had been so afraid he was going to lose her. All he wanted to do now, was to keep looking at her, holding her, touching her—reassuring himself that she was really back. "Does that mean I'm wearing out my welcome here?" he asked to no one in particular.

Becca smiled weakly and shook her head. "Not on your life, big boy." She turned her head slowly and looked back at the newcomers, through blessedly, non-swollen eyes. "Hi, Daddy. You, too, girlfriend…get on over here."

It was an hour later, when the nurse on duty insisted that Becca needed her rest and ran everyone out of the room. Becca rolled her eyes and asked if Macey could stay a few minutes longer. The nurse frowned, but agreed—provided it would only be for a few minutes. She tucked the sheets securely beneath Becca's battered body before she left the room.

Becca kissed her father and Carlton goodbye, and made them promise to eat a good meal, get some rest, and come back later, with her mother.

Macey stood off to the side, until the nurse left the room behind Alvin and Carlton.

Becca was already trying to loosen the tucked sheet from beneath her. "Man, I feel like a mummy wrapped in this damn sheet! Help me loosen it, Macey."

"Picky, picky, picky," Macey teased, but assisted Becca to a more comfortable, upright position. She sighed happily, noting that Becca was looking more—and acting more—like her old self every day. Macey could not have been more pleased.

"That's better," Becca sighed and leaned back against the pillows. "Now...sit and talk to me."

Macey looked doubtful. "I don't know, Becca. You look tired. Maybe I should go and let you get some rest. We can talk later..."

"I'll rest in my old age, girlfriend. Now sit your white ass down here before you make me pull a stitch loose somewhere."

Macey saluted and grinned.

"That's better," Becca smiled. "Macey? The man who did this to me..."

"Your father said you didn't remember anything," Macey mumbled.

Becca's eyes came alive with fire. "Bullshit! I just don't want him and Mama worrying about me any more than they already are."

"So, you do remember? God, Becca...do you think you can describe him to the police?"

Becca shook her head and grimaced at the slight pain she received from the effort. "I'm not sure. It was so dark outside, and...well, things are still a little fuzzy. Mostly, I remember his voice and his...hands."

Macey reached for Becca's hand when she became quiet.

Becca looked at her friend and suddenly began to cry. Her tough-girl image began to crumble around her. "Oh, Macey...it was awful...it was so...awful. God, he hurt me so bad...why? Why did he have to hurt me like that...?"

Macey offered comfort by sharing her friend's tears. After several minutes, she wiped her nose and asked, "Becca, why do you think he picked you? It wasn't robbery. The police said nothing was missing from your purse or car."

Becca looked at her friend and closed her eyes. "No, Macey...it wasn't money he wanted."

"Then you think he only meant to rape you?"

Becca opened her eyes slowly. "He raped me?"

Macey was stunned, uncertain of how to respond. If Becca didn't remember, she didn't want to hamper any future progress by telling her things she needed to remember on her own—in her own time.

Becca's thoughts twisted in turmoil inside her head. "Macey?"

"I...oh, Becca..." Macey stammered. She didn't want to reveal anything else that Becca might not have remembered.

Becca reached across and squeezed Macey's forearm. "Macey, listen to me. That man—that horrible, horrible man—wanted information about...YOU...."

Macey's tears ceased as quickly as they had begun. "Me!" She was more stunned than ever. Had her best friend been almost killed because of her? Who would do such a thing? And why, for God's sake?

Becca shifted in her bed. "I...I can't remember everything... obviously," she groaned and held tightly to the sides of the bed. "But, I do remember...how he kept drilling me over and over...about you."

"Oh, God, Becca...I am so sorry...so very sorry," Macey cried. She brought her friend's hand to her lips. "But, I don't understand...what... what did he want to know about me?"

Becca's exhalation was one of pure frustration. "Damn! I just can't remember. Why can't I remember?"

Macey leaned over and gently embraced her friend, hoping to calm her.

Both women were crying—Becca, in frustration for not having total recall of what happened—and, Macey, for feeling responsible for what had happened to her best friend.

Macey took a deep breath, pushed herself up, and wiped away the tears. "Becca, we're going to find the man who did this to you. I promise you that. I've already talked to a private investigator about finding my father. We'll just have him dig around and help the police do their job finding your assailant, too."

Becca stopped crying and wiped her nose on the back of her hand. "What do you mean...find your father? We both know where he is, girlfriend!"

Macey looked down at her friend and grinned. It felt good to smile about something. "Well, girlfriend," she mimicked. "A lot has happened while you've been napping this week. Why don't you lie back and let me catch you up on a what's been going on?"

CHAPTER 47

The Composite Sketch

Janet tapped her unpolished fingernails idly against the desk top. She sighed and stared at nothing in particular. Christmas week was always a slack time at CompuTech. Most of upper management personnel were encouraged to take paid leave to be with their families during the holidays. The paid leave ruling, however, did not apply to the lower echelon of workers.

It was Wednesday, December 28, and Janet was brooding because Jacob had yet to discuss any New Year's Eve plans with her. His Christmas present to her—a ten-dollar bottle of Chantilly perfume—had not been the gift she had expected. She—on the other hand—had presented him with a sporty, black leather jacket, that had cost her three "sessions" with Mr. Byce. She was so engrossed in her thoughts, that she didn't see or hear the front entrance door slide open, and close again.

Jacob stopped at her desk and smiled down at her. She seemed to be staring right through him. He cleared his throat. "Excuse me, Miss, but do you work here?"

Janet blinked hard, surprised to find someone standing before her desk. Three phone lines were also ringing. When had that happened? She hadn't heard anything. Her gaze began at the visitor's belt buckle and traveled slowly upward—past the starched white shirt, to the neckline where stray chest hairs competed to escape, to the clean-shaven handsome face smiling down at her. "Jacob!" she exclaimed.

He continued to smile and pointed at the blinking lights. "Don't you think you'd better answer those?"

"What?" Janet mumbled. She was totally unaware of her surroundings now that he occupied the same room.

"Those!" Jacob whispered loudly, pointing again to the blinking lights.

Scott came around the corner at that moment. A definite scowl was etched upon his handsome, weary face. "Janet!" he bellowed. "Can you help us out and answer some of those calls?" Scott noticed Jacob, and waved hurriedly in his direction.

Jacob suddenly felt guilty for having distracted Janet. It was obvious that Scott was extremely busy and needed her help. He didn't want Scott blaming him for Janet's momentary incompetence.

Janet reacted quickly to the suppressed anger she heard in Scott's voice, and instantly became the efficient worker that she could be— when the mood struck her. She answered and transferred the calls to the appropriate offices in a matter of seconds.

"I hope I haven't gotten you in trouble with your boss," Jacob said.

Janet looked back in the direction of Scott's office and shook her head. "He's just in a bad mood. Don't pay any attention to him," she flitted with a lack of discernment. "What brings you down this way, Mr. Wymer?"

Jacob also looked toward Scott's office. "Why is he in such a foul mood?"

Janet shrugged with indifference. "Who knows? He was supposed to have dinner with your sister last night, but, Mr. Byce called and had him pull together a bunch of figures on the international training project that Macey is supposed to be handling. Scott said there was something important he needed to show Macey, but, he was stuck here until about one o'clock this morning."

"So, he's carrying Macey's load as well as his own, huh?"

"Yeah, but don't tell her that. It'll just make her feel bad, and Scott doesn't want her worrying about anything else right now. He said she has enough on her mind, as it is."

"That's big of him," Jacob remarked. He was more impressed than ever with the man who might one day become his brother-in-law.

"Yeah, Scott's a nice guy," Janet nodded. "So, you haven't told me what brings you over here? Shouldn't you be attending to your Daddy's station?"

Jacob shrugged. "A friend's helping me out for a while. My mother is supposed to see a lawyer next week about her rights to sell the place. We thought the deed was only in Pop's name, but my mother found the legal documents a few days ago. It looks like Pop added her name to the deed at some point in time. Anyway, since we don't know..."

"You could stay and run it for her," Janet blurted.

Jacob exhaled softly. "We've talked about that before, Janet. I may have to delay my plans to move to Florida for a few weeks, but, I'm still going. It's time that I put my business degree to some use."

"So, you're still planning on leaving town?"

Jacob's eyes lit up with enthusiasm. "Yes! I can't wait to get to Florida." He felt a tenseness creeping between them, and immediately regretted expressing his eagerness to leave town. He suspected that Janet was much more serious about their relationship than he was. She had been using all her female trickery and wiles to get him into bed—for weeks now—but so far, he had been able to resist the temptation. It hadn't been easy. He had even lied to her—telling her that he was a virgin, with no intention of sleeping with any one until he married—something which he wasn't considering for several years.

Janet pouted and Jacob smiled.

He reached across the desk and lifted her chin. Her full, voluptuous lips beckoned an open invitation to him. "Janet, we have talked about this before, remember?"

"I remember, but that doesn't mean I like it," she sulked. "I'm going to miss you, Jacob."

"You can visit me in Florida sometime, and, I'll be coming back to visit Mama and Macey."

Janet shook her head and closed her eyes. She didn't want him to see her tears. "It won't be the same, and you know it. You'll get down there and fall in love with some blonde floozy in a string bikini!"

Jacob leaned closer and kissed her softly on the lips. "I can almost guarantee that there won't be anyone in Florida who will measure up to you, Janet. By the way, can I ask you something personal?"

Janet pouted again and batted her thick, dark lashes. "You can ask me anything, Jacob—anything at all."

Jacob stood back and perused her outfit. He lifted his hands and gestured toward her. "I've been curious about this for a while now. Why...umm...why have you been dressing like...this?"

Janet glanced down at her long-sleeve, high neck, pearl-buttoned white linen blouse, and the calf-length black rayon skirt. Her thick auburn hair was—once again—piled high upon her head, in Victorian fashion. "You...don't like it?" she almost whined.

Jacob scratched his head. "Well...yeah, I mean...it's okay, I guess, but, well, it's not really *you*...is it?"

"I thought this is the way you liked your women to dress, Jacob. I mean, you're so straight and everything...being a virgin and all."

Jacob was hard pressed to contain his laughter. He didn't want to lead her on in any way, but then again, it really wasn't fair to continue the charade about the state of his virginity. "Janet, about that...well, I...I have a confession to make. I haven't been completely honest with you about something."

"What do you mean, Jacob?"

Jacob scratched his head again and tried in vain to suppress a smile. "I...uh...well, this whole virginity thing? Well...I'm not a virgin...I haven't been since I was fourteen."

"But you said..."

"I know, I know," he nodded. "I just didn't want things getting too serious between us—with me getting ready to move away and all."

Janet looked at him for a long minute. She was stunned at his confession. She stood up slowly, and walked from behind the desk to where he was standing. "Why you lousy, no good, son-of-a..." She stopped in mid-sentence, picked up a steno pad, and hurled it in the general direction of his head.

He caught it in midair and returned her bewildered, wide-eyed look.

They stared at each other for a full minute before they both burst into uncontrollable laughter.

Macey was at The Medical Center again. She sat docilely beside Becca's bed, while Mrs. James spooned homemade chicken soup into her daughter's mouth.

Becca held up her hand when her mother dunked one of her high-rise biscuits into the broth and offered it to Becca. "Mama, please...I can't eat anymore."

Mama James looked perplexed. She was never one to waste perfectly good food—probably a major, contributing factor to her weighing in at two hundred forty-five pounds. "Well, then..." She looked at the dripping biscuit—momentarily puzzled about what to do with it—and quickly popped it into her own mouth. She licked her fingers and grinned at Becca. "You sure you got enough to eat, baby girl? The doctor says that you need to start eatin' solid foods now."

Becca glanced toward Macey for help, but received only a smile and shrug from her best friend. "I know, Mama, but I don't think he intended for me to eat a week's worth the first day. I'm so full, but thanks for bringing the soup. It was really good."

Mrs. James slowly pushed her ample body off the lounger, which creaked gratefully as the excess weight was lifted from it. She began gathering Tupperware bowls and silverware she had brought from home, and sighed heavily. "Okay, baby," she cooed. She bent forward and kissed Becca on the forehead. "I'm gonna head on home now and give you girls a chance to talk some."

"Oh, you don't have to leave on my account, Mrs. James," Macey offered. "It looks like Scott is going to be late again tonight, so I'm in no hurry."

"Well," replied Mrs. James. "I still need to get home and make sure Mr. James has eaten some dinner. You know how these menfolk can be sometimes. They'd work themselves to the bone if the womenfolk weren't there to make sure they got enough food and rest. I'll be going now. I'll see you tomorrow, baby. Good-bye now, Macey. You take care, you hear?"

"Bye, Mama...I love you," Becca waved. She couldn't help but smile, watching her mother's broad backside wobble from the room.

"Good-bye, Mrs. James. I'll see you soon," Macey smiled and waved.

Once the door closed behind her mother, Becca held her stomach with both hands and groaned. "Oh, Macey! She's not going to be happy until I'm as big as she is! She's going to do what that madman couldn't! She's going to kill me with *food*! If I ate everything she brought here today, I'd explode for sure."

Macey burst out laughing. "You're lucky to have her, Becca James, and you know it."

Becca smiled and slid a little lower down her pillow. "You are so right, girlfriend...so right. Hey...don't think that I don't appreciate you hanging out with me, but, don't you think it's about time you went back to your own life? I've already got one mother hen, remember? And trust me— one is more than enough!"

Macey smiled again at her friend. She was so happy to see Becca acting more and more like her old self. "Can I trust you to do what the doctors say?" Macey implored.

"You bet you can! I can't wait to get out of here."

"Have they told you when that might be, Becca?"

"Well, today's Wednesday, and I'd sure like to be home before the New Year, but, Dr. Mullins won't commit to a firm release date just yet."

"Well, don't rush it, okay? I know you're anxious to leave, but...you were hurt pretty seriously, Becca."

"Tell me about it," Becca replied softly. "You know, Macey...I remembered something else about the beating."

Macey allowed a quiet moment to pass between them before she raised her eyebrows and asked, "I'm guessing you want to talk about it?"

Becca nodded while a lone tear rolled unceremoniously down her cheek. She sniffed and tried to push herself up into a sitting position.

Macey assisted and waited for her to continue.

"He...uh...he used an old, rotted log...pushed it...inside me...over and over. That old log had so many splinters..."

"You couldn't have remembered that, Becca. The doctors agreed that you probably suffered a major concussion and blacked out before... before he did those things to you."

Becca choked up and Macey took her in her arms. Tears of anguish flowed down both their cheeks. Macey rocked Becca gently and kissed the top of her head.

"Oh, Macey, I wish that was true. I only pretended to black out—I wanted him to think I had passed out—figured maybe he would leave if he thought I was down for the count, you know? I didn't pass out, Macey. I saw him pick up that log at the same time he jerked my panties down. I really thought that, if I played possum and pretended I was unconscious, that he would just go away. Oh, God, it was so awful...it hurt so bad, Macey...it took everything I had not to scream, because if I screamed, he would know I wasn't passed out, and he might have..."

Tears flowed freely down Macey's cheeks while she continued to hold her friend. "It's going to be okay, Becca...it's okay...it's okay. He's never going to hurt you again."

Ruth Wymer felt like an intruder when she slowly opened the door to Becca's room and peered inside. She had knocked—timidly—and opened it when no one answered. She saw the two women embracing— and crying—so she began to retreat from the room before they saw her. She bumped right into Scott before she made her exit.

Ruth jumped and spun around.

"Excuse me," Scott almost grunted as the woman crashed against his chest and stepped on his foot. He looked down at the petite woman and, immediately, noticed the resemblance to Macey. The resemblance was remarkable. "You're...Mrs. Wymer, aren't you?"

Ruth's gasp was audible when she finally recognized Scott. She had extended Macey's Christmas dinner invitation to include him, but, she had been secretly relieved when Macey had declined. She wasn't sure if she believed—as her daughter and son obviously did—that Scott Pennell had nothing to do with Kacey's murder. She stiffened and drew away when he reached out to steady her. "Yes...I am, and, you're...Scott Pennell."

"Yes, ma'am," Scott professed. "It's...uh...nice to finally meet you."

"Is it?" Ruth quipped tersely.

Macey heard the noise outside the door and opened it to find her mother and Scott staring uncomfortably at each other. "Oh, my," she groaned. "I was hoping to have you two meet for the first time under better circumstances."

"I'll go," Ruth stated, and moved to walk around Scott.

"No, please, Mrs. Wymer," Scott pleaded. He touched her shoulder lightly, and felt her jerk away from his touch. "You stay, please. I'll leave."

Macey exhaled deeply and placed both hands on her slender hips. "Oh, for Heaven's sake, neither of you will leave," she commanded. "Please...you've both obviously come to see Becca, so come on in." She moved aside and held the door open for them both.

"Well, don't just stand there," Becca smarted from across the room. "Come on in. Hello, Scott."

Scott moved closer to the bed and smiled down at Becca. "Hello, Becca...it's really good to see you with both eyes open again."

"Not to mention my smart mouth, huh?" Becca quipped. "Scott... they told me that...you were the one who found me."

Scott nodded affirmatively while they all waited for the subsequent pregnant pause to pass.

Becca choked back the tears that threatened to return. "Thank you, Scott. Thank you for saving my life."

"Well, I really didn't do all that much, Becca..." Scott answered. He was embarrassed by her sudden and unexpected warmth.

Becca hushed him with a single look. "If you hadn't come by when you did, Scott, I'd be dead. There's no doubt about that. The doctors said if my injuries hadn't killed me, the exposure to the elements would have."

"Well...I'm just glad you're okay," Scott replied awkwardly.

Becca looked at the attractive woman standing beside Macey. Although Macey was several inches taller, their facial resemblance confirmed the familial relationship. "Hello," she smiled at Ruth. "You... must be Macey's mother?"

Ruth looked at Macey who smiled at her and nodded. She ventured to Becca's bedside and gathered the woman's larger, dark hand between her own tiny, white ones. "Hello, yes...I'm Ruth Wymer."

"You have a pretty terrific daughter here, you know," Becca pronounced. "She's the best friend I've ever had."

Ruth smiled at Becca, her own eyes now beginning to tear. "Yes, I'm finding that out more and more every day...she is pretty terrific."

Macey blinked in surprise at the admiration she detected in her mother's voice. Could it be that she really cared about Macey? Was it possible for them to form some sort of bond after all that had happened?

Scott flopped down into the vinyl arm chair that had been previously occupied by Mrs. James. The papers in his back pocket crumpled loudly, and he was embarrassed when everyone turned to look at him. He jumped back up and removed the copies of the killer's sketches that he had placed in his back pocket earlier. He wanted to be sure to show them to Macey, since the opportunity to do so had never presented itself the night before.

Becca rolled her eyes at Scott. "You sure make a lot of racket, white boy. Whatcha got there?"

Scott unfolded the pictures, but wasn't sure whether he should show them in front of Becca and Mrs. Wymer. He thought that Macey should have a chance to look at them alone.

"Scott?" Macey asked as she watched his brow furrow in thought. "What is it?"

"Uh...it's just the sketches—the ones done by the computer specialist..." he began.

"Oh, yes! I'd almost forgotten!" Macey exclaimed. "I'd forgotten you were going to do that. May I see them?"

Scott shrugged—still not sure of what to do—but, held them out to her.

Macey sat down on the bed, which allowed Becca and Ruth to look over her shoulder at the sketches. Macey did not immediately look at the sketches; instead, she watched Scott's eyes—tried to read what it was she saw reflected in them. She was not aware that the two women were peering over her shoulder at the sketches. She was about to explain to them both that this was the man who may have been responsible for Kacey's death, when she heard the two women gasp in unison.

Ruth's hand went to her throat, while Becca used both hands to cover her eyes.

Scott and Macey exchanged shocked and puzzled glances.

Becca recovered first and snatched the copies from Macey's hands. Fresh tears spilled across her cheeks and her entire body began to tremble. She looked at Scott—who didn't know what to do to comfort anyone. She looked back at Macey—who began crying over the obvious distress that Becca and Ruth were experiencing.

Macey had yet to look at the sketches. "Becca, you're scaring me!" she wailed and stared at her mother. "Mama? Please tell me what's wrong!"

Ruth took several deep breaths and leaned against Becca's bruised body. She looked at the sketches again—two different sketches, almost perfect images—of Lucas Dudley.

Becca kept her eyes closed shut for a long time, but finally opened them. She shook her head slowly. "Macey...I...don't know this man's name, but, he...he's the one who...attacked me...he's the one who hurt me..." Becca collapsed into fresh tears.

Macey gently pried the sketches from her friend's fingers. Her own face paled visibly as recognition of the man registered from within her deeply recessed memories. She looked at her mother, whose own tears had finally begun to fall.

Scott quickly observed the reactions from all three women. He didn't know which one to try to comfort first, so he rushed around to the side of the bed where Macey sat, and pulled her to him. "Macey, what's the matter! Do you know this man?"

Macey looked at her mother, and Ruth looked at Scott. Scott saw the same, identical emotions—shock, disbelief, and fear—reflected on both their faces.

Ruth was the first to find her voice. She swallowed hard and said, "I...I know this man. His name is Lucas...Reverend Lucas Dudley. I've...Dear God, forgive me, but...I've been having an affair with him for almost a year now. He's..."

Macey choked on her tears when she looked at Scott's worried expression. "Oh, Scott," she whispered. "He...he's the man who...raped me when I was fifteen. He...he's the father of my baby. . ."

Becca cried out and Ruth swooned.

Scott moved quickly to keep Ruth from falling off the bed. "Oh my, God..." he groaned.

It was quite possible that God was the only one who could help any of them now.

CHAPTER 48

LUCAS HIDES OUT

Macey arrived early at CompuTech at seven o'clock, Thursday morning. It would be at least another hour before any of her co-workers arrived. She sat at her desk and allowed the ceramic mug—filled with steaming black coffee—to warm her hands. She normally took cream and sugar in her coffee, but after everything she had learned last night, she needed the caffeine jolt that the virgin Java would provide. She stared into her mug and thought about everything that had happened in Becca's hospital room the night before.

"What are you doing here at this hour?"

Macey was startled at the unexpected intrusion. Her hands shook only slightly, but it was still enough for coffee to spill over onto the pile of papers stacked neatly on her desk. "What..." She looked up to see Scott rushing over to her desk.

Scott offered an apologetic grin. "Sorry, Macey...I didn't mean to scare you."

Macey smiled and thought how handsome he looked—although, he probably had not slept any better than she, Becca or Ruth had slept. She glanced appreciatively at his casual attire. He was dressed in gray slacks and a white turtleneck sweater. A slow warmness began to spread throughout her body at the welcomed sight of him. "Hey, you. No, don't worry, it's okay...you didn't scare me. I just didn't think anyone else was here yet." She found a tissue and dabbed at the spilled coffee.

"Let me help you with that," he offered. He grabbed a handful of tissues, and began to wipe spilled coffee from the edge of the desk.

Their fingers touched and Scott felt Macey tremble. He took her coffee cup from her curled fingers, placed it off to the side, and pulled her to a standing position. He watched her cast her eyes downward, but couldn't get a good feeling about why she was acting withdrawn from him. He lifted her chin and forced her to look at him. "Macey? What's wrong? Talk to me."

She withdrew her hands and went to stand before the large double window. The dreary winter weather—previously predicted—was determined not to disappoint the forecasters. The sun had risen a few minutes ago, but if the gloomy weather persisted, the coming day didn't look very promising. The weather matched Macey's mood perfectly. She turned to look at Scott and surprised herself by wondering what he might have looked like at seventeen—when her sister, Kacey, first fell in love with him. She shook her head and exhaled softly. "It's...well, it's a little bit of everything, Scott. So much has happened since you came back to Columbus."

"Are you blaming all of this on me?" he asked. It was incredulous, to him, that she might be thinking along those lines.

Macey looked up and saw the hurt in his eyes. "No, Scott...of course not...please don't think that. That's not what I meant, at all. These things probably would have happened whether you were here or not."

"I'm not sure about that. It may have taken a lot longer to learn the other truth about Dudley—that he was your sister's real murderer."

Macey shook her head and exhaled again. It was going to be impossible to concentrate on work today. "I still can't believe it, Scott— and, I'm not sure what it all means. He raped me, he killed my sister, he's been having a year-long affair with my mother, he beat my best friend almost to death trying to get information about my baby. It's all so... incredible and unbelievable. Why has this man infiltrated himself into my family?"

"I'm not sure if you're ready to hear this or not, Macey, but I'm going to say it anyway."

"What?"

"Well, I'm no expert by any means, but, I think all his actions have been very calculated and motivated by...the child."

"What child?"

Scott paused. He was surprised that she hadn't readily caught the drift of his comment. "His daughter..."

Cold, intense fury—unadulterated fury—quickly clouded her perfect face, at the insinuation that Lucas Dudley might have any rights to her child. "She is NOT his daughter! She's mine!" Macey screamed at him.

Scott pulled her into his arms and held on tightly when she fought against him. It took several moments, but he felt the moment her anger turned to fear and frustration. He continued to hold and comfort her while she cried into his shirt.

When the tears finally subsided, Macey looked up into Scott's eyes. "She's mine, Scott...and, she's all I've got. She's out there somewhere. That private investigator I hired tracked her to some small town in Tennessee—Hayden, I think it was. She's been there the whole time, living with an aunt I never even knew existed."

"Your father's sister?"

"Yes," Macey sniffed and grabbed another tissue. She blew her nose softly and continued. "She disappeared from Hayden about the same time Papa did."

Scott was confused. "Who? The aunt or your daughter?"

Macey looked at Scott with an exasperated expression. "My daughter, of course!"

"So, you think your father has her somewhere?"

"Well, he must! That's why we've got to find him, Scott. I don't think the police are focusing too much on finding him anymore, because they know Jacob doesn't want to press charges."

"I don't think it matters if Jacob presses charges. Your father tried to kill him. The police will still want him for assault with a deadly weapon."

"Not intentionally, and—for the record—in case you've forgotten...it wasn't Jacob that he was trying to kill."

"Whatever..." Scott shrugged. "The man is still dangerous. Besides, where could he have taken your daughter? Do you know of any place they might have run to?"

It was Macey's turn to shrug. "I don't know anything about my father, Scott. I have no idea what kind of man he is—other than what Jacob has told me over the years."

"Well, that's easy—I can tell you—the man's crazy!" Scott volunteered.

Macey smiled back. She had regained some composure. "No, I don't believe he's crazy. Besides...he's not the one I'm most concerned about right now."

"You're talking about the good reverend?"

Macey nodded and pressed her lips firmly together in thought. "Exactly...after the police came last night and everyone told them all that they knew about him, well, you know...you were there."

"Yeah, it is frightening. Did you hear anything else from the police after we got home?"

Macey shook her head. "No, but Mama called. I thought she was going straight home when we all left the hospital, but as it turns out, she convinced Detective Windham to let her ride with him to Reverend

Dudley's home. I think she wanted to be there when they arrested him."

"She didn't!"

Macey smiled. "She did. It was a pretty gutsy thing to want to do, don't you think? I've never known my mother to be so angry about anything before...except when Kacey was killed. I wasn't here, but, I heard that she went totally berserk. It's a good thing you weren't around, because she probably would have ripped your head off if she could have gotten to you. I don't know what her true feelings for Reverend Dudley were—prior to last night—but, I do know that she is furious at him right now—not to mention the guilt that she feels for blaming and hating you—all those years—for Kacey's death."

"I know he's the man from my memories, Macey, but we still don't have any real proof that he's the one who killed Kacey. I mean, what motive would he possibly have had?"

Macey shrugged and rubbed the back of her neck. "Who knows? The man is a sick pervert, but, worse than that, he's...dangerous. Men like that don't always need a motive to do the sick things that they do."

"Yeah, he's sick all right," Scott exhaled and rubbed the back of his neck. "So, the police...I'm guessing they've arrested him by now, right?"

Macey shook her head. "I'm not sure, but, Detective Windham called in a favor to some judge, who issued a search warrant. Mama went inside the Reverend's home with the detective, and she said it didn't look as though anything was missing. The police left an officer staked out in front of his house—just in case Dudley came back home in the middle of the night. The detective said he would also issue an APB on him today—for the assault on Becca—that's the only positive crime they have against him right now."

"The bastard..." Scott fumed. "I wish I had him alone for about ten minutes."

"I wouldn't need that much time," Macey muttered.

Lucas had known almost immediately when Macey hired the private investigator. The investigator's secretary was a devout follower of the good Reverend Dudley. She had been on the receiving end of his numerous, methodical spiritual cleansings, and, she had been more than eager to provide Lucas the answers to his questions. She told him that her boss had tracked Andrew to Hayden, Tennessee.

Hayden, Tennessee—that is where Lucas had been on Wednesday night when the police first entered and searched his home. He returned to Columbus in the early hours of Thursday morning, and immediately spotted the undercover cop parked across the street from his house. He wasn't sure what the police might have learned about him, but he didn't take any chances. He had parked his truck at a small shopping plaza, and walked to Ruth's home. He entered through the rear patio door, and was careful not to turn on any lights—he didn't need any. He knew where to find the objects he needed. They were located under his bed beneath a loose floorboard. He retrieved the 9mm pistol, and the metal box containing more than thirty thousand dollars in cash. It would be enough for him and Gabrielle to leave the country and start a new life somewhere else—possibly Mexico.

Lucas had learned all about Gabby from the private investigator's secretary, who was oblivious to any connection between Lucas and the girl. Lucas often charged the older women for his services—services that had provided him with more than thirty thousand dollars in cash over the past several years. However, he promised the investigator's secretary a free spiritual cleansing in return for all her help and information.

Lucas' hopes were short-lived, however, because Andrew and the girl had disappeared by the time he arrived in Hayden. He found Louise easy enough, and, although she had fought him valiantly—in the end—she provided him the information he needed. He knew that Andrew had returned to Georgia with Gabby—to a backwoods cabin he owned in Buena Vista. Yes, Louise had been difficult, and, as horrid as her facial disfigurement was, her body excited him enough for him to "cleanse her soul" before she died. He knew that sweet Louise was now in a happier place—finally free of all her scars and pain. He felt immense gratification in knowing that he had been personally responsible for ensuring her soul a place in Heaven...for all eternity.

Lucas planned carefully before he left for Hayden. He had visited a used car dealership, and traded in his beloved BMW for a more non-descript, 1972 Chevy pick-up truck. It tore at his heart strings to part with the more luxurious car, but, he knew he would draw less attention driving the truck. If there was the slightest chance that the police had any real evidence on him, he didn't want to risk being tracked by driving the BMW. He wondered how incriminating the evidence was against him, or, if they had any real evidence at all. How much did the police really know about his involvement with Becca James or Kacey Wymer?

Lucas decided there was one person who could provide the information he so desperately needed. Ruth would know. Somehow, he would find out how much the police knew about him, and, how much they knew about his past.

He left his truck parked at a small parking plaza and had walked to

Ruth's home. It had been easy to slip, undetected, through the basement window of the Wymer house at five o'clock this morning. Lucas knew that the basement was seldom used. It would serve as a good hiding place, while, it also allowed him the time he needed to plan his next course of action.

Lucas slept for a couple of hours and awoke at eight-thirty. He crawled to the top of the cellar stairs and listened to Ruth and Jacob moving around in the kitchen. His smile never reached his eyes while he listened to Ruth tell Jacob everything that happened at the hospital the night before. It didn't take him long to discover how much trouble he was in. It appeared that all his secrets were out. He decided to wait until dark before leaving the relative safety of the basement. That would give him time to finish formulating his plan—his plan to finally unite with the daughter who had been ripped so savagely from his heart and his life.

Lucas blamed several people for keeping him from his daughter, and, he offered a silent vow that they would all pay dearly. He had to find her. She belonged to him. Instinct told him that Macey was now the primary key to finding his daughter. He would follow her as long as it took. He was confident that Macey would lead him to his Gabrielle—to his destiny.

CHAPTER 49

LUCAS REMEMBERS HIS OWN PAST

Lucas remained hidden in the Wymer basement for two days. Jacob had not been home much during those two days. Lucas was careful—he always waited until Ruth left the house, before helping himself to their abundant Christmas leftovers. He used Jacob's shower to bathe himself, because it was important to always keep his body clean—something that had been drilled into his brain from a young age.

"A dirty body makes a dirty mind!"

Even after all these years, Lucas still shivered at the memory of his aunt's voice. His aunt's voice had taunted him from the early age of five—when his mother first abandoned him—until his sixteenth birthday. All those years—that voice had taunted, cowered, and shamed him into abiding her every demand.

Lucas sat at Ruth's kitchen table late Friday afternoon. He was dining on a cold ham sandwich and a large glass of milk. He didn't require much food, so he didn't worry about Ruth becoming suspicious. If she noticed the missing food at all, she would simply think Jacob had stopped by to help himself to the leftovers; and, Jacob—in turn—would think that his mother had eaten them. Neither would have any reason to question the other about a few slices of ham. The seven-layer chocolate cake—on the other hand—constantly beckoned to him, but, he resisted eating it because a quickly diminishing cake might be more noticed than a few slices of ham.

He had on the same black trousers he had worn since Wednesday, and this bothered him immensely. He had tried on some of Jacob's clothes, but they did not fit him. He took pride in his physique—he had worked hard to keep in top physical condition over the years—but, his waist line would never again compete with that of a twenty-four-year old. He had tried on Andrew's pants, as well, but they were too big for him. He did help himself, however, to a pair of Andrew's boxer shorts and a clean tee shirt. He even took time to shave and applied a small amount of Andrew's after-shave lotion to his face and throat.

Oh, but it so good to feel clean again.

"No amount of bathing can wash away the dirt that filters through your mind!" Lucas chewed absently on his sandwich, and allowed his thoughts to drift back in time—fifty years ago—when it all began. He remembered his aunt's constant, spiteful words, and the life she forced him to lead. Fifty years ago—but, at times, it seemed like only yesterday to him.

He had been only five years old when his father—Fred Dudley—left them. It was the typical scenario—a husband bored with the responsibilities of married life and a mundane job, becomes involved with a younger woman who persuades him to give it all up—to abandon his family—for *her*.

Juanita Dudley was devastated when her husband left. She was emotionally unprepared to care for herself, much less a five-year old child—a child she conveniently blamed for her husband's absence. She had loved her husband with every fiber of her being, but, she had been so fearful of becoming pregnant again—the idea was so repulsive to her—that she limited her sexual encounters with him to the bare necessity. She knew it was her wifely duty to service him, and she did so—once a month—and, only during the one week she believed she would not conceive. She blamed Lucas for causing the strain in his parents' relationship, and, she blamed him when her husband ran off with another woman.

One morning—six months after his father abandoned them—Lucas awoke to find himself all alone in the house. He called out for his mother, searched for her in every room, but, there was no trace of her, or any of her belongings. It was as though she had never lived there, never been a part of his life. He had sat alone in the house for two days. He did not eat, and, he urinated and defecated in one corner of the living room—his safe spot—where he had positioned himself since he first discovered he was all alone. He wanted to remain in the corner, so that he would be the first thing his mother saw whenever she returned. He knew that she would return to take care of him—she was his mother—and, it was her job to take care of him.

It was almost dusk—two days after his mother first left him alone—

when he heard the front door opening. His tiny, tear-stained face lifted, and hope returned to his heart. His mother had returned! She had come back for her little boy!

Lucas squinted his eyes and tried to make out the form of the woman who now stood in the shadows of the opened doorway. No, he was wrong—it wasn't his mother. It was his Aunt Martha—his father's older, spinster sister. She looked down at his filth and told him that his mother had gone away—that she would never return—and, that she never wanted to see him again. Aunt Martha moved into her brother's home that very night, and forever altered young Lucas' life.

"Keep your hands off that thing, boy, or it will rot off! And you had better make sure you never poke it inside a woman's thing, because a woman's thing is dirty! Dirty, dirty, dirty!

His aunt provided for them by cleaning other people's homes, and working part-time at the neighborhood Church of God. It was there that she became a fanatic about religion—a religion that she constantly forced upon her small, impressionable nephew. There was nothing wrong with the religion preached and practiced by the Church of God—it was a good church—and, the people who attended it were good people. However, it was his aunt's own insecure interpretations of everything she learned there, that distorted the religion for young Lucas.

Lucas grew up, convinced that his penis was a curse placed upon all men by God, and that women's vaginas were merely a cubicle for the curse to fester and grow. Sunday nights held a bizarre ritual for him and his aunt. Every Sunday night—before he said his prayers—his aunt would get on her knees, pull down his pants, and inspect the condition of his penis. Her sloppy, oral manipulation always followed the cursory inspection. She told him—over and over again—that *this* was what evil women did—that *this* was how the other woman convinced his father to leave them—that *this* was probably what that woman was doing to his father at that very moment. She told the young Lucas that she had to keep doing this to him, so that his manhood would grow to an enormous size, and, that—when he was old enough—he could use it to purge the evil from within a woman. His Aunt Martha performed this weekly ritual on him, from the time he was five, until shortly after his sixteenth birthday. Week after week, she brainwashed the young Lucas into believing that all women were evil, and that a spiritual cleansing of their womanhood was the only thing that could save their eternal souls.

Martha's warped perception of the spiritual cleansing concept, was that her nephew would grow into a man who sought out loose women— women like the one who had stolen her brother away from his family—

and, would, subsequently, punish them for the hurt and pain they had—or one day might—inflict upon another innocent family.

Martha taught her nephew well, but she never expected to become the first recipient of his learned sexual expertise. She was his first—the first to receive a spiritual cleansing of her sins and impurities.

It happened on the Sunday night after Lucas's sixteenth birthday.

Martha was in the process of performing her weekly gorging of his manhood, when something finally snapped inside Lucas. He didn't plan it. It just happened. He sat on the edge of his bed with his pants pooled around his ankles, and looked down at his aunt, who knelt before him in her usual position. Lucas had always been able to float outside himself in the past—pretending that what was happening to him wasn't real—but, on this particular Sunday night, that sense of detachment failed him. It came out of nowhere—the sexual stirring that any normal sixteen-year old would experience under such carnal circumstances. It had never happened before, but he couldn't stop himself this time. Lucas climaxed inside his aunt's mouth.

Martha jerked her head away, and spat out the bitter fluid—all the while—cursing his inability to control himself. She ran awkwardly into their only bathroom and vomited into the toilet. She stood up slowly and leaned over the sink to rinse her mouth. "Disgusting. . ." she sputtered incoherently.

She never saw Lucas follow her into the bathroom, and she gasped when she saw his reflection in the mirror. He was standing directly behind her. She continued to watch his reflection until an evil grin spread across his face, and she knew—instantly, and too late—what his intentions were. She, also, realized—at that moment—that what was about to happen was her own fault. She had done this to him—she had turned him into this...*animal!*

Tears coursed down her wrinkled face while Lucas had his way with her. Her pride prevented her from begging him to stop. She uttered neither a single word—much less a scream—in protest. She knew that she deserved whatever pain Lucas chose to inflict upon her.

Lucas had not been gentle with her. He pounded and grinded into her as hard as he could, and after he had climaxed for the second time that night, he bent forward and whispered, "Praise the Lord, Aunt Martha. Your soul has been spiritually cleansed."

Several hours later, Lucas packed his meager belongings into a duffel bag, stuffed the cash his aunt had been saving for years into his back pocket, and never looked back.

The police found Martha Dudley's body three days later.

Her employer grew concerned when she failed to report for work and didn't answer her phone. The police were contacted and asked to check on her. When a single policeman arrived, he found the front and back doors locked, as well as all the windows. He looked through the kitchen window and saw a body slumped over the table. He broke the glass window on the back door and unlocked it. He didn't need to check the woman's pulse. He recognized the permeating stench of death as soon as he opened the door. The woman sat slumped at the kitchen table, her right arm dangling by her side. A pool of coagulated blood covered the linoleum floor beneath her chair. It appeared that the woman had slit both wrists, and used her own blood to write two words on a white linen napkin—*FORGIVE ME*.

All efforts to locate the woman's nephew proved fruitless. There was no trace of him or any of his belongings. The police interviewed several neighbors and co-workers. Everyone they talked to told about Martha's devotion to her nephew, and the nephew's love for his aunt. After several weeks, the police concluded their investigation. They deducted that the nephew must have run away from home, and—in despair and loneliness—his aunt had taken her own life. There was no sign of foul play. An autopsy was not performed, so the sexual violation went undiscovered. Martha Dudley's death was treated as a suicide, and the case was closed.

The sound of a car door closing snapped Lucas' thoughts back to the present. He jumped from a sitting position, and knocked over the half-glass of milk. He peeked through the kitchen curtain, and saw Ruth unloading a bag of groceries from the trunk of her car. What was she doing back so soon? He had expected her to be away from the house most of the day—he had overhead her, earlier that morning, telling someone on the phone that she would be gone all day.

He quickly grabbed a dish towel and cleaned up the spilled milk, but, he failed to notice the small amount that had rolled off the table ledge onto the floor. He swiped away the crumbs from his sandwich, and looked around the kitchen for other signs of evidence that anyone had been there who shouldn't have been. The screen door opened at the exact moment that he dashed through the cellar door.

Ruth smelled it the moment she stepped through the door—Andrew's after-shave lotion!

She sat the bag of groceries precariously on the kitchen table. Her slender hand grasped at her throat, and she struggled to control her breathing. When had he been here? Was he still here? Was he hiding somewhere in the house? Had he been here all along? Her eyes traveled frantically around the kitchen, looking for more evidence to confirm her suspicions. Her hand touched something wet along the table's edge. She looked at her fingers and brought them up to her nose. She sniffed but couldn't detect any definite odor to the liquid. Her eyes moved along the table and gradually came to rest upon the small pool of milk spattered on the floor. "Milk," she whispered. "Andrew doesn't drink milk. He hates milk."

She took a deep breath and, acting much braver than she felt, slowly made her way into the living room, down the hall, and into the bedroom that she and Andrew shared. She checked each room for any noticeable signs of trespassing. She looked through the closet and his chest of drawers, but didn't find anything out of place. She walked slowly back down the hall and stopped at Jacob's bathroom. The smell of after-shave lotion was strong, and the sink was wet. She looked closer and saw a few tiny, dark whiskers trapped alongside the drain. They could have belonged to Jacob, but, she knew that Jacob would have thoroughly rinsed the sink after shaving—he always did. "I've got to call someone..." she spoke out loud. She was trying not to panic—trying to stay calm, but something did not feel right. "But who? Macey! Yes...Macey will know what to do."

She walked quickly back to her bedroom and picked up the phone to call her daughter's home. She forgot that Macey had said she was returning to work today—to catch up on her workload. Ruth waited for Macey's recorded message to end, so that she could leave word for Macey to return the call as soon as possible.

It came out of nowhere. A strong, hairy hand reached out and grabbed her right hand. She knew that hand—that firm grip. Oh, yes, she knew it all too well.

The phone fell to the floor just as the final beep signaled the okay for the caller to begin their message.

Lucas jerked her around to face him and smiled at the fear he saw in her eyes. This was what he liked to see in his women—raw, unadulterated fear. It was so important for them to fear his power over them. It was obvious to him that Ruth Wymer did, indeed, fear him. He reveled in the helpless, ravaged expression that consumed her face. He pulled her roughly against him and whispered, "Oh yes, Ruthie, you have reason to be afraid. You should be...very, very afraid."

CHAPTER 50

THE PROPOSAL

Macey was still working at eight o' clock on Friday evening. She had worked through lunch, and it looked as though she would, also, be working through dinner. Mr. Byce had called that morning to say that he would be returning the following Wednesday, and, he wanted an early morning meeting with her—a very early morning meeting. She was scheduled to meet with him in his office at six o'clock Wednesday morning, Macey had no doubt what the first thing on his agenda would entail. She shivered involuntarily.

Scott was working late that evening, too. He had stopped by at lunch for a quick hello—but, that was the last time she had seen him. She knew that he was working overtime to have everything in order for Mr. Byce's return on Wednesday. The incidents with Jacob and Becca—not to mention the turn of events concerning Lucas Dudley—had taken a lot of time away from their respective jobs. They both knew that George Byce would not be sympathetic to their explanations or circumstances.

Macey stopped what she was doing, leaned her head back, and stretched both arms above her head. She closed her eyes and inhaled deeply. She must be imagining things. She could have sworn she smelled the aroma of fried onions!

She inhaled once more before her senses correctly registered the aroma for what it was—the greasiest, best tasting burger in town—the tiny, but extremely satisfying, Krystal burger. The burger, itself, was almost paper thin, and was topped with grilled onions, a pickle, and melted cheese—all on a plain, unassuming four-bite bun. It was, without a doubt, the best burger in the Southeast. It smelled especially good now, because Macey had not eaten anything since a half-bagel and orange juice at six o'clock that morning. "I know that smell..." she sighed as she opened her eyes and spun around in her chair.

Scott stood before her, waving a paper bag in one hand and cup of coffee in the other. "We don't have anything like this in Pennsylvania, and, it's probably a damn good thing that we don't."

"Why do you say that?" Macey grinned as she eagerly accepted the offered bag. She walked over to the conference table and began to lay out their gourmet feast of three Krystal cheese-burgers each, chili fries, and coffee.

"Well, if I grew up eating these things, I'd probably weigh three hundred pounds by now and my arteries would be planning a mutiny, for sure. It's hard to eat just one, isn't it?"

Macey grinned again. "It's un-American to eat just one—eating only one is an injustice to the Krystal burger, because, to truly appreciate a Krystal you must consume a minimum of two, but preferably four."

Scott looked down at the spread of food and frowned. "I thought three each would be enough, but if you're still hungry after three, you can have one of mine."

Macey sat down at the table and smiled up at him. "Three should be plenty. Thank you so much, Scott."

"Well, I figured if I was hungry, you must be starving. Janet brought me a sandwich at lunch."

Macey nodded. "I know. She stopped by and asked if I wanted anything, but I wasn't really hungry then."

Scott sat down next to her. "Well, it looks like we should have everything caught up by the time he gets back, Macey."

The bite of burger stuck in Macey's throat. The thought of George Byce's eventual return physically sickened her. She wondered how much Scott really knew about what had happened between them. She managed to rinse the burger down with the hot coffee. "I hope so..."

They ate in silence for a few minutes. Scott wanted her to finish at least one burger before he said what was on his mind. "Macey?"

Her stomach was eagerly anticipating the arrival of the second burger. "What?"

"You don't have to be afraid of him any longer."

Macey hesitated before she asked, "Afraid of whom?"

Scott's expression was deliberate. He intended to make it hard for her to avoid direct eye contact. "You know damn well who I'm talking about...Byce."

Macey took a bite of burger, chewed it intently, and swallowed carefully. "Oh."

"I mean it, Macey. He will not be bothering you anymore. I told you before...I think I know what it's been like for you these last few months."

Macey was embarrassed. Her private life had always been just that... private. "We touched on the subject, yes, but tell me...what exactly do you *think* you know, Scott?" she asked. Her voice trembled in fear that the entire truth about her unsavory relationship with George Byce would come out now.

"I told you before...I've heard the office rumors." Scott finished his second burger and wiped his mouth.

"I never pictured you the type to listen to office gossip. That's a little beneath you, isn't it, Scott? I don't have to guess who you've been talking to about these rumors. Janet, right?"

Scott was taken aback at the sudden flare of anger that erupted on Macey's face. He had not meant to upset her. He had only wanted to reassure her that things would be different now. He intended to protect her from George Byce—at all costs—even his job if necessary. "Janet knows better than anyone, I suppose, about what it's like to be on the receiving end of Byce's lewd attention."

Macey pushed abruptly away from the table. "She doesn't know anything, Scott, and I resent you believing her idle gossip about me. If I wanted you—or anyone—to know anything, I would have told you myself. Oh, and, another thing...I certainly don't need you to be my knight in shining armor—to watch out for me. I have managed to take care of myself all of my life, and I can certainly handle the likes of George Byce!"

Scott stood up and moved to stand behind her. He pulled her back against him. "Macey...baby, maybe it's time that you allowed someone to help you. I have no doubt that you can handle Byce—all I'm saying, is that you don't have to do it alone anymore. I'm going to be there for you...always." He turned her around to face him and frowned at the tears sliding down her cheeks. "Macey? I told you before that I've fallen in love with you, but I'm not sure you know just how far I've fallen."

Macey sniffed loudly—and, rather unladylike—but managed to look up at him. She wanted—desperately wanted—someone to lean on, someone to trust, but, she had never afforded herself that luxury. "What do you mean, Scott?"

He grinned rather sheepishly and raised his eyebrows. "You need to hear it again, don't you? Okay, then—I love you, Macey Garner..."

Macey wiped her tears with the sleeve of her sweater and stared into his eyes for a long moment. "I know you've said it before, but, yes—I think I needed to hear it again. I haven't heard that from too many people in my life."

Scott shook his head in disbelief. "It's still hard for me to believe that I'm the first man to ever tell you that."

"Maybe that's because I've never let anyone get that close to me... until now."

Scott held a deep breath and finally released it. "Will you let me love you, Macey...really love you?"

They looked at each other for several moments, each of them weighing the consequences of her response.

"It won't be easy, Scott..."

"All I ask is that you let me try."

She took a deep breath and exhaled slowly. "And if I let you *really* love me, then I guess that means I won't have to keep my early morning appointment with Mr. Byce on Wednesday?"

Scott appeared to consider her question before he grinned back at her. "Well, I certainly don't want *that* to be the determining factor on whether you allow me to really love you. I'm still hoping that you meant what you said a few days ago—that you felt the same way. You do remember saying that to me, don't you?"

Macey closed her eyes. "I told you that I carry a lot of excess baggage with me, Scott. Are you absolutely certain that you want to become involved in all that?"

"Are you referring to Gabrielle?"

"For one thing, yes. I mean...you should know that I intend to find her, and to be a part of her life...if she'll let me. But, there's also the rest of my family."

Scott grinned again. "Hey, I like Jacob."

Macey frowned. "It's more than just Jacob, and you know it. It's taken me a lot of years, but, I know now that I do want a relationship with my mother. I'm not so sure about my father. I'm not sure that I could ever love or care for him again, but, well...I don't want to shut him out completely."

Scott shrugged. "Hey, I like your mom, too."

Macey frowned again and raised her eyebrows questioningly. "And..."

Scott nodded. "Hey, I like your best friend, Becca, and, I think she's finally coming around to liking me a little too, don't you?"

Macey stood with her hands planted firmly on her hips. "I wasn't referring to Becca; although, you're right, she is a very important part of my life, too."

"Yeah, well..." Scott sighed. "The man did try to kill me, and, I wouldn't exactly feel comfortable going coon hunting with your father; but, if he

347

could make the effort, then you have my word that I'll try, too..."

Macey suddenly burst out laughing. It was several moments before she could respond. "To my knowledge, Scott Pennell, my father has never been coon hunting in his life!"

Scott smiled and welcomed her into his arms. He sighed when she hugged him tightly around the waist. "So," he remarked casually. "It's okay, then?"

"Is what okay?"

Scott felt himself blush when he replied, a little too loudly, "Is it okay if I tell you that I love you and want to spend the rest of my life with you? I know I said it before, but it's...well, it's real for me now, and I need you to know that."

Macey clapped her hands against her ears and laughed. "You don't have to shout, Scott. I'm right here." She trailed her finger gently along his jaw line, and sensed the shiver that coursed quickly through his body. "And, yes, it is definitely okay if you tell me that. I'm ready to hear it now—I'm ready to believe that it's real for us."

"Oh, Macey..." Scott moaned. He pulled her into his arms so tightly that her breasts crushed against his chest. He lifted her off the floor until they were hip-to-hip, and groaned loudly when she instinctively wrapped her legs around his waist.

Their discarded clothing left a trail from the conference table to the soft, plush rug in front of Macey's desk.

The happy couple spent the rest of the night, in Macey's office, exploring each other's bodies and minds. It had been twenty years since Macey had lost her virginity to Reverend Lucas Dudley and—in one night—Scott had managed to erase all the memories of that painful, agonizing encounter. They made love, off and on, all throughout the night, and well into the next morning. They were both oblivious to the approaching storm that had finally arrived after several threatening days.

They were about to drift off to sleep again around four o'clock on Saturday morning when Scott rolled over and whispered into her ear. "Say it again, Macey..."

Macey barely managed to turn her head in his direction. "Mmm...say what again?" she asked sleepily.

He nibbled her ear lobe. "Tell me that you love me as much as I love you."

She was shocked to discover that her body could physically respond, so soon after the vigorous hours of lovemaking. She smiled at him and closed her eyes. "Oh, yes...yes I do..." she moaned.

Scott moved lower and nibbled on her neck. "Tell me again that you'll marry me?"

Macey's eyes opened slowly. "Is that what you want, Scott? Really?"

His lips ventured lower, to her breasts. "More than anything, Macey, so...will you? Will you be my wife and make me the happiest man in this room?"

The happiness she felt threatened to overwhelm her. She touched his face and laughed out loud. "Oh yes, Mr. Pennell. If you're sure that is what you really want, then...YES!"

"That's all I needed to hear," Scott smiled. "Now, why don't you just lie back and let me show you what married life with me is going to be like?"

The incessant ringing of Macey's phone shocked them both awake a couple of hours later. The storm outside was in full force as several bolts of acrid lightning and roaring thunder shook the windows.

A definitive chill crept throughout the room.

CHAPTER 51

JACOB SEARCHES FOR MACEY

Jacob was beside himself with worry. Where was Macey? He had been trying to reach her since late last night. There was no answer at her apartment—or at Scott's—and, he had gotten a steady, busy signal from her office until eight o'clock this morning. He had let it ring at least twenty times the last time he called, but had finally given up. Maybe she wasn't answering the phone because she was working on a deadline and didn't want to be interrupted.

He even called his mother to see if Macey might be with her, but her phone was obviously off the hook because he got a continuous busy signal at her end. He wasn't worried about his mother, though, because she was prone to forgetfulness. She often forgot to return the receiver fully to its cradle. He knew that his mother sometimes took the phone off the hook when she planned to take a long bath. If that was the case, she probably forgot to hang it back up afterwards.

Jacob was unaware of all that had happened during the past couple of days. He had called his mother on Wednesday, and left word on her answering machine that he would be staying with a friend for a few days. He failed to mention that the friend was Janet. Once he had revealed the truth to Janet about his virginity—or lack, thereof—she had only allowed him to leave her bed long enough for them to put in a few hours at their respective jobs. She called him every hour he was at the station to remind him of what she planned to do to him once he got home.

The girl was insatiable! She couldn't seem to get enough of him, and Jacob felt obligated to accommodate her as much as his body would participate. He worked late Friday night to make up for coming in late that morning—thanks to Janet. He felt obligated to keep the station running until his mother could make other arrangements—or until his father returned. Jacob had every intention of sticking to his original plan to move to Florida, so a few extra days really did not matter to him.

Jacob's thoughts returned to the late-night phone call he had gotten at the station the night before. He was reluctant to answer the call because of the late hour—a call a ten o'clock might mean leaving the station to rescue an abandoned driver somewhere—and, he was anxious to return to Janet's bed. The night had been filled with heavy thunder and lightning, so he assumed he had lost the connection when he first answered the phone—no one seemed to be on the other end. However—just as he was about to hang up—Jacob heard a raspy cough, as though someone was clearing their throat.

"Hello!" Jacob had yelled into the phone. "Is anyone there? Hello!"

Another moment passed before the caller finally responded. "It's me, Jacob..."

Jacob had never fully expected to ever hear his father's voice again, so, he was momentarily caught off guard. "Pop? Is that you?"

"Are...are you all right, Jacob? I mean...from the cutting..."

It was Jacob's turn to pause. "I'm okay, Pop..." He didn't know what to say to the man. He couldn't be sure if it was his imagination or not, but, it almost sounded as though his father really cared.

A cold had settled deep in Andrew's chest during the past couple of days. He coughed again. "I...never meant to hurt you, Jacob. You know that, don't you?"

Jacob did know that, but—more importantly—he believed it, too. He still wasn't sure who his father's intended victim had been, but it really didn't matter now. No real harm had been done, except maybe to his niece. "Yeah...I know. It's okay, Pop...really. Where are you? Everybody's been looking for you."

"The police too, I bet," Andrew responded gruffly.

"Yeah, probably, but, I don't think they're really looking all that hard, Pop. I told them that I wouldn't press charges, even if they found you."

"Someone tries to kill you and you won't press charges? Are you stupid, boy!"

Jacob bristled and inhaled sharply. His father had asked him that question—repeatedly—throughout his life, so much so that Jacob considered the fact that he, indeed, might be stupid. It had taken Macey's return—five years ago—to convince him, otherwise. Macey had helped him build up his confidence and self-esteem, in a way that his father never could.

Andrew heard Jacob's inhaled breath, and recognized his mistake

351

immediately. "Jacob...I'm sorry. That was uncalled for...I don't know why I do and say the things I do sometimes. I guess old habits die hard. Forgive me?"

Jacob was flustered. Who was this man asking his forgiveness? It surely couldn't be the father he had grown to love and hate in a singular emotion over the years—a father he had never felt close to—a father who never noticed him, never loved him.

"Jacob? Are you still there?"

Jacob cleared his own throat and closed his eyes tightly against the threatening tears. "Yeah, Pop...I'm here."

"I'm sorry I called you stupid, son."

Son! His father had called him *son!* Jacob could not remember his father ever calling him that before. "It's...uh...okay, Pop." Jacob sniffed and wiped at his nose. "You...uh...you never said where you were."

Andrew paused while another crash of thunder echoed in the background. "I'm not too far away."

Jacob took advantage of his father's strange mood and pressed forward. "Pop...do you have Gabrielle with you?"

Andrew was stunned! How in the world had they found out about Gabby? "How do you know about her, Jacob?"

The familiar, authoritative tone had returned to his father's voice. Jacob swallowed the lump that had suddenly formed in his dry throat, and wished that he had kept silent about his niece—at least until he had discovered where his father was hiding out. "I...uh...I found the pictures of her in your desk drawer, Pop."

"That drawer was locked."

"Yes, sir...I know, but, well, when it looked like we might never hear from you again, I started looking around the office for some legal documents on the station. You know, to see where Mama stood in all this. She's been a nervous wreck the past couple of weeks. She wasn't even sure if her name was listed on the title, along with yours."

"Of course, I listed your mother as co-owner. I'd always intended to provide for her in case..." Andrew became quiet long enough to regain control of the anger he felt rising within him. "We're getting off the subject, Jacob. Who else knows about Gabby?"

"Gabby?" Jacob asked. The nickname did not immediately register in his mind.

"Yes, it's short for Gabrielle. Who else knows about her, Jacob?"

"Well, Mama knows...Macey knows, and, Scott knows..."

"Scott?"

"Yes, sir. Scott Pennell...he's Macey's friend—they work together. He was the man with her that day in the station..."

Another moment of immeasurable silence followed before Andrew could speak. "I know who Scott Pennell is. He's the son-of-a-bitch who killed Kacey! I knew who he was the minute I saw him at the station. I couldn't believe my eyes when I saw him, and, then...Macey, too. He was the one I meant to stab...not you, Jacob...never you, son."

Jacob relished hearing his father refer to him as *son* for the second time. "Pop, he's really a pretty nice guy and, from everything I've learned about Kacey's death, it was never really proven that Scott was the murderer."

"Bullshit! His rich Mama and Daddy high-tailed it out of town with him before they could prove anything for sure! He's pulled the wool over all your eyes, hasn't he? The son-of-a-bitch...he killed my little girl...I know he did."

Jacob listened to his father's muffled sobs and felt helpless. "Pop, please calm down and tell me where you are."

Andrew's choked sobbing gradually turned into labored breathing, and another coughing spasm rocked through him. The shock and anger he felt, hearing about Scott Pennell, pulsated like poison through his veins. "I've gotta go, Jacob."

"No, Pop! Please don't hang up! You've got to tell me where you are!"

"No!" Andrew shouted. "I've got to go. I'll call you early tomorrow morning at the station. You be there."

"Sure, Pop, but..."

Another thunderous clap of thunder rocked the building and the line went dead. Shivers of impending horror coursed up and down Jacob's spine. "This can't be good..." he whispered as he listened to the dial tone.

Andrew called early Saturday—as promised—and gave Jacob a message to pass on to Macey. He stressed that the message be delivered only to Macey. He stressed that, under no circumstance, was Scott Pennell to become involved.

Jacob promised to deliver the message personally to Macey...if he could ever find her. He had been trying to contact her, since Andrew's call the night before.

He decided to try her office one more time. He didn't really expect her to be there at nine o'clock on a Saturday morning, but, she obviously wasn't at home. He had already left several messages on her answering machine. She was always very punctual in returning his calls, but, this time was proving to be an exception.

The phone was answered on the seventh ring—at least, Jacob thought it had been answered.

Scott had rested some and was ready to begin another passionate session with Macey, but she stopped him when her phone continued to ring. It could be important—someone calling on a Saturday morning—so, she persuaded him to hold off until she took the call.

Scott had every intention of honoring her request, but once she picked up the phone, he couldn't resist the opportunity to tease her—with his fingers and tongue. He decided to test her willpower—would she be able to talk to her caller, or would she have to hang up and receive what awaited her?

"Helllooo, ohhh..." she inhaled sharply. She bit her bottom lip and tried to ignore the stimulating sensations that coursed through every fiber of her body.

Scott's fingers began an extensive exploration of their intended territory. He smiled when he saw her closed eyes and determined expression.

"Hello!" she repeated anxiously, trying hard to suppress the moan of pleasure that threatened to erupt. Her inexperience and lack of willpower almost won out. She was almost ready to hang up the phone. If it was important, they would call back. Besides, it was Saturday...her office was closed!

Scott was having too much fun. He wondered how normal a conversation she would be able to carry on if he advanced his stimulations. He decided to test that thought.

His tongue vibrated inside her, and the phone dropped from Macey's trembling fingers, onto the onto the plush carpeting. The muscles in her thighs contracted and held his head firmly between her legs. She lifted her hips higher and shuddered. "Oh, God..."

Scott smiled mischievously. "Sorry about that," he whispered. "But, I couldn't resist."

"You're awful," Macey whispered back. Her lips were dry and swollen. Their marathon lovemaking session had left her totally exhausted, but also, deliciously exhilarated.

Scott's head still rested between her thighs and he grinned at her. "Hmm...I thought I was pretty damn good, myself." He looked at the dropped phone. "Who was that on the phone?" He began to nibble at the inside of her thigh.

Macey's eyes jerked open, and she pushed him unceremoniously off her. He landed on his backside, while Macey searched frantically for the dropped phone. She found it and sat upright. Her quaking thighs protested the interruption. "Hello? Hello? Is anyone there?"

Jacob had heard the commotion and noises from his end, and, his imagination was running wild. Had someone broken into Macey's office? Was she being attacked? "It's me, Macey! What the hell is going on over there? Are you okay? What's all that noise I heard? It sounded like something fell."

Macey tried to slow her breathing. "Jacob? Hi...no, sweetie, everything's fine. I'm sorry, I was...uh...rushing to finish up a project, and, I...knocked my coffee cup off the desk. I dropped the phone trying to keep the coffee from doing too much damage."

Jacob was skeptical of her explanation, but, he had more important things on his mind. "You're sure you're all right then? Man, it took you long enough to answer the phone. I've been trying to reach you since last night! I was about to hang up and drive over there."

"No! No...I mean, don't do that," Macey stammered. "Really, I'm fine. I'm just tired, that's all. I've been up all night...uh...working on this project."

"Well, sis, I suggest you put a skid on things there, because I'm about to tell you something that's going to rock your world."

Macey's world had just been rocked by Scott—several times—but, her spine tensed with unexplained anticipation. "What's wrong, Jacob?"

"It's about Pop, and...Gabrielle. He called me last night, Macey...he called me at the station last night—and again early this morning. Like I said, I've been trying to reach you all night."

Macey's throat constricted. "Gabrielle? What about her, Jacob? Tell me, please. Do you know where she is?"

"Yeah, Macey...I do. She's with Pop at some hunting cabin in Buena Vista."

"Georgia? They're here in Georgia?"

"That's right, Macey. They've been there for a few days now, and, Macey...Pop wants us to meet them there."

"He does? When? Now?"

"No, later today. He wants to spend a little more time—alone—with Gabby before everything changes for them. I'm not sure what he meant by that exactly. He gave me directions to the cabin. He said that we should meet him there at five o'clock this afternoon—just you and me, Macey—no one else."

"You mean..."

"I mean...definitely not Scott...not Mama, and—especially—not the cops. If anyone other than you and I show up, he said he'll take Gabby and leave for good this time."

"Gabby?"

Jacob smiled. "Yeah, that's what he calls her. Nickname, I guess. So... what do you think, Macey? Should we trust him?"

Macey closed her eyes to block out Scott's bewildered expression. "We have no choice, Jacob. No choice. I'll do anything to see her... anything."

"Okay then. It'll take about forty-five minutes to get there, but if this weather keeps up, it'll probably take us a little longer. How about I pick you up at three thirty?"

"Three-thirty? Yeah, Jacob...three-thirty is fine."

"Where will you be...your apartment or your office?"

Macey's mind was reeling with a dozen different possible scenarios— all of them involving what it might be like to see her daughter for the first time. She had a change of casual clothes in her office, and, she could use Mr. Byce's personal shower to clean up. Three-thirty seemed like a life time away. "Pick me up here, Jacob...at the office. I'll be waiting in the parking lot for you."

"Okay, sis. I'll see you then, and...Macey?"

"Yes, Jacob?"

"I'm really happy for you, you know? You've waited a long time for this day."

"Thanks, Jacob. Thank you so much for letting me know."

"I'll see you later this afternoon. I'll be at Janet's if you need me before then. Do you have her number?"

"What? Uh...no, I don't, but, I'm sure Scott does. He's working today, too, so, I'll get it from him if I need to call you. I'll see you later, Jacob, and, thank you...so, so much."

Macey hung up the phone and turned a wide-eyed look in Scott's direction. She knew she would have to tell him something. He had heard enough of her end of the conversation to probably figure most of it out on his own. She wished he could go with her, but, she wouldn't take any chances of jeopardizing the pending reunion with her daughter. Nothing would stop her from being at that cabin at five o'clock...not even her newly discovered love for Scott Pennell.

CHAPTER 52

Planning for the Rendezvous

Scott had retrieved most of his clothes before he turned back to Macey, who was still sitting dumbfounded on the sofa. "You're sure Scott does what?"

Macey sighed and looked at him. She had momentarily forgotten that she was not alone in the room. "What?"

Scott pointed to the telephone as he zipped up his pants. "That was your brother on the phone, right?"

Macey simply nodded.

"You told him you were sure I did something..."

Macey blew upwards at the stray, unkempt bangs that fell into her eyes. She made a waving motion with her hand as though swatting at a bothersome insect. "Oh...that. That was nothing, really. Jacob is with Janet at her place, and, he wanted to know if I had her number in case I needed him for anything. I told him that I didn't have it, but I was sure you did."

The innuendo—if that's what it was—caused Scott to flinch.

Macey smiled when she saw the uncertainty cross his handsome face. She stood up in all her naked glory—totally free of any self-consciousness around Scott. She ducked when he found her panties and used them in a slingshot-fashion to fast-forward them to her. "I didn't mean anything by that remark, Mr. Pennell. I know there's nothing serious between you and Janet."

"You sound pretty sure of yourself, Miss Garner," Scott joked back. He felt sure she was trying to distract him from her conversation with Jacob.

Macey pulled her sweater over her head—sans bra—and pulled her panties and slacks on. She placed her hands on her hips and grinned at him. "I most certainly am that—especially after last night!"

Scott lifted his brows and crossed his arms across his chest. "So, let me see if I understand what's going on here. One night of the best sex I've ever had—that either of us has ever had—and, you expect me to be completely in awe of this relationship?" he quipped.

Macey walked over to him, stood on her tiptoes, and planted a quick kiss upon his pouty lips. "Oh, there's no doubt about it, Mr. Pennell. You are—without a doubt—hooked!"

"Yep, she's trying to distract me, alright..." he thought. It was obvious, to him, that she was deliberately trying to detract his attention from her phone call with Jacob—buy, why? He caught her by the arm when she moved to walk by him, and pulled her to him. "Okay, Macey. All kidding aside—are you going to tell me what that phone call was all about?"

Macey had the good grace to blush. She didn't want to lie to him, but, there was no way she was going to chance her father running off— possibly forever this time—with Gabrielle. She looked up at Scott and offered a weak smile. "I'm sorry, but I can't tell you everything, Scott. You've already heard more than you should have."

"All I know for sure is that it involves your father, your daughter, and the fact that Jacob is picking you up in the parking lot at three-thirty. So—wherever you're going, Macey—I'm going with you—especially if your father is involved. He is still a fugitive from the law, remember?"

"I know he is, but you cannot come with me, Scott. I'm sorry...I wish you could, but, Papa has threatened to take Gabrielle and run off for good if Jacob brings anyone with him other than myself. You cannot go with me, and, if you insist on it, and something happened—well...I could never forgive you for jeopardizing my one chance to see my daughter. It would ruin everything between us."

Scott was crushed. "I can't believe you would think that, Macey," he shook his head. "I want to help. I want to be there to protect you from that...mad man. God only knows what he might try to do to you this time."

"You have to trust me on this, Scott. Please...I don't want to lose you, but, if I have to choose between you and my daughter..."

"You don't have to say it, Macey. I know who you would choose—and, you have every right to feel that way. I just wish it could be different." He turned his back on her and gathered up his shoes.

"Scott, please," Macey begged. "You've got to understand the predicament this puts me in. Please...please don't ask me to choose."

He stood at her door with his shoes in hand. He pointed to the stack of files piled high on her desk. His reply came out harsher than he had intended. "You've already chosen. I'll be in my office if you need any of those documents signed before you leave today."

Then he was gone.

Macey stood in one spot for several minutes, and cried softly into a handkerchief that Scott had left behind. She gathered together her change of clothes, smoothed back her hair, peeked into the reception area to make sure no one was loitering around, and quickly made her way to the elevators. She punched the button for the penthouse level, and spent the next hour soaking in George Byce's Jacuzzi. She washed her hair, dried it with his blow dryer, put on her clean clothes, and walked out of his office. She didn't bother putting on any make-up.

She knew that she should attempt to get some work done while she waited for Jacob, but, she felt the need to clear her head. She grabbed her keys and walked quickly to the parking lot. One place always helped her do just that—clear her head. It was the cemetery. Kacey would listen to her and lead her in the right direction.

She lowered the car window so that the cold air could hit her face. "Oh, Kacey," she whispered. "I know now why you must have loved him as you did. Please, please help me keep him, Kacey. Don't let this drive a wedge between us. Help Scott to understand..."

Macey tuned the radio to a station that was playing hits from the sixties and seventies. The deejay purred seductively to his invisible listeners. "And now folks, here's one of my personal favorites—a real blast from the past—*The Lion Sleeps Tonight.*" She sighed and leaned her head against the headrest. That had been Kacey's favorite song before she died. She tried to visualize the two of them standing side-by-side, faux microphones in hand, and singing in perfect harmony. "*Awemiwah, awemiwah, awemiwah, awemiwah....*" Macey smiled. That song on the radio—at just the right time—that was the sign she needed, to reassure herself that she was doing the right thing. "That's just the sign I needed, Kacey...thank you."

She was half-way to the cemetery when she realized there was no longer a need for her to visit there. Kacey had managed to ease her doubts and tension by riding shot-gun—beside her—in the car. Macey turned the car around and headed in the direction of The Medical Center. A visit with Becca would do wonders for her morale. She could visit Becca and still have time to return to work and finish up the work files she left piled on her desk.

It suddenly seemed like an interminable amount of time until three-thirty.

Lucas had driven Ruth's car to a motel in Phenix City, Alabama—a small, but infamous town—across the river from Columbus. He registered under the name of Jacob Wymer and stayed in his room until after dark. He drove to a small shopping plaza—empty now of shoppers and cars—and parked behind a retail drug store.

Lucas broke a back window and searched the pharmacist's shelves until he found what he needed— *Pyrrole*—a yellowish liquid that was similar to that of chloroform. He had used it before in some of his spiritual cleansings of young girls—but, only when the situation left him no other choice. He much preferred the girls to be awake whenever he performed the cleansings. The drug wasn't especially dangerous if it was used correctly, so, it should serve his purpose quite nicely.

He returned to the safe and secure confinement that his motel room offered, and remained there for the remainder of Friday night, and through mid-afternoon Saturday. He purchased a local paper to ensure there wasn't anything about him, or his connection to Becca James. He had hoped she would die, but, that had not happened. He had overheard Ruth speaking to Macey—during his stay in the Wymer basement—about the black bitch, and how her condition was improving every day. There had been a short article in Thursday's paper concerning Miss James' assailant—the identity of whom, was still unknown. The article simply stated that the police were looking for more clues, and questioning several suspected drug dealers in the area.

Lucas never suspected for a moment that the police had deliberately omitted any mention or description of him; nor, did he suspect that an APB had been issued on him for questioning in the cases involving Becca James and Kacey Wymer.

His hunger grew with his newfound confidence, so, Lucas ventured outside the motel at two o'clock, Saturday afternoon, and drove to a fast-food restaurant. Fast-food was not really his style, but, he couldn't risk being recognized at one of the finer eating establishments in the area. He would have to settle for a burger and fries. He sat inside the restaurant—a baseball cap pulled low over his forehead—and ate his meal, while he pondered the finalization of his plan.

It was a good plan. It would work. Even if the police somehow connected him to it, he and Gabrielle would be long departed from the great and mighty United States, before law enforcement officials could track them down.

Lucas' smile broadened as he thought about his plan. He was so deep in thought that he wasn't paying attention to the few people coming and going around him. It was simply a stroke of luck that he looked up from his paper at the precise moment Scott Pennell walked through the front entrance.

Lucas quickly hid behind his newspaper and glanced out the large glass windows to see if Macey had accompanied Scott. He spotted Scott's Porsche easily enough, and relaxed when he didn't see any sign of Macey. "*Too bad*," he thought. It would certainly have simplified his plan if they had been together, but, that was no problem. He was confident things would still turn out favorably for him and Gabrielle.

Lucas was sitting at a corner table—normally reserved for large groups—so Scott would, most likely, not have noticed him anyway. He smiled again as he watched Scott sitting alone at a table on the other side of the restaurant. Judging from the scowl on his face, it appeared that Mr. Pennell wanted to be alone with his own thoughts. Lucas thought that he looked like a man with a lot on his mind. "Tsk, tsk," he clucked. "Trouble in paradise, my friend?"

Lucas noticed that Scott kept looking at his watch—approximately every five minutes. Was he waiting for Macey to join him? It was three o'clock when Scott finally cleared away his trash and used the side entrance to leave the restaurant. Lucas waited until Scott backed the Porsche out of its parking space, before he folded his paper and left through the front entrance. He had a brief thought that if Scott were to look back through his rear-view mirror, he might recognize Lucas. "No," Lucas thought out loud. "He doesn't even know what I look like. Even if he did remember me, he wouldn't recognize me after twenty years. I'm so much more handsome now than I was then."

The reverend merged with the oncoming traffic and followed Scott across the Oglethorpe Bridge, one of three bridges that crossed the muddy Chattahoochee River and connected Columbus, Georgia to Phenix City, Alabama. "He must be going to CompuTech," Lucas mused thoughtfully. "I wonder...oh, wouldn't it be simply delicious if Macey was waiting for him there. No...that would make my job too easy. Oh well..."

Lucas kept a discreet distance between them until Scott pulled into CompuTech's vacant parking lot. "Well...not totally vacant," Lucas laughed out loud when he saw one other car—Macey's car—in the lot. He parked across the street from CompuTech. "It appears that my sweet Macey—mother of my precious Gabrielle—is, also, putting in some overtime today. How convenient for me," he laughed out loud again. "Oh...but, how unfortunate for the two of them."

CHAPTER 53

Respective Destinies

It was three-fifteen when Lucas parked across the street from CompuTech. He watched Scott lock the Porsche and walk around to the side of the building.

"Hmm..." Lucas mulled. "I wonder why he didn't use the front entrance?" He thought about returning to the motel—to rest until dark— but, he was convinced that fate had placed him and Scott at the same restaurant that day, for a reason. His intuition told him to stay put—to keep an eye on Scott Pennell. "Well, I suppose I can wait an hour or so. Macey's car is here, too, so maybe they've planned a rendezvous. I have no doubt that you know where our daughter is, Macey. She's certainly not in Hayden, Tennessee with her cold, dead Aunt Louise! Nosirree— our little girl is certainly not there. I think she's with Andrew, and, I think you—sweet, delectable Macey—can lead me to them both."

Lucas settled in to continue his watch. He eventually opened the glove compartment and withdrew a pair of binoculars—one of the items he had retrieved from the floorboard beneath is bed. His fingers caressed the other two items—a brand new 9mm pistol, and a nine-inch hunting knife—were tucked securely under the driver's seat. "We can't go hunting without a trusty, hunting knife," Lucas sang into the empty air.

The knife had been a gift from his aunt—one of the few real gifts she had ever given him— for his fifteenth birthday. He had used her gift—put it to good use—before he left home that last time. The knife had been instrumental in helping him to become the master of his own destiny. He had forced his aunt to use it on herself—to slit her own wrists—and then forced her to write her own suicide note before she bled out. Lucas had become his own man that day. It had taken tremendous self-control on his part, to fight the urge for one last spiritual cleansing on his aunt. It didn't matter to him that she was already dead when he wanted to do this. The urge had been strong—so strong—but he had fought the urge and won that battle.

A shudder coursed through his veins as he relived the memory of his aunt's murder. The memory had rewarded him with a miniscule erection. He stroked himself absently and looked around the parking lot. He doubted that fate would strike twice in one day, by supplying him a young, firm body to accommodate his sudden sexual appetite. The urges to perform spiritual cleansings had been increasing steadily over the past few years. Lucas found the urges to be neither unusual, nor unappealing. He looked forward to them.

A slight movement of the car interrupted his thoughts. His first thought was that someone must be outside, rocking the car back and forth, until—he suddenly remembered.

It was Ruth. She must have awakened again.

He would have to administer another dose of Pyrrole. She had been in the trunk of her own car since he had abducted her, late yesterday afternoon. The thought came to him that he could use Ruth to contain his gnawing, sexual needs. He contemplated the idea, and tried to think of a remote area of town that might accommodate them. There were still plenty of isolated, wooded areas remaining in Columbus—progress had not destroyed them all yet. He wondered if the spot where he had cleansed Kacey was still available. "Oh, my...what a sweet thought," he moaned, while he continued his light stroking.

Lucas blinked at the unexpected squealing of brakes. He exhaled deeply and looked around to see Jacob Wymer's pick-up truck come to a quick stop beside Macey's Rodeo. He saw that Macey was already standing beside her car. How long had she been there, Lucas wondered? Had she seen him sitting in the car? Lucas slumped lower in his seat and watched as she gave Jacob a quick kiss, and the two climbed back inside the pick-up. He turned his head away as the truck pulled from the parking lot and passed along side Ruth's Ford Taurus.

Macey's window was down and she glanced at the car as they drove past. She thought she had detected a quick movement before they passed the car, but she couldn't be sure. Her mind had been focused on one thing—one thing only—getting to Buena Vista, Georgia as quickly as possible. However, something about the Taurus still nagged at her brain. She looked out the back window and back at Jacob. "That looked like Mama's car, didn't it?"

Jacob glanced quickly into his rear-view mirror and shrugged. "I doubt it, Sis. She wouldn't have any business on this side of town, and, besides—do you know how many red Taurus cars there are in this town!"

"Yeah..." Macey answered. "I guess you're right." She turned around to face the front, and quickly forgot about the red Taurus. "So...how long do you think it will take us to get there?"

Jacob looked up at the dark clouds that threatened to erupt at any given moment. "Well, it's stopped raining for now...maybe an hour or more...it depends on what kind of weather we run into."

Macey closed her eyes and sighed. "Just get us there, Jacob...just get us there."

Lucas shifted himself slowly from his slinking position, and looked toward the retreating pick-up. He felt the car rock again as Ruth continued to kick from inside the trunk. *"She must be fully awake now,"* he thought. *"Damn bitch is going to kick a hole in the side of the car."*

He started the car, and prepared to follow Macey and Jacob. They could just be going to run an errand—maybe visit their sister's grave— but, then again—you never knew. Before Lucas could make a U-turn to follow Jacob's truck, he saw Scott's Porsche flash by him. Jacob was almost two blocks down the road by now, but it appeared that Scott intended to follow them.

Scott had never actually returned to his office after lunch. Instead, he had left his office radio turned on when he left at one o'clock that afternoon. He had locked his office door so that Macey would think he was inside working—that he did not want to be disturbed. He had left CompuTech long enough to grab a quick sandwich across the river in Phenix City, but it was more to kill time than anything else. He returned the Porsche to the side parking lot, after lunch, in case Macey checked to see if he was still there, when she left with Jacob. Scott had hidden in some bushes on the west side of the building and waited for Jacob to arrive. He gave them time to get a block down the road before he jumped into his car, fully intent on following them to wherever they were going. He did not know what he would do when they reached their destination. He had not planned that far in advance.

Scott was so intent on following the siblings, that he never noticed the red Taurus parked across the street from CompuTech. If he had paid closer attention to it, he would have seen it practically rocking on its side—instead, he sped past it without a second glance. "If she doesn't trust me enough to tell me what's going on, then I'll do what I have to do to protect her." He knew that Macey and Jacob were meeting Andrew and Gabrielle—he didn't know where—but, Scott did not trust the elder Wymer not to hurt Macey. *"Hmm...one problem would have resolved itself if only she had suffocated..."*

Lucas watched Scott speed away and offered up a small chuckle. He left the engine running and walked around to the back of the car. He soaked his handkerchief with the Pyrrole before he opened the trunk. He grinned wickedly when he looked down upon Ruth Wymer.

Ruth's mouth was still gagged, and her hands and feet bound tightly— just the way Lucas had left her almost twenty-four hours ago. She still managed to glare back at him when he grinned down at her.

The buttons on her blouse had popped open, and Lucas drooled at the sight of her limp, saggy breasts. "Sweet Ruthie, what is all the commotion about? I know, I know...you need to be cleansed, don't you, love?" He embraced the panic that spread across her face, and laughed out loud when she shook her head violently from side to side. Lucas leaned into the trunk and allowed himself one quick, hard squeeze of her breasts before covering her nose with the handkerchief.

The odor from the liquid stung Ruth's eyes and they began to tear. She tried to mumble something, but her lids grew heavy and, within seconds, she was knocked out again.

"There now—that should hold you for a while, my dear. Maybe you can help me alleviate some of my...frustrations...a little later." Lucas slammed the trunk closed, returned to the driver's seat, and put the car in gear. It took him about three blocks before he caught sight of the Porsche.

They were all on their way to their respective destinies.

Andrew and Gabrielle sat on the front porch of the cabin. They were enjoying a brief reprieve from the storm that had racked the area for the past couple of days.

He thought his granddaughter had been unusually quiet since their discussion about her mother. Andrew had held back very little. He told her the whole ugly truth—about making the decision to take her from her mother—about hiding her for twenty years in a small, desolate town that held no hope of a decent future for a young woman like her—he told her almost everything. He wasn't proud of some of the things he had done, but—in the end—he thought she believed that he had done those things out of love—for her, and for Kacey.

He was desperately searching for a way to make amends for all the heartache and humiliation he had inflicted upon his family. He had always seen Gabrielle as a source for his redemption—a chance to do it all over again—to do things right this time. He tried to convince Gabby that he would have reunited her with her mother years ago, had he known Macey's whereabouts. There had been times over the past few years when he thought he had seen Macey at the mall, or at the park, but, he always concluded it to be wishful thinking on his part.

He didn't want to interrupt her private thoughts, so he spoke softly. "I wish I knew what you were really thinking, Gabby."

Gabby sat cross-legged in a large rocking chair. She was dressed in a beige turtleneck sweater and denim overalls, and she looked more like a pre-teen than a recently turned twenty-year old woman. Her long, dark hair fell in a thick, single braid over her left shoulder. Her face was void of any makeup.

Andrew thought her to be the most beautiful creature ever put upon God's earth. He could only hope and pray that he had not destroyed the close bond they had developed and nurtured over the years. He didn't want to go on living if Gabby couldn't forgive him for the things he had done—things that had affected her life and her future.

He smiled awkwardly when his granddaughter looked over at him, and watched her closely when she inhaled the rich fragrance of the woods, that were damp with the mist from the previous storms. She returned his smile and it warmed him from the inside out. Her smile meant that everything would be all right between them. The rest of his family may never be able to forgive him for his past deeds, but, his precious Gabrielle had forgiven him—and, that was all that mattered to him. He could rest easy now—no matter what happened to him—knowing that her love for him had survived and would prevail.

"I'm thinking about what a brave and wonderful man you are, Paw Paw. It took a lot for you to tell me the truth about my mother. Yes, you have done some horrible things in your life, but, it's certainly not my place to judge you for any of that. My mother...oh, Paw Paw...I want to meet her so badly, but, I'm also thinking of how lucky I have been to have had you and Aunt Louise in my life." She sighed softly. "My mother—a woman I have always wondered about—wondered why she didn't love me—why she didn't want me—I've wondered about those things for a long, long time. I tried not to dwell on it too much, though, because I had you and Aunt Louise. You must know, that as much as I love the two of you—as much as the two of you love me—well, it just isn't the same as knowing a mother's love. I always felt like a part of me was missing. Does that make any sense?"

A single tear slid slowly down Andrew's cheek. He looked at her helplessly and shrugged. "What can I do, Gabby? I'll do anything to make all this up to you. I know I should have told you the truth about your mother years ago, but, I was so afraid I would lose you—that I would lose your love. I know now that I was wrong to try and keep you two apart, but..."

Gabrielle uncrossed her legs and walked over to the bench that Andrew sat on, with his head lowered into his hands. "Please don't cry, Paw Paw. You're doing the right thing now, and, that's all that matters. I'm going to meet my mother very soon now, and, that wouldn't be happening if it weren't for you. I love you, Paw Paw. Please, please don't ever doubt that."

Andrew lifted his head to see her kneeling before him. He knew that he didn't deserve her love, kindness, or understanding.

She wiped the tear from his cheek and leaned forward to replace it with a soft, gentle kiss. "Does she know she's going to meet me, Paw Paw?"

Andrew shook his head. "She knows that you're here with me, and, I'm sure she's *hoping* to meet you, but, no—she doesn't know that for sure."

"What kind of person is she, Paw Paw? Tell me more about her."

Andrew exhaled and raised his eyebrows in supposition. "I honestly don't know what kind of person she is, Gabby. I haven't spoken to your mother since she was sixteen years old. That night at the station...the accident with Jacob...that was the first time I've laid eyes on her since she gave birth to you. I don't know what kind of person she's grown into."

"What about my Uncle Jacob?"

Andrew smiled at the reference to Jacob as an uncle. "I'm ashamed to say I haven't given myself much of a chance to really get to know your uncle either, but, I have a feeling he's grown into the kind of man I wish I could be. He's kind...and honest...and, quite a good-looking young man."

Gabby smiled and sat beside him on the bench. She rested an arm on his shoulder. "Then he must look like his father," she concluded.

Andrew looked over at her and smiled. "Thank you for saying that, angel. Actually though, he probably looks more like your grandmother more than he does me. Your mom and her sister—Kacey—they got my looks, I think."

Gabby sighed dreamily. "A grandmother...I actually have a grandmother, too. Just think, in only a couple of days I've acquired a mother, an uncle, and a grandmother, to boot. How lucky can one girl be?" She reached over to hug him.

Andrew returned her hug and felt good about the plans he had made. He would reunite his granddaughter with her mother, make peace with his son, turn himself in to the police, and beg his wife to forgive him for his abominable treatment of her over the years. Maybe one day—after he was released from prison—they could continue to grow old together, pumping gas, and rebuilding motors at Wymer's Service Station. He knew he was hoping for a fairy-tale ending—one he did not deserve— that might never happen.

They both jumped when they heard the crunch of gravel along the half-mile driveway.

Andrew stood up abruptly and looked down at Gabby. "Well, it looks like judgment day has finally arrived, angel. You go on now...do like we talked about, okay? I want to spend some time alone with Jacob and Macey before I introduce them to you."

Gabby stood on tiptoe and kissed her grandfather on his bearded cheek. "Okay, Paw Paw...good luck," she smiled and jumped off the porch. She quickly dashed into the woods, taking the short path that led to the lake. There was a hunter's deer stand located near the lake's edge. She and her grandfather had planned for Gabby to wait there for one hour—after which—she would eagerly embrace her first meeting with the woman who had given her life.

CHAPTER 54

THE CABIN IN THE WOODS

Macey glanced down at Jacob's scribbled directions. They had already made two wrong turns that had cost them thirty additional minutes in travel time, but, they were still on time for the rendezvous with their father. It was ten minutes before five o'clock when they finally found the graveled driveway, that was almost completely hidden by overgrown bushes and weeds.

"There it is, Jacob! Look over there," Macey exclaimed and pointed to a dead tree to the left. "There's the old pine tree he said to look for—he said it had fallen just inside the driveway. She took a deep breath and looked anxiously around their immediate surroundings. There was nothing but forest—seemingly endless miles of Georgia pines—surrounding them. The driveway was extremely narrow, with tall pines neighboring both sides. It would be impossible for two cars, going in opposite directions, to occupy the driveway at the same time. There were no turn-around points along the driveway, so, one driver would have to completely back away in the direction they had come, in order, for an oncoming vehicle to get by.

"It sure is quiet out here," Jacob whispered.

"Why are you whispering?" Macey teased. Some of the tension and stiffness momentarily lifted from her back and shoulders when she spotted the fallen tree. "I don't think anyone can hear us," she whispered back.

Jacob blushed with embarrassment. "Sorry," he smiled. "But, doesn't this place give you the creeps...just a little? I wonder how long Pop's had it? Or, hey—I know—he's probably trespassing himself—it doesn't even belong to him. Yeah, that's probably more like it."

They continued moving down the long driveway until the lake suddenly came into view. Macey gasped at its captivating beauty. The wind sent tiny mists of rain dancing across the lake, and she was caught spellbound at its unsettling beauty. Jacob stopped the truck alongside the lake for a moment—to reassure himself that they had turned into the right driveway. Neither of them had noticed the small cabin that sat slightly back and to the left. There were dozens of red-tipped bushes—probably planted long ago by someone—that had been left to grow wild. They stood about fifteen to twenty feet high and practically covered the front half of the cabin.

It was the red Volkswagen parked close to the porch steps that finally caught Jacob's eye. "Hey, look!" he pointed—no longer whispering. "That's the car Pop was working on at the station. We had just finished overhauling the engine that day you and Scott came in. Man...I'm ashamed to say that—with everything that happened—I never even noticed the car was gone! Where has my head been?"

"My best guess would probably be between the sheets of Janet Braswell," Macey smirked. She had not intended for her comment to register as tersely as it did. Macey shivered when a sudden chill moved through her. "Don't park next to it, Jacob," she instructed. "There's something about that car...I don't know—it's silly—but, something about it...scares me."

Jacob pulled around to the side of the cabin, where a small clearing proved perfect for additional parking. The cabin was only about a hundred yards from the edge of the lake, and a trail had been cleared that wound down to the dark waters. Those waters were no longer dancing; the ever-increasing and cooler wind caused surging currents to ripple from one shore to another.

He jumped from the truck and stared back at her. "It's just an old car that Pop restored, Macey. He bought it from an old junk yard years ago, when I was real little. It sat up on blocks in our back yard for years—until a few months ago. Pop towed it to the station and spent all his free time fixing it up. I've gotta say...he did one helluva job, too. It's a classic now. He could probably get ten grand for it easy."

Macey closed the passenger door behind her and rubbed her hands together, to generate some heat. "It still gives me the creeps," she murmured. She wished she had brought a heavier jacket. The windbreaker she wore didn't offer much protection from the strong winds, but, it was the only one she had at the office. She had not wanted to take the time to return to her apartment for a warmer jacket.

She shoved her hands into her pockets and looked around her

nervously—half expecting her father and Gabrielle to appear at any moment, from any direction. Once you got past the initial depression presented by the overgrown driveway, it was easy to appreciate the beauty and serenity of the place. She could hear small animal sounds off in the distance, and the occasional splash from fish jumping in the lake—maybe they were trying to get out of the cold wind, too.

Macey squinted her eyes and looked at what appeared to be a tree house—or maybe a deer stand—at the bottom of the trail, near the lake. It looked sturdy and was enclosed—at least on one side—with a small opening for a window. There was a protective tarp across the top of the stand—maybe to protect the hunters during inclement weather. She supposed the deer must be abundant in these woods and the deer stand—if that's what it was—was probably used frequently. "Funny," she wondered aloud. "I never imagined Papa as a hunter."

Jacob smiled and stretched. "He's not—at least—I've never known him to be; but, then again, I never knew about this place either. What else do you think there is to do here—in the middle of nowhere—besides hunt and fish?"

Andrew allowed the screen door to slam shut behind him, to get their attention.

Jacob and Macey jumped and spun around at the sound.

"I don't use the place for hunting," Andrew spoke softly. He moved down the steps toward them, and never took his eyes off them. He was dressed in a flannel shirt and jeans, and, he sported a new salt and pepper beard. "I come here whenever I need to be alone...to think about things. He reached the bottom step and placed both hands in his pockets. Now that they were here, there was so much he wanted to say to them; but, he didn't know where to begin.

"Macey...Jacob...thank you both for coming."

The sight of her father—up close and personal—unnerved Macey more than she thought it would. The incident at the gas station had happened so quickly, that she had not had time to react to seeing him again after so many years. She took that time, now, as he stood before her, with his hands shoved deep inside his pockets. She took a deep breath and continued to stare at him—the man who had betrayed her so many years ago—the man who had been part of something that had changed her life forever. Her legs began to tremble. She thought they might buckle beneath her at any moment. She took another deep breath and walked around the truck to stand beside her brother.

Jacob instinctively put a protective arm around her as they stood united—if need be—against their father.

Andrew felt a little sick at his stomach. He wondered if this had been a mistake. Everything could, very well, backfire on him. He looked directly into Macey's eyes and tried to read her thoughts. Maybe she was thinking the same thing—that this had been a mistake. Maybe she hated him so much that all he would see in her soulful eyes, would be the contempt and revulsion that he deserved. She had every right to feel that way. He deserved all the hatred she could throw at him; however, for Gabby's sake, he knew he had to attempt to win her forgiveness— or—her understanding. He would not blame her if she could not forgive him for the part he played in what had happened to her. He knew that, if the tables were turned, he would never be able to forgive and forget.

A bewildering calmness came over Macey. It was almost as if someone was leaning against her, holding her up—supporting her—and, giving her the strength she needed to face her father. *"Kacey...'* she felt her sister's presence stronger than ever.

Macey returned Andrew's direct stare—all the while—watching his face carefully for any sign of trickery. She was determined to appear strong and in control. She no longer feared her father. She continued to stare at him. The longer she looked at him, the more confused she became, because she could have sworn that he was looking back at her with...*love* in his eyes. She must be imagining things. It must be this place—it's gentle and soothing serenity was causing her to let her guard down. The longer she stared back at her father, the more convinced she became that he meant her no harm. She knew that she had every right to hate her father as much as she hated Reverend Dudley, but, that feeling of hatred escaped her now. She just didn't have it in her to hate them, but, she did find herself pitying them both.

Andrew took two more hesitant steps toward them. "It's good to see the two of you together. A brother and sister reunited...that's wonderful. When did it happen? How did it happen?"

Jacob pulled his sister closer to him. "About five years ago."

Andrew's surprise was genuine. "Really...and, you managed to keep it from your Mama and me all this time?"

Jacob looked uneasy, and held his breath while he waited for the verbal abuse he had come to expect from his father. "Yes, sir, I did. I didn't think the two of you wanted anything to do with Macey."

Andrew's gaze drifted back to Macey, and his eyes misted over. He longed to take her into his arms and beg forgiveness for the way he had treated her all those years ago. He couldn't bring himself to do it, because he knew—instinctively—that she would not allow him to do it. He smiled weakly and nodded. "Macey...you are...beautiful, so beautiful.

You...uh...you've really been in town for five years?"

Macey's own eyes began to tear up—much to her surprise—and, she couldn't explain why. She didn't hate her father, but she certainly didn't like him either. She didn't want to be anywhere near him. She resented everything about him, but, somehow—at this moment—he didn't appear to be the same man she remembered from her childhood and teen years—the same man who had stood behind her thrashing head, reading scripture after scripture, hour after hour, while the good reverend raped her repeatedly. Macey quickly shook the old memories away—now wasn't the time to be thinking of the past. She had come here for one reason—and one reason only—to see her daughter. "Actually, Papa," she addressed him directly for the first time. "I've been in Columbus for the past ten years. It took me five years to get up enough courage to approach Jacob with the truth about who I was. I had to come back...to make sure he was okay."

Andrew shook his head sadly. There was so much he wanted to say to this beautiful grown woman standing before him. Seeing her standing there, strong and resilient, he had a precious glimpse into the woman that Kacey would have grown into. His gruff voice overflowed with emotion, when he asked, "Where were you all those years, Macey? I looked for you—everywhere."

Macey was shocked and dumbfounded. She had looked for her baby for almost ten years before deciding to return to Columbus, to see if her family still lived there. She had secretly hoped the baby might be living with them. "Yeah, I just bet you looked for me, Papa."

Andrew took a deep breath and pointed to the porch. "Can we sit and talk for a while, Macey? I know you must be anxious to hear about your daughter, but, there are things the three of us need to discuss first."

Macey looked around her, hoping beyond hope to capture a quick glimpse of her daughter. The last thing she wanted to do, was to sit and have a fireside chat with her father, but she didn't want to upset him either. He might change his mind about letting her meet Gabrielle. Macey watched a myriad of emotions pass across her father's weathered face. She knew that she had to put her personal feelings aside to get what she wanted—her daughter. She sighed and nodded. Her right hand reached out for Jacob's hand, and they followed their father onto the porch. She felt someone—or something—take hold of her left hand. She curled her hand, reflexively, around the invisible appendage. *"Kacey..."*

A shiver coursed through Macey's entire body, and she turned to look in the direction of the deer stand.

Jason sat down on the bench, and slid over to make room for Macey to sit beside him. "Where is Gabrielle, Pop?" He waited until Andrew seated himself in the large, rocking chair. "Is she even here?"

Macey looked all around her—turning her head from side-to-side, and strained her ears for any sounds coming from inside the cabin. Could her daughter really be only a few feet away from her at this very moment?

Andrew was watching Macey closely. He felt bad about delaying the reunion between mother and daughter, but, there were things he needed to say to both his children, and, he didn't know if he would have time to say everything he needed to say—after he went to jail. He fully expected to spend his golden years in prison for the attempted murder of his son. He wasn't sure what the statute of limitations might be for his involvement in the spiritual cleansing of his own daughter, but, he fully expected to serve time for that, too. He was sure that his participation in what he had allowed to happen, would be viewed as one of the most heinous forms of child abuse. There should never be a statute of limitations for crimes against a child. His only satisfaction was in knowing that the good Reverend would be sharing a cell with him.

Andrew nodded and saw the color drain from Macey's beautiful face. "Yes, she's here," he admitted. "And you will both meet her very soon. She's gone for a walk...to give us time to talk."

Macey's eyes were, once again, drawn to the deer stand. "You mean, she's out there in those woods...alone?"

Andrew smiled at the maternal concern in her voice. "Relax, Macey. Trust me, Gabby is just fine in those woods. She has more or less grown up in them."

"You mean she's been here—at this cabin—for twenty years?" Macey asked incredulously.

Andrew smiled again. "No, no..." he explained. "Not here at this cabin. She's only been here for a few days now. I meant that she spent most of her life growing up in a wooded area. After the stabbing, I took off to a small town in Tennessee..."

"Hayden, Tennessee," Macey offered.

Andrew's surprise was evident. "You knew?" he asked.

Macey shrugged. "I hired a private investigator after the stabbing. I just found out a few days ago, that you went to Hayden. I probably should have hired one years ago—I don't know why I didn't think to do that. I suppose I was trying so hard to keep a low profile, that I didn't want to do anything to draw attention to myself. I had to give Jacob time enough to grow up, so I could get him..." She stopped in mid-sentence. She would have been more than justified, but she didn't feel that the time was right to say, or do, anything that might antagonize her father.

Andrew's eyes remained wet with unshed tears. "Get him away from me, you mean?"

Macey nodded while Jacob looked on in silence. "She was in Hayden all this time then?" she asked. "I didn't know you had any relatives there, Papa, although, I'm sure I covered that town at one time or another—during those early years of searching for my daughter."

Andrew nodded to confirm her supposition. "Yes, you did cover Hayden, Macey. I was there the weekend you came through. I took the child into the hills, and we stayed there until I knew you had moved on."

"But who raised her?" Macey asked. "I know it wasn't you...you had a life back in Columbus."

"That's true, I did," Andrew acknowledged.

"But you did take an awful lot of trips out of town," Jacob piped in, understanding now where his father had disappeared to all those long weekends—and, why. "A lot of trips."

"I tried to visit Gabby at least once a month," Andrew explained. "It was my sister, Louise, who raised my granddaughter."

"Louise?" Macey repeated the name. "I never knew you had a sister named Louise."

"Neither did I," Jacob chimed in.

Andrew watched them both. He was suddenly so proud of the adults his children had become—with absolutely no help from him—he could take no credit for that. He wondered why neither of them had cursed him yet for all the abuse they had suffered because of him. Maybe they were holding it all inside—until they got their hands on Gabrielle. Either that...or they must truly be remarkable individuals—especially Macey—who had every reason in the world to hate him.

"Let me tell you about Louise," Andrew offered, "And about your child, Macey. There are some other things I need to say to you both. My hope is that—after I've finished—you will both find it in your hearts to forgive me for all the pain and suffering you've gone through, because of me."

"I don't think there is anything you can say to me that will make a difference, Papa," Macey countered. "I can't speak for Jacob, but, for me—too much has happened. However, if listening to what you have to say is the only way for me to meet my daughter, then—by all means—let's get on with it. Go ahead and try to wipe the slate clean—give it your best shot."

Jacob looked uncomfortable when he saw a single tear roll down his father's cheek. He had never seen his father shed a tear...never, not once.

His own eyes were suddenly brimming with the threat of reciprocation.

Andrew took a deep breath before continuing. "You have every right to feel that way, Macey, but, this is something I need to do, so I need you to bear with me. Please...will you listen to me? Jacob?"

Jacob and Macey looked at each other and nodded simultaneously— in silent agreement—before looking back at their father.

"Go ahead, Papa. We're listening," Macey sighed. "I've waited twenty years to see my daughter. I can wait another hour, if I have to."

Andrew wiped the back of his hand against his wet cheek. "Thank you, Macey...and, thank you, Jacob. Do y'all think we can...uh...go inside for this? It's getting a little cold out here, and I've got a fresh pot of coffee brewing. Please?" he asked as he stood and held open the screen door.

Macey entered first, followed close behind by Jacob. They were both instantly in awe of the homey, comfortable surroundings that greeted them inside the cabin. This was another side of their father they had never seen.

It was almost five-thirty, and for the next hour, Macey and Jacob listened attentively—without interrupting Andrew—as he walked them through his early childhood—through his marriage to their mother—all the way to the present day. He offered detailed suppositions as to why he had become the person he had, and he begged their forgiveness for the emotional and physical pain they had endured because of him— either directly or indirectly. He confided to them about his participation in Macey's spiritual cleansing, his inexcusable molestation of Kacey, his mental abuse of their mother, and, everything else that had happened in between.

Macey was surprised to learn about his childhood—the fact that his own mother had been the town prostitute, with each of her children having been conceived by a different father. She learned about the self-taught religious fanatic her father had become at the age of sixteen—the age he had been when he ran away from home and left his soiled and tainted parentage behind him forever. She could almost understand why it had been so important for him that his own daughters remain pure and wholesome. She, also, had a better understanding of how he might have been so easily manipulated by Reverend Dudley. There were no excuses, but, it felt good to finally have some explanations.

They had been talking and listening for an hour. The sun had set and the petty rain had begun again in fervor. Macey and Jacob held hands and exhaled in unison. The tears ran freely down their faces.

Macey remained seated when Jacob stood up and walked over to his father. He stood behind him, and wrapped his arms around his father's shoulders. He smiled at Macey, and tried to silently convey that he understood the emotional turmoil and reluctance she must be feeling. "It's okay, Pop," Jacob cried again when he looked into the tortured eyes of his father. "Everything's going to be okay now...you'll see...isn't that right, Macey?"

Macey looked at Jacob, and then back at her father. No, she could never forgive him for what he had done to her, but, she knew the time had come to close that chapter of her life. She could never move forward if she didn't first let go of the past. She had to find a way to let go of her father's involvement in her abuse. She couldn't forgive—yet—but, maybe she could forget. She had to, if she hoped to have any kind of a real life with Gabrielle and Scott. The words of forgiveness stuck in her throat, so she simply looked into her father's eyes—eyes so much like her own—and nodded in agreement.

Andrew began to sob uncontrollably. He did not deserve it, but—for the first time in a long, long time—he had hope that their forgiveness could be true. Maybe everything really would turn out for the best— for everyone involved. He had so many sins for which to atone, and so many people from whom he needed to seek forgiveness. He knew that he didn't deserve a second chance from any of them, but, he silently prayed that he would be given one. Maybe it wasn't too late to right all the wrongs he had done...maybe...

Andrew closed his eyes and sighed when he felt a feathery, light kiss placed upon his cheek. Jacob still stood behind him, and Macey still sat across the room at the kitchen table. *"Kacey..."*

CHAPTER 55

THE CONVERGING

It took all of Scott's willpower not to ride Jacob's bumper, but, he managed to maintain a half-mile distance between them most of the time. It was hard enough, in Columbus, to be inconspicuous in the Porsche; but, once they left the traffic of Columbus and Fort Benning behind, it really took some effort. There was not a lot of traffic along Georgia Highway 26, so Scott had to really concentrate and maintain a proper distance between him and Jacob's truck. He did this so well, that he never noticed the red Taurus, following at the same discreet distance behind *him*. If he had noticed the Taurus—even once—then the events that unfolded two hours later might have turned out differently.

Scott watched when Jacob stopped in front of a gravel driveway, and wondered if they had finally arrived at their destination. He hated the fact that Macey did not feel she could trust him with the truth; even so, he was determined not to let her face her father alone. He was positive that Macey and Jacob were meeting Andrew Wymer in these Godforsaken woods. He wondered if the man had Gabrielle with him—maybe using her as bait to lure Macey to him. He truly thought that the man meant to harm Macey.

Scott's imagination ran rapid, and his mind played a variety of scenarios—all of them ending in Andrew's devious murder-suicide plot. He probably intended to kill them all. "I won't let that happen, Macey. I won't let anything happen to you," he spoke out loud. He pulled off onto the grassy bank and looked around. "I guess I'll have to go the rest of the way on foot." He pulled his jacket tighter around him. There was something about dark woods that always gave him the creeps. He looked around him again and shivered. "I just hope these woods don't have any lions or tigers or bears, or...snakes. God, you know how I hate snakes. Please...don't let there be any snakes." Scott had read once that snakes hibernated in the winter, but he certainly did not want to be the one to test that theory.

He walked up to the dense, wooded driveway and looked up at the cluster of giant pine trees. He could barely see the sky at this point through the copious trees. He grimaced at the sound of gravel crunching beneath his Nike shoes—running shoes, thankfully—just in case it wasn't true that snakes hibernated in the winter.

He relaxed when he heard the loud noise that Jacob's truck made ahead of him, and felt reassured that no one should notice the slighter sound of the crunching gravel his shoes made. He knew how to eliminate the sound of the crunching gravel—all he had to do was move a foot off the driveway, and walk on the dampened pine needles. He shivered again and shook his head. *"Nooo...there could be snakes hibernating under those needles!"* No, he would take his chances. If anyone happened to hear it, he hoped that they would think it was some wild animal roaming the woods. "Oh great, wild animals...just what I need..." he mumbled beneath his breath. Could there be lions and tigers and bears in these Georgia woods? He wished he had watched more of those animal documentaries on the cable stations, or read more National Geographic magazines. "Okay, God...I'm going in now," Scott whispered. "You do your thing, okay? And...don't forget about those *snakes*..."

Lucas had stopped the Taurus about two hundred yards from where Scott had parked the Porsche. He grabbed the duffel bag that he had placed on the passenger seat. It contained everything he would need, and he was glad now that he had not stored it, earlier, in the motel room. He watched while Scott exited his parked car and ventured into the woods—very dark woods.

His plan was not going as he had initially formulated it—it had accelerated—but Lucas was more than ready to take advantage of the situation that presented itself. All the participants were readily available, so why not? Things might work out even better than they would have with his original plan. He was a stickler for detailed and efficient planning, but, there was also something to be said for spontaneity. "Oh, yes..." he smiled and nodded. "I can most definitely be spontaneous when the need calls for it. Tsk, tsk...too bad for all of you..."

Lucas worried that the abandoned Porsche might draw unnecessary attention. "No, no...I can't take the chance of someone seeing that car.

I'll have to do something about that," he muttered. "I wonder…"

He crossed the highway to where the Porsche was parked and tried the driver's door. He couldn't believe his good fortune—it wasn't locked! Not only that, but the keys were still in the ignition. "Poor, stupid fool…" Lucas grinned in mock sympathy. "He must not be thinking clearly. Why… *anyone* could come along and steal this wonderful machine…why, they might even decide to drive it into…maybe…that ravine over there. Oh, yes…that will do nicely, I think."

It only took mere seconds for Scott's pride and joy to slide noiselessly down the slippery ravine. It didn't make a sound until it crashed—fifty feet below—into a clump of sturdy pine trees.

"Ouch!" Lucas shivered dramatically. "What a pity—a terrible waste. Oh, well, I suppose I'll have to continue using the old Taurus for a while longer. Too bad…it would have been fun driving the Porsche— unfortunately, it is much too…eye-catching, shall we say?" He took one last look at the crippled Porsche. "Well…at least it *was* eye-catching."

Lucas returned to the Taurus and followed the dirt path that Scott had taken on foot. He drove a short distance past the driveway, put the car in reverse, and backed the vehicle in—far enough so that the car could not be seen from the dirt road. He got out of the car, stretched his arms over his head, and breathed in the clean, country air. He closed his eyes and a dreamy expression came over his face. "Ahh…I do love the woods…some of my best work has been completed in the woods…"

It took Scott about ten minutes to reach the clearing. He crouched behind a clump of bushes when he saw Macey and Jacob standing side-by-side, talking with their father. The hair on his arms stood straight up when he thought he heard a significant crunching sound, coming from a far distance behind him. *"Probably snakes following me…"* he thought. No—not snakes—it sounded more like far-off thunder. Little did he know that it was the sound of a very expensive automobile, making new friends with giant pine trees. He returned his attention to the trio that stood outside the cabin. He kept a close eye on Andrew. *"Well,"* he thought. *"The man doesn't look like a maniac right now, but, I'll just hang around to make sure. Macey will never know I was here…"*

The woods were Lucas' friend. He had no fears or qualms—unlike his predecessor—about using the soft pine needles to muffle his approach along the driveway. He stopped and smiled when he spotted Scott crouched behind a clump of heavy underbrush. He placed the duffel bag on the ground and quietly unzipped it. He fumbled around inside for the bottle of Pyrrole, but never took his eyes off the back of Scott's head. He reached inside his pants pocket for the handkerchief he had used to subdue Ruth. There was probably plenty of residual liquid on the handkerchief to accommodate Scott, but, Lucas did not want to take any chances. He re-soaked the handkerchief with the yellowish liquid. If Mr. Pennell had an extremely keen sense of smell, he might detect the medicinal liquid before Lucas had a chance to administer it. Lucas continued to watch Scott—no, the man was so focused on the familial reunion unfolding before him, that he would never see, hear, or smell him coming.

Lucas glanced quickly in the direction of the cabin. He couldn't see Jacob through the overgrown red tips, but, he could see Macey and Andrew. He gave the surrounding area a surreptitious and quick perusal. It was possible that Jacob had gone for a walk to allow his father and sister some time alone, but, where was Gabrielle? If Jacob had not gone for a walk, he could be inside the cabin with Gabrielle. So many possible scenarios filtered quickly through Lucas' mind. He did not want to advance upon Scott until he was sure of Jacob's whereabouts. His plan was coming together nicely—he did not want to do anything that could spoil it now.

Lucas' attention was drawn back to the cabin when he heard Jacob say, "*Neither did I.*"

"*Ah...very good...*" Lucas thought. "*Everyone is present and accounted for...*"

Scott was so intent on trying to pick up pieces of the trio's conversation that he never heard, felt, or smelled the threatening presence that crept up behind him. He never had a chance to react when a strong arm swept briskly around his throat, at the same moment a cloth was placed over his nose and mouth. The acrid smell assaulted his sinuses—his eyes began to burn and tear at the same time. He never had a chance to turn around, much less to struggle against his assailant.

Lucas caught Scott beneath the arms just before his victim crumbled helplessly to the ground. He looked anxiously toward the porch, relieved that the threesome showed no signs of having heard the slight disturbance. Something in the distance, near the lake—a deer stand, maybe—momentarily distracted him. He peered at it with unexplained intensity before finally shrugging the distraction aside. He dragged Scott backwards—deeper into the woods—and left him in a sitting position, against a large pine tree. He retrieved two pieces of long rope from the duffel bag. He used the shorter piece of rope to tie Scott's hands behind his back. The second piece of rope—a longer length—was used to secure Scott's whole body to the tree trunk. He removed Scott's socks and shoes, intending to use one of the socks as a mouth gag. He held the sock up in the air, by two fingers, and wrinkled his nose. "Whew! This smell, alone, should ensure you stay knocked out for quite a while..." He shook the sock before rolling it into a ball and stuffing it inside Scott's mouth. Scott's cheeks puffed out reflexively at the intrusion. "I'll take care of you and Ruthie later, my friend. There are much more enticing selections on the menu at the moment."

Lucas reclaimed Scott's previous hiding position behind the clumped bushes. He crouched down and watched until the three members of the Wymer family moved inside the cabin. Spontaneity had worked well for him so far, but, Lucas hesitated now. He was undecided whether he should approach the group now—or, allow them some quality time together before he enacted his plan. His plan would have to be modified from its original version, of course, but he never doubted that it would end successfully. He was so engrossed in contemplating his plan of action that he never noticed the red Volkswagen that was parked at an angle, with the passenger side facing the cabin's porch. Something— or someone touched his shoulder. Lucas jumped up from his crouched position. *"What was that..."* he thought frantically. He felt a slight, warm breeze move beside his face. It was so cold outside, but that momentary breeze had felt so warm. *"Kacey?"*

Lucas shook his last thought aside. It was ridiculous—he did not believe in ghosts. If he had, he was sure he would have already been visited by many of them. He decided to give the Wymers some time alone—why not—he could afford to be generous. He closed his eyes and smiled at the thought that his Gabrielle was being reunited with her mother at this very moment. He had gathered a lot of information from Louise before she died—the most important thing being, that Macey had not been a part of her daughter's upbringing.

Lucas thought it might be enjoyable to watch that reunion from a more advantageous viewpoint. He made his way toward the large windows on the side of the cabin that faced the lake, where he could watch everything going on inside. The cabin was relatively small, but its main selling feature had to be the four double-wide windows that offered a breathtaking view of the lake. There were two windows in the front room, and two in a back bedroom—probably the master bedroom.

Lucas made himself comfortable behind two azalea bushes, which still allowed him a birds-eye view of the interior of the living room interior. There were no curtains or shades on the windows—that would have spoiled the view—so, it was easy for him to leisurely observe his unsuspecting victims. One of the windows was opened about two inches, which allowed Lucas to hear almost every word that Andrew was saying. He listened with feigned interest while Andrew told his children the captivating story of his life. He paid special attention when Andrew rehashed the incriminating escapades involving the molestation of Kacey. "Ahh, Andrew, my friend..." he purred. "You and I are more alike than I thought. No wonder you found Macey's spiritual cleansings so... necessary. How delicious..."

He remained in his crouched position for almost an hour, during which time, the rain had slowed to a slight drizzle. Much to his surprise, darkness had silently enveloped the cabin while he had waited and listened. He was so engrossed in Andrew's story-telling that he never heard the soft footsteps coming up the path from the lake. He watched—slightly bored and emotionally unaffected—while Jacob comforted his father. It was only then that he realized the front door of the cabin had opened.

His gazed shifted, in slow motion, and rested upon the most beautiful specimen God had ever created and placed upon the earth. She stood just inside the door...a goddess dressed in overalls and a turtleneck sweater. He marveled at the thick, braid that fell across her shoulder—almost to her waist. He remained spellbound when the vision of beauty smiled at the group, apparently embarrassed at having interrupted their reunion. She spoke softly, "Did I come too soon, Paw Paw?"

Lucas gasped so hard that he felt a physical pain surge across his chest. His heartbeat increased rapidly, and his breathing competed with the tempo—he began to hyperventilate. He puckered his lips and blew out several short breaths, but never took his eyes off the focus of...HIS DAUGHTER! He closed his eyes and pushed the palm of his right hand against his chest. His breathing steadied and his rapid heartbeat began to slow down.

The rain had stopped, and Lucas inhaled the sweet, fresh smell of the forest. "I've waited so very long for this...so long. Oh, my sweet, Gabrielle...you are even more beautiful...even more pure than I ever imagined. You are a true vision...you are my *daughter*." He looked heavenward and closed his eyes. "Oh, God...thank you! Thank you for bringing her home to me. It's over...the waiting is finally...over.

CHAPTER 56

MOTHER AND DAUGHTER REUNION

Jacob took his father's trembling hands into his own. "Everything's going to be okay now, Pop...you'll see."

Macey watched them from across the room. She knew that her father wanted her forgiveness, but, there was too much history between them. She didn't think she could give him what he wanted, but, she was glad to see the fence being mended between father and son.

Andrew looked back and forth between his children. Tears were flowing freely and emotions were running high. Was it possible for his children to forgive him despite all that he had put them through? Did he dare hope for such a thing?

They were all so tuned in to one another's feelings, that they were not immediately aware that the screen door had opened and closed.

Macey was the first to feel another presence in the room. She turned to see a beautiful, young woman—a tentative smile upon her face—standing at the door.

The young woman was dressed in faded, denim overalls and a cream-colored turtleneck sweater. Her delicate hands were clasped loosely before her. "Did I come too soon, Paw Paw?" she asked timidly. Her question was obviously directed at Andrew, but her eyes and full attention focused intently on Macey.

Macey paled visibly and her vision blurred. She stood too abruptly and almost lost her balance. She felt she was on the verge of collapse, and was barely aware of Andrew's strong hands that reached out and stopped her fall. "Oh...my...God..." she moaned.

Andrew steadied her before handing her over to Jacob. He turned and held his hands out to the young woman while he smiled and walked toward her. "No, angel," he replied. "Your timing couldn't be better. Come here, Gabby. There's someone I want you to meet...someone who's waited a very long time to meet you."

Gabrielle smiled and approached slowly toward Macey. "And I've waited a long time to meet her, too." Her voice was so soft and low—only Andrew was close enough to hear.

Jacob stood directly behind Macey, but he was completely and utterly in awe of the beautiful creature—his *niece*—who stood at the front door. He didn't have sufficient words in his dictionary to describe the serenity that emanated from her very being. It was chilling to think that one person could have such an immediate effect and impact on someone. He felt Macey's shoulders tremble beneath him when her daughter took a step toward them.

Gabby took another step and stopped. Her hesitation became heavy and more evident when she realized her Mother was not moving toward her.

Macey's vision was still blurred from the tears, and she pressed her closed fist against her mouth to stifle the cry that threatened to escape. She exhaled, took a deep breath, and took her own step forward.

Less than five feet separated mother and daughter—it really was a small cabin. The two women stared at each other for several moments before they moved—simultaneously—slowly coming together in a fierce embrace.

Macey's entire body shook with uncontrolled sobs of joy at *finally* being united with the daughter she had thought she might never see. She hugged Gabby tighter against her—she never wanted to let her go. She tried her best to absorb twenty years of missed embraces into a single moment. She finally released her hold on Gabby, and leaned back to take a good, long look at her daughter. Gabby had inherited her mother's dark hair, but she was at least three inches shorter than Macey. The longer she looked at her, the more she thought that Gabby looked like Ruth. She took silent comfort in the quick observation that her daughter did not resemble her father—in any way. There was no physical trace of the good Reverend Dudley evident in Gabrielle Wymer—none, whatsoever.

Gabby sighed and released the breath she had been holding. She relished being cradled against her mother's chest for the first time. How she had dreamed of this day!

Andrew and Jacob looked on with broad grins, and tears flowing unabashedly down their cheeks.

Jacob looked over at his father and gave him a thumbs-up motion.

Andrew simply nodded and allowed the two women a few moments of quiet acceptance.

Macey stroked her daughter's head and looked over Gabby's shoulder at Andrew. She smiled at her father and mouthed the words, *"Thank you..."*

Her father simply nodded again and swiped the tears from his cheeks.

Macey held onto Gabby's arms and smiled. "Let me look at you. Oh, God...you are beautiful...so, very...beautiful."

Gabby smiled back and shook her head. "You're the one who is beautiful..."

Andrew's back was to the screen door and Jacob had moved across the room to join his sister and niece.

Nobody noticed Lucas' silent entry into the room...not until...the sound of his dropped duffel bag echoed throughout the room.

"Now isn't this a Kodak moment?" Lucas sneered.

Andrew spun quickly around—shocked at the abrupt intrusion—but, even more shocked to see Lucas Dudley standing in his living room. Good manners had never been one of his virtues, and they fully escaped him now. "What the hell are *you* doing here?" he demanded roughly.

Lucas feigned hurt and disappointment. "Now, Andrew, is that any way to greet a friend of the family?"

Surprise and anger clashed for control of Andrew's emotions. What *was* this man doing here? How had he found them? What could he possibly want?

Lucas' attention shifted immediately from Andrew, to the lovely creature he now knew to be his daughter—a procreation of his own flesh and blood—his contribution to God's great world.

Andrew followed Lucas' gaze and he bristled when anger surpassed surprise. He knew this man well, so he could imagine the lewd thoughts going through the reverend's mind at this very moment. "I'll ask you again, Dudley, what are you doing here? What is it you want? This is a private, family meeting."

Lucas ignored Andrew. His eyes were opened wide, and he unwittingly ran his tongue over his bottom lip as he stared at Gabrielle.

Andrew knew better than anyone—other than Macey—what might be going through Dudley's mind, and, his memory jolted back to a stormy, Sunday evening—twenty-one years earlier. It was the night when this man had convinced him that Macey was a whore in the eyes of God, and that he—Lucas Dudley—was the only one who could guarantee her salvation. The Reverend convinced Andrew that his daughter's soul was doomed to Hell, if she did not receive a spiritual cleansing from one of God's devoted servants. Andrew vividly remembered how Macey struggled, and her muffled screams of protest while the good Reverend performed the cleansing—repeatedly—that would drive the demons from every orifice of her adolescent body.

His memories of that repulsive night continued to unfold, and it was as though the gates of Heaven—or Hell, maybe—suddenly opened. The inexplicable truth about what had happened that night hit Andrew like a ton of bricks. He was twenty-one years too late to help Macey—but, he could still save Gabrielle. Another reality quickly dawned on Andrew—Lucas could be Gabby's biological father—one more thing for him to feel guilty about. Why hadn't he figured it out before now? How could he have been so easily manipulated into believing Lucas—that Macey bled because she was having her monthly curse? How could he have believed that his own daughter was the slut that Dudley purported her to be? He recognized the truth now. Macey had been a virgin that night—an innocent virgin—impregnated by Lucas Dudley, while her father looked on—if not with approval, then at least with acquiescence. "Oh, God... how could I have been so stupid..." he groaned and covered his face with his hands.

Macey saw the reality—followed by the regret—that spread across her father's face. She guessed that he must have figured out the truth of what happened that awful night, twenty-one years ago—the agony of that realization was written all over his tortured face. Papa...don't..." Macey cried helplessly.

Lucas was secretly delighted. "Yes, my friend," he reproached Andrew. "You were rather stupid, but, then again...I chalked that up to your rather limited upbringing—void of any real morals, as I recall you saying earlier this evening. Why, there was even a time when I thought that you and I could become...shall we say...*partners*...in my business of...spiritual cleansings. Who knows...maybe you could have kept my books for me, and in return, I would have given you a small commission. Oh, and lest we forget...maybe even a small discount for your own, very eager wife." Lucas sighed. "Yes...with all the young flesh available, you could have been a rich man today, my friend."

The bare, ugly truth was more than Andrew could stand. He growled and lunged angrily toward Lucas. "You...son-of-a-bitch—you...sorry... son-of-a-bitch!"

It happened quickly.

Lucas swung the pistol from behind his back and fired one calculated shot that caught Andrew in the left shoulder. He grinned with giddy expectation as Andrew clutched his shoulder and crumbled to the floor.

One down.

Gabrielle rushed quickly to her grandfather's side, in time to cushion his fall. "Paw Paw!" she screamed.

Blood trickled from beneath Andrew's fingers as he pressed hard against the wound, trying to ebb the flow. It stung like hell, but he was fairly certain that the wound was not life-threatening. I'm okay, angel..." he whispered hoarsely.

"Oh..." Lucas mocked. "I missed...I was aiming for the heart. I must be out of practice. Oh well, maybe I'll do better with the next shot."

Jacob took two steps forward, but Lucas was quick to wave the pistol fervently in his direction. "I wouldn't do that if I were you, sonny boy. I really hadn't intended on using this weapon—such messy results—but, do not think that I will not shoot you, too. I won't miss the next time."

Macey grabbed Jacob by the shoulder and pulled him back.

Lucas smiled and turned his direction on Macey. "Ahh...Macey. Why dear...you are even lovelier than I remember..."

Macey couldn't move. She felt frozen to the spot, and couldn't say anything to this man who had hurt her so badly all those many years ago. She felt, once again, like the scared fifteen-year old whose own father dragged her into the basement of the old church.

Jacob's face flushed fast with anger. "Leave her alone!" he demanded.

Lucas wrinkled his nose at the young man's obvious attempt at bravado. "Pl...lease," he exaggerated. "But, do you really think you are in any position to be making demands upon me?" Do you, boy?"

Andrew staggered to a standing position—with Gabrielle's assistance. He leaned against the dining table for support. His breathing was mildly-labored. "What...do you want, Dudley?" he demanded again—albeit—much weaker than the first time.

Lucas ignored Andrew's question. His gaze returned to Gabrielle. He recognized her for what she truly must be—a pure, angelic form sent by God to restore Lucas' soul. She was his destiny—his redemption. He knew and understood that, with her at his side, he could conquer anything life had to throw at him. "Gabrielle...come here...come to your father..."

Jacob's eyes grew wide in shock and disbelief. This could not be possible! This man had shared countless meals with his family—this man was worshipped by his mother—and, now—this man was telling them that he was Gabrielle's father? Impossible! It only took one quick look at Macey's pale and stricken face, however, to confirm the Reverend's proclamation to be true.

"No!" Andrew yelled. "You leave her be, Dudley! Leave her alone!"

"Oh, enough of that, Andrew!" Lucas snapped. He waved the gun in impatient dismissal of Andrew's protest. "Surely you don't think *you* can protect her? Any more than you could protect your precious Macey or... Kacey?"

Andrew froze in place. "What do you mean? What do you know about Kacey?"

Macey found her voice. "He killed Kacey..."

Lucas cast a sharp look at Macey. "Hush, now...this is my story to tell." He looked back at Andrew and sighed. "Oh...yes, I know so much more about Kacey than you realize, my friend. I did kill her though, but my one regret is that Scott returned to the car before I had time to administer her spiritual cleansing...as I did Macey's. Such a pity, too...I would have rather enjoyed that particular cleansing."

Lucas looked back at Macey, but spoke to Andrew. "Andrew...did you know that our sweet Macey is the reason that Kacey had to die that night—that Macey confided *everything* to her sister? Oh yes... everything...including *your* part in our little escapade."

"No..." Andrew moaned. On top of all the sexual abuse he had subjected her to—in the end—Kacey must have believed her father to be the monster that he was. She would have been right to believe that about him.

"Oh, yes..." Lucas purred. "She knew *everything*, and, the little bitch had the nerve to threaten me with what she knew—she was going to tell *everyone* about it. She never should have threatened to do that. Everyone believed her to be a quiet, meek little thing, but, she was braver than any of the rest of you. She followed me home one evening—shortly after Macey confided to her that she was pregnant, and that I was the father. The two of them were making plans to run off together before the baby was born—they were going to raise it on their own—they were going to deprive me of ever seeing my child!"

Andrew was trembling, but he forced himself to remain steady on his feet. He had heard it from the police, and read all the newspaper articles, but he needed to hear it from Lucas. "What did you do to Kacey?"

Lucas raised his eyebrows and titled his head slightly. "What did I do? Hmm...what *didn't* I do? Didn't you read the papers, man? Oh, well... fine...I'll tell you, then. Let's see now...when Kacey threatened to tell everyone what I had done to her precious sister—I still can't believe that a silly, fifteen-year old would attempt to threaten and blackmail *me*— she told me to leave town, or else. Well, I couldn't allow that to happen, now could I?"

"You...murderer!" rasped Macey. If she had any doubts before, she knew now that the man Scott had seen behind the Volkswagen twenty years ago had been Lucas Dudley.

Lucas pursed his lips together. "If it makes any of you feel any better, it was never my intention to kill her. I wish you could believe that—really, I do. I simply intended to scare her into keeping quiet about everything, but, well...the girl left me no choice. I had a good following in Columbus at the time—lots of new *prospects*, shall we say." He stared hard at Macey and shook his head. "No, it was not my fault, Macey—*you* were responsible for your sister's death. If you only had not felt the need to confide in her...she might be alive today. Anyway, that afternoon—when Kacey ran after me and told me what she knew—well, I simply could not take any chances of the truth coming out. I followed her and her young beau that night, and waited for the opportune moment. Young Scott tried like the dickens to get into her panties, you know, but our little Kacey held firm to her virtue—to the very end."

"Why...why did you have to kill her?" Andrew whispered hoarsely as angry tears continued to flow down his stricken, agonized face.

Lucas yawned—feigning boredom—but decided that it wouldn't hurt to tell them the truth—they would all be dead soon enough. "As I said, Andrew...I never meant for that to happen. I simply meant to scare her into submission...to give her a taste of what could happen if she ever breathed a word of what she knew to anyone."

Lucas' eyes glassed over as ancient memories moved front and center.

Halloween night, October 1969...

Lucas grinned at Kacey's surprise and vulnerability when he jerked open the passenger door. He could smell her fear as he dragged her from the car. *"Please don't hurt me...I won't tell anyone...I promise!"* Lucas recognized the instant that she must have realized that young Scott would not return in time to help her. *"What did you do to him? What did you do to Scott?"* He shoved her roughly to the ground and fell upon her. He brutalized her tiny breasts—squeezing them unmercifully hard, and pulling at them with his teeth. He used the same technique that his Aunt Martha had perfected upon his own, young manhood.

That was the instant when something snapped within him—that thought and image of his Aunt Martha. *"You're hurting me...please... please stop..."* He slapped Kacey hard against her temple to shut her up. He ripped off her remaining clothing, spread her legs, and attempted to force himself—roughly—inside her virginal body. *"Nooooo!"* He stifled her scream with one large hand. She bit down hard on his fleshy hand— hard enough to break the skin. His eyes flared in anger, and he hit her again—this time with his closed fist. He flipped a terrified and sobbing Kacey over onto her stomach and entered her from behind—anally—so as not to disturb her sacred virginity. He felt her warm blood against his thighs, but he did not remember anything else about the sexual act—he did not remember climaxing inside her.

He carried her limp and unconscious body back to the car and placed her inside the Volkswagen. He waited for her to regain consciousness—it didn't take long—and, when she did, Lucas spotted the lacy, white bra lying on the floorboard. *"You hurt me...so bad...hurts so bad..."* The reality of what he had done hit him hard when Kacey opened her eyes. He didn't think about what he was doing—he simply reacted to the situation. He reached for the bra and wrapped it tightly around her slender throat. *"Aghhh..."* She pulled at the bra, but Lucas pulled it tighter and tighter each time she tried to pull it away. He pulled and pulled until her hands fell limply into her lap. He released the bra and Kacey opened her eyes one last time. *"Macey..."* Lucas became hard again. He stroked himself harder and harder with each tightening grip of the bra around Kacey's neck. He waited—until she took her last breath—before he lifted her lifeless body upward and skewered her naked body—HARD—upon the car's stick shift. He shuddered again in an ecstatic climax.

Lucas enjoyed rehashing the sordid details of Kacey's last moments, but, he had the grace to grimace slightly when he noticed the sickened expression on Macey's face before she lowered her head. "Hmmm... maybe I shouldn't have been so graphic in describing it all to you." Truth be known, he was not proud of what he had done to Kacey—he had never intended on releasing the details to anyone. He had prayed for forgiveness for his rash and sadistic actions that night, and he truly believed that his God had forgiven him. He took comfort in blaming his aunt for what had happened to Kacey Wymer.

The truth of what Kacey had been forced to endure was more than Andrew could stand. "Agghh..." he wailed as he lunged, once again, for Lucas. He didn't care if another bullet ripped through him. He almost wished one would, and put him out of this horrendous agony. Tears blurred his vision as he pushed Gabby roughly aside and stumbled forward.

Lucas' reflexes were commendable, to say the least. He quickly swung the butt of the gun, and targeted Andrew squarely in the left temple.

Andrew collapsed and fell heavily onto the hardwood floor. His head hit hard against the floor and—this time—he was knocked unconscious.

Gabby rushed to her grandfather's side and cradled his bleeding head in her lap. Tears coursed down her ivory cheeks as she looked helplessly from Macey to Jacob, both of whom, were still visibly shaken after having heard Lucas's gruesome confession.

Lucas straightened himself and squared back his shoulders. He held his head high and spoke with unquestioned authority. "Leave him be, Gabrielle. Come over here. Do as I say, girl. NOW...or, I will shoot your mother and uncle where they stand."

Macey, pale and weak in her own right, made immediate eye contact with her daughter. Her heart was breaking—crying out for her sister and the pain, torture, and humiliation she must have suffered the night she died—blaming herself for Kacey's death—but, knowing that if any of them were going to survive this night, she had to regain control of herself and her emotions. She could never undo what had happened to Kacey, but, she would do whatever was necessary to protect her daughter. She nodded at Gabby to do as Lucas had instructed.

Gabby returned the nod and walked slowly toward the man who called himself her father. She did her best to veil the fear and confusion she felt. She was more than appalled at the story she had just heard, but, she also felt a strange obligation toward this man, who was her father. She felt inexplicably drawn to him. She wanted to hate him for the pain he had caused her family in the past—not to mention what he had just done to Andrew—but, she had been raised not to judge people for their sins. Gabby was more than shocked when she felt the need to obey her father's commands. *Honor thy mother and thy father.*

"Stop there...wait a minute," Lucas instructed as he bent down to unzip the duffel bag. He threw two pieces of rope at her feet. "Take these and tie your mother and her brother to those chairs. Macey? You and Jacob would be smart not to try anything stupid."

The shock of Lucas' confession still pulled at Macey's emotions. She realized that she and Jacob were both still in a state of shock. Neither of them saw any immediate option to the contrary, so, they abided by Lucas's instructions.

Gabby bent down to retrieve the ropes.

Lucas stepped forward quickly and caught her wrist, grasping it hard enough to cause her to flinch under the pressure of his hand. He pulled her tightly against him, so that she could feel the rapid beating of his heart. He pushed her away. No! He didn't want to feel lust for his own daughter! No! He would not allow that weakness within himself. He willed those emotions to immediately subside. "You have one chance to do it right, Gabby. If you don't tie them securely—hands and feet to the chair—then I promise...I will shoot them where they sit. Is that understood?"

Gabrielle looked up into her father's eyes and offered a weak smile. "Yes, of course, *father*."

Lucas smiled broadly at the paternal reference. "Good girl. Now do it!"

Gabby felt helpless, but she obediently followed her father's orders. She took the longer piece of rope and asked Jacob to place his hands behind him. She wrapped the rope twice around his wrists before running it behind and under the chair. She then asked him to cross his ankles where she wrapped and tied the final knot.

She proceeded to her mother's chair next. They stared at each other for a long moment. There was no need for words. Gabby telepathically understood what her mother wanted her to do. Gabby squeezed her mother's hands when Macey placed them complacently behind her chair. She knew what she had to do. She had done a good job securing her uncle to his chair, but she used the shorter rope to loosely tie Macey's hands to the back of the chair. "The rope's not long enough to tie her feet," she stated matter-of-factly.

"As long as it's secure around her hands, it should be fine," Lucas replied absently. He began moving aimlessly around the cabin. "We'll be long gone before either of them are able to loosen the ropes." He never once thought to question and check her handiwork. He trusted his daughter completely...after all, she was a part of him. He knew instinctively that she would never lie to him—she didn't have it in her to lie. She was too perfect. She was a part of his own perfection.

Lucas watched as Gabby rose and walked slowly back to him. He saw her glance down at Andrew, who had begun stirring once again. He watched his daughter's slow approach and appreciated the perfect creation that she was. There was nothing tainted about her—yet—either physically or spiritually. He had found her in time. He had created the perfect offspring deserving of God's love and acceptance.

Gabby stopped and stood directly in front of her father. She knew what she had to do. She had to find a way to distract him long enough for Macey to loosen her ropes. If she could persuade her father for them to leave now, maybe Macey could get loose in time to get help for her grandfather. "I've done as you asked, father. Can we go now? Please? I'll go anywhere you want, if you promise not to hurt any of them."

Lucas reached out to touch the softness of her cheek. He felt the dampness of tears and wiped them away. "You are so incredibly beautiful," he whispered.

"Thank you, father," Gabby responded shyly. "Can we go now?"

Lucas stiffened with suspicion. She was too eager to leave with him. "Why are you so anxious to leave, Gabrielle? We have plenty of time."

Gabby was nervous. She wanted to leave with her father, to prevent him from harming her newfound family. "I...I just thought you might want to get a head start...you know, to get as far away as possible before..."

"Before what, my dear?" Lucas asked with a dramatic flair. "Do you honestly think I can allow any of these people to live? Why it would just be a matter of days before they had the authorities breathing down our necks."

"But we could be far away before that happened!" Gabby cried. Fresh tears made her fluid eyes sparkle with renewed fear.

Lucas took a brief moment to contemplate what his daughter was saying. It was true—he could allow them to live—but, did he really want to do that? Would he being doing their souls any favor by allowing them to continue to live in their soiled, sinful shells? No...they would be much happier in Heaven—or Hell—free of their earthly burdens.

Gabby saw the chameleon expressions reflected in her father's face. From everything she had learned in the last half hour, she guessed that her father might be a highly sexual man. She had no personal experience in that area, but she had gained minimal knowledge from her years of reading hidden romance novels. She wasn't sure if she could pull it off, but she had to try. She would use the womanly charms the Good Lord had bestowed upon her—anything to save her family from whatever Lucas had in store for them. The only problem was—she honestly had no idea of how to go about it. She prayed a silent prayer that she wouldn't say or do the wrong thing. She moved closer to her father and timidly wrapped her slender arms around his waist. She looked up pleadingly into his shocked expression. "Please, father...do this for me. Please don't hurt them. I...really will do...anything you want...anything..."

Macey worked feverishly to loosen the rope around her wrist. She closed her eyes and hung her head when she heard Gabby speak those words. *"Oh, God, no! Please help her, God...don't let her do this."*

Lucas fought against the urge, but he felt the pressure of his desire as it pushed against the inside of his trousers.

Gabby felt it too, but luckily for her, she did not realize what it meant. She had never before seen a man's body, much less known the feel, functions, and intricacies of an erection. Although she had learned enough academically to obtain her GED, she had never been schooled in the ways of real life. Her Aunt Louise and grandfather had gone to great lengths to shelter her from life's more basic functions and desires. Gabby intuitively rested her head upon her father's chest and wept softly. She had seen old movies where a woman's tears could reduce a man to mush—something she hoped to accomplish with her father.

Lucas still held the pistol in his right hand, but used his left one to stroke his daughter's back. This surely must be Satan's test, he thought—a test to see if he could resist the temptations of his past—temptations of his own daughter.

His own daughter! Why the little bitch! She was no better than all the other women he had known throughout his life—worse yet—she was just like her mother! Lucas was so intensely focused on his daughter and her attempt to use her feminine wiles to win her way with him, that he did not see Andrew push himself up on his hands and knees. "You little harlot!" Lucas hissed. He released Gabby's arm and drew back his left hand to strike her. "You're no better than the rest of them! I had hoped and prayed you were different!" he yelled as the full impact of his hand sent her tiny body reeling backward.

Gabby cried out in pain, lost her balance, stumbled, and fell to the floor. She reached out to break her fall, but struck her head on the corner of the coffee table first. She emitted a weak sigh before she hit the floor—hard.

A large kerosene lantern provided sufficient light for the small living room, and, Andrew often kept it lit in case of power failure. The power had been out several times over the past few days while the storm had lingered on, so Andrew had lit the lantern after he had welcomed Macey and Jacob inside to talk.

"Noooo!" Andrew cried, after witnessing the brutal blow to Gabby's face. He pushed himself upward and forward, and used his head to butt Lucas squarely in the abdomen.

The surprise attack caught Lucas completely off guard. His attention had been totally focused on Gabrielle's ensuing fall. He had not wanted to harm his daughter. He had never really intended to harm any of them, but, something had snapped inside him—again—when Gabby came on to him like she had. It reminded him of the many times his aunt had used her limited womanly ways to seduce him and force him to do her will. Lucas fell backward—rather ungraciously—when his relaxed stomach took the full impact of Andrew's head.

A forceful bolt of lightning suddenly filled the room, and the power blinked off—on—and, then off again. Lucas' right arm waved frantically about him as he tried to break his fall. He knocked the kerosene lamp off the end table, in his attempt to stop his fall. Kerosene spilled onto the floor, creating a slow trail toward the large area rug beneath the coffee table. Flames from the lamp caught up with the traveling kerosene and quickly ignited the frayed edges of the carpet.

The flames provided Lucas enough light to make out Gabby's unconscious form, which lay a few feet from the wood coffee table—a wood table that beckoned the eternal flames. He began crawling on his knees toward her, but, quickly got turned around in the darkened, smoky room. He was unsure in what direction to move.

Macey screamed when the flames began moving quickly toward an unconscious Gabby.

Jacob rocked his chair back and forth, desperately trying to loosen his ropes. The only thing he accomplished was to secure a more horizontal position when his chair crashed backward onto the wooden floor. He coughed as he gulped in several breaths of smoke-filled air.

Smoke rapidly filled the small living room. The fire had jumped from the rug, to the coffee table, to the old cloth couch and—finally—to the curtains along one small window that faced the front porch. The old log cabin would not be able to contain the immense fire that was beginning to burn out of control.

It did not look hopeful that any of the inhabitants would escape alive.

CHAPTER 57

SOMETHING'S BURNING

Scott awoke in a groggy fog, just as a brilliant flash of lightning lit the surrounding area. His eyes grew wide with fear when lightning struck a second time—this time, hitting a deer stand located at the water's edge. The hit splintered the tree stand and sent it scattering to the ground in bits and pieces. *"Well, this is just great,"* he thought. *"I'm tied up beneath a bunch of trees in the middle of a lightning storm! I think I'd rather be dealing with snakes..."* He shook his head vigorously, which he regretted instantly when the movement triggered a searing spasm of pain between his eyes. His eyes burned terribly, but the taste of his dirty sock inside his mouth sickened him even more. He used his tongue and teeth to maneuver the sock from his mouth. He spat it out disgustingly upon the ground before him. He eyes immediately shot toward the cabin when he saw the lights flicker off—on again—and, then off for good. His eyes still stung from the whatever drug had been used to knock him out. He blinked several times when he saw a different kind of light coming from within the cabin. *"What the hell..."*

His subtle attention shifted from the flickering light within the cabin to the red vehicle parked in front. "Funny," he mumbled. "I didn't notice that car earlier. . ." Of course, he had been too worried about Macey to pay attention to his surroundings. Something about that car, however, momentarily captivated him. He continued staring at the Volkswagen—thinking that it looked a lot like the one his parents bought him for his sixteenth birthday. "Wow...where did that memory come from?"

Another bolt of pain penetrated his brain as he experienced a sudden flashback. Scott lowered his head and squeezed his eyes tightly closed. "Oh, God...no!" he screamed out loud. There it was—a memory from the night Kacey died—a vivid memory of the last time he had seen that red car. *"Kaceeeeeey...."*

Kacey! Impaled upon the stick shift of his 1969 Volkswagen Beetle—the memory came flooding back to him now. He saw it all again, especially her horror-filled eyes that appeared to stare straight at him—-blaming him for not helping her—for allowing it to happen.

Scott tried to swallow the lump that had formed in his parched throat, but, he couldn't generate enough spit to accomplish even that small feat. "Oh, God...Kacey...I am so sorry. So very sorry," he cried openly. "There was nothing I could do. I'm so, so sorry..."

A quiet stillness enveloped the immediate area surrounding the cabin—it was almost as if time was standing still. The wind stopped blowing, the light rain turned into a lighter mist, and, the darkness of the oncoming night was momentarily suspended. A feeling of peace—such as Scott had never experienced before—came over him. He closed his eyes and lifted his face upward toward the sky. His tears stopped, and all his senses—every fiber of his body—suddenly felt magnified ten times their normal capacity.

He couldn't explain what was happening to him, but, he felt certain it was something spiritual—or, maybe even supernatural. A feeling of calm and serenity coursed rapidly through his body. He opened his eyes and stared directly at the cabin. He would later attribute what he thought he saw to the side effects of the drug, but at that moment in time, Scott stared into the eyes of a fifteen-year old—Kacey Wymer. There was a sense of urgency about her as she floated about a foot off the cabin's front porch and beckoned him to follow her. She was dressed all in white, and her long dark hair fell thickly across her shoulders. A soft white mist—like a thin fog—seemed to be rising from the ground all around her.

Scott tried in vain to stand up. It took several moments before he realized he was tied securely to the old pine tree that he leaned against. He looked down at his bare feet and shivered at the thought of what may have slithered across them while he had been knocked out. That thought terrified him even more than his memories of Kacey. He tried again to get up, but Lucas had done an excellent job of securing him to the tree. His hands were tied behind him and they burned raw against the rope when he tried to twist them free. "Damn!" he shouted.

He strained hopelessly forward and stared at the cabin. Kacey was no longer on the porch, but the flickering light from within was brighter now than it had been a few minutes ago. Scott finally recognized it for what it was...FIRE!

The cabin was on fire and Macey was inside!

"Maceeeeey!" Scott screamed in despair.

Lucas roamed aimlessly on his hands and knees, searching frantically for Gabrielle. The smoke burned his eyes so badly that he had to keep them shut. Things were not turning out the way he had planned, but, he was still convinced that his plan would end in success. All he had to do, was to find Gabrielle and save her from the fire. The fire would turn out to be his saving grace—it would look like everyone inside had been unable to escape, and died in the fire. His preference would have been to be able to kill them all personally, but, their deaths by smoke and fire might work in his favor. There would be no evidence of any foul play. Lucas was no forensic expert, but, he hoped that Andrew's body would be burned badly enough to hide the bullet wound. Yes, this could definitely work in his favor. All he had to do was find his precious Gabrielle. He had to save her.

Smoke filled his parched lungs, and Lucas knew he was running out of time—he had to get himself and Gabrielle out soon—very soon. He stretched his hand out, felt the floor beneath him, and grabbed...*a foot!* Before he could get too excited, however, the foot kicked back viciously and sent him reeling backwards. His right leg twisted beneath him—at an unnatural angle—when he fell, and he heard the bone snap. "Agghh!" he screamed, the pain evident in his singed voice.

"You miserable son-of-a-bitch!" Andrew growled hoarsely. "You killed my daughter!"

Macey stopped her own fit of coughing when she heard the scuffling from across the room. "Papa! Where are you?" she yelled out between ragged coughs. She couldn't see him, but she heard him cursing Reverend Dudley. Her hands were almost free, thanks to Gabby's loose tying of the ropes. She had heard Jacob cry out when his chair fell over, but, but she hadn't heard anything from him since. That could only mean that he had been knocked unconscious from the fall.

Macey finally freed herself completely from the ropes and began feeling her way across the floor. She quickly found Jacob's overturned chair and grabbed for his dangling feet. "Oh, thank God! Jacob? Jacob?" There was no answer. He must have hit his head when he fell backward. Her hands moved to his chest and she felt it moving laboriously up and down. She knew she had to get him out of the burning cabin, but, he outweighed her by sixty pounds and she didn't think she could get his ropes undone in time. Gabby had, unfortunately, done a fine job in securing Jacob to the chair. Macey knew the only way she was going to get Jacob out safely was to drag him and the chair outside. She made the mistake of taking a deep breath and was rewarded with another coughing spasm, so intense, that it felt as though her lungs would surely burst from within their chest cavity. "Papa!" she yelled again while she struggled to pull Jacob's chair toward what she could only hope and pray was the front door. "Where's Gabrielle?"

The fire had spread faster than Macey thought was possible. It was everywhere. She willed herself to remain calm, but the fire and smoke played their own tug-of-war with her lungs. There had been no response from her father. She couldn't see anything—or anyone—through the dense smoke, and, she panicked when she saw the flames climb the walls and make their way quickly to the overhead wooden beams. "Gabrielle! Where are you, baby!"

Gabby moaned and began coughing. The thick phlegm racked through her lungs. She rubbed gently at the knot that had formed on the side of her head, but, she struggled to her knees and managed to cry out. "Mama? Where are you, Mama? Paw Paw?"

It didn't take Macey long to recognize the dire dilemma she faced. She could not save them all—not by herself. "Gabrielle!" Where are you, baby? Follow the sound of my voice, okay? I think you're only a few feet from the dining table. Feel your way over. I need your help with Jacob!"

Gabby sensed a sudden movement to her left. "Paw Paw? Is that you?" She heard shuffling and grunting noises, as though someone was dragging something—or someone.

Andrew's voice boomed voluminously through the room. "Gabby! Do what your Mama said! Get out of here!" he yelled. "Now!"

Lucas pushed himself up and swung a fist at Andrew's head, missing it by just a hair. "Gabrielle...child...I'm hurt...it's my leg—I think it's broken. You've got to help me, child. You can't leave your father to die..."

"Don't listen to him, Gabby..." Andrew began before a tremendous coughing fit came over him. He needed air desperately. He felt his lungs melting with every breath he took.

Gabby listened for a moment longer. She heard the sound of something being scraped across the floor in the direction from where her mother had yelled to her. She could also hear something else being dragged across the floor...much closer to her. It must be her father. "Paw Paw!" she yelled one last time, before turning and crawling toward the sound of what she hoped was a scraping chair. She reached out and grabbed the edge of it. "Mama? Please, let that be you..."

Horrendous coughing spasms forced Macey's burning throat to

constrict, but, she couldn't muster enough saliva to quench it. Her voice came out weak and raspy. "It's me, baby...over here..."

"You're going the wrong way, Mama! The door's over here!" Gabby's soft voice reached out to Macey. Their fingers touched and Gabby cried out in relief when her mother pulled her quickly toward her.

"I don't know how much longer I can hold out, Gabrielle," Macey whispered. "You've got to...help me...get Jacob out of here."

"Come on, Mama. Please, don't give up now. Come on...it's not far, Mama. The door's only a few feet away. Hold onto to me..."

Giant flames completely surrounded Lucas and Andrew.

Andrew finally surrendered to the intense pressure of his smoke-filled lungs, and collapsed in a fetal position, just a few feet from the front door.

Lucas had gotten turned around and had dragged himself away from the entrance—to the center of the living room—where he quickly became encased by shooting flames from all sides. "Gabrielle! Help me... you've got to help your father..."

Gabrielle and Macey somehow managed to pull an unconscious Jacob—still tied securely to his chair—through the door and onto the porch. They sucked in blessed amounts of fresh air that felt dampened by the recent misting rain. The demon fire behind them continued to roar its mighty wrath. The two women held onto each other and collapsed onto the porch.

Macey turned at the sound of crackling flames and pushed herself up on her hands and knees. She stared with horrid fascination into the burning furnace inside the cabin. She could hear Lucas Dudley screaming for someone to help him. "May you rot in Hell..." she croaked.

"Mama?" Gabby gasped as she tried to control her breathing. "Paw Paw's still in there. We can't leave him...we've got to get him out..."

Macey looked away from her daughter's pleading look, back into the burning inferno behind her. Her eyes darted quickly around the yard and landed on Jacob's truck. She was sure he had left the keys inside. "Baby, quick! Help me get Jacob down into the yard. Then I want you to take his truck and...go get help as quick as you can. Find a phone, call the police... an ambulance."

"What are you going to do?" Gabby asked as one of the ceiling beams crashed inside the cabin.

They both jumped up and bounced Jacob and his chair swiftly down the steps, into the yard.

Gabby looked at the truck, then back at the Volkswagen that her grandfather had only recently taught her how to drive. It was the only vehicle she had ever driven, and she didn't know if she would be able to handle's Jacob massive truck. She opened the door to the Volkswagen. "I'll take this car, Mama. The keys are in it and I know how to drive it. What are you going to do?" she asked again as Macey turned and started back up the steps.

"Maceeeeey!" a distant voice yelled.

It was so dark outside that Macey couldn't see anything past her nose, but, she instantly recognized the sound of Scott's voice. "Scott!" she yelled back, "Scott! Where are you?"

"Tied to a damn tree!" he shouted back.

Another beam fell inside the house and flames danced dangerously close to every window. If she was going to help her father, Macey knew it was now or never. She really didn't think she stood much of a chance at getting him out alive, but, she had to try—for Gabby's sake. She had to. She turned and looked back at her daughter—the daughter she had only known for a short while, but had loved for a life time. "Forget the car, Gabrielle! Go find Scott. He's a friend. He'll know what to do. Please, baby...hurry."

Gabby watched Macey. She wanted her mother to help her grandfather, but at the same time, she didn't want to risk losing Macey either—she had just found her. "Mama! For God's sake, what are you going to do?"

The door had slammed shut behind them when they escaped the cabin. Macey's fingers burned when she touched the hot door handle and she jerked them back. "We're wasting time talking about it, Gabby. I've got to see if I can help Papa. Go on now! Hurry and help Scott!"

"Be careful, Mama..." Gabby pleaded as she backed away from the cabin. "I...I love you."

Macey kicked the door open and yelled back before she re-entered the burning inferno. She dodged flames on both sides. "I love you too, baby. Don't ever forget that..."

Gabby quickly wiped at her nose before she turned and ran in the direction of Scott's voice. She found him, and worked to free him from the ropes. Her father must be an expert at tying ropes because Scott was bound much more tightly than Jacob's had been.

Macey involuntarily sucked in an unwelcome breath of acrid smoke when she kicked open the cabin door. "Papa! Papa!" she screamed as loudly as her lungs would allow. "Where are you?" She heard a weak cough coming from her left. Flames danced ominously all around her. The only fire-free area was the door from which she had just entered. "Papa! Is that you?" Macey lowered herself to her belly and began crawling toward the sound. Maybe it wasn't too late. She said a silent prayer to God and to Kacey to please not let it be too late. Her hand scraped against a boot at the same time another hand shot out and grabbed her forearm. "Papa?" she asked, terrified that it might not be him.

More coughing and gasping.

The hand tightened and slid to Macey's wrist. "You can't...help him, Macey...he's dead. You've got to help...me...my leg is broken..."

Macey gargled a sorry excuse for a scream and jerked her hand loose. She searched for the boot again—she remembered that Andrew had worn boots, while Lucas sported dress shoes. She found the boot again, and pulled herself forward until she felt Andrew's flannel shirt. She laid her head upon his chest, praying desperately to hear a heartbeat.

It was there! It was a faint one, but, it was there!

Macey slid backward, trying not to lose her bearings for the front door. She grabbed Andrew by his boots and began dragging him toward the door. "Please, God..." she whispered between ragged coughs. "Please give me the strength to get him out." She continued to inch backwards, on her knees. She lost her balance, when Lucas extended his good leg to block her progress, and stumbled backward slightly. She refused to give up her grip on Andrew's boots.

"Leave him, Macey!" Lucas yelled. His voice sounded suddenly stronger and more threatening. "You've got to help me. You can't let me die..."

Macey could barely make out the outline of his body through the smoke. He appeared to be laying on his side—the man who had made her life a living hell—the man who would have surely killed them all if he had gotten the chance. She would be doing the world a favor by letting him die. If anyone ever deserved to die, it was Lucas Dudley. It would make everything so much easier if she could hate him. She wanted desperately to hate him. Remembering everything he had done to her, to Kacey, to their mother—maybe she did have it in her, after all—that ability to hate. The temptation was great, but her faith in God...in His judgment, not her own...won out in the end. No, it was wrong to hate another human being—wrong to judge another human being—so, she did the next best thing. She leaned over, getting as close to him as she dared, and spat in his face—or, at least, in the general direction of his face. "Maybe that'll cool you off some, *Reverend.* You want out of here? Get yourself out. I hope...you burn in Hell, you...bastard!"

Lucas made one last feeble attempt to grab her, but Macey kicked his at his broken leg. His strength had been severely weakened, as had his lung capacity. He fell over on his side again. He looked at her shadowy silhouette. His croaky voice filled the night air—it sounded menacing and satanic. "You...will...all...pay..."

Macey ignored his cursed yelling, and reached the front door just as another ceiling beam crashed beside her.

She felt something wonderful—air—blessed, cool air!

Macey felt the cool air hit her backside, as she used the last of her strength to drag Andrew through the door and onto the porch. She rose shakily on hands and knees, and thought she saw Scott and Gabrielle running toward her. She, also, heard Jacob moaning on the ground below her, yelling for someone—anyone—to get the damn ropes off him.

Macey coughed and grinned. It was all right! Everyone was all right! She had thought that she would never see any of them again when she re-entered the cabin, but they had all made it. They were all alive!

The same sense of calmness that had enveloped Scott earlier—while he was tied to the tree—now surrounded Macey. The flames stopped dancing, the smoke stilled itself, and everything stopped. For one quick moment, her eyes were riveted on the Volkswagen. The passenger door had been left open, and for that one fleeting moment, Macey thought she saw Kacey—young and carefree—surrounded by a white misty fog. She sat in the passenger seat, and smiled and waved at Macey.

Time and motion were still suspended. Macey felt a bit foolish, but, she smiled at Kacey and returned the wave. She used a porch column to drag herself to a standing position, but she never took her eyes off her sister, sitting in the Volkswagen—waiting.

Time returned to normal—the flames began to dance again, the misting rain began to fall, and Macey's spasmodic coughing resumed. She sucked in a mouthful of fresh air, and that seemed to help. Tears pooled in Macey's eyes when she looked back at her sister. Kacey was still there—still sitting in the car—she really did seem to be waiting for something. The sisters shared a loving look, and they both lifted their hands—simultaneously—in a final wave.

Macey looked back at the burning cabin. She couldn't believe it. They had done it. They had all been saved!

All except...

Scott and Gabrielle were running toward Macey, but they were still about twenty feet away. "Maceeey!" Scott yelled at the top of his lungs, and pointed behind her. "Look out!"

Macey turned at the sound of Scott's voice, but immediately turned back to look at Kacey. Her sister's image—or ghost—was no longer with them. The stillness and serenity that had enveloped the night a short moment ago vanished completely. Everything returned to total chaos. She turned around in the direction Scott was pointing. "Oh, sweet, Jesus..." she cried out.

Lucas Dudley staggered and crashed through the opening that use to be the front door. His clothes were totally immersed in flames. He dragged his right leg awkwardly behind him, and Macey would later swear that she saw smoke seeping from the soles of his shoes. His entire body was smoldering from his burning clothes. He looked like Satan himself—straight from the pits of Hell.

Macey screamed when Lucas reached out for her.

He somehow managed to grab a handful of her hair, but he lost his grip. He stumbled and fell off the porch onto the ground below. His clothes continued to burn and the skin on his face bubbled with blisters. He tried desperately to extinguish the flames when he hit the ground, by rolling in the damp dirt.

Sparks from the flames on Lucas' clothing had jumped onto Macey's windbreaker when he had grabbed for her, and she pulled at it frantically—trying to get it off. She finally managed to remove the burning windbreaker and threw it onto the porch. She would have second-degree burns on her arm and hand—scars, for life, to remind her of this day.

Gabrielle's terrified screams echoed around them when Lucas fell to the ground. She covered her ears to drown out her father's heart-wrenching terror.

Scott pulled her face, protectively, against his chest so that she could not see Lucas' burning body.

Macey watched with horrid fascination as Lucas tried to stand up again. The man simply refused to relinquish his precarious hold on life. He just wouldn't die. She watched as he somehow managed an upright position. The skin on his once handsome face was blackened and the bubbling blisters began to pop and ooze. Macey thought she was imagining things when—like a magnet—Lucas was pulled backward toward the open door of the Volkswagen.

Lucas was facing Macey when he uttered his final words—before being sucked into the tiny red car. "I...condemn your...soul to Hell..."

Macey covered her mouth and fell to her knees as she watched what happened next. Once he had been sucked—or *dragged*—into the car, the flames on his clothing seemed to double, and engulfed him from head to toe. His burning hand reached out for something—as though he was grasping for something to hold onto—before being dragged down into the pits of Hell. He found something and grabbed onto it. It was the stick shift—the same stick shift upon which he had, long ago, impaled Kacey Wymer upon.

Lucas screamed again when the vinyl seats quickly caught fire. He shrieked like a girl when the car radio blasted out the words to Kacey's favorite song—*In the jungle, the mighty...jungle...the...lion...sleeps...tonight.*

Macey couldn't help herself—she felt hypnotized. She could not tear her eyes away from Lucas' burning body. It seemed like it was taking him an interminable amount of time to die. She jumped when his final scream reverberated throughout the woods—until an eerie silence finally prevailed. Macey could have sworn that she heard a young girl's scream coalesce with Lucas' soul as it orbited the perimeters of Hell, before finally being sucked through, for all eternity.

Scott released his hold on Gabby, and rushed to pull Jacob clear from the burning vehicle. He motioned for her to follow him, and, they quickly began undoing the ropes she had tied so efficiently less than an hour ago. He then hurried onto the porch, where he grabbed the semi-conscious Andrew under the arms and dragged him down the steps. "Come on, Macey!" he tried to coax her farther away from the burning cabin.

Macey felt paralyzed and she stared right through Scott.

"Mama!" Gabby yelled from several feet away.

It was the sound of her daughter's voice that finally brought Macey back from the brink of what she felt sure was temporary insanity. She jumped off the porch at the same moment the front window exploded outward. Shards of glass flew into her hair and stung her back.

Everyone quickly covered their heads with their hands, to protect themselves from the showering glass.

Scott jumped up and grabbed Macey in a rough embrace. He buried his face in her hair and held her so tightly against him, that he was sure he would do what the fire had been unable to do—suffocate her. He looked down at her soot-covered face and kissed her...long and hard. He never wanted to let her go.

"Can I get in on this?" Gabby asked shyly as she and Jacob slowly approached the couple.

Andrew, who had regained consciousness in time to see the human inferno being dragged into the Volkswagen, joined in. "Hey...don't forget about me..."

"Come on," Scott sighed. "Let's get the hell out of here. All that smoke is bound to wake up the snakes."

Scott, Macey, and Gabrielle piled onto the front seat of Jacob's truck, while Jacob insisted on riding in the bed with Andrew, who needed to remain lying down until they could get him to a hospital. Scott put the truck in reverse just as the final supporting porch column collapsed and fell across the burning Volkswagen. The car's gas tank suddenly exploded and the area was temporarily filled with excruciating heat, and an orange-red light as the good Reverend Dudley made his final descent home.

"The Lord does work in mysterious ways..." Andrew sighed as they drove slowly away. He was so thankful and relieved that Lucas Dudley would never again pose a threat to any member of his family.

Scott slowed the truck as they approached the entrance to the driveway, and found it blocked by a red Taurus. "That must be Dudley's car," he surmised. "I'll push it out of the way."

Macey grabbed his arm as she stared at the trunk of the car. "Scott, wait! I think that's Mama's car!" she exclaimed. "Oh my, God...look! It's moving..."

"Oh, great! This is just great," Scott sighed. "What now..." He put the truck in park and got out. He looked back at Jacob who was already assisting Andrew from the truck bed.

"That is Ruth's car," Andrew confirmed, holding his wounded shoulder and walking shakily toward the Taurus. "That son-of-a-bitch! He better not have hurt her."

"Look! It really is moving!" Jacob shouted. "Quick, Scott, see if the keys are in the ignition. We've gotta check the trunk."

Scott looked leery of the situation at hand. "Do we have to? I mean, what if it's a wild animal that Dudley was going to use for a sacrifice or something. Hell, it might even be possessed—after everything we've seen, that wouldn't surprise me," he mumbled. "No woman I've ever known could make a car shake like that!"

Andrew patted him on the shoulder and offered a weak, conspiratorial wink. "You don't know my, Ruthie! In her younger days, she made plenty of our cars shake, rattle, and roll!"

Scott was uncomfortable and embarrassed by Andrew's comment, but decided to take it in stride. Nothing much would surprise him now— not after everything that had happened in the past few hours. Nothing, that is...except the sight of Ruth Wymer's bare breasts hanging outside her open shirt as her husband assisted her from the trunk! "Oh, my God..." Scott moaned while he covered his eyes and turned around. "I can't believe I just saw my future mother-in-law's boobs..."

Ruth was oblivious to her physical appearance. She blinked her eyes repeatedly until her gaze finally rested on Gabrielle. She blinked back tears, felt the cold air brush against her breasts, and shoved them, nonchalantly, back inside her shirt. She held her arms out to her granddaughter.

"I think I'm going to like my new family," Gabby smiled and blushed simultaneously as she moved quickly into her grandmother's embrace.

Macey folded her hands in prayer beneath her chin and smiled. "Me, too, baby...me, too," she whispered as she watched her mother and daughter hug for the first time.

"Oh, Hell! No!" Scott was screaming behind them. He had walked over to where his car should have been parked. "No! Not my *car!*"

EPILOGUE

New Year's Eve - 1994

The white, colonial-style house—located in one of Columbus' more elite neighborhoods, and on a quiet cul-de-sac—was flanked on all sides by tall oaks and pines. It was decorated festively for the holidays. Mr. and Mrs. Scott Pennell were throwing a small New Year's Eve party. The guest list was very exclusive—only close friends and family had been invited. Scott and Macey stood together in the doorway to greet their guests, who were arriving in no particular style or order.

A Yellow cab pulled into the circle driveway, and, the driver walked quickly around to the trunk. He was more than eager to assist his beautiful, young passenger with her luggage. She had flown in from St. Paul, Minnesota, where she had just finished her last course before graduation at Luther Seminary. Her mother didn't know it yet, but she had decided not to go into ministry after all; instead, she had accepted a position as Assistant to the Associate Director of a regional women's and children abuse center in Atlanta. It would mean that she could visit her mother and the rest of her family every available weekend.

"Gabby..." Macey spoke the name softly and opened her arms to welcome her daughter's embrace. "I'm so glad you were able to get a flight out. I've been keeping a close eye on the weather channel, and, I was afraid you might get snowed in before your flight left."

"Trust me, Mama, I would've gotten here somehow," Gabby smiled and accepted her mother's offered kiss. "Hi, Scott," she smiled warmly. She gave him a tight hug. "It's so good to see you both."

Macey hugged her tightly against her. "Your room is ready, baby. Why don't you take your night bag on up. Scott will bring your suitcase up later.

The others should be arriving any minute now."

"Okay, Mama...I'll be right back."

"Oh, look!" Macey pointed. "There's Mama now! Hurry, Gabby..." she yelled over her shoulder. "You know who she's come to see!"

Ruth had used Lucas' thirty thousand dollars to buy a new car, and to make some small improvements to the gas station. After several days of deliberation and soul searching, everyone involved had agreed not to tell the authorities about the money, which had been stuffed into the trunk with Ruth on that last night. Ruth felt that she had more than earned her fair share of it. The rest of the family agreed wholeheartedly.

Judge Worsham had sentenced Andrew to five years of probation on the attempted assault charge. Probation had been offered as an alternative to prison due to the extenuating circumstances surrounding the case, the fact that Andrew had no prior record, and, the fact that Detective Windham—who was a good friend of the judge—put in a good word for him.

Andrew's luck at receiving probation did not extend to his personal relationship with his wife. He and Ruth filed for divorce a few months after Lucas' death. They had both tried to put everything behind them and start fresh, but, it just wasn't meant to be. The pain and embarrassment they both felt about their individual involvement with the good reverend had been more than any amount of counseling could remedy. Though divorced, they remained friends until Andrew was hospitalized with acute prostate cancer a few months after the divorce was final. He had never been one to visit a doctor, and by the time he finally got up enough nerve to see one, it was too late. The cancer had progressed too far at that point. The end came quickly, and, it was accompanied by extreme pain, but, Ruth knew that Andrew had made things right with his family before he died. That had been so important to him...to be forgiven for all his past sins.

Ruth honked the horn of her white Buick LeSabre and waved excitedly to her daughter and son-in-law. She smoothed out the wrinkles in the cream-colored pants suit that she had purchased as a Christmas gift to herself. She kissed Macey's cheek and motioned for Scott to help her carry something inside.

"Oh, Mama! You brought it!" Macey exclaimed. "It's too bad Jacob can't make it. He would have been *so* excited."

The aroma of the seven-layer chocolate cake that Ruth had baked the night before filled the foyer as the trio made their way inside.

"Forget Jacob," came the soft voice from the stairwell. "I know you made that cake for me!" Gabby had taken Andrew's death especially hard, and Ruth had been there for her every step of the way. She rushed into her grandmother's arms now and hugged her tightly. "It's so good to see you again, Gran!"

"You, too, angel," Ruth smiled. She had kept using Andrew's pet name for their granddaughter. "Although...it's only been a few months since we saw each other at the reunion—June...wasn't it?"

"It seems like it's been forever," Gabby grinned. "Happy New Year, Gran."

"Happy New Year to you, too, angel. Come on, let's get this cake into the kitchen."

Macey smiled and watched the duo walk past them into the huge kitchen. They looked so much alike. Part of her was sad when she thought about all the years they had missed sharing times like these with one another, but, she knew it wasn't her place to question God's will. She often wished her father had lived long enough to enjoy the peace her family had finally found. She had never really been able to offer him the forgiveness he sought from her, but, they had made their peace. She knew that it would be in her best interest to be able to fully forgive her father for his past mistakes, and she was making progress in that direction—it just had not happened yet.

Scott watched Macey while she was watched her daughter and mother. He kissed the top of her head and pulled her gently against him. No words were needed between them. He knew exactly what she was thinking.

They both turned back toward the front door when they heard the squealing of brakes. A brand new black and gold Ford Explorer had stopped only inches behind Ruth's LeSabre. Jordan High School's newly nominated Teacher of the Year—and Assistant Principal—was behind the wheel. Her husband, the new Director of the city's Parks and Recreation Department, sat beside her. He was offering unsolicited advice on how to drive their new vehicle, how far away to park it from the car in front of them, etcetera.

"Oh, shut your mouth, Carlton! You'd think I was some inexperienced sixteen-year old the way you're carrying on over this stupid car," Becca hissed. "I'm perfectly capable of parking the damn thing!" She was looking at him and not where she was going when she lightly tapped the rear fender of Ruth's car.

Carlton jumped out to examine the damage before Becca stopped the car completely. He held his hand over his heart, and came back to the passenger window. He leaned in and peered at his wife. He wanted to shout at her, but one look at her very pregnant belly pressed against the steering wheel changed his mind. "It's okay, baby," he soothed. "No damage done. It's okay. You okay?"

Becca unhooked her seat belt and slid ungraciously out of the driver's side. Her maternity dress rode up in the back, allowing her husband a birds-eye view of her ever-luscious derriere. "Of course I'm okay," she grumbled. "Help little Alvin out of his car seat."

"I got him baby, don't you worry none," Carlton said. He was doing his best to patronize his lovely wife, who was already two weeks overdue with the birth of their first child—a child the doctors all said would never be possible.

Becca and Carlton had married the weekend after her release from the hospital in January 1990. One year later, Becca's father died—peacefully in his sleep—from a heart attack. A year after that, Becca and Carlton adopted an African-American infant boy. They had been on the waiting list for almost two years, and were thrilled at the prospects of becoming parents. There was no doubt after whom the child would be named. Becca's mother sold the restaurant and moved to Opp, Alabama, where she and Carlton's mother decided to share living expenses since they were both widows. The two women got along famously and visited their children often.

Becca began experiencing sharp pains in her abdomen in March of 1994, and called her doctor. She thought she was having an attack of appendicitis. Routine tests were taken and the doctors determined that Becca was suffering from an anxiety attack. However, when the routine blood and urine tests came back two days later, they confirmed that she was pregnant! The doctors tried to warn the Browns that Becca would probably never carry the baby to term. She had been too scarred internally from Lucas' violent assault, but, here she was...nine and a half months pregnant...proving them all wrong.

"Hey, there, girlfriend!" Becca waved as she took little Alvin's hand and wobbled up the sidewalk to where Macey and Scott stood smiling and waving back.

Hey, yourself!" Macey grinned and hugged her best friend. "Are you sure it's safe for you to be traveling? I wouldn't want you to go into labor while we're singing Auld Lang Siene."

"Wouldn't be the first time I did something no one expected me to," Becca countered. She pulled Carlton alongside her. "Come on, baby, you can help pull me up off the sofa after I eat—I don't want to miss out on any of this good food."

"No," Carlton said, shaking his head and patting his wife's bottom. "It sure wouldn't do for you to miss a meal, now would it?"

Becca gave him a warning look as she made her way to the buffet table.

Scott followed them inside while Macey took one last look outside. She was devastated that Jacob couldn't make it this year. He had called earlier in the week to say he had to work on New Year's Day, and wouldn't be able to make the gathering. Macey had disguised her disappointment as best she could and said she understood, but it wouldn't be the same without him there.

The next several hours were spent in harmonious laughter and camaraderie among those present. Gabby played with little Alvin, which allowed his mom and dad some time to enjoy themselves. Dinner was casual and the men watched a college football game on television. The women talked about children, school, work, husbands, and boyfriends. It had been hard for all of them to get their lives back on track, but they had done it. A lot of tears and forgiveness had been spread around. In the end, they had all been able to put Lucas Dudley behind them once and for all...except in their dreams. They all still dreamed of the man who had so negatively impacted all their lives.

It was almost midnight when the group gathered around the Pennell's beautifully decorated Christmas tree. They watched Dick Clark on television and waited for the ball to fall—announcing the arrival of 1995.

Forty-five seconds to go.

The front door eased open and Jacob stepped quietly inside. His boss finally decided to close his electronic supply dealership that Jacob managed so successfully for him. Jacob knew that his entire family would be here tonight. It had been an eight-hour drive—in holiday traffic—from Clearwater, Florida, but, he decided at the last minute to make the trip. He had missed the family reunion in June and he desperately wanted to see everyone. He also wanted to introduce them to his fiancée—or rather—to *reintroduce* them to her.

He and Janet Ward had parted as good friends when he left Columbus for Florida in 1990. They corresponded for several months, but gradually stopped writing each other. Janet married and divorced while Jacob enjoyed the anatomical scenery that Florida so graciously offered. Then, several months ago, Jacob had assisted a beautiful woman with the selection of a digital satellite system. Two of his salesmen were out sick that day, and Jacob was always quick to jump in wherever he was needed.

The beautiful woman turned out to be Janet, who had recently moved to Clearwater. She had lost track of Jacob a few years earlier and didn't think he would still be living in the area. Her three-year old daughter from her first marriage was with her that day, and, it had been love at first sight for Jacob. The little girl, whose name was Nicole, had stolen his heart from day one; and, her mother provided the icing on the cake. Janet had done a lot of growing up over the years, and had surprised everyone by embracing motherhood with gusto and enthusiasm. She was a saleswoman in a prestigious women's clothing store. She no longer wore the gaudy, risqué outfits, which had been her trademark while a receptionist at CompuTech.

Jacob had dropped Janet off at her parents' home so she and Nicole could sleep in Janet's old bed. They planned to break the news to everyone tomorrow. It was a big step for Jacob and he hoped his family would approve, but, he wasn't worried. They wanted Jacob to be happy, and, Janet and Nicole made him very happy.

Ten seconds to go.

Everyone had their backs to him while they watched the ball descend. Five...four...three...two...one...

"H-A-P-P-Y N-E-W Y-E-A-R!" everyone shouted.

"Happy New Year!" Jacob shouted back gleefully.

They all turned to look at him, and before he knew it they were all over him—kissing him—hugging him—patting his back. Man, it was so good to be home!

Macey pulled him aside and hugged him again. "Oh, Jacob...I'm so happy you made it. I've missed you so much."

He pulled her to him for a hug and noticed, for the first time, the barrier between them. "Hey! When did this happen?" he asked looking down at her slightly protruding belly.

Macey put her hand protectively upon her belly and smiled up at her brother. "About five months ago, actually...not too long after the last reunion."

"Wow, that must've been some reunion, all right. Oh, Macey," Jacob whispered hoarsely. "I know how long you and Scott have been trying to make this happen. I'm really happy for you guys."

"Thanks, little brother," Macey sighed. "I had almost given up hope that it would happen. Scott has been so busy since he became CEO of CompuTech, and—with me taking over the Technology Department—well, we forgot about it for a while. That's probably what helped me to get pregnant—forgetting to constantly take my temperature, charting this and charting that."

"Is it...uh...okay? I mean..."

"You mean, because of my age? Am I too old?" Macey laughed at Jacob's obvious embarrassment. "No, little brother, everything is fine. The baby is healthy and due to arrive sometime in April."

"Your birthday is..."

"The twenty-seventh of April, yes...and, I will be forty-two then, but the doctors have assured us that all is well." Macey paused a moment before continuing. "It's a girl, Jacob..."

"Oh, Macey...man, that is so great. You'll finally get a chance to really be a mother...I mean, you know...from the beginning and all."

Macey sighed and rubbed her stomach. "That's right, Jacob...and I can't wait for her to arrive."

"Have you guys thought of a name, yet?" Jacob asked, looking back over his shoulder at the group of friends and family hugging one another, and offering well wishes for the new year.

"I'm surprised you even have to ask, Jacob."

Jacob closed his eyes and nodded. "Kacey..."

Macey smiled. "Yeah...Kacey Irene Pennell. She'll be named after someone who would have loved her just as much as I will."

Jacob rubbed his chin thoughtfully. "Kacey Irene Pennell...K-I-P! I think I'll call her Kip!"

Macey smiled at him and nodded her head. "Yeah, I think I like that... Kip Pennell."

Brother and sister walked outside together, onto the patio, and looked up into a sky that was clear and alive, filled with an abundance of sparkling stars. One star—in particular—caught their attention; it appeared to be blinking double-time.

Jacob pointed upwards and whispered in Macey's ear. "What do you think? Do you think Kacey approves?"

Macey looked upward and focused on the dominant, blinking star. Tears of happiness flowed slowly down her cheeks. "I know she does, Jacob. I know she does..."

THE END...*Correction*...Make that...THE BEGINNING!

Our Father in heaven,
Hallowed be Your name.
Your kingdom come,
Your will be done
On earth as it is in heaven.
Give us this day our daily bread.
And forgive us our debts,
As we forgive our debtors.
And do not lead us into temptation,
But deliver us from the evil one.
For Yours is the kingdom and the power and the glory forever.
Amen.

Matthew 6:9-13 (NKJV)

www.ingramcontent.com/pod-product-compliance
Lightning Source LLC
Chambersburg PA
CBHW020504260626
47156CB00006B/1859